I0722921

HIDING IN PLAIN SIGHT

BARBARA A. LUKER

Black Rose Writing | Texas

©2025 by Barbara A. Luker
All rights reserved. No part of this book may be reproduced, stored in a retrieval system or transmitted in any form or by any means without the prior written permission of the publishers, except by a reviewer who may quote brief passages in a review to be printed in a newspaper, magazine or journal.

The author grants the final approval for this literary material.

First printing

This is a work of fiction. Names, characters, businesses, places, events, and incidents are either the products of the author's imagination or used in a fictitious manner. Any resemblance to actual persons, living or dead, or actual events is purely coincidental.

ISBN: 978-1-68513-541-6
PUBLISHED BY BLACK ROSE WRITING
www.blackrosewriting.com

Printed in the United States of America
Suggested Retail Price (SRP) $21.95

Hiding in Plain Sight is printed in Garamond Premier Pro

*As a planet-friendly publisher, Black Rose Writing does its best to eliminate unnecessary waste to reduce paper usage and energy costs, while never compromising the reading experience. As a result, the final word count vs. page count may not meet common expectations.

Edited by Tyra Erickson

The love of a true friend is worth more than winning the lottery.
I dedicate this book to my dear friend and lottery partner Matt Grochow.
Rich or poor, you will be in my heart always and forever!

Praise for
Hiding in Plain Sight

"A titillating ride, *Hiding in Plain Sight* by Barbara Luker, is a delicious blend of romance and thriller. While reading the book, I had so many theories as to what was going to happen, and none of them turned out to be right. A testament to her creativity and expert storytelling, I was still guessing up until the heart pounding climax. Women's fiction doesn't always have to follow the same formula, and Luker has once again broken the mold with her unique blend of the two genres. With a relatable and sympathetic protagonist like Jordan Wheeler, readers will feel compelled to root for her at every turn. And of course don't forget her trusty sidekick, Pete, whose growls act as a proxy for the readers who will surely be growling along with him. A refreshing read that I highly recommend to those looking for the perfect combination of wistful true love and heart stopping chills."
–Lisa Febre, author of *Round the Twist* and *Welcome to the Bright*

"An emotionally charged novel replete with uncertainty and complicated obstacles, Luker's *Hiding in Plain Sight* will keep you on the edge of your seat as you anxiously wonder how things will turn out in this thrilling and nail-biting ride of suspenseful romance."
–Lucille Guarino, author of *Elizabeth's Mountain*

"*Hiding In Plain Sight* tugs at your heart like Nicholas Evans' *Safe Haven* and spikes your adrenaline like Anna Quindlen's *Black and Blue*!"
–Cam Torrens, award-winning author of *Stable, False Summit,* and *Scorched*

"*Hiding in Plain Sight* by Barbara Luker had me hooked from the very first paragraph—in fact, it pretty much prevented me from getting things done once I began reading it. Jordan Wheeler has started a new life for herself in Wyoming by disappearing and leaving her wealthy, powerful, violent, and criminal husband in New York. Terrified that he will find her someday, she

keeps to herself and leaves no paper trail. Her only insurance is the USB she holds, that contains evidence of her husband's criminal activities. An accident has Jordan crossing paths with her neighbor Ben, who has also moved to remote Wyoming for reasons of his own. Against her better judgement, she opens herself up little by little to Ben and begins to hope and dream of a normal life with him. Unfortunately, someone from both Ben and Jordan's past shows up and betrays them. Jordan's husband, of course, seeks revenge. And the evidence. I was on the edge of my seat the entire time I was reading this book. The author skillfully wove a suspenseful story with clever dialogue and compelling characters. This is a must-read for anyone who loves a good page-turner but who doesn't like graphic violence. This would make a fantastic movie! I can't wait to see what Ms. Luker comes up with next!"
–Diane Hawley Nagatomo, author of *The Butterfly Café* and *Finding Naomi*

"With the perfect balance of romance and suspense, *Hiding in Plain Sight* kept me turning the pages, alternating between sweet, swoony moments and heart-racing drama. When Jordan Wheeler ran from her abusive husband, she never expected to find Ben, the love of her life. But the secrets she carries form a wall between them, trapping Jordan until she is forced to face the past. Barbara A. Luker crafts such realistic forbidden love stories, once you read one of her books, you'll want to read them all."
–Anna Daugherty, author of *Outside of Grace*

"Page after page, Luker's story, *Hiding in Plain Sight*, is an engaging read, a story that doesn't let up right down to the fulfilling ending. When the last page is closed, I'm satisfied with the ending, and looking forward to more from this author."
–Paulette Mahurin, author of *Two Necklaces*

Thank you to my dedicated beta readers Susan, Maureen and Nancy.
You've been with me from the beginning with good advice, sharp eyes and
gentle critiques. I hope you enjoy this newest story!

HIDING
IN
PLAIN
SIGHT

CHAPTER ONE

All was silent when Jordan woke before dawn in the small cabin in the woods. Having long ago become immune to the cacophony of garbage trucks, car horns, and other sounds that accompanied the hustle and bustle of New York City mornings, she never would have expected to adjust to the quiet of this part of the world.

At first, the silence had seemed ominous. Each day found her waiting for something horrible to happen as feelings of dread enveloped her and everything in the glade. Yet time passed and she realized her fears, even considering her situation, had been silly. The juxtaposition of moving from a magnificent penthouse in the big city to a cabin so small it could have fit in her New York closet had taken even more change, but now she quite liked the solitude and comfort offered by her little corner of the woods.

Her night had been yet another like so many others since her escape; full of nightmares about Richard. Waking in terror, she slept little the rest of the night leaving plenty of time to think about her life's sad turn of events.

The rising sun that would flood this side of the house for most of the day hadn't yet made it high enough into the sky to pierce the dense foliage of the woods, and a slow smile spread across her face as the gentle sounds of nature filtered through the open window.

Stretching and rubbing the sleep out of her eyes with one hand, the other stroking Pete's long, dense fur, she luxuriated in the knowledge that for the first time in over a decade she alone was in total control of her life.

Subtle as they were, her movements roused the sleeping dog and soon a cold wet nose pushed against her arm, urging the pair to start the day. Without an immediate response, the nose pushed a little more insistently before a soft chuckle escaped Jordan's lips.

"Good morning to you too," she said before turning on her side to gaze into the dark chocolate eyes staring back at her. A quick look at the clock on the bedside table showed it was much too early for breakfast. "So just what do you have against sleeping in?" she asked the German Shepherd.

Cocking his head for just a moment in the endearing manner common to the breed, he looked like he would respond.

They had only been together a few months, but already it seemed they had developed an unspoken communication. Talking to the dog as if he understood what she was saying was lunacy, but after weeks of solitude, it had become a habit.

She had never set out to have a dog, but a single woman living alone in the woods had made Jordan something of an enigma to the locals and as little as she made her way into town, gossip had been rampant about the woman in the woods. Having come so far in her quest to leave behind an unhappy and dangerous past, being talked about was the last thing she wanted. She stuck out as the outsider she was, which had led to the snap decision to get a dog. Whether perched in the back of a pickup truck, tucked away in a large purse, or roaming loose in the yard behind a strong chain-link fence, it seemed everyone in the little town had a dog or two and it didn't take long to realize having a dog just might be a way to fit in.

It was her third time at the local pound that did the trick. The two previous had ended in disappointment after being unable to find the one dog that tugged at her heartstrings. Wandering from one dreary kennel to the next, her heart had broken at the sadness on each furry face as she passed by. The poor dogs seemed to know that an unfamiliar face meant a chance to escape from the pound, but what had started as genuine excitement with tails wagging and dogs jumping at the kennel fence, soon became desperate whimpering when she moved on to the next kennel. In another time and place they all would have come home with her, but it was impossible with her current situation.

Head hanging low in disappointment, she had walked past two empty kennels before coming to the last one where she saw him. Unlike the other dogs who readily rushed to greet her, this one cowered in the back of the space and it seemed he would have knocked over the concrete blocks behind him to move even further away from her if he could. Covered in filthy, matted fur, the large tan and black dog had barely been recognizable as a Shepherd. Bedding ripped to shreds, the toys scattered throughout the small space ignored, the dog's lips curled back as a low and menacing growl emanated from him. Stopping for a better look and grasping the wire fence serving as protection between them, something drew Jordan to the dog in spite of his threatening look and ever-increasing growl of warning.

"What about this guy? What's his story?" she asked the volunteer who had been shadowing her.

"We're getting rid of him today. He's just too aggressive to adopt out," the woman said without an ounce of regret.

The large red warning sign on the top of the cage showed the dog would be put down that evening and Jordan looked back at the dog with pity as something changed in him. The snarl was gone and the ears were now perked up.

"He doesn't look aggressive," she insisted.

"Trust me. I've worked here a long time and looks can be deceiving with dogs. This guy has tried to bite every one of us at one time or another. We just can't take a chance of adopting him out and something happening. Even if we could find someone brave enough to take him on, it would have to be someone who knows how to beat the aggression out of him. We tried, but it's just no use. Best to just end it."

"You can't be serious," Jordan exclaimed. "Are you telling me you beat this dog? No wonder he tried to bite you. What kind of place is this?"

"Look lady, if you think you can handle him, more power to you. You can even have him at no charge but we'll make you sign a waiver of liability. We don't want anyone saying we didn't warn you."

Glaring at the woman with a venom she hadn't realized she possessed, Jordan turned back to the dog, unable to comprehend that this beautiful animal was going to die because the shelter didn't know how to handle him.

Grabbing a handful of treats from a nearby container, she opened the door latch and eased into the small space. Remembering the woman's words and knowing her entrance into the cage could prove to be a colossal mistake, she pushed her fears aside. There was something in his eyes that begged for someone to understand him, and she just couldn't let him die.

"His name is Pete," the woman said as she watched from safe a distance before muttering to herself about crazy folks.

Locking the kennel door behind her, Jordan spoke softly. "Hello Pete."

Dropping to a crouch before breaking off a small portion of one of the dog treats, she tossed it to him. His head swiveled from the treat on the floor to her face and back while she offered whispered words of encouragement. Throwing one more piece his way, she smiled with excitement when the dog reached down and gobbled up the food.

"What a good boy," she whispered before repeating the action.

This time there was no hesitation in his eyes and after downing the treat, he stood from his sitting position, head up and ears alert, albeit with his tail still between his legs.

Reaching out her hand, she offered another treat.

"I wouldn't do that if I were you," the shelter woman warned. At her voice, the dog froze in place, his eyes locked on the woman as he growled menacingly once again.

Eyes locked on the dog, hand unwavering in front of her, Jordan spoke softly.

"Stop talking and go away please."

"Lady, he's going to attack you and we won't take responsibility for it."

"Go-a-way," Jordan said as quietly as possible.

It took a few moments before the sound of the woman's footsteps faded away. The dog had watched the woman the whole time before turning his attention back to Jordan and the treat in her hand. He took a hesitant step forward. Knowing how they had been handling the dog, Jordan couldn't fault him for not trusting her, but doubt began to creep in and her hand shook just a bit before the dog took another step forward. Before she could pull it back, the dog took the treat gently from her hand.

Her heart had just started to beat again when the dog's tail began to wag and he sat down in front of her, looking expectantly at the other hand holding the remaining treats. Faces mere inches apart, the dog could have torn her to shreds, but instead he cocked his head as if to say, "Now what?"

That simple gesture sealed the deal and they had gone home together that same day.

The smiles on the faces of the pound people expressed their relief at having the dog taken off their hands and the aggressive behavior they claimed was so apparent had never materialized. From the moment Jordan clipped a leash on his collar and they walked out of that horrible place, Pete had been a happy, obedient dog and her constant companion.

It took several attempts to remove the matting from his fur, but once completed, a beautiful, show-worthy Shepherd emerged; a dog that to Jordan's dismay attracted attention from all who saw him. She wasn't able to relax until realizing that when confronted by a dog of such size, many people crossed the street rather than approach them on their walks. Pete helped her assimilate into the community while at the same time serving as a barrier to engaging in any meaningful discussion about her past. It was a win-win.

Another shove from Pete's cold nose brought her back to the present and Jordan threw off the bedcovers as he hopped over her, stopping at the bedroom door before turning and looking back.

"I'm coming," she assured him with a laugh before grabbing an old sweater from the foot of the bed and following Pete down to the kitchen door.

An overnight freezing rain had coated everything in a thick layer of ice causing tree branches to hang low to the ground and utility lines to sag.

Racing past her into the cold, dark morning, Pete's back legs slipped before he regained his footing and began circling the yard to investigate every smell that was different from the day before.

Wrapping the sweater a bit tighter around her slim frame to ward off the morning chill, Jordan noticed yet another hole in the sleeve and wondered what Richard would think if he could see her in a garment in such disrepair. Back then she wore nothing but designer clothing dripping with expensive jewelry. At first, it had all seemed glamorous, but like with so many things in life, the luster soon wore off to the point where she longed for the simple comfort of a pair of jeans and a sweatshirt. She had spent a decade serving as window dressing for Richard's life as the woman she had been before they met was erased when Richard molded her into the wife he expected. Although she had been a willing participant in the change, she discovered how uncomfortable life was when pretending to be someone else.

Things were changing though. Having shed the privileged lifestyle that Richard so embraced, the small-town girl was finding her way back to herself.

"Come on Pete," she encouraged from the doorway. "Do your business and let's go inside. It's freezing out here."

His outdoor responsibilities taken care of, Pete raced through the open door into the comfort of the tiny kitchen. It had taken some time to learn how to deal with the temperamental stove which all too often went out overnight, but this morning a gentle warmth permeated the kitchen.

Dancing underfoot as she prepared his breakfast, Pete gobbled it up almost immediately before picking up his favorite toy and curling up on his bed near the stove. Learning to appreciate the joy of dog toys was new to him and more than once Jordan had wondered what his life had been like before ending up in the pound. Was his family out there somewhere? A nagging fear that someday his original owners would come back to claim him haunted her and if that happened she wasn't sure she could let him go.

Hands wrapped around a cup of coffee, she watched the dog settle in on the large soft bed and wondered if her daily run was such a good idea with so much ice. Even with his strong claws, Pete had slipped more than a few times as he tried to make his way around the yard. It wouldn't be much better on the roads, but if she waited for the sun to do its magic, she might be okay. She would run alone. She might take a chance with her own well-being but Pete was another story. As much as he would hate it, Pete would have to stay home.

Keeping busy tidying up the already immaculate house while waiting for the weak sunlight to melt some of the ice, she took a mental inventory of all the needed repairs. As much as she'd like to fix things, cash was tight after purchasing the property and repairs would have to wait until she could find a way to bring in extra money.

That wouldn't happen anytime soon. Her lack of marketable skills and inability to provide documentation under her original name had turned even the thought of gainful employment into nothing but a pipe dream. She'd have to find a way to fix her own life before she could fix the cabin.

Before meeting Richard, Jordan's future plans were many and varied. Constant doodling as a child had showed real promise as an artist. Family and teachers alike had expected great things from her, but it was one thing to stand out in a small town and another when pitted against more talented individuals in New York. The avant-garde art world of New York had been uninterested in a conservative Midwestern girl and doors that should have opened based on her talent alone hadn't budged. It wasn't until a friend suggested she reinvent herself that doors began to open for her.

Parting with some of her quickly dwindling bank account, she had changed her name and Jordan became Victoria Stevens; a woman destined for great things in a great city. As Victoria Stevens, she felt like she fit in the high-class, high-octane art world of New York and more importantly, she felt like someone.

As pleased as she had been by the name change, those back home were anything but. Her father, beside himself with anger when he learned what she had done, had disowned her and neither he nor any member of the family had spoken to her in years. The few attempts she had made to reach out to them had all been disastrous and after more tears and harsh words than she could cope with, she gave up trying.

It took time to get over their rejection, but she was in New York and it was intoxicating. The sights, the sounds, the hustle and bustle were like nothing the small-town girl had ever experienced and she had loved every bit of it. Doors that had been closed to her now opened and she became part of the art community in trendy SOHO even if she still was making no money. It hadn't taken long before the city that had at first so enchanted her had beaten her down and she was ready to pack her few meager belongings and head home with her tail between her legs to beg her father's forgiveness. That is, until Richard appeared in front of her at a friend's gallery show. He was years older, but the pair were smitten and it didn't take long before her hopes of an art career were left behind and Richard became her life.

Having already divorced two wives, Richard wasn't looking for love or marriage. He was looking for a beautiful young woman to prove to the world how virile and successful he was. Only when she threatened to walk away had he agreed to marriage and that became the first of many mistakes she made. Before long she had allowed him to change who she was.

He had claimed to be attracted by her bohemian lifestyle, but once married, he expected a socialite wife. To be part of his circle she needed to be worldly, sophisticated, and unlike who she was.

At first, to make Richard happy, she went along with his wishes, but all too soon, she realized that changing who she was had only succeeded in making her unhappy. It took even longer to understand that even with the transformation, Richard had never loved her the way she loved him and with those insights came the realization that she was floundering in a way she never could have imagined. It needed to end.

The one thing she hadn't allowed herself to admit in all those years together was that Richard would never let her go. She had become his possession and no matter how unhappy she was or how disappointing the marriage was turning out to be, she was to keep her mouth shut and accept her fate. It was a lesson that would be drilled into her in the harshest of ways.

The first time he struck her, it came out of the blue. In an effort to salvage what she could of their fading relationship, she had suggested they seek counseling. While Richard had always had a temper in his business dealings, there had been no indication of it in their marriage. The blow came like the strike of a cobra, knocking her to the ground while he towered above her with such rage on his face she feared for her life, yet, as quickly as his anger had manifested, it was gone and he reached out to caress where his blow had landed as if he could make it all better with just a simple touch. As she backed away from him in fear, he had simply shrugged his shoulders and walked away leaving her with a cheek that was swollen and purple for days.

In the days that followed, Richard's words and actions were attentive and loving and the memory of his blow faded as she convinced herself his reaction was an anomaly. For a time, things were back on track, but it wasn't long before things changed once again for the worse and Richard had lashed out at every perceived transgression.

The blows began to occur on a near daily basis leaving her bruised and bloodied. She longed to curl up in a corner but social obligations meant she must ignore her injuries. In public at least, she must act as if nothing was wrong even as the compounding bruises and black eyes became impossible to hide no matter how skillfully applied the makeup.

More than a bit fearful as the attacks began to escalate, she suggested it was time they consider divorce only to be thrown into a wall as the mirror above crashed to the floor with shards of glass littering her body with cuts.

"No woman leaves Richard Harvey," he had snarled as he towered above her, his fists clenched at his sides. "You're not going anywhere. Try it and not only will I kill you, but I'll send the rest of your sad little family to the grave along with you."

He had left the room without a backwards glance as a cold wave of clarity washed over her. He was never going to change and she could either accept it and deal with the escalating physical abuse, or leave him and start her life over. There was no question what the decision would be. The hard part was how to do it.

She couldn't just pack up and leave. Extremely wealthy and powerful, Richard had already proven she would pay for disobeying him. Failure to escape would ratchet his anger even further. To be free she would need to become someone else. It was the only way to save her life.

Painstakingly biding her time, she had waited for just the right opportunity to slip away into anonymity while saving every penny she could from the funds Richard provided her each week. It wasn't long before she had a substantial nest egg tucked away. When the time came for her escape, Richard would unwittingly finance her new future. It was ironic and the one thing that gave her any satisfaction about her plans.

The only thing still undecided had been when that escape would occur. The day came as Richard prepared for an unexpected business trip to South America that would take him away from the city for three weeks. His absence would provide the head start needed if her plan was to succeed. Lying in bed, sleep eluding her as the promise of an escape dangled enticingly before her, she had figured out the last piece of the puzzle. The next morning all it took was a casual suggestion of a trip to Paris to improve her French. At first he seemed hesitant to agree until being reminded the trip would also give her a chance to soak up some of the international culture he so envied in others.

"I suppose it would do you some good to get a bit of education. Take Anthony's wife with you," he had ordered without even looking at her. For months, her only contact outside the marriage had been with the wives of his trusted business associates.

"You know none of the other women have interest in anything except shopping," she reminded him. "If I go by myself I'll have more time to browse through all the museums and get more out of the trip. Besides, you don't want your friends knowing how inexperienced I am with that kind of culture do you?"

That was all it took to convince him to let her go on her own. His assistant had made all the arrangements and the day after Richard left for South America found Jordan in the back of a limo on her way to the airport. Her luggage was the only thing heading to Paris, however. She walked in the terminal through one door and out another before hailing a cab to the train station. With just one small bag and her carefully hoarded stash of cash, her escape was underway.

It might have seemed rather clandestine and exciting to a casual observer, but the reality was much different. Richard didn't like to lose and the minute he discovered her absence, his henchmen were sure to be hot on her trail. The thought of being caught was terrifying.

Unable to risk discovery, she had spent hours planning each minute detail. Traveling first by train to Charleston, then hopping a bus to Des Moines, her travel on public transportation ended. She began to use a network Richard would never think of—college students heading home for semester break.

Central message boards on any college campus offered ample opportunity to find rides and for Jordan, it was easy to blend in as just another student looking for a cheap way home for the holidays. Using different names each time, and always paying in cash, it became an untraceable mode of travel. Before long, she had covered almost every corner of the continental United States in a confusing maze of directions all designed to throw anyone who might be looking for her off the scent. If Richard ever did find her, it wouldn't be for lack of planning on her part.

So how had she ended up in a remote corner of Wyoming? She'd closed her eyes and pointed to a spot on a map. There wasn't a single connection in her past to the town or even the state and it was the perfect place to hide in plain sight. A few short days after her arrival, the woman now known once again as Jordan Wheeler had paid cash for the dilapidated cabin in the woods and she was finally home; the haven close enough to town that on nice days she could walk the five miles, but secluded enough to be off most people's radar.

In the months since moving in there had been little indication Richard was even looking for her, but she knew better than to let her guard down. Frequent trips to the public library to use free internet service turned up little mention of her disappearance. If he was concerned she hadn't returned to New York after her trip to Paris, there was no public mention of it and as the weeks passed she let herself hope she might finally be free.

·　　·　　·　　·　　·

Eventually the sun's warmth did as she hoped. The slow ice melt meant it was safe enough to run and Jordan paused briefly on the stairs to lace up her shoes while Pete paced between the stairs and the kitchen door anxious to get going. He had seen the pattern too many times not to know what it meant and he went to the door, grabbed his leash in his mouth and dropped it at her feet as he danced excitedly in front of her.

"Not today buddy," she told him before rubbing behind his ears. "It's still too icy out and I don't want you to get hurt. But I'll be back in a couple of hours and we can play."

Putting his leash back on the hook, she expected that would be the end of it but Pete had other ideas. Parking himself in front of the door, he barked sharply and blocked her way.

"I'm sorry pal, but you can't go today. Trust me; it's for your own good."

He was quick to obey as she called him to her side and he took up his spot on her left and looked up expectantly. As she took a step forward so did he and she noticed a slight limp as he got up from his sitting position. Running her hands gently over all four legs, she saw nothing of concern until a barely noticeable flinch when she moved his back right leg.

"Looks like you need to see the doctor," she said as she sat back on her haunches. It might not be anything serious, but Pete was the most precious thing in the world to her and she didn't want to take a chance. Reaching for the phone, she placed a call to the vet.

A typical small-town vet, Dr. Norris struggled to pay his own bills while never turning down a client who couldn't pay. He also was the one person in town who wasn't afraid of Pete and that alone should have endeared him to Jordan, but he was a man and having had her fair share of interest from men over the years, she wasn't oblivious to the fact that he was attracted to her.

Each interaction with the man brought with it the distinct possibility he would ask her on a date and she knew it was only a matter of time before the words would come out of his mouth and she would inevitably have to disappoint him.

"Dr. Norris, it's Jordan Wheeler."

With barely enough money coming in to feed himself, staff was out of the question and she wasn't surprised he had answered the phone himself.

"Jordan, what a nice surprise, but didn't I ask you to call me Kevin?"

"I know you're probably busy, but Pete is limping a bit. It doesn't appear to be anything too serious, but I'm not sure. Any chance you can squeeze us in?"

"For you? Of course! Do you want me to come to your house? You're at the end of Cedar Ridge Road correct?"

A flash of panic went through her when she realized he knew where she lived. To avoid a paper trail Richard could discover, she had made a point of using cash for everything.

"That's okay. I have to pick up a few things in town so I'll come to you. We can be there in twenty minutes."

"Perfect. I'll see you then," he told her. "Drive carefully. It's icy out today."

If she had still been living with Richard she would have spent the next two hours getting ready to leave the house. Now a five-minute shower, running a brush through her hair and throwing on a pair of baggy jeans and a sweatshirt was all it took. There was little resemblance between the woman living in the cabin and the socialite from New York and that was just fine with Jordan who now worked hard to downplay her natural beauty.

Being pretty opened doors for women but being beautiful made a woman memorable and that was the last thing she wanted. The long, wavy, peroxide blond hair Richard had insisted on was gone, replaced by the natural auburn she had been born with. She knew she should have cut her hair to make a more dramatic change, but she was just vain enough that she couldn't bring herself to do so.

Jade green contact lenses, insisted on by Richard not to correct any vision problems but rather to hide the "ordinary" brown eyes she had been born with, were long gone. Now the eyes reflected back at her in the mirror were the dark chocolate eyes of her childhood.

Even more dramatic was the lack of makeup. A professional makeup artist had been part of their staff back then. Richard demanded perfection and having grown up in a home where his mother was never without a full complement of makeup, he had expected the same from his wife but while skillfully applied, the makeup had nonetheless aged her.

That was behind her now and blessed with natural beauty, the makeup and all the other artificial enhancements Richard had demanded became a thing of the past. Her porcelain skin was now slightly tanned from her daily runs and the freckles she vaguely remembered hating during her childhood once again adorned the bridge of her nose adding yet another dimension to her transformation.

Camouflaging her figure was proving to be substantially more difficult, however. Tall and lean with a dancer's grace and elegance, her physique attracted attention wherever she went. In fact, Richard had told her more than once that he loved watching other men stare knowing they could never have her.

To successfully hide from her husband, she needed people to forget about her, so she had taken to covering her body in nondescript clothing that was far too large, hoping no one would notice the trim figure beneath.

Even with as little preparation as it took to get ready these days, they were late as she had struggled to carry the hundred-pound dog to the truck while trying not to slip herself before starting the slow and torturous drive into town on roads still sporting a hopscotch pattern of ice.

The ancient pickup truck, her only extravagant expenditure beside the cabin, bucked and slipped along the road until she pulled into the driveway where Dr. Norris was waiting. The smile on his face was as charming as ever and she wondered how long he had been standing in the cold waiting for them.

"Let me help you Jordan," he said as he offered his hand. "It wouldn't help to have you fall now too would it?"

"Thank you. I'm sorry we're late. The roads are worse than I expected." Turning to Pete, she reached out her arms to lift him out of the truck before Dr. Norris stepped in.

"I can get him," he said as he wrapped his arms around the wriggling dog. Unlike a lot of dogs, Pete loved his trips to the vet and he was excited to see one of his favorite people. "Hey there big guy. Let's get you inside."

As he placed Pete gently on the ground, she waited for the inevitable compliment.

"You look lovely today Jordan."

It was the same every time they saw each other, even when Jordan knew she looked anything but.

"Thank you, but I think Pete's limp is even more pronounced than when I called." One thing she had learned was if she acted like the words hadn't been spoken, it usually got him off the subject.

"Hum, well let's have a look then shall we?" Trying to be professional after Jordan's brush off, he still couldn't hide the disappointment on his face.

Minutes later, they were in the clinic's single exam room. Rather than hoist Pete up to the slippery steel exam table, Dr. Norris crouched down as his fingers started a slow and thorough probe of the area around the injured leg. He would never show it willingly, but Jordan knew Pete was in pain and yet he never tried to pull away or act aggressively. How wrong the shelter people had been.

"He definitely did something, but I can't tell how serious it is without an x-ray and I'm sorry to say mine is on the fritz. We can take him up to Smith's Mill in the morning to the emergency hospital, but in the meantime, I'd like to keep him here overnight so we keep him off that leg. That way I can keep an eye on him and make sure he's comfortable and pain free."

"Can't I do that at home?" Her hoard of cash was still pretty substantial, but having reverted to her maiden name and unable to get a job without a social security number that wouldn't lead Richard right to her, it wouldn't last forever and she wanted to save money wherever she could.

"You could, but even when he goes out to relieve himself I want him off the leg. I'll carry him out and hold him up while he goes. I think that might be a bit too much for you to manage. I know money's tight for everyone so I won't charge you boarding costs."

He was right of course but it didn't make her feel any better about leaving Pete. Kevin lived in an apartment behind his office and would have easy access to Pete when needed so it was the sensible thing to do, still Jordan couldn't help but feel she was abandoning her best friend.

"I wouldn't normally do this, but seeing as how it's so icy and all, you could stay here for the night. You'd be close to Pete and we could leave for Smith's Mill first thing in the morning."

Startled by the boldness of his suggestion, her head snapped up at the words. Was he asking her to sleep with him? But that's not what she saw on his face. Instead of lust, it was hope. Nothing but hope at the thought of spending some time with her.

Even if she hadn't been working so hard to stay off Richard's radar, the answer would have been the same. As nice as Kevin was, and as much as he and Pete loved each other, Jordan couldn't muster even an ounce of interest in the man beyond friendship. He was certainly attractive, but the only interest she had in him was that he was safe; an unassuming man who wanted nothing more than a wife and family and to be happy in the little corner of life he had carved out for himself. She had learned months ago that he had no ambition for anything other than what he currently had and with no better word to describe it, his life was safe. But it was also boring.

Boring should have been what she wanted after the high stakes, high energy, and high society world she had lived in for a decade, but faced with it, she knew that wasn't what she wanted. She wanted and needed a man who would excite her on many different levels and who she was deeply and passionately attracted to. That was no longer Richard, but it definitely wasn't Kevin either. None of that mattered though because she was still legally married.

"As much as I hate to leave him here, if you think it's for the best that's what we'll do. And I appreciate the offer but it would be too hard on Pete to hear me in the building while he's stuck in a kennel for the night, so I guess I'll go home and come back first thing tomorrow. You'll take good care of him, right?"

Kneeling down she took the dog's face in her hands and looked into sorrowful eyes as if he too realized he was being left behind.

"I'm sorry Pete, but you're going to stay with Dr. Norris tonight. I'll be back first thing in the morning. I love you buddy."

It would be their first separation since becoming a family and emotions overwhelmed Jordan at the thought.

"Don't worry about a thing, Jordan. He'll be fine."

Not wanting to cry in front of either of them, she left the clinic and hurried out to the truck before dropping her head to the steering wheel and erupting in tears. Pete had only been part of her life for a few months, but already the world seemed lonely without him. Leaving him behind felt like she was abandoning him.

With no other option, she started the drive home. The now setting sun and dropping temps were refreezing the water on the roads, making the drive even more nerve rattling. It was a welcome relief when she finally pulled up to the cabin. Wandering from room to room, stopping to straighten a knickknack or wipe away an imagined speck of dust, she was restless and more than lonely without her canine companion, but there was a solution. Changing into the running gear she had discarded before the trip to the vet, she left the cabin on a quest to find some peace of mind.

The freezing rain still coating much of the countryside had transformed the landscape into an enchanting scene when the coating of ice caught the fading rays of the sunset. The entire countryside was now a magical wonderland. But for the few places left in shadows, the weak sunshine throughout the day had cleared the ice from most of her usual route and she ran without hesitation.

It was a cool and crisp evening, the kind she enjoyed the most, but she had already worked up quite a sweat. Stopping for a moment, running in place just long enough to remove the hooded sweatshirt and tie it around her waist before putting her reflective vest back on, she continued on her route.

Nearing the halfway point of her run, she looked up at the big old house on the hill as she always did. Like a gothic mansion, it towered over the rest of the town, surrounded by heavy, dense foliage that blocked passersby from viewing the property. Only the very top level of the house was visible from the road and she wondered not for the first time what the occupants were hiding behind their living wall.

The wall wasn't totally impregnable. Nearly hidden from view was a small wooden door painted in the same green hue as the foliage surrounding it.

At the very back of the property with nothing to indicate the door's reason for existing, Jordan had often let her imagination run wild. Was the door used in generations past for the lady of the house to receive unlikely suitors? Was it a secret door for bootleggers to deliver outlawed whiskey? Or more likely but far less exciting, it may have been placed there as a convenience for anyone wanting to access the back road without having to travel all the way around the property.

Nearing the house, she noticed for the first-time lights peeking out through slight breaks in the foliage. It was the first time she had seen lights in the house since the new owners had moved in almost a month back. Only the occasional barking of a dog had broken the stillness that seemed to envelop the property each time she passed and on those occasions, a sharp command by an unseen male voice quickly stilled the barking.

The hilly road leading past the house seldom saw traffic making it the perfect place to run, especially in the dark, but it was one of those areas that were often in shadow for most of the day and Jordan knew she would need to be extra cautious.

Stopping again for a moment, running in place to stay warm, she surveyed the icy road before deciding that a slow and steady descent should be safe enough.

Concentrating on staying upright, her mind at first didn't register the large black and white mass that launched itself towards her. Lurching away from the object at the last minute, she felt a millisecond of self-congratulatory pride before losing her balance, slipping on the ice and falling towards the deep ravine bordering the far side of the road.

She grabbed for a low-hanging branch in a desperate attempt to slow her fall, only to strip the branch clean while shredding her palms in the process and tumbling headfirst down the ravine. Rocks and branches tore at her body as she somersaulted further down the hill until landing near the bottom in an ungraceful heap of pain and blood, and everything went black.

When she could open her eyes again, filtered starlight shone from above. Confused by her surroundings, her thoughts disjointed and fuzzy, she felt the cold, damp chill that had enveloped her body as she lay on the wet ground. Wedged between two large boulders that had apparently prevented her from tumbling all the way to the bottom of the steep ravine, even the smallest of movements caused searing pain, leaving her struggling to catch her breath. It was at least twenty-five feet back up to the road and she knew she could never make it on her own.

Using what little strength she had, Jordan called out for help, only to discover the sound coming from her mouth was little more than a whisper.

"Help me please," she called with as much volume as she could muster before a dark shape appeared on the road above her.

"Help," she called weakly again, unsure if she was actually seeing something or if her aching head was playing tricks on her. Just when she was about to admit she was seeing things, the sharp bark of a dog echoed above her. Surely the owner wouldn't be too far behind. A sliver of hope entered her thoughts before the pain and cold overwhelmed her and she once again slipped into unconsciousness.

CHAPTER TWO

"Ben?" Staring out the window, he didn't hear her calling at first.

"Ben, dinner's ready." The voice was more determined this time.

"I'll be down in a minute Helen," he responded before turning back to look out the window once more, hoping for a quick glance of the woman.

She was late. She was never late. She had run past the house each morning and each evening for the past month as regular as clockwork, but today she had yet to appear and he chided himself for still standing there. In an even sadder footnote to his current situation, the highlight of his day had now become standing in the dark in front of the one window that overlooked the desolate road bordering the back of the property, waiting for the few precious seconds when a complete stranger ran by. He had seen her many times since moving to the house, and the pattern never changed. Her face shrouded by the hoodie she always wore, pulled low over her eyes, an oversized sweatshirt hung from her slight frame, and more often than not, a yellow reflective safety vest flapped in the wind to help passing drivers see her in the dim light.

The first time she appeared he only caught a fleeting glimpse, but there was something about the way she ran that intrigued him. Her long strides ate up the pavement as if she was floating above the ground and even though she had worked up a sweat; her steps appeared effortless and graceful. He marveled at her dedication while wondering what demons were chasing her as she ran.

Easily keeping pace at her side, the dog never seemed distracted by the occasional squirrel or rabbit that darted across the road in front of the pair. His own dog, Bear, would have been after it in a flash, but the German Shepherd never wavered from her side.

"Ben, your dinner is getting cold." Helen's call was even more insistent, and he realized he was probably holding her up from going home for the day.

The house, inherited from a long-lost maiden aunt, had been the perfect escape from the fiasco in Washington. With few other options, he had packed his meager belongings in a secondhand truck for the cross-country trip. The house was old, but in good shape and clean as a doctor's office, all thanks to Helen. In her late seventies, she had lived with and cared for the aunt he had never met until the woman died at the ripe old age of ninety-eight. With her own family scattered across the country, Helen had stayed on after his aunt had passed away, keeping the house in perfect condition until Ben inherited her services.

He couldn't pay her. Heck, it wouldn't be much longer before he wouldn't be able to feed himself—but it didn't seem to matter to Helen. She lived in a small cottage at the far corner of the expansive property, insisting it was more important to her to have someone to take care of than to receive a paycheck and thus the unlikely pair had slipped into a seamless arrangement.

Used to busy days, the move to a little town in the middle of nowhere had been a bit of culture shock for Ben, but having Helen in the house offered companionship and as they got to know each other, a friendship was already developing.

Unsure what to make of the big city lawyer who lived in the house, Helen had at first served his meals in the large and overly formal dining room while she ate a solitary dinner at the kitchen table; until the evening when he picked up his plate and joined her in the kitchen without a word of explanation. From that moment, their relationship changed. It wasn't long before he thought of Helen as a surrogate mother.

In fact, it was Helen who had suggested he start his own law practice in a town that had none.

The last attorney had gone bankrupt after less than a year in business, but Helen insisted there was a need for legal services even if the office might never be profitable. And thus, without fanfare, the firm of Ben Anderson Attorney at Law came to be in the house's library with Helen serving rather unwillingly as secretary and paralegal.

Helen's concerns that her additional duties would interfere with care of the house became moot as the sum total of the new firm's clients was an elderly farmer in need of a will. It wasn't until the will was executed that the man admitted an inability to pay Ben's fee and had instead offered vague promises to do so upon his death.

Laughing at Ben's naiveté regarding how locals conducted their finances, it had been Helen who assured him the man and his heirs would keep his word.

"Sorry for being so late," Ben offered as an apology when he finally joined Helen at the kitchen table.

She was clearly irritated. Dinner was always precisely at seven and it was well past.

"Were you standing at the window watching for the woman again?" she asked before ladling a hearty portion of stew into the bowl in front of Ben. "I don't know what you find so fascinating about her."

"Honestly, I don't know either," he admitted. "But someone who runs that hard must have a story. I guess I'm just curious about her. Are you sure you don't know who she is?"

"Not exactly. I asked around in town and Molly at the market told me the woman lives just outside of town in a run-down cabin tucked into the woods. The old Olson place, I think. . . oh I forgot; you wouldn't know where that is now, would you? Anyway, she moved in several months ago, lives alone with a big dog, and keeps pretty much to herself."

"That's pretty specific for 'not exactly'," he told her with a laugh.

"Molly said there was something strange about her, though."

"What's that?" he asked between bites of food.

"She pays cash for everything. Paid cash for the house, paid cash for the old beat-up pickup she drives, pays cash for her groceries. Apparently, she doesn't have a checking account. Don't you think that's unusual?"

"Maybe a bit, but some people don't trust banks. Where does she work?"

"She doesn't, as far as anyone knows. Spends a lot of time at the library, I guess, but if she has a job, it's nowhere in the county or Molly would know."

"What else does Molly know about her?"

"They say that the dog that runs with her is a trained killer. She adopted him from the pound. They were going to put the dog to sleep because it kept attacking the staff there. But she came in and hypnotized the animal with some voodoo or something, and next thing they knew the dog was as docile as a kitten. What do you think of that?"

"I think that some people in town have pretty vivid imaginations," he told her with a laugh. "Say, speaking of dogs, where is Bear?" A large black and white Husky, dinner time most often found him begging for table scraps.

"He was getting under my feet when I was making dinner, so I let him outside. I'm surprised he hasn't been scratching at the door to come back in. Let me go call for him."

"Don't worry. I'll go out after dinner if he doesn't come back before then."

After being cooped up in the house most of the day because of the freezing rain, a little fresh air would be good for the dog and the heavy, dense stand of shrubbery surrounding the property would keep him from wandering.

By the time the meal had finished and Ben helped Helen with the cleanup, she was ready to head back to her cottage.

"Would you mind walking me to the cottage?" she asked as she hung the dish towel near the sink. "It's still a little slippery out and I don't want to fall."

"Of course," he told her before helping with her jacket and taking her arm to steady her as they walked together.

For a brief moment, he wondered if his own mother, a socialite who lived for the prestige and social status his parent's wealth afforded them, would ever admit to needing help. Their wealth had allowed her to never age and he couldn't imagine her admitting to a frailty.

"Good night, Helen," he said warmly as they reached the cottage. "See you in the morning."

Bear had still not appeared and, searching the grounds with hands shoved deep in his pockets against the night chill, Ben called his name. Nothing. Walking around the back of the house where it bordered the road, he froze in place. The gate door tucked ever so secretively into the foliage at the back of the house stood wide open.

Picking up his pace, he raced to the gate, calling Bear's name even louder as he looked up and down the desolate road for him. Just when he decided to get the truck to search, the dog's head appeared over the edge of the ravine bordering the opposite side of the road.

"Bear, come," he called from across the road.

Normally well trained and responsive to any command, the Husky didn't move from where he stood staring down into the ravine.

Curious as to what had captured the dog's attention, Ben carefully stepped onto the roadway, mindful of the patches of ice, and tried again.

"Bear, come now." Whimpering but unmoving, the dog continued to look down into the darkness before Ben crossed the roadway to grab his collar. As he did, strong barks replaced the whimpers.

"What in heck are you doing?" Ben asked in frustration before Bear broke free and tried to go down the hillside. Looking more carefully, Ben noticed a faint path through the brush, as if something large and heavy crashed through breaking branches and dislodging dirt and rocks as it went. Near the bottom, he saw something yellow that had flown in the ravine.

Apparently spooked by the site, Bear continued to take tentative steps down the slope.

"It's nothing, boy. Just an old piece of material. Come on. Let's go back to the house."

Turning for home, a slight movement caught Ben's eye. He stopped for another look. Something had definitely moved in the ravine. An animal? Was that why Bear was so interested in going down there? Taking a step or two down the hillside and using the light on his phone to provide some illumination into the darkness, he gasped at the sight. Wedged between two large rocks was a body twisted at an unnatural angle.

Quickly dialing 911, he provided what little information he had before making his way carefully down the slippery hillside.

Bear had been commanded to stay at the top of the hill, in part to help emergency responders find the location, but also to prevent him contaminating a potential crime scene any more than Ben would be doing. Slipping and sliding down the hill, he followed the now much more visible path of destruction littered with pieces of sweatshirt and a running shoe that showed just how forceful the fall had been. He dreaded what he would eventually find.

Slowing down as he neared the body, the reflective yellow vest covered in mud, he gasped yet again. The victim appeared to be the very woman he had been hoping to see from the upstairs window. Whatever movement Ben thought he had seen from the road was gone and an unexpected sadness washed over him before he placed his fingers on the woman's neck, surprised to discover a weak but steady pulse.

"Help is on the way," he said, even though the woman was obviously unconscious. A slurry of mud and blood covered her face and the parts of her body he could see and he reached out to take her hand, startled by the unnatural coolness of her skin. Covering her delicate hand with his own, he willed some of his body's warmth to go into her as he waited for help to arrive. It seemed to take forever before the high-pitched wail of an emergency siren pierced the night and Bear began howling in time with the siren.

Soon enough, the roadway became packed with emergency vehicles, their flashing lights bouncing off leaves in the dense stand of trees lining the road, creating an eerie atmosphere as the first responders made their way down to the woman and Ben climbed carefully back up the hill.

By the time they had the woman securely attached to a stretcher and could make their way up the treacherous slope, significant time had passed. Ben and Bear watched from the sidelines and only Ben's firm hold on Bear's collar kept him from going to the woman's side. The dog's agitation was unusual, but maybe to be expected with all the surrounding strangers.

"So, tell me again how you found her?" the Sheriff's deputy asked as he took out a notepad and pen and approached Ben once again.

Ben wasn't old, but the Deputy looked young enough to still be in school and from the way he tugged at the tie around his neck, it was easy to see he would be more comfortable in a t-shirt and jeans.

"It's like I told you before," he started with a mild level of annoyance at having to answer the Deputy's questions yet again, "my dog was standing at the side of the road and when I went to bring him home, I looked down the ravine and saw her."

"How do you know her?" he asked.

"I don't know her, well, not really anyway. I think she's the same woman who runs past my house every day, but I never met her and don't know her name."

"Her name's Jordan Wheeler. She lives in the old Olson place south of town. I'm sure you've seen her around town with that big German Shepherd."

"Actually, I've only been in town a few weeks myself."

"Oh, that's right. You're that big city lawyer who opened up an office here, right? I heard about you from the Sheriff. He thinks you'll be broke within six months."

Ben didn't admit it, but if he was a betting man, he wouldn't even give it that long the way things were going.

"So where are they taking her?" Ben asked as the ambulance doors closed and the vehicle pulled away.

"To the hospital in Smith's Mill," the Deputy said. "But she looked to be in pretty bad shape, so I wouldn't rule out her being airlifted to the big hospital in Cross Lake. Say, you seem awfully interested in her for someone who claims not to know her. You don't know how she fell, do you?"

"I'm not sure I like what you're implying, Deputy. I already told you but I'll say it again. I don't know what happened to her. Maybe you should do your job and figure it out."

A few months ago, Ben wouldn't have lost his temper with the man and he regretted it as soon as the words were out of his mouth. After all, an attorney never knew who might be a potential client, but he was right about one thing—Ben was interested in the woman and hoped she would be okay.

Locking the gate securely behind him as the remaining emergency personnel packed up their belongings, Ben continued to keep a firm grip on Bear's collar until they were once again in the house. The dog's agitation continued and Ben realized he felt equally unsettled after what had just happened, unsettled but happy that he finally knew something about her.

"Jordan. Her name is Jordan," he said to the empty room. For weeks now, he had referred to her as "the woman" and it was a relief to know her name. It suited her, well, at least as much as the very little he knew about her, but he wanted to know more. Making a snap decision that was so unlike him, he grabbed his truck keys and headed to the hospital in Smith's Mill.

.   .   .   .   .

"I'm inquiring about a patient brought in by ambulance a little while ago. Her name is Jordan," he told the receptionist in the emergency room.

It was only on the thirty-minute drive that Ben had realized medical privacy laws would prohibit him from getting any information about her condition, but he had to try.

"Are you family, sir?" the woman asked without looking up from her computer.

"I . . .," he said before hesitating. As much as he wanted to know how Jordan was doing, if his current situation had taught him anything it was that nothing good comes from a lie.

"You're looking for Jordan Wheeler?" a nurse said as she hurried towards him. "Come with me please."

For reasons Ben would never know, the woman seemed to have made an assumption about his being family and he said nothing as she escorted him into a treatment room. Attached to a myriad of monitors Jordan lay deathly still as activity continued around her. She still appeared to be unconscious but judging by the calm demeanor of the medical staff, she didn't appear to be in any immediate danger. He stood by the door transfixed by the sight of her. They had cleaned away the mud and blood that had covered her body and with his first genuine look at her face, he found himself captivated by her beauty.

"Dr.? Miss Wheeler's family is here."

"Perfect," the doctor said as he guided Ben to a corner of the room and shook his hand. "She should be okay, but that was a heck of a spill she took. I think the cold weather actually helped her a bit, but she has several injuries that will keep her out of commission for a while. She dislocated her left shoulder and we've popped that back in already. Shouldn't need surgery, but you never know. She broke a couple of fingers and some of the smaller bones in her hand and we're putting a cast on that now, and she has a pretty badly sprained knee, but from what they told us about where they found her, she's pretty darn lucky that she didn't have more serious injuries."

"So, is that it?" Ben asked, unable to contain his surprise that she wasn't more seriously injured.

"Well of course there is the head injury," the doctor said almost as an afterthought. "She's got a pretty severe concussion and will need to be watched carefully for a few days."

"Has she woken up yet?"

"Briefly when they brought her in, but she was pretty much just babbling ... talking about a cow that hit her and knocked her down. Really she was making no sense and as soon as we gave her pain medication she went out again. We'll keep her overnight for observation, but tomorrow she should be able to go home with you. Someone will have to be with her for a few days because of the head injury, but with time and rest, she should make a full recovery."

"Can I sit with her for a while?" Ben asked. The question just slipped out of his mouth.

"She's going to sleep through the night so why don't you come back say late morning tomorrow? She should be ready to go home by then. Leave your name and number with the nurse and we'll call you if that changes, but she'll be in expert hands tonight."

"Thanks doctor," Ben said as they shook hands. The nurses were already preparing to move Jordan to another room and Ben quickly handed over one of his new business cards before walking out the door with only a quick backwards glance.

Walking out of the hospital, he wondered why he hadn't corrected everyone who assumed he was Jordan's family. Helen had said she lived alone and maybe, just maybe, she had no family. It certainly didn't justify his deception, but tomorrow he would stop by just to ensure she was going to be okay and that would be the end.

Driving home from the hospital in what was now the middle of the night, a smile covered Ben's face; it had been there since learning Jordan would be okay. She was a stranger to him and yet in all the drama of the last few months, she had, for some reason he couldn't figure out, become important to him. Other than Helen and Bear, he really had no connection to another human being in his new hometown and it was just beginning to dawn on him how much he missed adult companionship. Whatever the case may be, he couldn't get her out of his mind.

Just a few short months ago, Ben had been an up-and-coming lawyer with a prestigious Washington D.C. law firm. Graduating from Harvard Law near the top of his class and recruited by firms across the country, his future had seemed bright and he eagerly put in a hundred hours or more each week to secure that future.

Whispered in hushed tones throughout the firm was talk of a partnership and as much as he had tried to contain his growing excitement at the possibility, the realization that he may be the first new partner in over a dozen years made all the sacrifices worthwhile.

It hadn't taken long for him to become the newest golden boy in the firm and why not? According to a senior partner, Ben was a new, handsome face that clients immediately trusted and after years of living in his brother's shadow, he had finally come into his own. Women loved him, men wanted to be him, and everyone in the firm wanted to work with him. Big money corporate deals fell into his lap bringing prestige and wealth to the firm and with each victory he moved one step closer to the coveted partnership.

Having already sacrificed so much to get to that point, he couldn't imagine a better payoff, but late nights of burning the midnight oil had ruined more than one promising relationship and as his forties loomed on the horizon, he had doubted a wife and children would be part of what had finally become a fairy-tale life. Yet he continued on, working all hours and giving up time with friends and family to reach the goal of seeing his name on the firm's letterhead.

Who would have thought that just when it seemed the brass ring was within his grasp it would all come crumbling down around him?

That he let it happen was what kept him up at night. D.C. had been Ben's world, one where he was his own man. He had flourished in the capital and had achieved a well-earned reputation that had nothing to do with his brother. Then Brandon came to Washington and with one phone call it all came crashing down around him.

Brandon was the twin brother he had once loved more than anything in the world but who had so often been the bane of his existence. Physical appearances aside, the two were as different as night and day. Big brother by two minutes, Brandon was rebellious and mischievous and a schemer from day one with a singular goal of gaining as much power and wealth as possible by any means possible.

Easily navigating the maddening social structure of high school, Brandon had been the most popular boy in their elite private school. Everyone wanted to be his friend yet in reality, the only genuine friend of Brandon's was Ben.

Overshadowed by Brandon's gregarious and outgoing nature, Ben had, by high school standards at least, faded into the woodwork. A thoughtful student, he kept his head down and worked hard. While Brandon partied, Ben stayed home so often that some in the large school never even realized Brandon had a twin.

Still, being overshadowed by his brother had not been an issue until Brandon got himself into the first of many situations he needed Ben to get him out of.

Being a star running back on the high school football team did nothing to help Brandon in the classroom and for years he had skated by academically. That is until a new coach showed up. The old school coach who only cared about a winning season had been replaced by a man who understood that football was just a small part of high school and actually learning something was more important.

Suspended from the team for poor grades, only their stepfather's plea for a do-over on his math and science finals provided Brandon a second chance, although his odds of passing were slim. He needed his brother's help. As with many twins, the boys had pranked friends and family many times in the past with one boy pretending to be the other, but those had been the harmless pranks of children. This time was different and Ben knew he shouldn't be part of the plan, but Brandon's persuasive skills ultimately convinced him to take the tests in his place.

The dramatic improvement in the test results should have been a clue the boys had switched places. Ben was an exceptional student, yet no one questioned the results. Reinstated on the football team, Brandon quickly fell back into his old ways reveling in how easy the deception had been. Ben was another story. Guilt gnawed at him with such intensity he threatened to come clean about what they had done and only Brandon's threats to expose Ben's complicity in the incident had kept Ben from telling the truth. He might never be smarter than his brother, but Brandon was smart enough to know how important Ben's reputation was to him. In the end, Ben kept his secret.

After years of similar situations, Ben's resentment and anger at being used by Brandon ultimately eroded the bond of brotherly love. Vowing to never again bail his brother out of a jam, he thought his life would finally be free of guilt, but the vow didn't hold and in the end it cost Ben everything when Brandon showed up in Washington as the nation's newest senator.

The pundits and indeed the party chairs on both sides of the aisle were left shaking their heads over how it happened, but as with everything else in his life, Brandon had charmed his way onto the ballot and into the hearts of voters and eventually into the office of U.S. Senator in a landslide victory over a long-term incumbent.

His arrival in D.C. set off a media firestorm, and he quickly became the darling of a town bursting with wealth and power. It was high school all over again, but on a much grander scale.

That he was a married man with two small children went unnoticed by the public as Brandon was photographed time and time again with beautiful young women who were not his wife.

While Brandon basked in the attention, Ben watched from the sidelines as the brother's paths continued on their separate ways until one late-night phone call that would change the course of Ben's life.

"Hey Benny my boy, long time no see."

As much as Ben tried, he couldn't help but cringe and wonder why his once beloved brother was reaching out after so long.

"Brandon. Hello," he said flatly. It was the best he could do.

"Sorry I didn't call you when I got to town, but how have you been?"

Small talk wasn't Brandon's usual conversation starter and the hairs on the back of Ben's neck went up. Something was definitely wrong.

"What's wrong?" he asked with a sigh.

"What do you mean? Can't I call my little brother just to say hi?"

"You haven't talked to me in months and now you call out of the blue? I'll ask you once again. What's wrong Brandon?"

"Well since you bring it up, I am in a bit of a jam and I wonder if you can help me out."

"What have you done now?" How could he possibly have gotten in trouble in the few months he had been in the capital?

"Remember how you and I used to prank on people and convince them you were me and I was you?" he asked. Actually the "prank" as Brandon called it, had only been one sided as he well knew.

"Brandon just tell me what you did. I need to get back to work."

"Oh, that's right. Mother told me you're up for partnership. I'll never understand why you went into corporate law. Sure, the money's good, but the amount of work you have to put in . . . what a waste. Politics is where the big money is Ben, trust me on that one."

"Damn it Brandon, what do you want?" Too tired to play Brandon's games, he wanted nothing more than for the conversation to be over.

"Well, you'll probably see it on the news tomorrow; that is, unless you're willing to help me out. You see there's this girl . . ."

As long as Ben could remember there had usually been a girl involved somewhere in his brother's misdeeds.

". . . and, well, it turns out she is a little underage and even though we were being careful, somehow the media got wind of it and, well hell, they have pictures okay? Pictures of her and me coming out of a hotel room together."

"Jesus Christ Brandon. You're married! Or did you conveniently forget that?"

"Come on Ben, you know how it is here. Women are everywhere and they are young and ambitious and well, you know I've never had a problem attracting the good-looking ones. She came up to me and I didn't want to hurt her feelings."

"So, you took an underage girl to a motel, screwed her, and got caught. Is that what you're telling me?"

"Well, I wouldn't put it so crudely, but yeah I did. And it turns out she was only sixteen and a hooker on top of it. Some reporter from the Post has the pictures, and he's threatening to go public with the story if I don't pay him off. Do you know what that will do to my career? You've got to help me little brother."

"Just what the hell do you want me to do? Pay the guy off and be done with it and then keep your dick in your pants and go home to your wife." Crude language wasn't the way Ben normally expressed himself, but something about this seedy conversation brought it out in him.

"I can't pay him off. He's asking for two million. I don't have it and I know you don't either. I could ask the folks, but we really don't need to drag them into this. Besides, even if I paid him he would just keep coming back for more."

"Just what do you expect me to do?" Ben asked even though he knew full well what was coming.

"Be me."

There it was. Brandon's solutions to all of life's problems. He wanted Ben to step up and take the blame for him.

"You can't be serious," Ben said with just a faint laugh.

"That's not exactly what I mean. We can tell the reporter it was you coming out of the hotel. No one cares what a lawyer does in this town so it won't be a big deal for you. In fact, it might end up being a great thing. There's no bad publicity, right? So, little brother, can you do me a solid on this one?"

"Let me get this straight," Ben said slowly. "You are asking me to pretend it was me that took an underage girl, no let me get this right . . . an underage hooker, both of which are a crime in every state in the nation, to a hotel and had sex with her?"

"Damn it Ben, don't get all high and mighty on me. I made a mistake okay? We've always been there for each other and you know how much this could cost me. If you tell the reporter it was you and not me he'll go away because there's no story okay. Nobody cares what a lawyer does in this town and that will be the end of it. We can each go our separate ways and you'll never have to hear from me again."

Unfortunately for Ben, in a moment of weakness, the only part of Brandon's plea he could focus on was the last part. The thought of not having to deal with Brandon again was enticing if they could get away with it. After all, no one would care enough about what Ben was doing to publish the story and since no police had been involved, it wasn't much of a story, anyway.

Ben's momentary hesitation was all Brandon needed, and he quickly laid out the plan for how they would proceed.

Against all reason, Ben found himself sucked into Brandon's drama once again and it wasn't long before he was on the phone with the reporter setting up a meeting in an all-night coffee shop a few blocks from his law firm.

Like all hastily thought-out plans however, it ended as the worst mistake of Ben's life. The reporter, whose usual beat was the courthouse, immediately recognized Ben and with very little effort connected the twin angle and once he did, there was no convincing the man Ben had been with the girl. The story made the front page of the biggest newspaper in D.C. and within twenty-four hours the wire services had picked it up. Ben's old school partners, wanting nothing to do with such a public scandal, had sent him packing without so much as a backwards glance. As far as the legal profession was concerned, Ben was now damaged goods and no one would even talk to him about a job. Before long and with his savings dwindling fast, the fancy car, and condo had to be sold and, unless he wanted to be homeless, he was left with one option—the long-abandoned house he now called home where he would try to rebuild his life.

He left D.C. in the rearview mirror while, after a mostly symbolic vote of censure by the Senate, Brandon went on with his life as if nothing had happened. There truly was no justice in the world and Ben wondered how long it would take before those memories became less painful.

CHAPTER THREE

"Mail for you, Ben," Helen said as she walked into his office the next morning and placed a stack of envelopes on the corner of his desk.

"I don't suppose there is a check from Mr. Bennett in that pile is there?" he asked with a wry smile. Try as he might he hadn't given up hope the elderly farmer would pay his fee before the man died.

"I'm afraid you'll be waiting quite a while before you see a fee from that man. Folks in his family have lived to be well over a hundred. But I have some good news for you," she said. "There might be a case on the horizon."

"What do you mean?"

"Didn't you hear all the sirens last night? Sounded like they were awfully close. A good accident case would bring in a lot of money from the insurance company."

"I think you've been watching too much TV," Ben said with a laugh. "Besides, that's not exactly what happened."

"What do you mean?"

"Remember that woman? The one who runs by here all the time?"

"You mean the one you're a little fixated on?"

Her accusation made Ben feel like a stalker, but she had a point.

"Let's not go there okay? Anyway, she had some kind of an accident right behind the house. I was looking for Bear, who by the way somehow got out of the back gate, and found her all busted up at the bottom of the ravine. When they got her out, they took her over to the hospital in Smith's Mill."

"What happened to her? Is she dead?"

"No, in fact, for such a terrible fall, she's in pretty good condition. The doctor told me . . ."

"What do you mean the doctor told you?" Helen interrupted. "Why would the doctor tell you anything? Did you go to the hospital?"

"Well, yeah, but . . ."

"But what? What reason could you have to be there?" Standing with hands on her hips, she glared at him in frustration.

"If you'll let me explain," he said to stop her from yelling at him, "you said she lived alone and I figured if it was me I wouldn't want to be all alone in a hospital, so I went just to make sure she was going to be okay. One thing led to another and next thing I know the hospital staff thought I was her family and I guess I didn't dissuade them of that idea."

"So you lied to them?" she said in a manner that made him feel ashamed of his behavior. He hadn't shared the details of what went down in D.C. with her but she was an avid fan of all the news outlets and he suspected that she had checked up on him before he moved in. She probably thought lying was a way of life for his family.

"Again, I didn't lie, but I also didn't clarify my position when they made the assumption."

"A lie of omission then."

"Yes, I guess so."

"What happened to her? How'd she end up at the bottom of the ravine?"

She listened patiently as Ben relayed what little he knew about the evening's events.

"And this Jordan, is that what you said her name was? She never regained consciousness?"

"Not when I was there, but the doctor said she was awake when they brought her in and she claimed a cow knocked her down the hill."

Helen directed a funny look his way but said nothing.

"Why are you looking at me like that?" he asked.

Nodding her head in the direction of the large dog sleeping contently in front of the fireplace, she cocked an eyebrow at him and waited for Ben to connect the dots.

"No . . . you don't think . . ."

"It makes more sense than a cow wandering on the road," she said. "You said Bear was standing at the top of the ravine when you found her and you know how excited he gets when he sees new people. I'm not saying he did it maliciously, but it was pretty icy out last night and maybe it was just a freak accident."

"A freak accident that could cost me what little I have left," he said sadly. The evidence against the black and white dog was circumstantial but realistically it was the only explanation that made sense.

"So what are you going to do about it?"

"I had planned on stopping by the hospital again. She's supposed to get out this morning and now it appears I might have to ask her some questions. Maybe Bear had nothing to do with it."

"Don't get your heart too set on that," she offered. "Something tells me as innocent as that dog looks right now, he's the cause of all this."

As she got up to leave the room, the phone rang startling them both. Calls had been few and far between since opening the office.

"I'll get it," Ben told Helen as she went back to the kitchen. "Anderson Law Firm"

"Is this Ben?"

"It is. How can I help you?"

"This is Dr. Burns at the Hospital in Smith's Mill. I'm calling about Ms. Wheeler."

"How's she doing?"

"Quite well all things considered, but she certainly is eager to be released. It's my preference that she stay for observation for a few more days, but as long as you're there with her all day it should be safe enough. Can I assume that won't be a problem?"

"I don't think . . ."

"You will be with her right? If she doesn't have that support system in place I'm afraid I won't be able to release her and she seemed very stressed over not having any health insurance. She is quite insistent that she leave. What should I tell her?"

Suspecting Bear caused the woman's injuries, Ben couldn't let her continue to rack up a huge hospital bill.

"It won't be a problem. I'll be over in about an hour to take her home. Thank you, Doctor."

Guilt over what Bear had apparently done to the woman weighed on him but knowing that she had no insurance, he couldn't in good conscience let her worry about the cost of her care much less having to pay someone to stay with her for the next several days. Even if it meant asking his mother and stepfather for a loan, he would have to make this right. Grabbing his keys, he headed to Smith's Mill.

.   .   .   .   .

"Great news," the nurse said as she breezed into Jordan's room. "Your family should be here in an hour to take you home."

The nurse's words caused Jordan to catch her breath as she looked back in horror at the woman. How had Richard found her so easily? Had one stupid decision destroyed her future?

"My family?" she asked.

"Well, your husband. I saw him when he was here last night and honey I can tell you, he's one of the most handsome men I have ever seen. You sure landed a good one there. Muscles on top of muscles and those piercing blue eyes. I've been married for fifteen years, but I'd leave my husband for yours in a heartbeat. Oh my God, I'm so sorry. I shouldn't have said that out loud. Let's get you unhooked from all this equipment and dressed for the trip home. I brought some scrubs you can wear since we had to cut everything else off you last night."

As the nurse continued her work, Jordan thought about what she had said. Richard didn't have blue eyes and while he was in good shape for his age, he certainly wasn't built like the man she was describing. Obviously he couldn't be bothered to bring her back himself and had instead sent one of his security minions. No matter who had come to bring her back, she knew the injuries from the fall didn't compare to the punishment Richard would dole out when he saw her again. The thought of going back to him made her skin crawl.

"There you go dear, free to go. We're sending you home with a cane so you're a little more stable with that bum knee. I scheduled a follow-up visit with Dr. Burns in three weeks. Now you just sit here and wait for that hunky husband to collect you and when you're ready press the nurse call button and I'll come back to wheel you out to the car."

The woman had no way of knowing that now Richard had found her she could never recover the freedom she had enjoyed for these few precious months. Almost as soon as the nurse left the thought came that she should flee—walk out of the hospital and away from whomever Richard had sent to collect her. But with no real clothes, no money, and her injuries, where would she go?

Standing at the window, staring out into the more seasonable brilliant sunshine that had appeared as a welcome relief from the dreariness of yesterday's freezing rain, Jordan felt trapped and afraid. Although her life here wasn't much to speak of, at least she had been safe and happy. Now she would be back under Richard's thumb and fear of his abuse. Tears filled her eyes, and she did nothing to wipe them away as they cascaded down her cheeks.

"Jordan?" came a deep male voice. Her escort had arrived.

Hastily wiping the tears from her face, she turned to face the man, shocked to see he looked nothing like she expected but everything like the nurse had described. Then her breath caught in her throat. She knew him. He was one of the many shady men Richard had brought into their lives throughout the marriage, but unlike most of those men, this one had assaulted her at a party years before. The sight of him standing in her hospital room was terrifying, but she was also confused. She remembered every detail of the terrifying assault but she hadn't remembered him being one of Richard's security detail.

A touch over six feet tall, with dark wavy hair and piercing blue eyes framed by thick dark lashes any woman would kill for, he was definitely an upgrade in the looks department from the security people Richard normally employed, but knowing what she knew about the man, Jordan would have preferred to deal with one of the others. The dark hint of a beard accented the sharp angle of his jaw but didn't quite hide the slight cleft in his chin. There wasn't an ounce of extra fat on the man and the nicely tailored cut of his suit couldn't hide the muscular build underneath. He could have been a model for any designer and yet here he was doing Richard's dirty work. Her skin crawled at the thought of being alone with him for the trip back.

"So, you've come to take me back have you?" she asked as she reached for the cane propped against the bed. "Nice touch telling them you were my husband."

"Sorry about that and for the record I didn't actually tell them that. They assumed that and I didn't correct them," he said with a brilliant smile. "My name is Ben. Ben Anderson."

The hand he extended to her was unexpected, but she made no move to shake it and he slowly pulled it back. There was something different in his eyes from the last time they had seen each other. When he had his hand up her skirt at the party, his eyes had been dark and cold, but today his eyes sparkled with happiness. But that wasn't the only thing unsettling.

"You don't have to introduce yourself. It's not like I care after all and I don't imagine Richard would be pleased you are being so nice to the prisoner."

"Excuse me? Am I missing something Miss Wheeler?"

"Why are you calling me that?"

"That's your name right? Jordan Wheeler?"

"Wait a minute," she said as she realized that Richard and his henchmen would never have called her by that name. "Who exactly are you and why are you here?"

"Ah, as I said my name is Ben Anderson and I was the one who found you after your accident. The ravine is just on the other side of my property. I came to see if you're okay and if I can help."

"You mean Richard didn't send you?" she asked in surprise. What was he doing here if Richard hadn't found her? Was it possible he wasn't the man from the party and just looked like him?

"No and I'm sorry but I don't know who Richard is. I'm here because I heard you were getting out today and I thought maybe I could give you a ride home. The doctor told me you shouldn't be alone and I've been told you live alone so I thought maybe I could help."

"What in the world are you talking about and how do you know I live alone?"

None of this was making any sense to Jordan, but she knew she didn't want to go anywhere with this man whether or not he was admitting to his true identity. Just when she was about to tell him so, the doctor walked in.

"Oh great, I got here just in time," he said cheerfully as he shook the man's hand. "So, as I told you this morning, because of her head injury she can't be alone for the next three days. You'll make sure of that right?"

The man and Jordan looked at each other as he nodded his agreement to the doctor. What was going on?

"You, young lady," the doctor said as he shook her good hand, "take it easy for a few days and let this guy pamper you. If you change your mind about the pain killers, just give my office a call, but otherwise keep up with the acetaminophen and I'll see you in three weeks for a follow up."

Obviously she was missing something in this conversation and as soon as the doctor left she looked up into the steel-blue eyes of her assumed "husband" demanding answers.

"What exactly is going on here?"

"I'm sorry, but it was the only way I could get you released today," he said.

"What are you talking about?"

"The doctor told me you have to be with someone at all times for the next few days. I was told that you live alone out in the country and that you don't have health insurance and can't afford to stay in the hospital so I told him you would come home with me."

"How would you know all that? Oh, wait a minute. I forgot. You're my husband. Just what else have people told you about me?"

"Please let me explain. I think I caused all this. Well at least I think my dog did."

"Look mister, my head is throbbing and nothing you are saying is helping with that. Will you just tell me what you're doing here and why you think I'm going to leave with you?"

Now that it was obvious this guy wasn't connected to Richard, her confidence was back even if his uncanny resemblance to her attacker still unsettled her.

"If you'll sit down before you fall down and give me a few minutes, I'll explain it all."

Still in enough pain that standing for so long was causing her to become woozy, she quickly took a seat on the edge of the bed.

"Thank you," he said as he pulled up a folding chair across from her. "I'm pretty sure my dog Bear is involved in how you ended up at the bottom of the ravine. He's a large black and white Husky and the doctor told me you were saying a cow knocked you off the road. Since Bear had gotten out of the gate from my property and he was standing at the top of the road where I found you, it appears he was the cow and I am so very sorry. And because of that I don't want you to worry about paying for any of this. I'll take care of all your expenses."

As he talked, she tried to remember what had happened before she fell. He might be right. It may have been a dog that had rushed at her causing her to fall. In a perfect world she would expect him to pay her hospital bill, but she didn't know this man and didn't want to have that kind of connection to Richard if he was indeed the man from so long ago.

"If you're worried I'm going to sue you, don't be. What happened was just an accident and I can pay my bills myself. I don't need your help."

"Yes, I understand that, but it's my responsibility, and it's the right thing to do. I've already told the hospital to send the bills to me so you won't have to worry about it. But there's another thing."

"Now what?"

"Doctor's orders. You can't be by yourself and I thought maybe you could stay at my house for a few days."

"Are you kidding me? I don't even know you."

"It wouldn't just be the two of us . . . I have a housekeeper. Her name is Helen. She lives on the property too."

"I don't think so," she told him as she got up intending to find her own way home.

"Look, I'm not a crazy person. In fact, I'm a lawyer."

"That explains the suit," she told him sarcastically.

"What's that supposed to mean?"

"Look mister, around here, the only people who wear suits are lawyers and the guy from the funeral home. You don't look like a mortician so you must be a lawyer and you stick out like a sore thumb in that suit."

He actually looked a bit hurt by her comment and she recognized how mean it had been even if it was the truth.

"If you're done criticizing my appearance, can we get back to the issue at hand? You need a place to stay for a few days and I have plenty of room. We won't even have to see each other in the house if you don't want, but at least there will be someone there if you need help."

"I don't need help with anything," she snapped uncharacteristically. Her pain level was going through the roof and she just wanted to go home. "I have Pete . . . oh my God, Pete!"

How could she have forgotten! She was supposed to have met Dr. Norris this morning to get x-rays for Pete.

"Do you have a cell phone?" she asked as she struggled to stand.

As he held his phone out she grabbed it and quickly dialed the vet's office. There was no answer.

"Do you have a car? Can you give me a ride?"

"I do and I'm happy to take you home with me," he told her.

"That's not it. I need to go to the emergency animal hospital here. Do you know where that is?"

"No, but this is a pretty small town and someone will give us directions. My truck's just out front."

Stopping only to ask for directions to the animal hospital, they hurried to his truck as fast as her hobbled condition would allow.

"Can I ask why we're going to the animal hospital?" he said as she drummed the fingers of her uninjured hand on her lap.

"My dog Pete should be there. He got hurt on the ice yesterday."

"I'm so sorry. Of course, I should have known he would run with you. I never even looked for a dog."

"What? No. He wasn't with me. It was too icy for him to run. Hey, how do you know he runs with me?"

"Pretty hard not to know," he said with a chuckle. "You've run past my house twice a day every day since I moved in and that dog is hard not to notice. So how did your dog get hurt if he wasn't with you?"

"He slipped on the ice when I let him out in the morning. The vet doesn't think it's anything serious but wanted him to have x-rays. I was supposed to meet him at his office first thing this morning to drive to the animal hospital. There was no answer when I called his office so I hope that means he and Pete are here. Look, there it is up ahead."

Spotting Dr. Norris's battered van parked in front of the building, she breathed a sigh of relief.

Just as the attorney was opening the door to help her out of the truck, Dr. Norris came out of the building with Pete by his side. Once the dog recognized his owner, he pulled away and raced to Jordan's side, nearly knocking her off her feet in his excitement.

"Hello buddy," she said as Pete covered her face in dog spit. "I missed you so much."

"Oh my God Jordan," Dr. Norris said when he finally saw her. "What happened to you? And who is this?"

The sheer number of bruises and a black eye that had nearly swelled her eye shut would have been enough to cause concern, but add to that the cane, the cast on her hand, and shoulder sling and she looked like a truck had hit her.

"Ben Anderson," the attorney said as he extended his hand to the obviously stunned veterinarian. "As you can see Jordan had a minor accident and spent the night in the hospital. I'm taking her home."

The mix of confusion and disappointment on the veterinarian's face was hard to hide and Jordan actually felt sorry for him. After all the times she had put him off, it was apparent he thought there was something going on between her and the lawyer as he looked at her for more explanation. As tired as she was of putting off his advances, she knew his interest in her well-being was genuine and she quickly tried to put him at ease.

"I'm fine. Took a little tumble during my run last night, but nothing too serious. I'm sorry I couldn't let you know before now, but the important question is how's Pete? He doesn't seem to limp anymore."

"X-rays were negative. I think he just twisted that back leg on the ice. He slept comfortably through the night and there's no sign he's in any pain this morning so I think he'll be just fine. But if you can keep him kind of quiet for the next two days just to make sure he doesn't re-injure his leg that would helpful. Doesn't really look like you'll be doing much running or much of anything else for a while though. I can stop out at the cabin and help if you like."

"There's no need," Ben said. "Jordan, and Pete of course, will stay with me for a few days."

Torn between confusion as to why Ben thought she had agreed to his plan but not wanting to deal with Kevin showing up at the cabin, Jordan said nothing about the situation.

"Was there anything else Jordan needs to know about her dog?" Ben asked.

"I guess that's everything," Kevin told him.

"Thanks for taking such good care of Pete," she told him as she reached for Pete's leash. "If you give me a couple of days to get a bit more mobile, I'll drop off payment at your office."

"No hurry," Kevin assured her before giving Ben a skeptical look. "You know I really am happy to take you and Pete home. It's on the way."

"We've got it handled thanks," Ben said dismissively. "Jordan if you're ready I think it's time we get you back to the house and settled in. You're looking a little tired."

For someone who was in such good shape, she was indeed tired and her head continued to throb. She just wanted to crawl into bed with Pete by her side and sleep the day away.

"Thanks again Dr. Norris and I'll see you in a few days."

Driving away from the animal hospital, Pete on the seat between them, Jordan cast furtive glances at Ben. The interaction between the two men had been strange. In fact, they had acted like two teenagers fighting over a girl, neither one of them realizing that there was nothing to fight about. Pete was settling down after the excitement of seeing her again and as he turned around twice on the seat, she expected him to lie down with his head on her lap. Instead, he turned to Ben and carefully placed his head on the man's leg as Ben reached down to pet him.

"That's odd," she said as she watched Pete's unexpected behavior.

"What's that?

"Pete. He's really taken to you."

"Doesn't he normally like people?"

Hesitating to frighten him, she explained Pete's situation at the pound.

"Interesting. You know my housekeeper told me there are stories going around town about how you did some kind of voodoo on the dog so you could handle him when they couldn't. You're not some kind of voodoo princess are you?"

"Not hardly," she said softly. "As you can see, Pete is the sweetest dog ever, and he's never been aggressive. But if people choose to stay away from him because they think he might bite, well that's okay with me too."

"Why is that?" he asked in surprise.

"It's just that I value my privacy and where I come from people didn't stick their nose into my business. I know people talk about me here and I just wished they weren't so concerned about my life."

"Where are you from?"

The innocent question caught her off guard. Answers to those types of questions had been part of her pre-escape planning, but to hear someone actually ask made her hesitate for a moment and she hoped he didn't realize it.

"East of here."

As she gave the vague answer, he turned to look at her and she quickly looked away. Lawyers were inquisitive as she well knew and she didn't want to get into a more detailed discussion with a stranger.

"I live about five miles outside of town and we're going to go right by my driveway. You can drop us off on your way home."

"Can't do that," he said with a smile. "You need to have someone with you round the clock for the next couple of days so you'll have to come home with me unless you have somebody else to stay with you. Do you want me to call the Vet? He looked like he'd be happy to stay with you."

Choosing to ignore his dig at Dr. Norris, she argued the point.

"I feel fine and I know what the doctor said, but really there's no need. I'll be fine on my own."

"You might think that, but I promised your doctor. If you don't come stay with me, then I'll have to take you back to the hospital."

"You wouldn't do that," she said angrily.

"Oh, but I would. So, it's up to you. Back to the hospital or you be my guest for a few days."

Folding her arms across her chest she could feel the anger building. What was it with men who thought they could control her life? Casting a sideways glance at the man, she could see he wasn't kidding.

"Fine, but what about Pete?"

"He comes too. Bear would love to have a friend to play with."

That seemed to settle it and silence overtook them as he started the drive back to his house. Overwhelmed with tiredness from all the activity of the morning and the waves of pain that kept flooding across her body, Jordan drifted off to sleep, waking only as the truck pulled to a stop.

"You live here?" she asked in surprise looking up at the two towers framing the front of the house—the same two towers she passed every day on her runs. He had told her she ran past his house, but it wasn't until they arrived that her pain riddled brain actually connected it with this place.

"I do, but I've only been here for a month. It belonged to a spinster aunt I never met, and she left it to me when she died. Pretty gruesome looking isn't it?"

Trying to be nice, she also wanted to be truthful. "Well, it's old, but with a fresh coat of paint and maybe some flowers out front it wouldn't be so bad. I always wondered who might live in a house like this."

"And was I what you pictured?" he asked as he helped her down and handed her the cane. Pete jumped out behind her to start a thorough investigation of the yard.

"Not exactly," she said diplomatically.

"Think you can manage the stairs okay?" he asked as she followed him up to the porch.

"If I take it slowly. You know I really can go home. You don't have to do this. I'm sure the last thing you need is a stranger in the house."

Before he could answer, the front door opened and a small woman with perfectly white hair and glasses perched on the end of her nose walked out to greet them. She looked over the top of the glasses at Jordan.

"Who do we have here?" she asked before directing a stern glance at Ben.

"Helen, this is Jordan Wheeler. She's the woman I told you about who had the accident behind the house last night. She's going to be staying with us for a few days. Jordan, this is Helen Patterson."

"Hello," Jordan said shyly, reaching out her one good hand as the woman looked her up and down. She could feel the disapproval flowing from the woman and wondered what she had done to earn such dislike. Casting an accusatory look at Ben she clarified, "This isn't my idea I assure you. I'm perfectly happy to go home, but apparently I am not allowed a vote."

Ben smiled in return before helping her into the house and depositing her in a chair in a large and sunny room.

"Now you're going to need some things for the next few days I imagine. If you put together a list and give me your address I'll drive over later and put a bag together for you."

Tricked into staying with him, Jordan hadn't considered she would need things from the cabin. The mere thought of letting a stranger in the house seemed too much of a risk.

"That's okay. I appreciate your willingness to do it, but I'd rather collect the things myself if you can drive me."

"Sure, if you'd like. We'll go later this afternoon if that's okay. Helen, please make up the first-floor guest room for Jordan. I'm sure she would like to lie down for a bit."

Just as he finished talking, a large Husky walked into the room, stopping just long enough to survey the new arrivals before his gaze landed on Pete, who without Jordan noticing had found his way into the other dog's comfy bed by the fireplace. For a moment both dogs tensed and the hairs on Jordan's arms stood up expecting there to be a fight, but the Husky gave Pete a sniff, started wagging his massive tail and settled in beside him. It was as if the dogs had known each other for years.

Pete might have felt comfortable in this strange house, but Jordan was anything but. While Helen went to attend to the guest room, Ben settled in on the sofa across from his guest and stared at her as she looked around the room.

"Why are you looking at me like that?" she finally asked turning back to face him.

"You look awfully familiar to me, but I can't seem to place you. Where did you say you came from?"

"I didn't."

This time her answer caused him to raise his eyebrow, but he didn't pursue the line of questioning and she turned the tables on him.

"What brought you here?" she asked.

"Like I mentioned earlier, I had a relative who left me this house. I lost my job in D.C. and needed a fresh start and this was about as far away from my old life as possible so it seemed like a good option. I didn't know until I arrived that the last attorney to try to open a practice here went bankrupt in just a few months. You'd think with no lawyer within a hundred miles that it would be a lucrative business, but so far I've only had one client and he couldn't even pay my fee. Helen seems to think that people around here don't trust lawyers. What do you think?"

"I think she's right. Most folks seem to be working class and having someone come in from the outside wearing an expensive suit with a fancy education probably makes people nervous."

"That's the second time you mentioned my suit. Are you saying if I dress a little less professionally they might accept me a bit more?"

"I guess I am. Lose the suit jacket. It makes you look unapproachable. You probably can keep the tie but loosen it up a bit. You'll be surprised at how people will accept you if you don't look quite so intimidating and buttoned down."

It wasn't in her nature to tell others what to do, but something about the man seemed to bring it out in her; either that or it was the pain she was in that was becoming worse with all the activity and she hoped it was the latter. It just wasn't in her nature to be so contrary.

"Thanks for the advice. I'll try it."

"Miss Wheeler, your room is ready if you'd like to come this way," Helen said from the doorway.

"Thank you and please call me Jordan," she told her as she struggled to stand from the deep chair before Ben jumped up to help. "Could I trouble you for a glass of water? I think I need to take a couple of aspirin and lay down for a bit," Jordan added.

She had always had a high tolerance for pain but had never experienced the type of full body pain that had been coming in waves for the last hour. She was finding it hard to concentrate and as she downed the aspirin Helen provided, she doubted the wisdom of having turned down the prescription pain medication offered by the doctor. Pete had already made himself comfortable on the double bed and she joined him, being careful to move slowly to minimize the pain that had already drained her. By the time her head hit the pillow, she was out like a light as Pete settled closer to her.

.　.　.　.　.

Night had fallen when she finally woke and for a moment she struggled to remember where she was until a persistent scratching at the door preceded a sliver of light and the door slowly opened. Pete raised his head at the intrusion but seeing the Husky at the side of the bed he settled down again.

"Jordan are you awake?" Ben asked in a soft voice.

"Yes."

"I don't want to bother you, but I wanted to make sure you were okay. You've been sleeping for hours and missed lunch and dinner. Helen is keeping some food warm for you in the oven if you're hungry."

"Thank you. I need to get Pete's food from the cabin."

"He's already had some of Bear's," he assured her as he came into the room. "While you were sleeping, I came in to check on you and then took Pete and Bear out to the yard for some exercise. I hope that's okay. We didn't want to disturb you."

"What time is it?" she finally asked.

"It's almost nine."

Had she really slept that long? A small pile of what appeared to be her clothing was visible on the dresser across the room.

"Are those my things?" she asked in surprise.

"I hope you don't mind, but when it looked like you were going to sleep through the night, Helen drove out to your cabin and picked up some things for you and Pete for the next few days. We can always go back tomorrow if there's something she didn't think of."

"How did she get in my house?"

"She said there was a key in the flower box by the front door."

She was right of course. With no place to carry a set of keys when she ran, Jordan had fallen into the habit of placing a spare key near the door. Apparently it wasn't such a good hiding spot if Helen had found it so easily.

Pete hopped down from the bed and the two dogs left the room as she struggled once again to get up. Ben came quickly to her side as dizziness overwhelmed her.

"Are you okay?" he said as he grabbed her arm to prevent her from falling.

"I think so. I was just dizzy there for a minute, but it's going away now. It's probably because I haven't eaten."

"Do you think you can make it to the kitchen?" he asked.

"Yes, thanks."

The walk to the massive kitchen at the back of the house was a painful one. Everything had stiffened up while Jordan slept and she sank into a chair as Ben took the food from the oven and placed it on the table in front of her before taking his own seat. Ravenous after a couple of days of not eating, Jordan dug in; stopping only when she realized Ben was staring at her again.

"What?" she asked as she put her fork down.

"Nothing really. It's just that I can't shake the feeling that I've met you somewhere before. Did you ever live in New York? That's where I grew up."

As hard as she tried, she couldn't control the look of suspicion that crossed her face and knew he had seen it too. New York is a massive city, but Richard moved in elite circles and that community was smaller than one might think. Was he really the man from the party? If so, it was like he had completely changed his personality, but something told her this wasn't the same man. They had definitely not met, but he was digging for information about her that she had no intention of sharing, so she lied.

"No."

"Hum, well then it must have been someone that looked like you. They say that everyone has a doppelgänger somewhere right?" Little did he know.

Trying to change the subject, she asked after Helen. "I'd like to thank her for collecting my things and for the food."

"She doesn't actually live in the house," he reminded her. "There's a small cottage on the far side of the property and she lives there. She left a couple of hours ago but she'll be back in the morning and you can thank her then."

An uncomfortable silence descended on them. It had been a long time since Jordan had a normal conversation with a man and it didn't help matters he was a stranger to her.

"What kind of law do you practice?" she finally asked.

"In D.C. it was corporate law but I'm kind of resigned to the fact that my practice here will be wills, divorces, and maybe a land dispute or two. The stuff that any first-year law student knows how to do, but I have to pay the bills somehow."

"Why did you leave Washington?"

As innocent a question as it was, she could tell it struck a nerve by the change in his posture and facial expression.

"I'm sorry, it's none of my business and I'm the last one who should ask people to spill their secrets."

As soon as the words were out of her mouth, she realized she had just drawn a large bullseye on the fact that she had her own secrets to hide. He raised an eyebrow at her but said nothing about it.

"You know I wasn't sure I wanted to tell people that story, but I suppose it's going to come out at some point." He stared out the window before finally getting up and pouring himself a cup of coffee.

When he finally spoke, the entire story came out as he shared what had cost him his job and about his lifetime of covering for his identical twin brother. Suddenly it all made sense to Jordan. The man she met so many years ago at the party, the one who couldn't keep his hands to himself, had to be the brother. They truly were identical in almost every way, but then again, the eyes never lie.

"So I packed everything up and moved here because short of asking my parents for help, it was the only option left to me. No law firm worth a dime will hire me after what happened in D.C."

"Why didn't you ask your family for help?" she asked even though people could have asked her the same question. Her family, even if they had been able to help, had severed ties with her years ago. Not only had she turned her back on the family name, but her parents had despised Richard. By the time they were married, her parents had officially cut Jordan out of their lives. Turning to them for help when she left Richard had never been an option.

"If I had I'm sure they would have helped, but that's not the man I am. After everything with my brother, I promised myself I would never ask someone else to get me out of trouble. Besides, after everything went public, I had brought enough shame to the Harrington name."

"I thought you told me your last name was Anderson?" Having now caught him in a lie, she was instantly on alert.

"It is. My dad passed away when I was just a baby and my Mom remarried and now her last name is Harrington. James and Lillian Harrington. Maybe you've heard of them? My stepdad is one of the wealthiest real estate tycoons in the country. Anyway, my brother changed his last name to Harrington, I supposed to cash in on the connection to my stepdad's money, but I kept my father's name."

Not only had she heard of his family, she and Richard had attended many events in their mansion across from Central Park. Although she didn't remember seeing Ben at any of those functions, it certainly was conceivable that he had been there and seen her. No wonder she looked so familiar to him.

"Ah, I don't think I've ever heard of them," she lied. "Thanks for dinner, but my head is pounding and I need to go back to bed. Come on Pete. Good night."

Her abrupt departure aside, she had been enjoying talking to the man, but his questioning proved he was dangerously close to discovering her secret and that just wouldn't do.

CHAPTER FOUR

Pete snoring peacefully at her side, Jordan slept little that night while trying to come up with a solution to prevent Ben from connecting her to Richard. The doctor had ordered two to three days of observation meaning just one more day before she should be able to go home to the solitude of the cabin.

She longed for the tranquility of the cabin even as her physical condition remained unchanged. In fact, as the night wore on, the headache had subsided, but all the bumps and bruises became more painful than ever causing her to regret her snap decision to avoid pain medication over worries that not keeping a clear head might lead to accidentally saying something that would give away her secrets.

Turning for yet another look at the bedside clock she was relieved to see it was near dawn. Home at the cabin she would get up for a morning run soon, but from the sounds outside her bedroom door, she wasn't the only early riser in this house. Slowly getting up from the bed, she stretched as much as her painful condition would allow to try to loosen the muscles that had tightened overnight, happy to discover Helen had selected clothing that would be simple to slip on.

Looking in the full-length mirror across the room, her eyes filled with tears. The dozens of deep purple bruises and her swollen and discolored face would have sent children screaming into the night and she finally realized that only the grace of God had spared her life.

Pete's wet nosed nudged at her hand. He was hungry. They made their way to the kitchen guided by the smell of fresh brewed coffee.

"Good morning," she said softly so as not to startle Helen who was standing with her back to the door as she cracked eggs into a sizzling pan.

"Jordan, good morning," she said before wiping her hands on her apron. "Oh my, you certainly are colorful today."

Having already seen her reflection in the bedroom mirror, Jordan couldn't disagree and smiled back hoping to gain a little more acceptance from the woman.

"It's not as bad as it looks," she assured Helen although her pain levels were still elevated. "I wonder if I could trouble you for a glass of water."

"We can do better than that. Have a seat and I'll have breakfast ready for you in a minute. Ben is usually not up this early, but I heard him moving around upstairs so I expect he'll be down shortly. Were you able to get much sleep last night?"

"Not really, but I slept almost all day yesterday, so that's expected I guess. I wanted to thank you for picking up my things and for keeping food warm for me last night. I know you don't want me here and I'll be gone as quickly as I can."

"You're very welcome and I'm sorry we didn't get off to such a good start. It's not that I don't want you here, but Ben has an enormous heart and I just hate to see someone take advantage of him."

"But this wasn't my idea . . .," Jordan began before Helen cut her off.

"I know that and I'm sorry, but it's my job to protect him. Ben had a hard time before he came here and it's been difficult for him. He hasn't made any friends until he met you."

Unsure whether the story Ben had told her last night had been shared with Helen, Jordan said nothing as Helen placed a plate of food and a glass of juice in front of her. Seconds later Bear and Pete were sitting on either side of her, staring hopefully at the plate even though they had both already polished their food bowls clean.

"Pete, you know better than to beg," she told him sternly. "Lay down." As if she had made the command to both dogs, they lowered to the ground in tandem while still looking expectantly at her.

"You certainly have a way with dogs," Helen said before taking a seat across from Jordan, her gnarled and seemingly arthritic hands warmed by a steaming mug of coffee.

"I never had a dog before adopting Pete and didn't know how we would get on, but now I don't know what I would do without him," Jordan admitted as Ben walked into the room. He appeared to have taken her advice because there was no sign of the suit coat and his tie hung loosely around his neck.

"I feel the same way about Bear," he said as he gave Helen a kiss on the cheek before dishing up his own breakfast and joining the ladies. "And let me apologize once again for the trouble he caused you. He's always been too friendly for his own good and I'm sorry you suffered because of it."

"It's okay. It was just an accident. He's a sweet boy." Reaching down to scratch behind Bear's ears, the dog licked Jordan's hand before she pulled it away.

"He can actually be a bit of a troublemaker, but I've noticed how protective he's become of you. You probably didn't realize it but he slept outside your door all night."

That was a surprise to Jordan, but she had also noticed that whenever she got up from a sitting position, Bear and Pete were both right next to her as if they were trying to prevent her from falling.

As Helen got up from the table and left the room, Ben once again began staring at Jordan. It was exasperating.

"Why do you do that?" she finally asked.

"Do what?"

"Why do you keep staring at me? Didn't your mother ever tell you how rude that is?"

"Sorry. I guess I didn't realize I was doing it again, but I'm still trying to figure out who you remind me of and it's driving me nuts."

"I probably look like a hundred women," she said to convince him to let it go.

"That's absurd," he said with a smile. "Women as beautiful as you are pretty rare."

Lowering her eyes to conceal her reaction she could feel the flush spread across her cheeks and for the first time she was grateful for the bruises that would hide it from view.

"Thank you," she said, "but you should just let it go. I don't like it when people pry."

For a moment he said nothing, but she could feel his eyes boring into her before she finally looked up to see just the hint of a smile on his face.

"Duly noted," he said. "Have you thought about what you'd like to do today? I'm still working on getting my office set up in the house, but maybe we can go for a walk around the property or if you're not up to that we can watch movies or something."

"Could you use some help?"

"With what?"

"Getting your office set up. I'm pretty good at organizing and I'd like to do something other than just sit all day."

"Are you sure you're up to it?"

"I told you I'm fine."

"From the looks of you I'm not so sure I'd agree, but I could sure use the help. My office is the one with the French doors. When you're done with breakfast, that's where I'll be."

Remembering the area from when she had first entered the house, Jordan knew he was right about needing help. The room was packed with boxes.

"I'm ready now if you are," she said before standing carefully with Bear and Pete close behind.

Walking like an eighty-year-old because of the pain and stiffness she felt, Ben's eyes continued to follow her. The constant scrutiny made it even more imperative she get out of his house and back to the cabin before he figured out how he knew her. Trying to shield her face from his prying eyes Jordan was grateful she had let her hair fall loose this morning.

For the next few hours they worked side by side in relative silence organizing the mess in his office. The room, having previously served as a library, would now house the hundreds of law books from the boxes. A bit too unstable to climb a ladder, Jordan filled the lower shelves while Ben worked above her head. By the time they unpacked all the boxes, the room appeared much larger.

"This is terrific. I didn't think I would ever get those books unpacked. It seems you instinctively know how to organize them. Why is that?"

"My Uncle Ronnie was a lawyer and when I was a little girl, I used to help my Mom clean his office on weekends. When she wasn't looking I'd sneak into his law library and page through the books. For a while I even thought about becoming a lawyer, but as I grew up and discovered other things in life, being stuck in an office seemed too confining."

"There are times I feel that way too, but for me the challenge of figuring out my case and convincing a judge or jury to see my client's side of the story is such a high that I don't think I could ever give it up."

Drawing gave her the same high and she understood what he was saying but doubted the clients he might get in this area would provide that same challenge.

"I imagine the work you did in Washington was much more glamorous than what you'll be doing now," she pointed out. "I've only been here a short while myself, but nothing exciting seems to happen around here."

"Admittedly I've had to adjust my expectations about the job, but if I ever get any clients at least I'll have the satisfaction of helping someone. For now let's take a coffee break," he suggested.

"If you're suggesting a break because of me, there's no need. I actually feel better being able to move around." It was the truth. The more they had worked, the better she felt.

"Actually, I'm the one who needs the coffee. In D.C. I worked long hours and coffee got me through the day. Full transparency? I'm guess I'm a caffeine addict."

Sitting together once again in the kitchen, they could see Helen out back hanging freshly washed laundry on the line, the wind gently swirling the clothing around her as she clipped the garments to the line. Jordan had a vague memory of her mother doing the same thing throughout her childhood reminding her how much she missed having her mom in her life. It had been years since she had heard her voice. Sure, it would be easy to pick up the phone and place a call, but if Richard was looking for her, he might have gone looking in her hometown. Any calls to her parents posed too much of a risk to not only her, but them as well.

"If it's not prying," he said giving her another curious look, "why don't you tell me a little about yourself. Do you have brothers and sisters? What do you like to do with your time? Do you work?"

As much as she didn't want to share private details of her life, it had been years since anyone cared enough to ask and with thoughts of her mother still swirling through her mind, she discovered she wanted to talk.

"I don't work, well at least I haven't for years. I didn't need to before, but pretty soon I won't have a choice."

"Money problems?" he asked. "Trust me; I know exactly how you feel. If I don't get some clients soon the utility company will be very unhappy with me. What was your line of work, I mean before?"

"At one point in my life I considered myself a gifted artist, but once I got out of my sheltered small town, it didn't take long to realize my talents were a dime a dozen. I might as well have done paint by the numbers as far as buyers were concerned."

"You painted?"

"Nothing as grand as that. I did pencil and charcoal drawings, mostly. A bit of graphic design for friends of my father who wanted to promote their business; certainly nothing that was going to show up in a museum or anything."

"Can I see some of your work?"

"There's nothing to see. I haven't sketched anything in over a decade."

"Why not?"

"There was no point. I wasn't any good, and it was a waste of time when I should have been bettering myself."

"That sounds like a father talking," he told her. "Was he the one who said you weren't any good?"

"No," she quickly assured him although most of the time Richard had acted like a father instead of a husband. "He had nothing to do with it and I haven't seen my father for years. I just realized one day that I would never be as good as I thought I was so I stopped wasting my time."

"Would you sketch something for me?"

"What would be the point?"

"Why does there have to be a point? Come on? For me?"

"I don't think so. That's all in my past. The next time I sketch someone it would have to really mean something to me otherwise it would just be a waste of time."

"I don't think I'd agree that doing anything that brings you joy is a waste of time. Did I tell you I play the piano?" he asked. "Well, I should clarify that I try. Had lessons when I was a boy, but never really put the time into it like I should. Back when I actually owned a piano I played just for the sheer enjoyment of making music. It was a great creative outlet for me from my, what did you call it? Buttoned down life?"

As he threw her own words back at her she tried to decide if he was angry with her. He seemed anything but. The charming smile he directed her way sent a thrill coursing through her body. Shirt sleeves rolled up above the elbow, tie loosened at his neck, hair mussed slightly from the work they had been doing, his smile stirred a desire within her that had been missing for a very long time. It wasn't just his obvious good looks she found so attractive as much as the way he truly seemed to care about a complete stranger.

He continued to probe for information, but the more he asked the more she shut down. Was he trying to trap her or just get to know her? Flashing back to the look of lust on his brother's face as he had manhandled her at the party, it seemed even identical twins could be as different as night and day. Maybe someday the memory of that unpleasant encounter with the brother would fade leaving only the memory of the caring look Ben now directed her way.

She wasn't naïve enough to believe Ben's only interest in her was guilt over Bear knocking her down. He was definitely attracted to her and in another time and place, his attention would have flattered her. The day she married Richard however, she had thrown away any chance at true happiness with a man and as with Dr. Norris, she couldn't give Ben any hope of there being more between them as much as she might want otherwise.

"I'm sorry, I've kept you from your work long enough. Please excuse me."

Getting up from the table as quickly as her battered condition would allow, she walked back to the bedroom to get a sweater and compose herself a bit. Interacting with Ben was unsettling in many respects and more than anything she wanted to walk out the front door and go back to the peace and security of the cabin, but even if she could do so, it was a long walk that her current condition made nearly impossible. What she could do however, was go outside and take a slow walk around the property. Calling Pete to her side, the pair slipped quietly out the front door.

The sun was shining and the slight breeze carried with it the scent of apple trees and lilacs that were just beginning to bloom. Turning her face to the sunshine, Jordan breathed deeply. In this remote part of the west, Mother Nature's handiwork was pure and untainted by human interference and she breathed in again to fill her lungs with the pure goodness.

Pete raced around the yard investigating every new smell as Jordan walked slowly behind. Taking in the myriad of colors beginning to appear in the flower beds and lawn that was sporting a lush green carpet of grass, she reached the gate to the road opposite where she had fallen.

Reaching for the latch, she hesitated for a moment, her hand stopping in midair. Was she ready to see where her life could have ended? Like a witness to a car crash, the need to see for herself was overpowering and before she talked herself out of it she was through the gate and standing at the top of the ravine.

In the clear light of day, it was easy to see the path she had created during the fall. Subconsciously cradling the still tender palm that had been ripped to shreds in her desperate attempt to stop her fall, she shivered in the sunlight. The ravine was steep and strewn with large boulders she had probably bounced off of on her way to the bottom. It truly was a miracle she hadn't died. Pete's nose pushed into her hand and she reached to pet him. As always, he seemed to sense her emotions and sat quietly as she looked down into the ravine. A moment later, Bear joined him.

"Jordan, are you okay?" Ben asked softly. She hadn't heard him walk up behind her, but oddly enough his presence, standing so near she could smell the faint aroma of his aftershave, was comforting.

"Did you see me fall?" she asked without looking at him.

"I'm sorry, I didn't. In fact, I almost didn't see you at all. It was already dark by the time we found you and I almost walked away until I saw something move down there. If it hadn't been for that I might never have known you were there."

"And I might have died."

"I guess so, but you didn't and we should focus on that blessing."

"Things would have been easier if I had you know. At least it would be over."

Taking her shoulders in either hand, Ben spun her gently towards him with anger in his eyes.

"You shouldn't even joke about something like that. Listen Jordan, I'm not stupid. I know there is something going on with you that you don't want to talk about. We all have our secrets I suppose, but I wish you would realize you can trust me. If you're in some kind of trouble, please let me help."

The look of pleading on his face was profound and she would have given anything at that moment to tell him everything and accept the help he was offering, but he was one of them; one of the golden circle of wealthy families that Richard was part of and that meant he wasn't to be trusted.

"I don't know what you're talking about," she told him sadly before leaving him behind as she walked back to the house with both dogs at her side. She went straight to her room and closed the door behind her, unable to get the concerned look on Ben's face out of her head.

Sure, she had told him too much, but how had he figured out she was in trouble? Pacing back and forth in her room it finally came to her that as a lawyer he was used to reading people and as prepared as she thought she was for hiding her past, she didn't stand a chance against someone so adept at getting the truth out of people. It was time for her to go home whether or not the doctor thought so. Quickly gathering her few personal things she opened the door casting a quick look down the hallway and, seeing no one, she hobbled to the front door.

"Going somewhere?" Ben said from behind, his words stopping her in her tracks. "You should at least have lunch first if you're thinking of walking all the way home."

"Look, I'm sorry," she said before turning back to face him as he leaned against the kitchen doorframe. Her face was red with embarrassment beneath the bruises, but she was determined not to be talked out of her decision. "Yes, I know I should have said goodbye, but I didn't want you to try and stop me because I'm going home. I appreciate everything you've done for me, but I've made my mind up."

"Having gotten to know you just a bit, I can see that in you, but be realistic. Do you really think you can walk all the way home? If you're determined to go, and I think you're making a mistake just so you know, at least let me give you a ride."

Was this some sort of trick? Why was he giving in so easily?

"What's the catch?" she asked suspiciously.

"No catch. I apologize for asking so many questions when it's obvious you don't want to trust me. Whatever's going on with you is your business and I promise not to pry anymore. I'll take you home and you'll never have to see me again if that's what you want, but we're both outsiders here. I know I could use a friend and I think you could also, so all I want is for you to promise that if you need anything or if you ever want to talk about what's bothering you, you'll call me."

"That's it. You just want to be friends?"

How many times had she heard that from a man before being accosted by them?

Richard's friends were intimidated by him, but apparently not enough so that they worried about hitting on his wife. On more than one occasion she had made the mistake of trusting one of them who claimed to want to be her friend only to want so much more.

"That's it. Just friends."

Searching his face for any sign that he might be lying she came up empty. The tension she hadn't realized had been in her since entering Ben's house slowly evaporated and the corners of her mouth turned up slightly.

"That's nice," he told her.

"What?"

"Your smile. I think it's the first time I've seen you smile. Now how about that lunch and then I'll take you home?"

Knowing it wouldn't be long before she would be safe and sound in her own home, her smile grew even wider.

·   ·   ·   ·   ·

"Boy you're really tucked back in here aren't you? Are you sure it's safe?" Ben asked as he turned off the main road and drove further into the woods.

"Safe enough with Pete at my side I expect," Jordan told him. "Besides, I like the privacy. Most people probably don't even know there's a cabin back here."

"That's kind of my point. Anything could happen to you and no one would ever know."

"Are you only saying that because I'm a woman?" she asked raising an eyebrow at him.

He couldn't have known how right he was. If the day came when Richard discovered her whereabouts, he could do anything to her and no one would ever know. But it was that same seclusion that made her feel safe. Richard would have to know the cabin existed in order to find her and the odds of that happening were slim.

"Not completely although that's part of it. There's a lot of crazy people out there and I want you to be safe."

"Look Ben, I know you want us to be friends, and I'll admit that's not a totally abhorrent thought . . ."

"I don't know if that statement should flatter me or not."

"But it would have to be on my own terms and that means don't ask so many questions. My private life is my private life and either you accept that or we part ways right now."

He studied her for the longest moment before responding.

"You are the most confounding woman I have ever met but I accept your terms. The next time I ask you something you feel is over the line just say so. I want you as my friend."

As the truck pulled to a stop in front of the cabin and Ben killed the engine, the silence of the woods engulfed them. The polite thing would be to invite him inside, but was she ready for that? It surprised her to realize the condition of her home embarrassed her. Sparkling clean though it may be, it was a far cry from Ben's house. Still, if she was ever to make friends, she would have to trust someone.

"Would you like to come in?" she asked finally.

"If you're sure."

It must have been the last thing he expected to hear from her, but she nodded and offered a quick smile as Pete and Bear jumped from the truck ahead of them.

"You can just put my things on the bench there and I'll put them away later," Jordan said as she moved to the stove to start some coffee.

The small kitchen seemed cramped with Ben's enormous frame filling the room, but as he looked around, his presence was comforting.

"Your house is nice," he said as he moved into the living room.

"No, it's not and I know it. It's a dump," she told him before placing a couple of mismatched mugs on the table. "About the best thing you can say is it's clean, but it was private and the only place available in my very limited price range."

"If you like I could help by fixing some things for you. Even if I say so myself, I'm pretty good with a toolbox and you wouldn't have to pay me."

"Thank you. I appreciate the offer, but I'm not a charity case. I pay my way and I'll get repairs made when I can afford to pay for them myself," she insisted.

The thought of having Ben in her house regularly was unsettling. He was far too attractive, and she had been alone far too long. It would be too much of a temptation to resist even if she wasn't ready to trust him.

"Well, if you change your mind the offer is still there. Say, how come you don't have any photos?" he asked as he looked around the small space.

"There's no one to have pictures of."

"Was that question over the line?" he asked as he came back into the kitchen and took a seat at the table.

"I guess not. I already told you I haven't seen my family in years."

"Why is that? Did they die?"

"No, at least I don't think so. Honestly I'm not sure. My parents cut ties with me a very long time ago when I made some decisions they didn't agree with."

"Do you realize that the lawyer in me is just itching to know more? Every time you say something like that it makes me wonder what the rest of the story is. Maybe someday you'll realize that you can trust me."

"How many times have I heard that from a man before," she snapped. "Everyone who has ever said that to me has been a liar."

He had definitely touched a nerve and anger seethed within her as her hands clenched into fists so tightly her nails dug into her bandaged palms. Surprised by her extreme response to a rather benign statement, Ben looked at her sadly from across the table.

"I'm sorry that men have treated you badly in the past," he said softly, "but not all men are like that and you're being unfair by assuming I would treat you the same. I've done nothing except help you and offer my friendship. Maybe I should just leave."

He got up from the table and turned to leave, stopping only when she spoke.

"I'm sorry. But I'm damaged goods and getting involved with me even as just a friend isn't fair to you. Maybe it's for the best."

Turning back to her, hand still on the doorknob, he looked confused, as if he was trying to decide whether to ask more questions, but in the end, he just left.

· · · · ·

"Did you get Jordan all settled at home?" Helen asked when he walked in the house.

"I suppose," he said sadly. The entire drive home he had regretted walking out.

Something about the woman continued to draw him to her and it wasn't just because he couldn't shake the feeling he had met her before. From all outward appearances she was one tough woman, but hidden behind those dark eyes he sensed a real vulnerability that called out to him.

It was obvious Jordan was in some kind of trouble, but what exactly? The little clues she dropped each time they talked might be inadvertent, but unintentional or not, it seemed she wanted someone to come to her rescue. There had to be a way to crack the façade she had built to protect herself.

"Is it just me or does there seem to be a lot more to her story than she lets on?" Helen asked.

"Honestly I was thinking the same thing," he admitted. "But if she isn't willing to let us in, maybe it's best we just stop asking questions."

"Best for whom?"

"What do you mean?"

"It seems to me that each of you were brought here and thrown together for a reason. Jordan might not be talking, but I have a feeling you might be just what she needs in her life."

"You mean a lawyer?"

"No, although maybe that too. I think she needs a friend."

CHAPTER FIVE

Being home again worked like a tonic on Jordan's battered and bruised body and each day she felt better than the one before. At first the stairs to her bedroom had proven difficult, but taking it slow and with Pete at her side, she managed them and within days was well enough that it tempted her to run. Remembering the doctor's orders she quelled the desire and settled instead for long walks along the country roads surrounding the cabin. The peacefulness of the countryside allowed ample time to think and it was on one of those walks it came to her that something had changed.

It had been two weeks with no one for company except Pete and after months of being on her own, she was lonely. It was a different loneliness than what she had experienced with Richard. In New York, surrounded by people, she was often ignored and isolated from the surrounding conversation. Things were different now and it was Ben who had triggered it. His kindness and sincere interest in getting to know her, something she hadn't been subject to in years, had made it harder to be alone now. It was only now, when she had closed the door on a friendship with him, that she discovered what she had lost.

She wanted and admittedly needed someone who loved her and cared about her. In marrying Richard she had thrown away any chance at not only the love of a good man, but the love of her family. Sitting on the front steps while Pete chased squirrels up a tree, her thoughts drifted to home and her mother. Over a decade had passed since she had last spoken to her parents and it wasn't a pleasant memory. Name change aside, her father was incensed not only by her decision to marry a man over two decades older, but one whose reputation as a ladies' man had reached all the way to their hometown. Their last call had ended with her dad calling her a whore as he slammed the phone in her ear.

As painful as that was, the memory had never left her although years later she realized it had been her dad who decided to cut her out of the family. While he was delivering his edict, her mom had said nothing and in fact, other than asking questions about why Jordan was marrying Richard, she had not passed judgment at all.

Was it possible that after all this time her mom might accept her back?

The threat of Richard lingered of course and moving back home would never be an option, but would one little phone call hurt? Emotionally fragile after everything with Richard, it was a risk to open herself up to her parent's disdain again, but at this point she really had nothing left to lose. Reaching for the phone, she slowly dialed the number.

"We're sorry. The number you have dialed is no longer in service . . ."

What did she expect? It had been too long, but she wasn't ready to give up and tried one more call to her mom's office.

"Larson Accounting," a cheerful voice announced.

"Ah hello. I'm looking for Nancy Wheeler. Does she still work there?"

"Of course, I'll put you right through."

Her heart raced in her chest and her hands shook. For the briefest of moments she was tempted to hang up.

"Nancy Wheeler."

The soft comforting tone of her mother's voice came over the line and all the love she felt for the woman cascaded through Jordan at once. Just two simple words and she had been transported back to her childhood. Afraid to lose that feeling, she said nothing.

"Hello, is someone there?" her mother asked. "Hello?"

"Mom?" she said hesitantly. "It's me, Jordan."

Dead silence greeted her words, but at least her mother hadn't hung up. The sound of soft crying filtered through the line.

"Mom please don't cry."

"Jordan is it really you? Oh, honey are you all right?"

How did she answer that question?

"I'm . . . well, I'm okay, I guess. How are you . . . and Dad?"

"I'm fine and Dad is fine. Honey where are you? Did Richard find you? Some men have been here looking for you."

Jordan's blood ran cold. Obviously it had been wishful thinking to assume he couldn't find her. The man who knew her as Victoria Stevens had somehow discovered her real name.

"Mom listen to me carefully. You can't tell anyone that we talked. Not even Dad. I left Richard and it's a long story but if he finds me I'm afraid what he might do to me. I'm sorry I didn't listen to you and Dad," she said before bursting into tears.

"Jordan, please don't cry. I've waited for this day for over ten years and I'm just so grateful that you're away from that man. Do you need anything? I can send you money."

"No Mom. I'm fine. Really I am. But I'm sure Richard's men are watching you, so I probably won't be able to call again soon. He will not give up on punishing me for leaving him and I don't want you and Dad to get hurt."

"You need to go to the police Jordan. They'll protect you."

"I wish that were true," she said sadly. "But you don't understand just how powerful Richard is. It's better this way for all of us. I'll try to call again in a few months to let you know I'm okay, but it means so much to me you didn't hang up."

"Oh honey, your Dad will regret it to his dying day. He was just so hurt that you seemed to want to leave us all behind that he said and did things he shouldn't have. If he could just hear your voice again . . ."

"Mom, I just can't. You want to believe he's sorry, but after everything with Richard, I just can't have another man treat me that way. I love you more than you know and I miss you every day but I have to go."

"Please Jordan, don't go. I love you too, but please . . ."

Ending the call before her mother could finish her statement, Jordan started crying happy tears. She was no longer alone.

. . . . .

After weeks of limited activity, Jordan was hoping for good news during her follow-up doctor's appointment. Her shoulder felt healed, and the knee was as strong as ever with only the lingering yellow discoloration of her skin where the deeper bruises remained. In fact, looking into the mirror these days, she was pleased with what she saw.

"I think you and I will run tonight," she told Pete before racing down the stairs to the kitchen. "Just need to get the all clear from the doctor and then it's back to the road for us both."

There was an extra spring in her step and a smile on her face as she prepared to leave for the doctor until Pete looked at her sadly. She hadn't reached for his leash. The bout of unseasonably warm weather had led Jordan to the decision to leave the dog at home rather than risk the heavy coated dog overheating as he waited in the car for her.

"Sorry pal, but you have to stay home this time," she said before his ears perked up and he ran to the window overlooking the front of the cabin and issued a few warning barks.

It took a minute before Jordan heard what his sensitive canine hearing had detected. Someone was driving towards the house.

Had Richard found her after the phone call with her mother? Reaching for the baseball bat she kept as protection near the door, the flaw in her escape plan, which hadn't included what to do if Richard showed up, became apparent and her heart raced until she recognized the truck and all thoughts of fleeing into the safety of the woods evaporated. It was Ben with Bear riding shotgun. Pete instantly recognized the pair and began to bark and wag his tail furiously. Putting the bat down she went out on the porch.

"Good morning Jordan," Ben said cheerfully as they got out of the truck and Pete and Bear raced after each other in the yard. Used to seeing him in a suit, he looked decidedly casual today in jeans and a polo shirt. It was still a bit much for this part of the country, but the short sleeves of the shirt struggled to contain the massive biceps he sported and she could see the faint outline of his abs confirming her original suspicions that he was no stranger to working out.

"What are you doing here?" she asked as he walked closer before stopping at the bottom of the steps. It had been over two weeks since they last saw each other and it surprised her when her stomach started doing flip-flops at the sight of him looking up at her.

"Today's your follow-up appointment right?"

"So?"

"So, I'm here to drive you."

"Why?"

"Don't you remember? I promised your doctor I would bring you back and you know I'm a man of my word."

"No, I don't remember," she admitted. "Thank you but I can drive myself. In fact, I was just going to leave."

"Then my timing is perfect. Your chariot awaits my lady," he said before sweeping his arm towards his truck. "The dogs will keep me company while you're with the doctor."

"Thanks for coming all this way, but you probably have better things to do and besides I was going to run some errands after the appointment."

"Not a problem. I have the whole day free. Now we better get going if we're going to get there in time."

Waffling with how to get out of the situation, she couldn't help but stare at the man and once again she felt a warmth course through her body. His eyes never wavered from her own and his smile, creating just the slightest bit of a dimple, was intoxicating. Surprising them both, a smile of her own reflected back.

"I probably shouldn't say this, but you look terrific. I mean now that all the bruising is gone," he told her. Despite the implication that she had looked horrible before, Jordan turned the slightest shade of crimson before looking away.

"At least I won't scare small children today," she said with a laugh.

"Jordan Wheeler did you just laugh?" he asked giving her a surprised look. "It really suits you so I hope I hear it more often. Well let's get going."

With the dogs stowed safely in the truck's bed for the relatively short ride to Smith's Mill, Jordan spent most of the drive looking out the window waiting for Ben to say something, but he seemed content enough to just cast occasional glances her way.

Finally, she could stand the unnerving silence no longer.

"How's Helen?" It was the safest topic she could think of.

"As bossy as ever," he replied with a chuckle. "She said to send her best wishes and to remind you to stop in the next time you're in the area. Are you running again?"

"Not yet, doctor's orders, but I'm hoping to get the all clear today. Pete and I have been limited to long walks."

"I've been thinking I should start running. Maybe we can go together some time?"

"Not to discourage you or anything, but I run about ten miles a day."

The look on his face was priceless.

"No kidding? That's like running to Smith's Mill every single day! Why would anyone subject themselves to that kind of torture?"

It was a question she had asked herself many times, and she had to laugh yet again. It was coming easier these days.

"Once you get past the initial pain it's liberating—at least for me. Maybe it's the endorphins or whatever but running helps me let go of whatever's bugging me. It helps me feel free."

"Having seen you run I get that. I think that's what intrigued me about you. You run like someone is chasing you, but it looks almost effortless."

"I intrigued you?" she asked giving him a raised eyebrow.

"Please don't be upset, but the very first time I saw you run by the house there was something about you that made me curious and I found myself more often than not standing at the window watching for you. Don't ask me to explain why I felt the need to do it because I really didn't understand it myself, but having met you it makes sense."

She probably should have been concerned that he was apparently stalking her on her runs but she too was curious. "In what way?"

"Well, there's your obvious beauty," he started, "but it's more than that. You only have to look in your eyes to see there is so much more to you. There is definitely something extraordinary about you as I'm sure men have told you your entire life. You've probably had no shortage of suitors."

Sure, she had been told she was attractive before, but what pretty girl hadn't? Obviously he was seeing something in her she couldn't see in herself. While other girls dated incessantly, high school had been mostly a never-ending series of sitting at home with her parents. There was nothing more difficult for a girl to accept than knowing no boy wanted to ask her out and Jordan had spent years thinking there was something wrong with her. It wasn't until well after high school that she was told by a friend that boys were afraid to ask her out. Apparently being pretty and yet shy had made her seem unapproachable.

"Not really," she admitted. "Being good looking isn't a guarantee guys are interested in you and I found that out the hard way in high school, but I can guarantee that a good-looking guy has no shortage of women after them."

"No, I'm sure that guys can have the same problem, but would you perchance be saying I'm good looking?" he teased with a sparkle in his eye.

"Don't get so full of yourself. You know you're attractive and you obviously work hard to keep it that way judging from those biceps."

Even her hand flying across her mouth to cover her embarrassment at the overly personal statement couldn't hide the crimson stain appearing on her cheeks as Jordan inadvertently flirted with him.

"Thank you for that," Ben said with a laugh, "but what do you say now that we have established the fact that we each find the other attractive, we remember we're just friends and move on to a topic that's a little less personal?"

"Agreed. So, something nice happened to me this week," she offered shyly even as she wondered why she was sharing her news with him. Could it be as simple as she was thinking of him as a friend?

"After everything you've been through in the last month you deserve it. So what happened?"

"I talked to my mother."

"Didn't you tell me you hadn't talked to your family in almost a decade? But you never told me why."

"That's not true. I said they had disagreed with some decisions I made."

"Oh, right. Now I remember. So, they're okay with those decisions now?"

"Not exactly," Jordan admitted. "My dad still wants nothing to do with me, but I found out my mom never felt that way. It was just easier for her to do what he said. But she still loves me!"

"How could you have ever doubted that? Even after everything my brother has pulled, my mother still loves him. I couldn't imagine what a child could do that would make a parent stop loving her."

"It's not always that black and white you know," she said peevishly.

He barely knew her and might never understand why speaking to her mother was such a big deal. Surprisingly, it disappointed her.

"Explain it to me. What could you possibly have done that made your dad mad enough to cut you out of his life?"

"I've already said too much," she insisted with a touch of anger. "As my friend, something you insisted on if I remember correctly, I just wanted to share some good news with you. Nobody asked for you to give me the third degree about it."

"Come on Jordan, that's not fair. I'm just trying to understand what you've been through. You don't have to tell me if you don't want."

"Good, because I don't."

"But we can still be friends right?" he asked hopefully as he pulled into a parking space at the hospital.

The thought of finally having someone as a friend was enticing, but how long could she keep volleying the slew of questions about her past? Would she ever trust him enough to tell him the truth?

Turning in her seat to look at him she realized his eyes were once again locked on her. She decided to take a chance.

"Yes, we can be friends."

"Took you long enough to say," he teased with a wink of his eye. "Now, while you're in with the doctor, I'll take the dogs across the street to the park and get some exercise. Just honk the horn when you're done. Good luck."

. . . . .

By the time she came out of the hospital, this time without her cast, sling, and cane, there was no sign of Ben or the dogs and shielding her eyes from the bright sun, she spun around looking for them. Hearing Pete's bark she spotted the trio at the side of an ice cream truck where Ben was feeding cones to both dogs. Within seconds, the tentative licks had turned into giant bites and the cones disappeared as the dogs licked the remaining evidence from their lips. Giving Jordan a wave before turning back to the truck, Ben emerged once again with two more cones and started walking towards her.

"Jordan, there you are. I bought us ice cream to celebrate. We have reason to celebrate correct?"

"If you're asking if I got an excellent report from the doctor, then yes. We have reason to celebrate. I am definitely going to live and even more exciting, I can start running again."

"That's my girl," Ben said excitedly before he realized what he had said. "Sorry, I didn't mean that the way it sounded."

"It's okay. You don't have to apologize. But I don't know if my good checkup warrants an ice cream celebration."

"Aha, but it's not just your good news we're celebrating!" he announced. "I didn't tell you earlier, but I got a new client yesterday and this one can actually pay so that does warrant ice cream. Not knowing what you like, I got one vanilla and one chocolate."

Offering both to her, and looking ever so pleased with himself, she had a bit of fun.

"Thanks, but I'm more of a strawberry type of girl," she said with a shrug of her shoulders.

"Oh," he said as all the excitement seemed to ooze out of him and his smile faded. "Well, I can see if they have strawberry. Just give me a minute."

He looked so disappointed she couldn't carry on with her charade and laughed. "I'm just kidding. Chocolate is my favorite. Thank you very much."

As the dogs wrestled for control of a large stick they had found, the pair wandered through the park before eventually finding a bench in the shade. Warmed by the early summer sun, Jordan kicked off her shoes and wiggled her toes. This day was turning out much better than she expected and for at least this one moment in time, she let her troubles fade away.

"Tell me about your client," she asked as they watched the dogs play and tried to stay ahead of the dripping ice cream.

"I don't want to jinx it, but I think there might be some good money from this case. It's a land dispute. The client has farmed his property for a very long time and his ownership is now being challenged by a neighboring property owner who also is a distant relative."

"That sounds interesting."

"Yeah it might be, but it's going to be a ton of work. I just wish I had money to hire a paralegal to do some of the research for me. Most of it can be done online, but it will still take hours and it's going to be hard to prepare the case and do the research by myself, especially if the other side pushes for a speedy trial."

"I might know someone who could help," she suggested softly.

"Wow that would be great. Is he a paralegal?"

"Not exactly, and it's not he."

"I didn't mean to imply . . . well he or she it doesn't make a difference to me as long as they can put in long hours and expect little pay."

"How about me?" Her options for working were pretty limited by her unwillingness to leave a paper trail Richard would use against her, but she wasn't looking to be paid.

"You? Are you serious?" he asked with a perplexed look on his face.

"I know I'm not a paralegal but I know my way around a law book and I have plenty of time on my hands and you wouldn't have to pay me and I'm smart and detail oriented and . . ."

"Wait, Jordan, stop!" he exclaimed. "I know you could do the job, but I honestly can't pay much and I know you need the money."

"Didn't you hear me? I said you didn't have to pay me. I just need to get out of the cabin and do something constructive for a change."

"But I'd have to pay you something," he insisted although she could tell the idea of free help was enticing.

"How about this? I'll work for you for say twenty hours a week if you let me bring Pete to work and in exchange you do some handyman work around the cabin for me. We'll call it fair and square and no money has to exchange hands. You get help and I get some improvements done at home that I can't afford. It would be a win-win for both of us."

"If you remember I offered to do those improvements for you for free," he reminded her.

"I know, but this way it won't be charity. I'll be giving you something that I hope will be of value. So do we have a deal?"

"We do and thank you. I admit the thought of taking on this case with no help was daunting and it will be nice to have someone to bounce ideas around with. Now how about we get to those errands you needed to run?"

It was feeling like something changed between them and they might actually become friends. Jordan hadn't lost sight of the fact that being friends with someone who had a connection to Richard, even if he didn't understand the significance of that connection, was dangerous. If Ben hadn't realized who she was by now, odds were slim he would and she really needed a friend these days. If she was ever going to take a chance on trusting someone, now was the time and Ben might be that someone.

It hadn't taken long to discover Ben was even more intelligent than she initially thought.

He had a quick wit and a natural affinity for observation, especially about people; all traits that would be helpful in his line of work but a little dangerous in her present situation.

"You know when I walked into your hospital room that first day you looked like a deer in the headlights, but today, not so much. Does that mean you're feeling comfortable around me?" he asked on the drive home.

"Partially," she admitted. "That first time I saw you I thought you were someone . . . well it doesn't matter. Suffice it to say you were nothing like what I was expecting from someone claiming to be my husband."

"Oh yeah, that. I suppose I should have come clean to the hospital folks about that, but thinking I was your husband was actually helpful to me when your nurse set her sights on me."

Jordan couldn't help but laugh remembering the comment the nurse had made about leaving her husband for Ben.

"You laugh, but guys have feelings too and that woman had predator written all over her. Thinking that I was your husband was the only thing that saved me from her."

"I understand what you're saying, but it's still funny. At least you can defend yourself. For women it's not so easy and sometimes it's downright frightening."

"Sounds like you've had some bad experiences."

If only he knew his own brother was at the heart of the one she remembered the most. That night she was sure she was going to be raped. That's not something a woman forgets.

"It's not just me. I'm sure most women, at one time or another in their lives, have been put in that position," she said sadly.

"I'm sorry Jordan."

"What for?"

"For whatever has gone so wrong in your life. For whatever you're hiding from. I wish I could make it all go away for you and see you smile all the time."

Little did he know she wished for the same thing.

CHAPTER SIX

Jordan's new job started the next day and came after a night of disturbing dreams she attributed to nervousness about working for Ben. Whatever had possessed her to offer her services for a job she knew next to nothing about? It was out of character and she prayed she wouldn't embarrass herself or Ben.

"Morning Jordan. Wow, you look terrific!" Ben exclaimed when he answered the door. The casual dress and conservative pumps she wore were nothing special, but there was a look of desire behind his eyes that, knowing he would never act on it, Jordan ignored. "Come on in. Would you like some coffee before we get started?"

"Thanks, but I'm fine. What is the first thing you'd like me to do?"

"Aren't you the eager one," he said with a laugh. "I set up a table for you in the corner of my office until we figure out a more suitable option and in the next couple of days the cable company will be here to put in another phone and internet line. If it's okay with you, I was thinking the music room next door might be a suitable spot for your desk. Of course, you'll still need access to the law books in my office but we'll figure that out later. Besides, it's not like there are a lot of client meetings scheduled right now."

"If it's a big hassle, I can always go to the library to use their internet."

"Thanks for thinking of it, but I was going to suggest that I would also pay to have internet brought to the cabin so that you can work from home. I have an extra laptop you can use. Since you're not getting a paycheck, I want to make this as easy as possible for you."

Disappointed at the idea he might not want her working from his house, she tried to smile back at him, but must not have succeeded.

"What?" he asked. "Did I say something wrong?"

"It's nothing. I think I just misunderstood. I thought I was expected to come to the office."

"You are, but I wanted to give you the option to work from home if there was bad weather or you have something else to do so we'll get computers set up for you both here and at the cabin. Now let's get started."

Pulling a chair next to his so she could see his computer screen as he went through the list of things he wanted her to research, he explained.

"I was up late last night putting this together and it's going to change as we go, but this is a good start to some of the research I'll need to get done before we file our response. Now that you're officially on the payroll, I can tell you more about the suit. My client has been farming his property since the early 1990's. Before that, the property was owned by his parents and his grandparents and subsequently passed down. The opposing party has publicly claimed for years that they illegally transferred the property to my client's side of the family. It wasn't such a big deal for him to be making these accusations before, but now that my client is looking to sell the farm, the bogus claims are causing potential buyers to withdraw their offers. So, my client wants this settled once and for all and is litigating to prove he's done nothing wrong. As soon as word got out that we were moving ahead with asking the Court to litigate the matter, the other guy filed suit of his own claiming ownership. There are two suits going at once, each filed by someone claiming they are the rightful owner of the property even though the opposing party has yet to share with our side any evidence of his rightful ownership."

"Doesn't the law require the claimant to share their evidence with you?"

"You're right, it does and the motion I'm going to file in the next few days will be on that very thing. But the opposing counsel's office is hundreds of miles away and from what I understand, they are very good at stalling. It's a tactic I used myself once or twice and it's very effective. They find reasons to delay providing the other side with information resulting in less time for preparation and rebuttal. It's not exactly legal, but it happens."

"I see."

"If there's anything you don't understand or you're not sure how to proceed, just let me know. Do you think you have enough to get started?"

"I'm good. Thanks."

"Help yourself to whatever's in the kitchen. You know where the coffee is by now. Helen went into town early this morning and she'll make lunch for us when she returns. If that's it, I guess I'll leave you to it."

For the next several hours, they worked without saying much. Pete and Bear, after spending an hour playing together in the yard, had stretched out in front of the office door and promptly fell asleep. Except for regular chimes from the grandfather clock in the hallway and an occasional question from Jordan, the house was quiet.

"This might be a dumb question," she said as she looked up from the mountain of law books on the table, "but could this be something as simple as a chain-of-title dispute? Should I be looking at the conveyance documents or the abstract to see if they have made a mistake along the way?"

Ben looked up from his own work and his eyes were sparkling back at her. It seemed having a challenging case to work on had woken something in him.

"Frankly, I'm surprised you even know what those things are. From what the client has told me, if our guy is in the wrong that might just be the case, but before we waste hours going down that road I want to make sure we have thoroughly researched the specific laws of this state. Although litigation over ownership rights is fairly standard in all parts of the country, each state puts their own spin on it."

"You don't want me to go to the county and check their records?"

"Eventually, but not yet. Now that I finally have a paying client I want to be sure and do this logically so we charge only what is really necessary. This type of litigation isn't something I'm experienced in so I don't want to make any mistakes."

"If you don't mind I'm going to take a break to let Pete out and maybe grab a cup of coffee."

"That sounds like a great idea. Mind if I join you?"

"You're the boss," she said with a smile.

Taking their coffee to the back yard where they could enjoy the mid-morning sun, they watched both of the dogs romp together.

"I saw you and Pete run by this morning," Ben told her. "You sure didn't waste any time getting back to it did you?"

Surprised that he had seen her at such an early hour, she felt a little thrill until reminding herself that he was now her boss.

"Don't you ever sleep?" she countered.

"You should talk. What time did you get up, anyway?"

"We left the house at four. I wanted to get in a run and not be late for work."

"And you're going again tonight?"

"Probably not. I realized the days of running twice a day are behind me when I figured out I was just doing it out of boredom. Besides, being so inactive for the last three weeks has been a set back to my conditioning and I paid the price this morning. I better take it a little easier for a few days until I get back to where I was."

"I hear what you're saying. When I left Washington, I had a regular work out schedule at the gym, but money got tight and the gym membership had to go. I hoped there would be a gym here, but discovered the closest one is in Smith's Mill. Even if I had the extra cash, driving that far to work out wouldn't make much sense."

"I probably shouldn't say this, but if you haven't been working out, I can't imagine how fit you must have been before.

"Thank you, I think," he said with a warm smile. The man was most definitely growing on her and having let her guard down at least a bit, she had to work hard to stifle any more thoughts about how attractive he was.

"Ben, Jordan? Lunch is ready when you are," Helen called from the kitchen door.

After a quick lunch, they were back at work before Jordan finally looked at the clock to see it was almost six. Leaning back in her chair she noticed Ben was nowhere to be found while Pete was quick to get on his feet and push his nose against her leg.

A quick search of the house for Ben came up empty until she spotted him out the window pacing back and forth. Gathering her things, she headed outside.

"Ben, sorry to bother you, but would it be okay if I went home for the day?"

Looking up from the law book in his hands, he seemed surprised to see her.

"What? Oh Jordan. I'm sorry. Of course you can go. You don't have to ask. Our deal was you put in hours when you want and if I need you at a certain time, I'll let you know. You've worked hard today and I'm really impressed with how quickly you're catching on."

"Maybe I shouldn't ask, but just what are you doing out here?"

In the brief time she had been watching he seemed to talk to himself as he wandered around the yard with the heavy book in his hands.

"It's a bad habit I got into in law school I'm afraid. I pace when I need to concentrate extra hard on something. This case can be tricky and I'm worried I'll miss something and my client will pay the price."

"Corporate law must be equally challenging and you succeeded there so why would you think this will be any different?"

Closing the book in his hands, he took a seat on the front steps and motioned for her to join him. It had been a long day and she really just wanted to go home, kick off her shoes and relax, but he was the boss, so she settled in next to him as Pete sat on the step in front of them.

"When I graduated and joined the firm, there was a built-in safety net around me. All the Associates had partners we worked under and nothing went out of the office without their review. Any mistakes we might have made were caught before it could impact a client and eventually we learned how to do things without supervision, well at least as far as the cases we dealt with at our firm. Here I'm on my own and as much as I hate to admit it, it's a little nerve-wracking because I've never dealt with these types of cases before. There are no guarantees when you run your own practice and I hadn't really considered that before this case came along. The legal system is a step-by-step, very detail-oriented process and if I mess even one thing up, it's my client who pays the price. I just can't let that happen."

"I barely know you, but something tells me the fact that you feel that way is going to make you an exceptional lawyer for these people. I used to know a man who couldn't have cared less what happened to the people he did business with and it was a horrible thing to watch. More people should be like you."

"So, this man, was it your father?"

"No. My dad was the complete opposite. He was so worried about what other people might think of him that it kind of paralyzed him. He never took risks and wanted nothing to change. His idea of happiness was maintaining the status quo. As a kid I suppose having such a predictable life was a good thing, but when I grew up I realized that you have to take a chance now and then because how else would you ever know what your limitations are?"

"Is that how you live your life?"

If only he knew.

"Once upon a time maybe, but that was a long time ago," she said wistfully. The tears clouding her vision had nothing to do with Richard and everything to do with the opportunities she had wasted in her life. "Once upon a time I thought I could be a great artist. Not just good you know, but great. When I left home, I had a head full of dreams and a desire to make those dreams come true, but I got talked out of it and I gave up trying. If things had been different, I might have . . . well it doesn't really matter anymore I guess. I better get Pete home. See you tomorrow."

She might have shared too much and her heart raced as she stood up and called Pete to her side. The stare she was becoming so used to from Ben was changed this time. Instead of curiosity about her past, his look seemed to be a mixture of sadness and empathy.

One good thing had come from that discussion though. Having admitted his own fears about the case made Ben seem less intimidating to Jordan and after a nerve rattling first day, she was actually looking forward to going back.

·　·　·　·　·

Determined to be helpful to Ben, the half-days Jordan had originally expected to put in soon turned into more because she had so much to learn. The legal system was complex and often frustrating, but Ben proved to be a capable and patient teacher even with her never-ending questions. Where others might have objected to the constant interruptions, he seemed to welcome the questions.

"Ben, I'm sorry to bother you . . .," she began after yet another day filled with questions.

"Jordan you don't have to keep apologizing. The only way to learn is to ask," he said as he turned away from his computer for the umpteenth time.

"Sorry," she said before they both laughed. "I couldn't help but wonder why these two property owners don't just talk to each other to settle their differences. Didn't you tell me they are related?"

"What are you trying to do? Put me out of business before I even get started?" he asked with even more laughter. "If everyone actually talked to each other to settle their differences, lawyers would go broke. The one thing I've learned in my very shortened career is that right and wrong is never black and white. People's egos and feelings always get in the way. One guy might know legally they are wrong, but because it's more important for him to win, he doesn't care if the law isn't in his favor and will spend thousands of dollars trying to win only to still lose in the end."

"I guess I never looked at it that way," she admitted. It was as if he was describing Richard. "I used to know someone who always had to win. Get in his way and he'd roll right over you without looking back. There are many people in this world so intimidated by men with power that they let them crush the little people and they don't fight back. If more people fought back against men like that, the world would be a much more civil place."

Expecting a snappy comeback to her statement, she instead received the dreaded stare once again.

"What? Why do you always stare at me like that?"

"I'm sorry, I know you don't like it when I do, but sometimes you make the most extraordinary observations. I guess I'm just trying to figure you out."

Relieved that for once he wasn't dwelling on how familiar she seemed to him, she relaxed. "I better let you get back to work."

"It's already been a long day and I could use some fresh air. Any chance I could convince you to go for a walk with me?"

Although they had strolled around the yard a few times since she started work, they had never before left the property. The thought of being seen in public together was a bit outside her comfort zone and her initial reaction was to decline his invitation, but he looked so hopeful she just couldn't. Before she knew it, they had closed shop for the day, clipped leashes on both dogs and walked into the midst of downtown.

More than a few surprised looks were directed their way as they strolled through the small commercial district. Although Jordan was by far the most tenured resident of the pair, Ben happily greeted each person they passed while she kept her eyes to the ground, unwilling to engage in conversation with complete strangers.

Her lack of engagement didn't go unnoticed.

"You've been awfully quiet. Is anything wrong?" he asked.

"No, I'm fine."

"One thing I've learned over the years is that when a woman says she's fine what she really means is there is something on her mind. So, what's wrong?"

"You've sure made a lot of friends in your short time here," she pointed out as they continued on their walk after one particularly long discussion with a woman.

"What do you mean? I don't know anyone but you."

"Oh, but I thought . . . well I mean that woman. You talked to her like you knew her. How is that possible?"

Stopping to look at Jordan he couldn't help but laugh. "You know back in D.C. that never would have happened, but here it just seems to be the neighborly thing to do. Are you telling me you've never had a conversation with anyone in town?"

Lowering her head to shield her eyes, she was hurt that he seemed so appalled by the possibility.

"Just you and Dr. Norris," she whispered.

"Come on Jordan, that can't possibly be true. You're smart and beautiful and seem to be aware of everything and everyone around you. Why wouldn't you talk to people?"

If only he knew. Talking to people, being on their radar, was dangerous. Having a conversation made her memorable, and she wanted to fade into the woodwork. It was the only way to remain safe from Richard.

"Okay, so you don't want to talk about it," he said when it was apparent she wouldn't answer the question, "but humor me and try something will you? The next person we meet, I challenge you to engage them in conversation. Say hello and give them a compliment. Nothing more than that. Just say something nice."

"Why?"

"Just humor me. I want to show you that interacting with others isn't as scary as you think. Here comes a couple with their kids. Try it."

Looking ahead, Jordan spied a small family walking towards them. The young parents were holding hands and smiling as they pushed one child in a stroller and a boy of maybe two or three walked in front of them. Within seconds the boy spotted Bear and Pete and raced to their side until he crashed headfirst into Pete and fell to the ground. The parents hurried to the child and quickly pulled him away from the dog.

"I'm sorry. Is he okay?" Jordan asked hurriedly as she reached for Pete's collar. A child getting hurt by Pete would only fuel the community's already prejudiced view of the dog.

The child giggled and reached out his hand towards Pete again. "Play with puppy," he cried.

"Well apparently he's just fine," his father said before scooping the child up into his arms. "I hope he didn't hurt your dog. That's a nice-looking animal you have."

Pete had not moved from Jordan's side and she looked down at him with pride.

"Thank you."

"I don't know if you're aware of this or not, but we've heard rumors in town that your dog is aggressive, but he seems anything but. Billy has always wanted a dog, but we weren't quite sure having one around such small children was a good idea. Seeing how well behaved your dogs are though we might rethink that. We're Casey and Charlotte by the way."

"Please, call me Charlie," his wife said.

Introductions having been made and now convinced that the rumors were untrue, Casey put his child down next to Pete who immediately began licking the boy's face as the child laughed with unbridled enthusiasm.

"You're the attorney we heard had set up shop in town is that right?" Charlie directed to Ben.

"That's right, although judging by how few clients I've had I don't know how long that will last," Ben said with a chuckle.

"When I took over the newspaper I thought the same thing," Casey said. "In fact, I didn't think we'd make it to the end of the year, but that was a few years ago and we're still here. It's not something that will ever make us rich, but it puts food on the table. I just wish I could keep staff. I can't afford to pay much and it seems as soon as I get someone great, they find something else that can offer more money."

"What positions are you looking for?" Jordan asked. She had been quiet to that point and it surprised them all when she spoke.

"No one right now luckily, but it's usually graphic designers I can't keep."

"Jordan can help," Ben said suddenly. "She's a wonderful artist and I'm sure you'd love her work."

Snapping her head around, a look of horror filled her face. Why would he say that?

"I'd love to see some of your work," Casey said.

"Sorry, but Ben was confused. I'm not a graphic designer," she hurried to clarify. "I sketch is all and I haven't done it for years."

"But an artist is an artist, right? I'm sure if you were in a pinch Jordan could help you out. You can reach her at this number." Handing over one of his business cards, Ben looked awfully pleased with himself.

As Casey pocketed the card, his wife spoke up. "It was nice meeting both of you, but we're on our way to a doctor's appointment and if we don't leave right now, we'll be late."

"Pleasure meeting both of you," Casey said. "And Jordan, I might just give you a call."

As the family walked away, with Billy throwing kisses back at Pete, Jordan turned to Ben in anger.

"Why did you do that?" she demanded when they were far enough away to avoid being overheard.

"Because you need the money of course. Look Jordan, I might not have seen your work, but I trust you and if you think you're a skilled artist why not put it out there? No sense in hiding your light under a bushel if you know what I mean. And if he calls, you can always say no. But tell me, how did it feel?"

"How did what feel?"

"Having a conversation with a stranger. It was okay right?"

"I guess . . . at least until you offered me up on a platter!"

As they turned back towards Ben's house, a familiar voice called out to them from down the street.

"Jordan, wait up."

Turning in tandem to see Dr. Norris running towards them, Jordan felt herself tense up.

From her perspective at least, the last interaction between the two men had been uncomfortable, and she wasn't looking forward to a repeat.

"Dr. Norris is something wrong?" she asked when he reached them.

Apparently winded from his quick sprint towards them, she had to wait for an answer as he caught his breath, but what caused her own breath to catch in her throat was something completely unexpected.

"It's so good to see you," he said as he drew her in for a hug releasing his hold only when Bear growled menacingly at him.

Both Jordan and Ben looked at the man; she with a confused look and Ben with a smirk on his face. She moved a step back when he released his hold.

"Was there something you wanted?" she asked, her tone measured because of the strange greeting.

"Ah, I guess I just wanted to remind you it was time for Pete's flea and tick medication. I can drop that off at your house tomorrow if you'd like."

"Thank you, but there's no need. I'll swing by tomorrow at lunch and pick it up."

With that sorted it would seem their conversation had ended, but Kevin remained where he was, looking uncomfortably from one face to another.

"I . . . could I maybe speak with you for a moment Jordan? Privately I mean?" he finally stammered.

Risking a quick look at Ben, the same amused smirk still on his face, she nodded her head to show he should leave them alone.

"Come on dogs, let's give them some privacy," he said as they walked down the block far enough to show he had complied, but still within earshot of the conversation.

"Dr. Norris what is it?" she asked. His overly personal greeting had thrown her off her game.

"Please . . . call me Kevin. I wonder, well I mean I . . . well darn it Jordan. Would you have dinner with me tomorrow?"

After months of dancing around the question, he had finally spit it out. His face a brilliant shade of red as he nervously twirled his cap around in his hands, she almost felt sorry for him. Almost.

"That's very nice of you . . . Kevin," she started, ". . . but I'm sorry, I can't."

"It wouldn't have to be a date. We can just go as friends if that helps."

"I'm sorry, but I really don't think that's a good idea. You're a nice guy and everything, but I'm not . . ."

"Available. That's it. You and that lawyer are together now. I don't know why I didn't realize that before. I'm sorry."

Without giving her a chance to correct his assumption, he turned on his heel and almost ran down the street towards his office. As she watched him flee she didn't hear Ben come up behind her until he whispered into her ear.

"You didn't turn him down because of me did you?'

"Of course not," she said indignantly. "Didn't your mother teach you it was impolite to eavesdrop?"

"I didn't have to hear what he said to know what was going on. I'm willing to bet he's been panting after you for a very long time, but I can't say I blame him."

While his compliment should have made her happy, she couldn't get past the hurt look on Kevin's face when she had turned him down. He was such a nice man and had taken such good care of Pete and now every interaction with him would be awkward.

Turning for home they walked side by side as the dogs raced ahead stopping every so often to look back and make sure Ben and Jordan were within eyesight. Ben carried on a one-sided conversation as Jordan thought about the entire exchange with Kevin. Was there something she could have done to let him down easier?

"You've probably never been turned down by a woman, but is there a nice way to say no?" she asked out of the blue.

"Oh, I've been turned down plenty of times and with some very creative excuses. Trust me, when a guy finally works up the courage to ask a woman out, there is never a good way to be rejected. I remember this one girl in high school. She was my dream girl—beautiful and smart—and my brother kept telling me she liked me. It took me the entire school year to work up the courage to ask her out. When I finally did, she laughed at me. She said I might look like my brother, but I would never be as cool as him and even if there were no other boys left on earth, she would never go out with me. That's not something a guy gets over in a hurry I'll tell you. It was years before I asked another girl out. Lucky for me that girl had never met my brother."

"So you didn't date in high school?"

"No. I was lucky though . . . I had a large group of friends, guys, and gals, and so there was always someone to go to a dance or movie with. But it was just friends. How about you? Any serious boyfriends in school?"

"Not really. My parents had pretty strict rules about dating and after meeting my father and the third degree they got when they did, well, let's just say the very few boys who asked me out didn't stick around long."

"Surely in college there was someone?"

Coming from a family of privilege and wealth could he ever comprehend that for some people higher education was just a pipe dream? For Jordan, art school had always been in the plans until discovering the cost. Her parents had made just enough money to put financial aid out of reach and not enough to fund even a year's tuition.

"I always wanted to go to art school, but we couldn't afford it," she admitted. "So no, there was no one in college."

"But somewhere along the line there was someone important to you right?" he asked.

The way he stared at her after offering the question suggested it was important for him to know about her past relationships, but even if she was willing to share that information now, how could she ever make him understand why she had been with Richard?

Luckily they had reached the house, and she could make her escape.

"It's getting late and Pete and I should head home."

"But you never answered my question," he pointed out.

"See you tomorrow Ben."

. . . . .

Opening her eyes each morning she discovered she was looking forward to going to work. At first she attributed it to having something to do each day, but it was more than that. Her lonely life at the cabin, which had been so welcome after the stress of her life with Richard, had worn on her. At Ben's house she found human companionship and little by little she was rediscovering what it was like to have adult conversations. But it was more than that. The research she was doing for Ben had opened up a corner of her mind and both the theories and purpose behind the law were fascinating. Like so many things in her life, if things had been different, she would have enjoyed a career as an attorney. For now though, she would settle with spending each day challenged by the work Ben asked of her.

"Done for the day Jordan?" Helen asked as she walked into the room.

"I'm not sure. Do you know where Ben is?"

"He's outside on the phone."

"Outside?"

"He probably didn't want to disturb you when the call came in. It's been my experience that these calls can get pretty heated."

"What do you mean?"

"I know I'm not telling tales out of school; Ben told me he filled you in on what happened with his brother back east. Anyway, whenever Brandon calls it usually ends up in an argument."

"He's talking to his twin brother?"

"Yes."

The hair on the back of her neck stood up at the thought of that man. She had assumed they no longer had contact.

"Are you staying for dinner Jordan?"

"Thanks, but I think it's time Pete and I were on our way. Can you tell Ben I said goodbye please?"

"Sure. See you tomorrow morning."

Back home, Pete fed, wilted flowers surrounding the cabin having received a nice long drink of water, Jordan's thoughts were of Ben's twin brother.

Maybe she had become too complacent believing Ben would never put two and two together, but if he continued to have contact with his brother, the risk of discovering her connection to Richard might be too great and the realization made her heart heavy with sadness. Having Ben as a friend and working for him was something she wasn't ready to just walk away from, but if she couldn't take the risk of being around Ben any longer, she knew staying in town would also be out of the question. The cabin had sat empty for almost two years before she bought it and the odds of recouping that investment were slim to none. Without that money she could never afford to move. It was a vicious circle that most likely would keep her right where she was with no choice but to make the best of it and try to limit saying anything that would bring Ben closer to the truth.

CHAPTER SEVEN

"Helen said you were talking to your brother when I left last night," Jordan said when they took a break for lunch the next day. All morning she had tried to find just the right time to bring up the topic without letting Ben know how interested she was in why they were talking.

"With Brandon, it's never as simple as having a conversation. It usually ends with an argument."

"She told me that too," she said with a smile. "Why do you keep talking to him if he's that difficult?"

"I've asked myself that a hundred times," he admitted. "But you know how happy you were when you talked to your mom? I think I'm waiting for something to change so Brandon and I have that type of breakthrough. But he's never going to admit his behavior is wrong and he'll keep coming to me to get himself out of trouble."

"Is that what he wanted this time?"

"In a manner of speaking. He's finding the cost of living in Washington D.C. to be substantially above his pay grade. He was looking for money."

"Why would he ask you? Surely he realizes how much you lost because of him?"

"Oh, I'm sure he does, but after our parents turned down his request and my stepdad told him to live within his means, he's apparently running out of options. It seems his biggest worry is the heavy hitters he's been courting in D.C. finding out about his money problems."

"Do you still love him?" she asked. Even with all the horrible things Richard had done to her, a small part of her still loved him.

"I know I should say yes, but honestly, I don't know. I'd give anything to have my brother back, but I don't think he's ever going to change and I'm never going to accept him the way he is. Does that make me a bad person?"

The look of pain in his eyes said everything about how much the situation with his brother had hurt him. Her heart went out to him and she surprised herself by hugging him. As much as they both tried to deny it, they were two very damaged people, hurt by those who should have loved them and looking for a way out of their sorrow.

Her cheek pressed against his chest as the faint scent of musky cologne filled her nose and the steady beat of his heart pulsed in her ear. She felt safe for the first time in years. This was a man who seemed to have the same values and dreams that she did, and yet they could never be together. In another time and place there may have been something between them, but not today. She pulled away, offering only an enigmatic smile in her sudden nervousness about her action.

"If you don't mind, I think I'm going to head home early," she told him as she turned to hide the sudden blush that had appeared on her cheeks.

He seemed equally flustered and stumbled over his words in response.

"Ah, yeah, whatever you want. The cable company is supposed to stop by later this afternoon anyway and after they're done here, I was going to send them to your place. It's probably best if you're there when they arrive."

He was obviously uncomfortable and a little distance might be just what they both needed. It might have been just a hug, but Jordan found she was having a hard time shaking the feelings it had stirred in her.

Determined to put any such romantic thoughts about Ben out of her mind, she headed home and weeded her flowerbeds until after the cable company finished their work and she could fire up the borrowed laptop. But it wasn't research for Ben she was doing. It had been almost a month since she had been at the library checking up on Richard and with everything that had changed in that month, she was nervous about what she might find.

Unknown to Richard, she had long ago discovered the access codes to his private, off-the-book financial records. Over the years it had yielded a treasure trove of information about his questionable business dealings yet, for a man so careful about covering his tracks, it was a mystery why he had never once changed the password on the account. Having stumbled on the password early in their marriage, it only benefited Jordan that he was too stupid or careless to make a change.

It wasn't the only thing she had discovered. One day, late in her marriage, she had wandered into the extensive library of their home, trying to find something to occupy her time.

Like so many things about Richard, the library was a sham designed to imply a certain lifestyle and level of culture and taste. It was unused space in the large apartment, but once discovered, it had become a sanctuary for Jordan to hide out in when dealing with Richard and their failed marriage became overwhelming. On that particular day, she walked around the room full of shelves packed with never-read books until something caught her attention. Slightly ajar, as if someone had recently read it, one particular volume was so out of place she couldn't help but pull it from the shelf and open the cover. That's when she discovered the flash drive nestled securely in the hollowed-out pages of the book. She instinctively knew she had found something of great importance.

It took days before she could slide the drive into her laptop without Richard or one of his men noticing and she waited excitedly to see what secrets Richard was hiding, but unlike the other files, the drive was heavily encrypted.

Her intermediate computer skills were no match for the safety features. Deep down, she knew that the information she had previously discovered was only the tip of the iceberg. Whatever was on the flash drive must be even more damning.

She hadn't intended to take it, but minutes before she made her escape, something prompted her to sneak into the library and pocket the drive. Now, months later, she still didn't know what information was on the device, but it was tucked away as an insurance policy, just in case Richard found her.

The financial information she had been able to access from Richard's accounts were copied and hidden in a place known only to her. The information was a safety net should something happen to her. The steps she had taken had seemed melodramatic, but the more she had learned about Richard and his business dealings, the more she realized she probably hadn't gone far enough.

Between whatever was on the flash drive and the records she had already copied, she was sure there was enough to put him away for a very long time if she used it against him, but that was yet to be determined. The last thing she wanted was to become entangled in an even more acrimonious dispute with Richard, but if he found her, she would use it as leverage for a divorce.

Now, with all the information safely hidden away, she continued to watch from the fringes of the internet as Richard went on with his shady business dealings.

It had been weeks since discovering anything new, but on this day a series of obscenely large checks made out to a name she didn't recognize caught her attention. The checks seemed to start when Richard would have returned from South America.

"Tracer LLC," the payee of each of the checks, led her to a website for a company by that name in Queens. Public records showed Tracer LLC was a private detective agency registered with the State of New York and the man behind Tracer LLC was none other than Richard's former head of security, Dick Simmons. It didn't take a great leap of faith to suspect Richard had hired the man to find her.

She knew Simmons well enough to know he would be tenacious about getting the information Richard wanted and would never give up the hunt which meant Jordan would never be safe. She had been hiding in plain sight until now, but was that about to end?

The shrill ringing of the phone startled her and although there was no one to see what was on the screen, she quickly closed the laptop before answering.

"Hello?"

"Jordan, it's Ben. How did the install go?"

"It was fine. They left about an hour ago, but I'm sorry to say I haven't done any work yet."

"That's not a problem. We got a lot done this morning, and I'm feeling good about where we are right now."

"Then why are you calling? I mean, was there something else you needed?"

"Nothing work related, but I wonder if you might like to go see a movie with me tonight?"

It was unusual that such a small town could keep a movie theater in business and odds were big name blockbusters weren't on the marquee.

At her hesitation, he was quick to clarify they would just go as friends. "You've worked hard this week, and I know I could use a night out."

"What's playing?"

After their lingering hug earlier, she wasn't so sure being alone in the dark with Ben was such a good idea, and she was stalling for time before answering.

"Honestly, I don't know, but Helen told me it's dollar night. One dollar to get in. One dollar for popcorn and one dollar for licorice. You get the picture. The price is certainly right, but I don't want to go alone. If money's tight for you, I can certainly give you an advance on your wages," he said with a chuckle.

"You aren't paying me anything, remember?" she countered.

"Then I guess the movie and popcorn's on me. So, what do you say? Would you like to go with me?"

"I guess you've persuaded me. Should we meet there?"

"Why don't I pick you up? Helen asked me to drop off some food she made for you and I better not leave it in the truck in this heat. I'll be at your place in an hour if that's okay."

"All right, I'll see you then."

Trying not to read too much into his invitation, she couldn't stop her heart from racing.

"Stop being so foolish, Jordan. It's not a date," she told herself before racing upstairs with Pete hot on her heels.

With only minutes to spare, she made her way downstairs dressed in her nicest dress. Having left all her designer clothing behind and with little money to spare for luxuries like dress shopping, the simple, sleeveless wrap dress was nothing special, but she looked and felt terrific in it. The best she could do to dress up the look was to step into a pair of her favorite designer heels, the one thing she hadn't been able to part with from her previous life. The heels made her legs look especially long and for the first time in a very long time, she felt every inch a woman. Running a brush through her thick hair, she added just a touch of lipstick before doing a quick walk through a mist of perfume and she was ready.

Pete sniffed the air when he picked up the scent of the perfume. It really had been a long time since she looked and felt like a woman, and even Pete sensed something was different before he bolted to the door at the sound of Ben's truck pulling to a stop in front of the cabin.

Watching through the window as he got out of the truck, a wave of nervousness washed over Jordan when she noticed Ben had taken extra care of his appearance as well. Hair slicked back, face freshly shaven, sleeves rolled up on what looked to be a new dress shirt and wearing jeans that looked recently ironed, he started for the front door before going quickly back to the truck. When he emerged again, he carried a bouquet in his hand and her heart pounded in her chest. The only thing missing from this "non-date" was a box of candy.

Pete raced to the door at Ben's knock.

"Pete, stay."

Opening the door to Ben smoothing back his hair, he seemed as nervous as she, but still offered his most charming smile before looking her up and down. He seemed surprised at her appearance, and she wondered if she had chosen the wrong outfit. Smoothing down her skirt, she lowered her face to mask the embarrassment.

"Jesus Jordan. You're absolutely beautiful," he finally said.

Certain he was teasing, she looked him in the eye, seeing only unadulterated adoration.

"Thank you," she said softly, moving aside to let him in. There was so much more she wanted to say about how handsome he was, but she held her tongue.

"These are for you," he said, offering the bouquet. It had been ages since a man had given her flowers, but she worried he was spending money he shouldn't.

"They're beautiful," she said as she reached for the flowers and turned to find a vase. Settling for a canning jar left behind by the previous occupant, she filled it with water and placed the bouquet in the middle of the kitchen table. "I just wish you wouldn't have spent so much money when I know things are tight for you right now."

"Time to confess. I didn't buy them. They're straight from Helen's rather extensive garden, with her permission, of course."

"Of course," she said. "But I thought we agreed this wasn't a date?"

"It's not. Just two friends who dressed up for each other, brought a few flowers, and unless my nose is deceiving me, put on a bit of perfume. You smell very nice, by the way."

"Thank you. I like it too, but Pete's a little confused by it all."

"Oh, I almost forgot the food," he said before racing back outside and coming back into the house with a bag. "Helen said everything is marked with reheating instructions."

"That's so nice of her, but I couldn't eat all this in a month if I tried," she told him. The entire grocery bag was full, and she placed its contents in the fridge.

"She also said you'd say that and that most of it can go in the freezer," he said with a laugh. "If there's one thing I've learned about Helen, making sure people eat is one of her biggest concerns. She thinks you're too thin, but I told her you're perfect the way you are."

"Thank you for that I think," she said, wondering at the compliments he was showering on her tonight. He had insisted this wasn't a date, but his words said otherwise.

"Are you ready to go?" he finally asked. "Movie starts in a few minutes."

Reaching for the doorknob, they were both surprised when the knob fell off in his hand.

"Sorry about that," she said, her face red with embarrassment. "That's one of those things I've tried to fix myself, but it keeps happening. Obviously, I don't understand how the mechanism works."

"They can be tricky," he assured her with a smile as he fitted the knob back onto the door. "If you want to put together a list of things that need fixing, I'll pop over tomorrow night after work and get started on my end of our deal. This should hold it for now, though. Well, we better go or we won't get popcorn before the film starts."

.   .   .   .   .

By the time the credits rolled, Jordan was thoroughly enjoying the evening. Relieved to discover the movie was a comedy, they both laughed along with the rest of the sparse audience.

"You know, it's still pretty early. Would you like to go for a walk or maybe get something to eat at the diner?"

"I don't know," she teased, "I'm pretty full of popcorn, but the diner sounds like a good idea and we could walk since it's such a nice evening."

"As you wish," Ben said before gallantly offering his arm.

The diner was only a few blocks away and a little bell tinkled above their heads as they walked into a mostly empty dining room.

"Why don't you get us a booth? I'm going to go wash up," Ben suggested.

Turning away from him, she slid into a booth furthest from the door and looked around the place to find the sole waitress giving her a suspicious look. Her behavior wasn't new; it was the same look Jordan had been receiving since arriving in town. As the woman approached the table, she slapped a menu down, apparently none too pleased to have customers at this time of the evening, even though the diner was open all day every day.

"What can I getcha?" she asked before Jordan even opened the singular menu.

"If you can give us a few minutes, my friend is washing up," Jordan said with what she hoped was a warm smile. The laughter she and Ben had shared through the evening was wearing off in the face of the woman's snippy attitude.

"Whatever," she said before shuffling away. The sound was so strange Jordan's eyes went to her feet, expecting to see her in slippers. Instead, she saw swollen ankles and flesh that spilled over the top of the woman's shoes. She didn't appear to be an old woman, yet she walked as if she was and the thought came to Jordan that her attitude was because her feet hurt.

Studying the menu as much to shield her face from the waitress as any actual interest in food, Ben's return startled her.

"So, what looks good?" he asked before Jordan handed over the menu to him as he slid into the booth. "Helen said their burgers are pretty good."

Tired of being treated like she wasn't part of the town by the locals had made her grumpy. "I'm not so sure I would trust them not to spit on mine," she told him.

"What are you talking about? Did something happen?"

"It's nothing. Just a waitress with an attitude problem."

As if she had heard Jordan mention her, the woman materialized at the table and one look at Ben was all it took to change her from an overworked, underpaid waitress to the world's biggest flirt. She nervously adjusted her glasses and licked her lips before offering him a smile.

"Good evening. How are we doing tonight?" she asked pleasantly before Ben looked at Jordan in confusion and Jordan settled back to watch the show.

She'd witnessed similar instances with Richard. Women had looked at her with suspicion and disdain, but the minute a good-looking man appeared, they were all charm and sunshine. Once Ben's beautiful eyes caught their attention, any woman would get lost in them. She knew because it happened to her every time she looked at him and for that alone, she couldn't fault the waitress.

"Can I get you some coffee to start?"

"Jordan, what would you like?" Ben asked politely. The moment he directed his attention to her, Jordan could see a sneer on the woman's face, but it was gone before Ben turned back to her.

"Decaf and a glass of water would be nice."

"One decaf, one regular coffee, and two glasses of water please," he told the waitress who quickly left to prepare their drinks.

"She seemed perfectly fine," Ben said when she was out of earshot before Jordan burst out laughing.

"Have you ever met a woman who didn't smile back at you?"

"Well, there was you, but I think that's changing," he teased. "What's your point?"

"Before you came to the table, the woman was downright rude to me, but then you show up and suddenly she is all smiles but only to you."

"I'm sure that's not the case."

"Oh no? When she comes back to take our orders, please make your order really complicated. I'm going to order something simple, but you watch her face when I'm ordering. You'll see what I'm talking about."

"Okay, but I think you're wrong," he said just as the waitress came back and carefully placed a full cup of coffee in front of Ben before nearly dropping a half-full cup of decaf in front of Jordan, spilling most of what was in the cup with no apologies or attempts to wipe up the mess.

"Now, what can I get you, sir?" she asked with a smile as she turned towards him.

"Before we get to that, I think you spilled my friend's coffee. Can you get something to clean it up and bring her a fresh cup?" he asked.

"Of course," she said before directing a biting look at Jordan. "I'll be right back."

"Did you see that?" she whispered excitedly. "Did you see the look she gave me as if it were all my fault? If you wouldn't have asked her to clean it up, she would never have done it."

"Come on Jordan, be fair. It looks like she's tired after a long day, is all."

"Why is it men are so clueless when women fawn all over you?"

The waitress's return saved him from having to answer and they sat silently while she wiped up the mess she had made and this time gently put down a fresh cup of coffee.

"Now, what can I get for you, sir?" This time, she actually turned her back on Jordan as she waited for Ben to order.

"Jordan, what would you like?" Ben asked yet again.

"Could I please have a chef's salad without tomatoes?"

"It's still going to be the same price," the waitress snapped.

"That's fine," Jordan responded with her most charming smile. "And could I have Thousand Island dressing on the side, please?"

"It comes with the salad," she snapped again.

"I understand that, but could you put it in a little bowl so I can decide how much to use?"

"Fine," she said with a dramatic sigh. Jordan had simply asked her to do something every waitress had been asked to do hundreds of times.

Turning back to Ben once again, a smile reappeared on the face of the waitress.

"And for you, sir?"

"I'd like the cheeseburger special, but instead of American cheese, can I get a couple of slices of Swiss? If that costs more, that would be fine." The menu had been perfectly clear that there were no substitutions allowed for the special and Ben expected her to tell him no.

"For you, no charge, sir," she said with a wink. Jordan could barely control her laughter as he continued with his special order.

"I'd like that burger done medium well and could you have them toast the bun? Then I'd like a couple of tomato slices on the burger, and extra crispy fries. And instead of pickle chips, could I get a couple of pickle spears instead? That would be great."

"Is that all, sir?" she asked, writing furiously to get all the details of his order down on her pad.

"One more thing. I'm not a big fan of these little containers of imitation creamer. You wouldn't have any of the genuine stuff in the back, would you?"

"I think we do," she said excitedly. "Let me see if I can find some for you. I'll be right back."

Casting a quick look of disdain Jordan's way, she shuffled back to the kitchen. How she would explain all of Ben's special requests to the cook was a mystery.

"Do you see what I mean?"

"Yes, and I'm sorry I doubted you," he said. "And I'm sorry she's treating you that way. Do you want to leave?"

"We don't have to. I know you're hungry and besides, it's nothing I haven't dealt with before, especially since I've kept myself pretty isolated since I got here."

"Why is that? And before you get all closed up on me again, I know that's a personal question, but remember we're friends now."

As the waitress returned and with a triumphant presentation of real dairy cream in a little cow server, she considered telling him the truth, but then realized how dangerous it could be and instead offered a version of the truth.

"I've never been the most open person, and coming to a new town, it seemed simpler at first to just keep to myself. A few folks have been welcoming despite my reluctance to be part of the community, but others, like our waitress, have treated me with suspicion. About the only person who was really nice to me was Dr. Norris, and you and Helen, of course."

"Ah, the good Dr. Norris. The poor man has such an obvious crush on you I actually felt sorry when you turned him down."

"You have to know I did nothing to encourage his attention and after he saw us together that day I got out of the hospital well . . ."

"It was easier to let him believe we were together."

"Well, yeah, but you practically flaunted it in his face that I was going home with you that day."

"Hey, it was the truth, and he was pretty quick to suggest he take you home despite what he might have thought about the two of us. And now here we are together."

"Lest you forget, this isn't a date," she reminded him.

"I know, but I'll bet the good doctor wouldn't see it that way and our waitress doesn't either. Here she comes with our food."

Placing the plates in front of them, Ben finally understood the full impact of what she had been saying.

While his order was prepared exactly as he had asked, Jordan's salad came with diced tomatoes buried underneath a river of salad dressing. The waitress stared at her as if daring her to complain before haughtily striding away.

"Do you need any more proof?" Jordan laughed.

"Let me call her back and have her do it correctly," he offered, while raising his hand to signal the waitress.

"Don't bother. I actually don't mind the tomatoes and I can scrape most of the dressing off, so it's fine. Somehow it would all become my fault and she'd tell everyone what a bitch I had been to her. I don't need that kind of reputation."

"Are you sure?"

"I am. Besides, your food looks great, so let's just dig in."

As they ate, they never stopped talking and it was close to midnight before either of them noticed the time.

"I suppose I better get you home to bed or your boss won't be too pleased with me in the morning," Ben said as the waitress dropped off the check. They had been the only customers in the place for the last hour, and she probably was tired of dealing with them.

"Yeah, my boss, he's such a slave driver," she teased. "How much is my bill?"

"It's on me," he told her as he placed a few bills on the table.

"You don't have to do that. You already paid for the movie and popcorn."

"Consider it a perk of the job. In fact, it might be the only one," he teased as they walked back to the truck and started the drive back to the cabin. "I have to be honest with you, Jordan. I wasn't sure you could do this job, but I've looked at the research you've done so far and you really have a mind for the law. Maybe you should have gone to law school."

"Thanks, but I think that ship has sailed. However, I appreciate your confidence in me and I won't let you down."

Pete's barking heralded their arrival back at the cabin and she realized what an excellent watch dog he was. If Richard ever showed up, she would have plenty of warning.

"Well, thanks for a great evening," she said as Ben walked her to the front door.

Standing just inches from each other under the soft glare of the porch light, the lingering scent of her perfume mingled with the muskiness of his aftershave, and everything in Jordan screamed for his touch. He apparently felt it too and leaned in to kiss her before she remembered she was a married woman and jerked away from him at the last minute.

"What are you doing?" she asked as her hands flew to her face and a confused look appeared on his.

"I'm sorry, I thought, well hell. I don't know what I thought. Jordan I'm sorry. I better go. I'm really sorry."

Stumbling over his words and obviously embarrassed by his actions, he hurried to his truck, spinning the tires on the loose gravel as he backed up in a hurry to get away from her.

"Oh my God what have I done?" she asked herself.

It wasn't just Ben that wanted that kiss. It had been a mistake to agree to go out with him. Feeling the way, she did about him she doubted they could ever be just friends.

CHAPTER EIGHT

The next morning came much too quickly and Jordan had slept little. Her insomnia that night, which she had initially attributed to stewing over what had happened on the porch with Ben, instead seemed to be thanks to the vengeful waitress giving her caffeinated coffee instead of what she had asked for. By the time she arrived at Ben's house, her lack of sleep was plainly evident.

"Good morning Helen. Thanks so much for all the food you sent over. I'm going to be eating well for a month."

"You're welcome, my dear. Did you and Ben have a good time at the movies last night?"

"Yes thanks and speaking of Ben, I didn't see his truck outside. Is he here?"

"Afraid not. He got up extra early and said he was spending the day in the law library at the college in Casper. You'd think with all the books he has in that office he wouldn't need to go somewhere else, but he seemed in a hurry to get out of here."

"Oh, well, I'm sure there must be a reason."

She was the reason. He didn't want to be around her after the way their evening ended.

"Would you like some coffee, Jordan? I just made a fresh pot. I don't want to be cruel, but you look like you could use it."

"Thanks, but I better get right to work."

"You've got plenty of time and I could use a bit of conversation. Please join me."

What could she say?

Pete had already made himself comfortable in the sunny corner of the kitchen along with Bear, and with Ben apparently gone for the day, there was no reason to decline the invitation.

"Now that it's just us women, why don't we get to know each other better? Tell me a little about yourself," Helen asked.

An innocent question to be sure, but Jordan suspected there was more to this little coffee chat than Helen let on.

"There's not much to tell unfortunately," she said, hoping Helen would take the hint.

"You know Jordan, I've been on this earth a very long time and you can't fool me. Behind that beautiful face is a story. Now I know you don't know me or Ben that well, but I also know that at some point you're going to need to trust someone. I'm not one to pry, but when that time comes, I want you to know that if you're going to trust anybody, Ben is the man. Even after everything he went through back east, he is the kindest, most giving man I have ever met and I know he thinks the world of you. This house is a safe place and you should never forget that."

Knowing she felt it important enough to provide such reassurance was touching and before Jordan could stop it, tears started falling and her head dropped to stare at the mug in her hands.

It was some time before she could compose herself enough to speak, and Helen waited patiently without saying a word.

"I know you and Ben want to know what's going on with me," Jordan said, "but I just can't. It's complicated and I can't put you guys in the middle of it." It was the closest she had ever come to admitting her fears out loud.

"You know there isn't much that surprises me in life anymore, but I can't imagine what you might have done that you needed to run here and hide. A beautiful young woman like yourself should enjoy life to the fullest instead of being trapped in this backwater town, living all by yourself out in the woods. Did you kill someone or rob a bank? I can't believe you would, but Ben could help you if you're in that kind of trouble."

"No, it's not that, and I'm not alone. I have Pete." At the sound of his name, the dog raised his head before lying back down again.

"That dog can't replace the love of a good man, and I should know. I had a wonderful man to keep my bed warm for over thirty years and I miss him every day since he passed. A lot of the wonderful things about my John I see in Ben."

"You're right. Ben's a wonderful man, but we're just friends."

"From the way he looks at you, I think Ben might want more from you."

She was right. The look was in his eyes when he tried to kiss her last night, and she knew he wanted much more than she could give him. There might not be a ring on her finger anymore, but she was still married.

"That's never going to happen, and I already told him that. I can't help it if he's got other ideas. Maybe it would be better if he just forgot about me."

The thought of never seeing him again was surprisingly painful.

"Now don't go jumping the gun here. Ben would never forgive me if he thought I put that idea in your head. Just ignore the ramblings of an old lady. I've probably read too many books that filled my head with romantic notions."

"I better get to work," Jordan said before taking her mug to the sink. "Thanks for the coffee."

Being alone in the office made the day go slower, and Jordan's thoughts kept drifting from what she was reading to the hurt look on Ben's face when he had made his hasty exit the night before. He was the last person she wanted to hurt, but she had done nothing wrong and yet she felt compelled to make things right between them. With his face fresh in her mind, the long dormant urge to sketch came to her.

Since meeting Richard, she hadn't sketched so much as a doodle, but the desire was back stronger than ever and within minutes Ben's face took shape on the page. In her mind's eye she envisioned the strong cut of his jaw, the way his hair framed his face and the slight cleft in his chin, and she worked hard to transfer it all to the paper before stopping suddenly. A black and white sketch made it nearly impossible to capture the ice blue of his impressive eyes and she paused with the pencil in midair.

Faces had been her specialty and she would draw complete strangers on a napkin or scratch piece of paper, often resulting in amazing likenesses, but they were strangers with no need for her to convey the person behind the drawing.

With Ben, she felt a strong desire to portray the complex man behind the eyes—his strength, his compassion, and even the way his laughter touched everyone around him. Tapping her pencil on the table, she tried to imagine a black and white version of Ben's eyes, but nothing came to her and hearing Helen's footsteps, she shoved the unfinished sketch into the desk drawer.

"Jordan, I'm going to be starting lunch soon. Is there anything in particular you would like?" Helen asked as she poked her head in the office. Jordan had wasted the entire morning on the drawing.

"Actually, it's such a beautiful day out today I was thinking of skipping lunch and taking the dogs for a walk, if that's okay with you."

"It's up to you, but if you're hungry later, there's fixings for sandwiches in the fridge. Just help yourself. Bear's been under my feet all morning, and I think he could use a good long walk to expel some of that energy."

Bear wasn't the only one with excess energy and spending her lunch hour with the dogs helped Jordan relax a bit too, at least until returning to the house and seeing Ben's pickup. Letting both dogs off their leashes as they quietly entered the house, she expected to find Ben in the office but could hear him talking with Helen at the top of the stairs. Wrong as it may be, she stopped out of sight to listen.

"So, tell me the truth. Why did you sneak out of here this morning? I get the distinct impression you didn't want to be around Jordan today. Did something happen between you last night?"

"You're imagining things," Ben said. "I needed to do some research, is all."

"Not only is that Jordan's job, but did you forget about all the books in your office? Sounds to me like you made an excuse to avoid her."

"Helen, it's not what you think."

"And what exactly would that be?" she asked. It was easy for Jordan to picture her glaring at him, hands on those slim hips, daring him to lie to her.

"Honestly, I don't know, but I didn't sneak out. We had a misunderstanding last night, and I thought it might be easier if I put a little distance between us."

"Ben Anderson, what have you done?"

"Nothing really, at least nothing I hope has done any lasting damage."

Bear's playful barking interrupted their conversation.

"Sounds like Jordan's back. We'll talk more later and until then, try not to do anything that will hurt her. I think she might be in more trouble than you suspect," Helen told him before they both started downstairs and Jordan ducked into the office so they wouldn't see she had been eavesdropping.

"Afternoon Jordan."

"Hello," she told Ben, without looking up from the book she had quickly opened. "I'm surprised to see you. Helen said you were out for the day."

"That was the plan, but I have a meeting with a new client later this afternoon. Thanks for taking Bear out. It sure was a beautiful day for a walk."

They were now reduced to discussing the weather. The stilted conversation was the complete opposite of the prior evening.

"I thought that since you have a client coming in and all, I'll work from home this afternoon. If it's okay with you."

Without waiting for an answer, she stood and gathered her things.

"You don't have to do that," he said.

"No, I think you'll need the privacy and after all, isn't that why you paid all that money to have internet put in the cabin?"

"Jordan wait. If this is about last night, I'm sorry."

"I don't know what you're talking about," she lied. "I'll see you tomorrow morning."

Without giving him a chance to stop her, she called for Pete and they were out the door. Driving home she realized how childish she was being, but hearing Ben say he wanted distance between them had hurt more than she cared to admit.

Being cooped up in the cabin in front of a computer was the last thing she wanted on such a beautiful day, but not wanting to give Ben any more reason to be upset with her she worked all afternoon and was making real progress on the list of items he had asked her to research.

There was a genuine sense of satisfaction about the work, as tedious and detailed as it was, and if her life had been different, she would have enjoyed what she was doing. Instead, she felt guilty for running out the way she had, which would only make tomorrow morning even more uncomfortable.

Shutting down the computer, she finally looked at the clock to see how late it was.

"Come on Pete. Let's get you some supper."

At the sound of his name, Pete's ears perked up, and he followed her into the kitchen, where she filled his food bowl and put out fresh water. Having skipped lunch, she was hungrier than usual, but thanks to Helen's generosity, she had a surplus of options as she stared into the now jam-packed fridge.

The sound of an engine interrupted the silence and once again her heart began to race thinking Richard had found her, but before she could even reach for the bat, Ben's truck appeared in the clearing. While relieved it wasn't Richard, Ben wasn't much lower on the list of people she wanted to avoid and she peeked around the curtains hoping he would think she wasn't home, forgetting for a moment her early warning system. As soon as Pete recognized the truck, he began barking in excitement and the jig was up. Ben exited the truck carrying a toolbox with a tool belt slung over his shoulder.

"Jordan, it's Ben. Can you let me in?"

Taking a deep breath, she opened the door.

"What are you doing here?"

"Repairs, remember?" he told her as he raised the toolbox. "You forgot, right?"

"I guess I did, but that's okay. We can just skip it."

"Why would we do that?" he asked. She couldn't look him in the eyes and knew he would figure it out. "Oh, I see. Last night, right? Look, I'm sorry if I made you uncomfortable. I guess I was reading you all wrong, but I don't want that to ruin our friendship. I promise never to make that mistake again. If you want me to kiss you in the future, you're going to have to come right out and say it. I won't be making any more assumptions, okay?"

Raising her eyes to look at him, she could see the twinkle there and his smile soon followed. Darn but he was good at reading her. Since he would figure it out eventually, she came clean about what she had heard at the house.

"I heard you and Helen talking upstairs. I didn't mean to eavesdrop, but couldn't help it. You said you didn't want to be around me after last night, so that's why I left."

"I'm so sorry. Yes, it hurt my feelings when you pushed me away last night, but it was all my fault. You've made it perfectly clear you're not interested in a relationship. We'll just be friends."

"But if you're feeling something more..." she trailed off.

"It doesn't mean I'm going to act on those feelings. Look Jordan, whatever demons you're running from don't have to ruin your life. You're safe here and I hope you know you'll always be safe with me. You can tell me to go away, but I hope you don't and besides, there's the matter of holding up my end of the bargain and making some repairs here."

"Are you sure?"

"I am. Now if you'll let me in, I'll get started with that pesky doorknob."

The smile he flashed at her was genuine and to Jordan it felt like they were back where they had been before the ill-fated attempt at a kiss. She moved aside to let him in as Pete mobbed him looking for some attention.

"You didn't bring Bear with?" she asked in surprise.

"Helen took him for a walk. I think you put the idea in her head earlier today. She said you're an inspiration for her to be more active."

"I don't know about that, but good for her. I was just going to make something for dinner. Have you eaten?"

"Actually, I haven't but don't let me interrupt you."

"Don't be silly. If you remember Helen provided plenty of food and while you work, I'll get something heated up for us both."

"Thanks, I'd enjoy that. Now did you have time to make a list of things that need doing?"

Handing him the list with a shy smile, she let him get to his work while she set the table and worked to put food out. Standing at the stove hearing him whistle while he went about the repairs, a feeling of happiness washed over her. Her entire childhood had been like this...her mother in the kitchen cooking up something for dinner and her dad working around the house or even sitting quietly in his favorite chair reading the paper. Oh, why had she been so quick to throw her life away on Richard? He would never give her a divorce and she would spend the rest of her life in hiding, alone and unloved.

Sneaking a quick glance at Ben, his back to her as he struggled to fit a new knob onto the door hardware, she could see the outline of his shoulder muscles through his shirt and an ember of desire built in the pit of her soul. It had been a long time since a man had held her close and she could imagine the feel of his powerful arms. As if he realized she was thinking of him, he turned to catch her watching him and gave a quick smile before she turned back to the stove trying to compose herself.

Thirty minutes later he had already checked two things off her list just as she announced supper was ready.

"Let me just wash up first," he said as he set his tools on the bench by the door. "Is the kitchen sink okay or would you prefer I use the bathroom?"

"Here is fine," she said as she pulled out a fresh towel and handed it to him. "I didn't know what you'd like so I made the pot roast. It smells delicious."

"Helen's famous for her pot roast, but pretty stingy with the recipe. She considers it a treasured family secret."

Dishing up plates for both of them, it pleased her to discover Ben was right about the roast. It was so tender it melted in her mouth as she moaned in delight.

"See, was I right or what?" he asked with a laugh.

"My mother was an excellent cook but nothing as good as this," Jordan told him as she took another bite with Pete staring at her feet hoping she would drop a morsel or two. "How did you ever convince her to work for you?"

"Don't you remember? I thought I told you she came with the house. Not literally of course, but she had worked for years taking care of the relative who left the house to me. When my great aunt died, Helen had nowhere to go. I didn't even realize she lived on the property until the first morning when I came downstairs and she was in the kitchen making breakfast. One thing led to another and here we are—can't survive without each other."

"It must be nice having someone who needs you."

"I probably need her more than she needs me but it works for us. Honestly, if she wasn't here, I don't know if I still would be. It's only been a couple of months but it's been difficult to adjust to living such a solitary life after D.C."

"I suppose you had a lot of friends there."

"At the time I thought so, but after the scandal they all found reasons to distance themselves from me so I guess they were never genuine friends. I haven't always had many friends. Brandon was always more outgoing than I. He was constantly surrounded by friends of both sexes, but I kept to myself. I have a few college buddies but they've all started families and have careers around the country and I don't see them except for one friend who reached out to me after the scandal broke. Turned out he only reached out so he could repeat the story to everyone we knew."

"I'm sorry. It must have been difficult with everyone knowing what happened." Although her drama was equally hard, at least it hadn't been in the public eye.

"I heard a saying one time. *What doesn't kill you makes you stronger.* If that's true, I should probably be the strongest man alive."

"I've always thought there are different ways to be strong," she said so quietly she could have been talking to herself. "Sometimes having a will to get through difficult situations is the best kind of strength."

"And are you one of those people?"

Uncomfortable with the turn the conversation had taken she hesitated to speak, but then again Ben had opened himself up and shared something deeply personal.

Wasn't it about time she did the same?

"In some respects, I guess I am, although I'm not sure I'll ever be through it. But I'm still trying."

"You know you can tell me anything right?"

Looking up there were tears in her eyes at the kindness in that simple statement. "I know and I thank you for it. But it wouldn't be fair."

"Fair to whom? What aren't you telling me Jordan?" He was pleading with her to open up to him, but it was too dangerous.

"Please, just let it go. I appreciate everything you've done for me and even though it doesn't seem like it, your friendship has become very important to me. But that's all I can say, at least for now."

"But ..."

"Please, as my friend, just let it go."

The muscles in his jaw clenched and unclenched and she could tell he was thinking about what she had said. He didn't answer for the longest time. Finally, he nodded his head, but from the way he looked at her she knew the respite from his questions would only be a temporary one.

CHAPTER NINE

Ben's questioning aside, Jordan's comfort level being around Ben and Helen had grown exponentially as the days and weeks passed.

In some respects, they had become a little family, drawing Ben and her even closer. Being together every day also allowed them to discover how compatible they truly were. At night, they gravitated together for dollar movie night, long walks with the dogs, picnics in the small park in the center of town, or the occasional trip to Smith's Mill to go bowling or have a meal somewhere other than the diner. Soon she couldn't imagine a day without Ben in it, and she suspected he was feeling the same. Never classifying their time together as a date, she began to accept that she could be friends with a man even while she still felt a pull towards him that had nothing to do with friendship.

Physical attraction aside, Ben was charming, polite, funny, and considerate—all of which made it easy to imagine a future with the man who was so unlike Richard in all the ways that really counted.

He cared about her opinions and knowing that allowed her natural confidence to shine through, even when her opinions were the polar opposite of Ben's.

"What do you mean you don't believe in religion?" he asked in surprise as they strolled through the park with the dogs. "Seriously? You don't believe in God?"

"No, I believe in God, but organized religion is another thing. All you have to do is look around at the beauty that's in nature to know there is some higher being who created all this, but organized religion is too much of a business for me to believe it's a good thing. Churches seem to exist only to make those in charge wealthy and powerful, and something tells me that's not a good thing."

"But that's the fault of man, not the religion. Trust me, people are the root of all evil. Whatever religion you believe in didn't set out to create the television preacher dynasties. Corrupt people allowed that to happen and some people forgot the message of religion in a quest to use the church for their own benefit. All you have to do is look at churches that feed and clothe the poor and tend to the sick and ailing to see the good those religions do."

"Do you go to church regularly?"

"It's been years since I was in a church for Sunday service, but as a child we never missed attending as a family and I think it formed the basis for who I am. Didn't your family attend church?"

"On and off, but when I grew up, I stopped going. Besides, you only have to look at the news to see all the scandals associated with the church. For goodness sake, people even use it as an excuse for wars. Can you honestly say that God intended us to go to war over our beliefs?"

"Again, that's men using their religious beliefs as an excuse to do wrong. We've taken having freedom of religion and twisted it to our own purposes, but there are millions of people in the world who follow the teachings of their God to do good and live good lives. I know I've made a lot of mistakes in my life that go against those teachings, but I hope I'm learning from them and trying my best to make reparations."

"So those mistakes—you've forgiven yourself for them?" she asked. Knowing the mistakes she had made in her own life and the hurt she had caused her family because of it, she doubted she could ever forgive herself.

"It was hard, but I had to," he admitted with a sad look on his face. "I certainly will never forget the people I hurt by my actions, but the first person I had to forgive was myself."

"And Brandon? Do you forgive him?"

"That's a lot harder to do and I'm still working on it. It's easy to say he caused me to lose my dream, but then I realize how much better my life is here and I know I never would have had this life if he wasn't such an ass. I almost feel like I should thank him."

"Oh, I don't know that I'd go that far," she said with a laugh.

"Yeah, you're probably right." For the first time since they had begun the discussion, the corners of his mouth turned up in a smile.

"You still talk to him, right?" The day Ben had paced outside in a heated exchange with his brother wasn't a one-off. There had been at least two other calls between the brothers, each ending with Ben hanging up on Brandon.

"Unfortunately, I do."

"Why don't you just block his number so he can't call you?"

"That would be the sensible thing to do, of course, but I just can't do it. He's my brother and I tell myself that someday he'll realize what he's doing, but every time we get into another argument, I understand how futile that hope is."

"You and I have a lot more in common than it seems."

"In what way?"

"There was someone in my life for a long time that was kind of my Brandon. It was a different hurt, but I haven't forgiven him either."

The bluntness of her statement after weeks of silence about her past caused Ben to stop dead in his tracks to stare.

"I'm sorry," he told her as he took her hand.

"Don't be. I don't deserve your pity."

"Jordan, it's not pity. If you haven't figured it out by now, I care for you. I care for you a lot, and it's beyond me how someone could hurt you knowingly. I'm sorry you had to go through that is all."

"Yeah, well, it was my fault for letting it happen."

"Stop it," he said angrily before grabbing her by the shoulders to face him. "Don't let someone else's actions be your fault. Damn it, why do women do that, anyway? Why do you always make excuses when someone treats you poorly? No matter what this guy did to you, it's not your fault."

Tears sprang to her eyes before she jerked away from his hold and walked away. "You don't know what you're talking about," she said just as angrily as he hurried to catch up and her steps got quicker to distance herself from him.

"Will you just stop for a minute?" he asked. "Jordan please."

"Why? So you feel you can make another glaring assumption about all women? We make mistakes too, but at least I will admit mine. I'm the reason my life is so messed up. I'm the reason my family wants nothing to do with me. No one held a gun to my head and told me to do the things I've done. It was all me and now I'm paying the price for it."

"For God's sake, Jordan, what the hell are you talking about? For months you've talked in circles about what it is you're hiding from me and I can't take it anymore. Just tell me what you're hiding."

The truth was on the tip of her tongue as they stood toe to toe, each breathing heavily in frustration. She was tempted to just lay it all out for him until realizing it would just end up hurting yet another person.

"God, will you just let it go?" she begged. "It doesn't matter anymore, anyway. I can't change anything, and it just doesn't matter."

"How can you say that? Look at how upset you are just talking about it. You're never going to be free of whatever's in your past until you can talk about it. Hell, if you won't talk to me about it, then at least talk to someone. Helen or maybe even a priest."

The absurdity of telling a priest about Richard and how a still very married woman was now getting involved with Ben was more than she could take and she started to laugh uncontrollably as he stared at her in abject confusion.

"I already told you how I feel about that. No priest can solve what's wrong with me and neither can you. If you can't accept that then I think we should just part ways."

"You can't be serious. Running away from me every time we have an argument isn't the solution and you know it. I'll give you some space since that's what you seem to want, but please, stop pulling away from me every time we disagree."

"Don't you see?" she said so softly he didn't catch it at first. "Don't you see I can never be the person you want me to be?"

"I think it's you that doesn't see Jordan. You don't see that all I've ever wanted was for you to be happy, but you never will be until you let go of whatever you're hiding and move on with your life."

"So why do you even bother with me if that's your diagnosis? Tell me that. Why do you care about me at all?"

"Because it's obvious. You need someone to care about you, even if you don't see it yourself."

.   .   .   .   .

That one conversation said more about what was between them than any other, and all of Jordan's frustration with Ben's questioning melted away that night. From that moment on they were seldom apart. The suspicious looks and whispered comments when Jordan entered a store or passed someone on the sidewalk diminished and after months of treating her like a pariah, people smiled at her.

More surprising still, people who had previously crossed the street to avoid contact with Pete now openly approached her to pet him or scratch behind his ears. Ben's charming smile and instinctively caring manner towards everyone they encountered had opened doors for her and finally she felt like part of the community and it wasn't long before Ben felt the same.

If the people in town knew of Ben's past, it was never mentioned and little by little, she could see him relax when he introduced himself and there was no mention of the scandal back east.

In a town with more churches per capita than most any other city in that part of the country, she could only imagine their reaction if they somehow discovered the truth about his scandal. Though it might eventually come out, knowing Ben and respecting him before his past came to light would help him weather the storm, and she was glad for him.

But for her, it was a waiting game to find out when her suddenly happy life would come crumbling down around her. Her entire life she had sensed when trouble was on the horizon and the feeling was worming its way into her subconscious. Everything was going smoothly in her life, but as the feeling grew, she found she was waiting for the other shoe to drop. Would Ben figure out who she was? Would he decide the bother of trying to get her to confide in him wasn't worth it? Her life was the opposite of charmed and someday she knew all the happiness she was now feeling would come to a crushing end. Until it did though, she was determined to enjoy today.

. . . . .

"Jordan, do you know where the Lucas file is?" Ben asked as he walked into her office to leaf through the mess of files on her desk.

The smile, which these days was always on Jordan's face, got even bigger when she noticed the clearly labeled file already in his hands.

"You mean this Lucas file?" she laughed, tugging at the corner of the file.

He looked down at the file before laughing at himself.

"I'm such an idiot," he said with a wry grin. "What would I do without you? Say, I should have mentioned this earlier, but I have to run up to Casper at the end of the day to file some paperwork at the courthouse and I wondered if you might want to come along? We've both been working so hard I thought maybe we could go for a nice dinner at a restaurant with real cloth napkins and maybe a nice wine cellar, maybe one with music we could dance to. I know you don't want me to say it's a date, but maybe, just this once, you could let me believe it is and give me a chance to feel like a real man again?"

They had been working non-stop for weeks now and things were going well between them, even though it was becoming more difficult to quell the attraction Jordan felt for him. The thought of a romantic dinner with wine and dancing was certainly enticing, but could she agree it was a date? She decided to throw caution to the wind and let him call it whatever he wanted.

"If it's going to be a date, even a pretend one, I have a few conditions," she said, surprising him. "First, if it's a date, you have to pay."

"Not a problem," he said excitedly. "What else?"

"You can hardly expect me to go dressed like this. I need the afternoon off to figure out what to wear. If we're going to pretend we're on a date, then I want to feel feminine for a change."

Seeing the sparkle in his eyes at her request, she should have realized she had taken it a step too far, but unfortunately, that realization wouldn't come until much later.

. . . . .

She spent the rest of the afternoon in a mad dash to Smith's Mill to find a new dress to wear for the pseudo-date. With only one women's clothing store in town, her choices were limited, but eventually she found the perfect dress even if it seemed better suited for her prior lifestyle.

The designer certainly knew how to show a woman's body to its best advantage and she wondered for just a moment if the snug fitting dress sent the wrong statement to a man she was constantly having to remind herself was nothing more than a friend.

In the end, and with few other options, she parted with some of her carefully hoarded cash and the dress came home with her. Stepping into it, she felt more like a woman than she had in all the designer gowns and jewels Richard had filled her closets with. Slipping on the heels that had collected dust since the night she and Ben went to the movies, butterflies filled her belly as she imagined what would go through Ben's head when he saw her for the first time. Hearing his truck coming up the road, she didn't have to wait long.

"Come on Pete, Mom's got a date," she said before applying the lightest touch of perfume and heading downstairs to answer the door, unprepared for the sight that greeted her. Ben stood before her in a beautiful black suit, crisp white shirt and black silk tie with a matching pocket square and dress shoes shined to a high polish. His blue eyes sparkled and his normally effusive smile seemed even larger. He took her breath away.

Seconds passed as they each took in the other and when their eyes finally met, she didn't know what to say. He was simply the most attractive man she had ever met, and nervousness overwhelmed her.

"Good God Jordan. I've told you many times how beautiful you are, but tonight, well tonight you've taken it to a whole other level. You're stunning."

Her first instinct was to make a snappy comeback to lighten the mood, but hearing him say such nice things, she just couldn't. Richard had taken away every ounce of her confidence, and Ben's simple words brought it all back. There was no way she would make light of it.

Looking up at him through hooded lashes, she smiled tentatively and offered her own compliments. "Thank you. That suit looks terrific on you. Is that Prada?"

"It is, and I'm surprised you knew that. When I left D.C. I almost got rid of all my suits, but just couldn't bear to do it. It's nice to be back in one of the expensive ones again. Are you ready to go?"

After a stop at the federal courthouse in Casper, where she could only assume Ben, dressed in his finery, received even more attention from the clerks than usual, they made their way to what looked to be a very expensive seafood restaurant.

Even though it was still early, the full restaurant should have meant a long wait. But that wasn't the case.

"Reservation for Ben Anderson."

"Mr. Anderson, welcome," the hostess said, giving him a look Jordan had seen several other women give him. It was a mixture of awe and desire all rolled into one. But who could blame her? Jordan's own temperature had yet to come down from the heat that erupted in her when she opened the door and saw him. "We have your table all ready if you'll follow me."

Ready to follow the woman, Jordan felt Ben take her hand in his own and she looked down at their now joined hands before looking into his eyes.

"It's a date, remember?" he said with a wink.

Every part of her head said she was treading in dangerous waters, but her heart overruled it and she didn't pull away.

As the woman directed them to a table in the most secluded part of the dining room with champagne already chilling in a nearby stand and a small nosegay of roses gracing the center of the table, she couldn't help but notice that only their table had flowers and her pulse ratcheted up.

The hostess had barely left when the words tumbled out of her mouth.

"Ben, what's going on?" she asked, trying to keep her composure.

"Please don't be mad at me. I just wanted to do something special for you to say thank you for everything you've done for me."

"I don't know what you're talking about. I was just doing my job," she told him as he poured them each a glass of champagne while she watched carefully.

"It has nothing to do with the job," he said as a waiter headed their way before Ben waved the man away. "All this is for being my friend. If it wasn't for you, I probably would have moved away a long time ago, but you make this place tolerable. Well, more than that really. You've made it my home, and I don't know how to thank you for that."

"I don't understand. Of course it's your home."

"No, it wasn't. At least not until you came into my life. I don't think you realize what you've done for me. I arrived here a broken man; ashamed of the man they chased out of Washington and ashamed I let myself get drawn into Brandon's drama. It's hard to admit even now, but I honestly thought all of my dreams were over until I met you and things changed for me. The practice picked up. I learned to loosen up a bit and the community accepted me. All those dreams that I had for a career, a partnership—they're gone now, but that doesn't mean my life went with it. In fact, I have finally realized that the life I have now is what was meant to be. I'm my own man here and I'm actually helping people who need it."

"But that's all on you," she argued.

"Sure, but only in part. You've helped in ways you might never imagine and without you here, I might have packed up and left. Having you as a friend made me realize that there's more to life than working hundred hour weeks and getting promotions."

Reaching across the table, he took her hand. She didn't pull away.

"The time we've spent together has meant more to me than anything else in my life, and I wanted you to know how important you've become to me."

"I don't know what to say," she told him. The heat from his hand warmed her entire body.

"You don't have to say anything," he told her. "After all this time, I know opening up is hard for you and as far as I'm concerned you can keep all the secrets about your past as long as I'm part of your future. I don't care what you're running away from, as long as you don't run from me. Whether you like it or not, you've become the most important part of my life and I know you're not ready for this—hell, you might never be ready—but I'd give anything to be more than just a friend to you."

His eyes held her own with such intensity she knew she would have to choose her words carefully, and she tried desperately to collect her thoughts. This man, a man she knew without a doubt she could spend her life with, had just opened up his heart, and the wrong word from her could devastate him.

"I've waited a lifetime for someone to feel that way about me, but..."

"Please don't say but," he asked as he pulled his hand away before she grabbed it back.

"But," she started again, "I never thought it would happen to me. Against my better judgement, I've developed feelings for you too, but I don't think I can give you what you want . . . what we both want. There's just too much about me you don't know."

"God, Jordan, you're killing me here. Please tell me. Let me help you. I'm sure there has to be a way we can be together, especially since we both want it. What could you possibly have done that was so horrible?"

"I made a mistake and will spend the rest of my life paying for it," she told him as the tears fell. "Can you just take me home?"

"But . . . ?"

"Please, just take me home."

The promise they had both felt about their evening evaporated as quickly as it had appeared and without another word exchanged between them, Ben did as she asked.

.   .   .   .   .

Coming in to work the following Monday, after a weekend with no contact between them, Jordan considered handing in her resignation.

Being around Ben and feeling as she did about him, knowing nothing could ever come of those feelings, was becoming unbearable. It was best for both of them if she just ended their friendship now—even if he didn't realize it.

What she hadn't counted on, however, was his behavior.

Their pseudo-date, which they both knew had been anything but, had ended so badly she was afraid Ben would fire her even before she quit, yet to her surprise he acted as if the night had never happened and with their friendship seemingly intact, her intention to resign disappeared. Business and their friendship, both in the house and outside of it, continued as if the date had never happened and the sense of relief she felt at Ben's continued companionship was immense.

As Ben became more accepted by the townspeople, his practice had picked up, resulting in changes at the house. They converted the music room into an office for Jordan, even though the pair continued to find their way to each other throughout the day to bounce ideas off one another or just to have a cup of coffee together.

Even Helen had commented on the perfect fit their friendship seemed to be, but Jordan knew Helen was too astute not to sense the underlying tension that popped up each time she and Ben were within arm's length of each other. More than once Helen had witnessed Ben reach out his hand to touch Jordan's arm before pulling back at the last minute. His guilty look didn't tell the entire story of what was between the couple, but it said enough for Helen to know there was more than friendship brewing in the house. To her credit, however, she said nothing as she waited for nature to take its course and when it did, it was just in time for a celebration.

They had finally adjudicated the land dispute case in front of a judge. Ben had presented a masterful case with the courtroom gallery hanging on his every word. In the end, the inexperienced trial lawyer soundly thumped his more credentialed opponent and Ben easily won the case.

His assurances that the case had been a slam dunk from the beginning didn't fool Jordan. He was a natural in the courtroom and all those years dealing with corporate law had been a waste of his natural abilities. She couldn't have been happier about his success.

Arriving at the house after the big verdict, Ben spun Jordan in the air as their laughter filled the house.

"Can you believe that? What a rush!" he said excitedly.

"I am so happy for you, even if I didn't understand half of what you said up there. You had them eating out of your hands."

Putting her down, he continued to hold her close as the laughter died away and they stared into each other's eyes. The uneasiness she should have felt was non-existent, and she didn't move from his arms.

"I couldn't have done this without you, Jordan. I hope you know that."

"Thanks, but it's not true. I think this is what you were born to do. Do you even realize how much you've changed since I met you? You've come alive working on this case, and I'm so happy for you."

Without thinking, she reached up and placed a soft kiss on his cheek that instantly changed the demeanor between them. His hands came to either side of her face and the look of desire in his eyes, the look he had so carefully hidden away for weeks, was front and center.

"Ask me," he said softly.

"What?"

"You know. Ask me."

A spark of desire leapt within her. Of course, she knew what he was asking; she had never forgotten.

Lowering her head to avoid those piercing eyes, he used his finger to raise it again.

"Isn't it about time we both admitted what we're feeling? Ask me Jordan, please."

"Kiss me," she requested so softly she wasn't sure she had said the words aloud.

"Say it like you mean it."

"I want you to ki . . ."

The words were barely out of her mouth before his lips claimed hers. Nerve endings erupted from the desire that had been building within Jordan from the moment she saw Ben in her hospital room. The feel of his late day beard, the warmth of his lips, and the playfulness of his tongue all mingled together until her knees threatened to buckle and she clung to him with all the strength she had left until the sound of dogs barking at the back door brought them back to reality as they looked at each other with a new understanding.

"That would be Helen back from grocery shopping," he said softly as his hand caressed the side of her face and she pressed her body against his, unsure whether she could stand on her own yet.

"So it would seem."

"Can we continue this later?"

Her answer should have been no, but still swimming with desire for the man, she could only shake her head affirmatively before he gave her a quick kiss on the forehead and went to let Helen and the dogs in while she collapsed into her office chair. Her sketch of Ben had remained carefully tucked out of sight, although she had been working on it on and off for a few weeks, and still awash with a jumble of emotions, she pulled it out once more. The fine details already completed, the space where his eyes should have been stared back at her, but this time when she closed her eyes, she knew just how to finish the drawing. It took only minutes before she had captured his eyes perfectly.

Brilliant blue or black and white, it didn't matter. That one kiss had opened her eyes to the fire and passion in him and by some miracle, she had transferred it to the paper. Whatever happened between them in the future, she would always have the sketch and the memory of this day. Carefully placing the sketch under a law book on her desk, she joined the others in the kitchen.

"Jordan, there you are," Helen said as she worked in tandem with Ben putting away the groceries. "Isn't it wonderful news about the court case?"

"It's terrific and you should have been there to watch Ben. He was wonderful."

"You two sound like you're surprised we won," he said with a wry smile. "Did you have that little faith in me?"

"It's not that," Jordan was quick to point out. "The only courtroom drama I've ever seen has been on television, and this was so much better than that."

"Thank you," he said, laughing. "I have to admit, that was a lot more fun than corporate law. Being in front of a judge with all those eyes on me was nerve-wracking, but once I realized the defense didn't have a leg to stand on, my nerves disappeared and the case just flowed out of me."

"Maybe all those late nights you spent practicing your summation had something to do with it?" Helen offered with a warm smile. "I don't know if he would admit this to you Jordan, but he practiced so much I think I could probably recite it word-for-word myself."

"And in the end, all those hours paid off. But I said it earlier. I couldn't have done it without you Jordan, and you too Helen. You both helped tremendously and as a thank you, I am taking us all out for dinner tonight."

"But I just bought a roast," Helen protested.

"Save it for Sunday," Ben said. "Tonight we're celebrating and I won't take no for an answer."

"Oh my, then I better get back to my cottage and get cleaned up," Helen said before rushing out the door.

"Now where were we?" Ben asked as he reached for Jordan's hand and pulled her into his arms. "Now I remember." Lowering his head for a kiss, he met no resistance. The kiss was slow and sensual, leaving both of them breathless when it ended.

"How did I ever get so lucky to have you in my life?" he asked huskily as his hands roamed her backside, pulling her even closer to his body and sending shivers up and down her spine.

"Lest you forget, your dog tried to kill me."

"Oh yeah. I'll have to remember to give him an extra treat tonight for that and maybe something special for you too—to say I'm sorry about Bear and all."

His cheeky smile elicited her laugh, even though she was just beginning to realize what she had opened herself up for by asking for his kiss.

"Helen's not the only one who needs to get ready," she told him as she pushed him away so she could think clearly. "What kind of place are you taking us?"

"You might be disappointed, but Helen's favorite place is a dive bar about halfway between here and Smith's Mill. It's not much to look at, but it has the best ribs, a full bar, and live music every night. Would that be okay with you?"

"Sounds like fun," she assured him. "Let Pete and I run home so I can change, and I'll be back in an hour."

"No need. We'll pick you up on the way. I'll see you in an hour."

. . . . .

Dive bar might have been a generous description of their destination for the evening, but Ben was spot on in his assessment of the food and the live music. Unsure how to act together in front of Helen, Jordan was relieved when Ben seemed to know not to flaunt what happened between them even if that didn't stop him from sitting close enough their legs touched and his hand could caress her thigh every now and then. As with the kiss, his touch caused cascading shivers through her body, making it hard to concentrate on what everyone was saying. If he was trying to keep the fire burning in her, he was succeeding.

Meal finished, Helen rose to her feet, wine glass in hand.

"Ben, thank you for a wonderful evening, but I have something to say," she said dramatically enough to make them suspect she had imbibed one too many cocktails. "As much as you may try, you can't hide anything from me."

Ben and Jordan immediately looked at each other. How had she figured it out so quickly?

"I know this was the last place on earth you wanted to be and I know what you've been through in the last year, but you're a fighter. I saw that in you the first day we met. Just like your aunt, bless her soul, you belong here and whether or not the people in these parts know it, they need you. Not just because you're an amazing lawyer, but because you're an even more amazing man and you make all of us better for knowing you. Jordan, don't you agree?"

"I do," she said enthusiastically as they all raised glasses. "To Ben."

Ben leaned across the table and planted a kiss on Helen's cheek.

"Oh my!" she exclaimed as she pressed her hands to her now blushing cheek. "If I was fifty years younger, I wouldn't let you stop there!"

Her unexpectedly saucy comment caused smiles all around.

"I think someone has had a bit too much to drink," Ben told her kindly. "How about we get you home to bed?"

"Nonsense," Helen told him. "You and Jordan haven't even danced."

"We can always dance another time," Ben insisted.

"Helen, do you need a ride home?"

Looking up, they recognized the couple standing next to Helen as Ben's next-door neighbors.

"We're going that way and we can give you a ride," the man said as his wife nodded her head.

"Herb, that would be lovely," Helen told him as she struggled to stand before Ben helped her to her feet. "Now you two stay and have a good time. Don't do anything I wouldn't do," she said with a final wink.

Watching them walk slowly through the crowd, Helen looked every inch of her almost eighty years, mostly because of over imbibing.

"Helen was right," Ben said, turning his attention back to Jordan and extending his hand. "It's time for us to dance."

He didn't need to ask twice, and they joined others on the dance floor, working their way through a country line dance. After a few initial missteps, it didn't take long to get the hang of things and the fast-paced dancing provided a chance for the desire coursing through Jordan's body to dissipate. Before long, she was having more fun than she had had in years.

"You're a superb dancer," Ben said when they finally took a break. "Did you have lessons or something?"

"Not really. My mom and I spent hours in the living room dancing to her old records. I guess I just picked it up from her. But it's been ages since I danced."

"Not even around the house? You seem to enjoy it so much I figured you'd be the type to dance around in your underwear, singing your lungs out into a hairbrush."

His question was innocent enough, but how could he know there hadn't been enough happiness in her life since meeting Richard to want to dance? She looked up at him with sadness filling her eyes.

"I'm sorry Jordan. Once again, I didn't mean to pry. I'm happy though that things seem to be changing for you and if it's not too presumptive of me, I hope maybe I had a little something to do with that."

But for the possibility of ruining a wonderful evening, it might be the perfect moment to pour her heart out to him, but she just couldn't.

For the first time all night, the band switched to a slow ballad and without a word Ben took her hand and pulled her back onto the dance floor, his strong arms holding her close as they swayed to the song before he started singing the lyrics softly into her ear. For that one moment in time, she let all of her worries about Richard go and luxuriated in the feeling of safety and contentment she felt with Ben. It lasted all of a few minutes before she was brought back to reality. As they stood together, swaying to the music that had ended without their notice, every eye in the place seemed to be on them and Jordan pulled back in embarrassment.

"I'm sorry, I don't know what came over me," she whispered. Neither one moved and Jordan could feel her heart threatening to burst out of her chest. She had let herself get wrapped up in the possibility of a future with Ben; a future that would never be, and she was ashamed of herself. "Please take me home?"

"I don't understand," he said in confusion. "Why are you doing this again? What's wrong?"

"Nothing," she told him quickly. "I just think it's best if I went home. I'm sorry."

"But... "

"Please?" she begged before walking to their table to gather her things and walking out the door.

Those who had witnessed Jordan's abrupt departure directed undisguised looks of sympathy his way before a sudden anger washed over him. He didn't understand what had just happened. A perfectly lovely and romantic evening was in ruins and he couldn't for the life of him figure out what had gone wrong.

Stopping just long enough to throw a few bills on the table, he hurried after Jordan, half expecting to find her walking home on her own and relieved to see her standing next to the truck waiting for him.

"Jordan, please, at least tell me what I did wrong?" he asked as he approached her.

"It's not you," she said angrily. "I just want to go home."

"Not until you explain to me what's going on! You owe me an explanation, don't you think?"

"I don't owe you anything," she spat back at him. Her embarrassment at letting herself get carried away had manifested itself as anger at him and he didn't deserve it, but she couldn't help herself. "You're my boss and that's it. I just let myself forget that for a minute is all. But I don't owe you any explanation. Now do I walk home, or will you at least give me a ride?"

They completed the ride to the cabin in silence and, with the truck barely at a stop, Jordan opened her door and bolted for the safety of the cabin. Slamming the door soundly behind her, she left no doubt there was to be no further discussion about the abrupt conclusion to their evening. Breathing heavily, her face became flushed with the jumble of emotions coursing through her as she prayed Ben wouldn't follow her to the door. The sound of the engine fading into the night as the truck drove away was a relief.

For the briefest of moments as they had danced together, Jordan had let herself believe she could have a lifetime of love and happiness and a house full of children with Ben. Realistically, it was nothing more than a pipe dream with Richard the roadblock right in the middle. She had finally realized the price she would pay for putting her life of misery with Richard behind her and now it seemed Ben would be made to pay, too.

Overcome with sadness and anger for all the poor decisions in her life that had brought her to this point, she collapsed to the floor in tears as Pete sat down beside her. Whining softly in sympathy, his muzzle pushed towards her face until she finally sat up and put her arms around his enormous body.

It wasn't until he stiffened that the sound of a vehicle approaching the cabin caught her attention and she peeked through the curtains to see Ben's truck slam to a stop in front of the cabin in a cloud of gravel dust before he jumped out and ran to the door. Expecting to hear a deafening pounding on the door, there was nothing but silence until finally his voice, so soft she could barely make out the words, came through the old wooden door.

"Jordan, please. I'm sorry, but please talk to me. Let me help you. There's nothing we can't sort out if we do it together."

What could she say? The pain in his voice was profound, but once she opened the door, there would be no going back and Jordan knew it.

"Please, don't you at least owe it to me to look me in the face?"

He was right, of course. She owed him that, and so much more. Wiping the tears away, she got to her feet and reached for the doorknob, taking one last breath before opening it to see a man who looked as miserable as she felt. Neither said a word as they stared into each other's eyes. She moved back to let him come in as his phone rang. He ignored it.

"Thank you. I'm sorry for coming back when you made it perfectly clear you didn't want to talk to me, but damn it Jordan, I thought our friendship meant more to you than this."

"It does. I mean, our friendship is important to me also," she sputtered.

"Haven't I shown you I'm trustworthy? Haven't I been nothing but loyal and kind to you?" he asked.

"Yes, but..."

"No buts. Jordan, you either trust me or you don't and if you trust me, then why won't you let me help you? Why won't you let me show you how much you mean to me?"

With each question, he had moved closer to her until finally he was in front of her, close enough she could feel the heat from his body. She dared not move for fear of falling into his arms.

"And why won't you let me do this..."

Before she could make sense of the question, his lips lowered to claim hers in a kiss that took her breath away, making her head swim and her knees go weak before she pushed him away.

"Ben, stop please."

He backed away from her as soon as the words came out of her mouth, his face a mass of confusion and desire.

"I just don't get you. How could I be so wrong about you? You look at me like you want the same things I do and that kiss? Well let's just say it wasn't just one sided. Or are you that good of an actress? Have you been playing with me this whole time? Is that what this is?"

"Of course not," she said angrily. "How could you even think that?"

"Then why all the mixed signals, Jordan? Why does every fiber of my being tell me you want me as much as I want you?"

"Because it's true," she whispered, unable to look him in the eye.

"Well then, what's going on?" he asked as he reached for her again before she walked across the room, intent on putting as much distance between them as possible.

"Ben, I can't be with you. As much as I want to, as much as you mean to me, I just can't be with you in that way."

"That makes no sense. We're here together, we're two consenting adults, and it doesn't matter what happened in your past. We can figure that out as long as we are together. Please, just let me hold you and I promise I'll make it all better."

More than anything, she wanted to believe he could fulfill the promise, but even he was no match for Richard. The only way to end this before it hurt him even more was to tell him the truth. Taking a deep breath, the words finally came out of her mouth.

"I'm married," she said quietly.

"What? What did you say?" The abject shock on his face was more than she could bear, but she said it again.

"I'm married," she said loud and clear as Ben stared back in shock.

"That's not true. You don't have a ring or even a tan line. You can't be married."

"I'm so sorry, but it's the truth," she said as tears formed in her eyes and anger formed in his.

"I don't believe you. Why would you lie about something like that? You're just making it up because you still don't trust me enough to tell me the truth. Damn it please tell me you're making this up?"

Taking a step towards Jordan, he grabbed her arm harder than either of them expected and she wrenched away uttering an exclamation of pain which immediately caused Pete to jump between them.

Ears flattened, fur on his back standing on end, he issued a low growl of warning that surprised them both and Ben immediately stepped back as Jordan rubbed her arm where he had grabbed her.

"Jordan, I'm so sorry," he said before his cell phone, which had been ringing incessantly since he walked into the cabin, rang yet again.

"You better get that," she said quietly before reaching for Pete's collar in case he felt the need to protect her further. It was the first sign of aggression the dog had shown since she adopted him and if she had really been in danger, she would have been glad of it, but she didn't want Ben to get hurt.

"Ben Anderson," he said in clipped tones. "When? Is she alive? I'll be right there." The fear in his voice said more than his words. Something was horribly wrong. Ending the call, he turned to leave before Jordan stopped him.

"What's wrong?" she asked with no response. "Ben, what's wrong?"

Tears filled his eyes causing Jordan's blood to run cold.

"It's Helen. She was walking Bear, and a truck hit her. They're airlifting her straight to Casper. I have to get to the hospital to be with her. I have to go."

"Not without me," she said angrily. "I love her too. I'm going with you."

Stopping only long enough to grab her things, they raced to the truck and started the long drive to Casper, each of them praying they wouldn't be too late.

CHAPTER TEN

The monotonous hum of the ICU equipment had lulled Jordan to sleep at Helen's bedside and although Ben had been with her since entering the room, there was no sign of him when she opened her eyes. It was a relief. Their death-defying overnight trip to Casper was done in stony silence, each lost in their own fears for the woman lying so still in the hospital bed. Swathed in bandages, the tube down her throat and a bank of machines keeping her alive, Helen was hanging on by a thread and Jordan reached for her frail hand, its warmth providing the smallest glimmer of hope. With no windows in the ICU room, she had no way of knowing how much time had passed, but Helen was still alive and that was all that mattered now.

The night before had been a blur. Expecting to learn more when they arrived, they were instead directed to a waiting room as an hour wait turned into two and two turned into more. Each sitting on opposite sides of the crowded waiting room, the time passed so slowly the clock barely seemed to move and as the room slowly emptied with still no word on Helen's condition, Jordan hadn't known what to do. Ben's face was devoid of emotion but she knew him well enough to know if Helen didn't make it he would be devastated. She had longed to put her arms around him, but in light of their earlier disagreement, she did nothing. She suspected they were both preparing for the worst possible news and by the time the doctor finally walked into the waiting room they were beside themselves with fear.

The doctor had deemed it a miracle that Helen had survived not only the flight to Casper, but the lengthy emergency surgery that followed, yet he had been unwilling or unable to give them even a shred of hope that she would pull through.

At his words they had instinctively joined hands, their earlier fight forgotten as they focused on the woman they both loved.

"Can we see her?" Ben asked. It was the first words he had spoken since they arrived at the hospital.

"She's being moved to ICU right now. A nurse will come and get you when you can go in. I'm sorry I couldn't give you a better prognosis, but she's alive and fighting and that's something."

With a slight nod of his head, the doctor was gone, and the room was quiet once more. Ben released Jordan's hand and paced around the room as she sat once more and bowed her head. Ben didn't seem to realize that the woman he had once accused of not believing in God was now focusing every breath on praying for Helen to recover. It was another hour before a nurse walked into the room to announce they could see Helen and they both moved towards the door.

"I'm sorry, but we limit ICU to one visitor at a time."

Exchanging looks of disappointment, Jordan suggested Ben go.

"It should be you," she told him. "I can wait."

He turned to look at the nurse. "Surely there's got to be a way we can both see her. It might be the last time we do. Can't you please make an exception?"

Bombarded by Ben's baby blue eyes, the woman didn't stand a chance and Jordan could see she was weighing her duty to follow the rules and her desire to give Ben whatever he wanted.

"Please," he asked again.

"I really could get in trouble for this, but if you don't tell anyone I suppose it would be okay for a little while. Follow me."

Giving Ben a rather coquettish look, she headed towards ICU as they hurried to follow. There was no hand holding this time and Ben barely looked at Jordan. They walked side by side down the hallway, but they might as well have been miles apart.

The quiet of the ICU wing had been foreboding—as if death waited around every corner—and Jordan's spirits sank with every step she took until finally they were in front of the glass door at Helen's cubicle.

The nurse motioned for them to hurry lest someone see them and she slid the door closed behind them and pulled the curtain.

"There's a chair against the wall there and I'll bring another one in a minute. She's heavily sedated so she won't fight the intubation. Talk to her if you like. Studies show that patients can hear sometimes."

While they both stared in horror at the small, frail body in the bed in front of them, the nurse checked a few things before leaving them alone.

Each moving to a side of the bed, they reached for her hands; Ben's enormous expanse of hand encompassing Helen's much smaller one. He gently smoothed her thick white hair away from her forehead before placing a kiss where his hand had been and leaning down to whisper something into her ear as Jordan watched with tears rolling down her cheeks. When Ben looked up again there were tears in his eyes too and Jordan's heart broke.

"She's going to be okay," she whispered. To say any differently was to tempt fate. "I just know she's going to be okay."

The pain in Ben's eyes was more than she could handle and she moved to his side to wrap her arms around him as he did the same to her. Lowering his head to her shoulder his body shook with his silent sobs. In that one moment Jordan knew without a shred of doubt that she loved him and she cried also until the nurse returned with a folding chair and their moment of intimacy was interrupted. They pulled apart and they each wiped tears from their eyes and took a seat at Helen's bedside.

Now it was hours later and Ben was nowhere to be found. Muscles aching from sitting for so long, Jordan stood and stretched, her eyes never leaving the bank of monitors surrounding Helen's bed. She had a vague memory of nurses coming and going throughout the night, but no way to know if that was a good sign or not.

"Good morning," said a quiet voice as a nurse entered the room. "How's our patient doing?"

"Shouldn't you be the one telling me that?" Jordan asked with more impatience than was necessary. She was tired and hungry and scared and while her tone might be understandable, it was also unnecessary. "I'm sorry. I didn't mean that," she said quickly. "But how is she doing?"

"She made it through the night and that's always a good sign. The doctor is talking to your husband right now if you want to join them. They are at the end of the hallway."

It wasn't the first time someone in a hospital had mistakenly called Ben her husband, but this time the assumption was more painful than the first.

"He's not my..." Jordan had been about to correct her before stopping. If they learned Jordan was of no relation maybe she could no longer see Helen. She hurried out of the room to see Ben shaking hands with the doctor.

By the time she joined him at the end of the hallway the doctor was already gone.

"What did he say? Is she going to be all right?"

"Nothing we didn't already know. It's still touch and go. Apparently the pickup that hit her did a good job of it and the only reason she is still alive is because the driver stopped and called 911 immediately. He said she was alert and talking until the ambulance got there which sounds like a good sign, but really it wasn't because she was in shock. She was worried about Bear and kept trying to get up to see him."

"Oh my God! Bear! Is he?"

"He's fine. According to the Sheriff, they think he might have saved her life. The driver reported seeing Bear tugging at the leash just before he hit her and that helped him avoid hitting her head on. I figured you wouldn't want to go home until Helen's out of the woods so this morning I called your vet friend and asked him to take care of Bear and Pete until we get back."

The way he referred to Kevin as her friend sounded like it should have had air quotes around it, but she was too tired to argue the point with him.

"Thank you for that," she told him. "Did you get any sleep last night?"

"Not much. I just couldn't stop thinking about what will happen if . . ."

"Stop it. We can't let ourselves go down that rabbit hole. We need to be strong so Helen can be strong. I can't let myself believe we will lose her. I just can't."

He seemed surprised by the strength of her conviction and he took a deep breath, stood up straighter, and nodded.

"Then neither will I."

"Thank you. Now why don't you go check on our girl and I'll find something for us for breakfast?" She began to walk away before he reached for her hand and stopped her.

"Jordan, thank you."

"For what?"

"For coming with me last night. For your words just now. For loving Helen as much as I do. It means a lot to me."

Overcome with emotion, she simply squeezed his hand and headed towards the cafeteria. She loved him so much, but now that Ben knew part of her secret, nothing would ever be the same between them. Telling him she was married had been devastating for him. If it hadn't been for Helen's accident, Jordan doubted she would ever have seen him again and yet now here they were, providing support for each other.

Sitting in the ICU, watching the loving way Ben held Helen's hand, she couldn't help but imagine how it would feel to be the object of Ben's affection. But once Helen was on the mend and safe at home again Ben would go back to his life and she would go back to the life she had before they met. She would change her running pattern to avoid the painful memories of the house on the hill and the love she felt for the man inside and if that wasn't enough, she would leave town and this time she would take Ben's happiness with her. She had left Richard behind with barely a thought whether it would hurt him. If she left Ben, it wouldn't be that easy and she not only knew it, but she was already dreading the pain it would cause both of them.

·   ·   ·   ·   ·

The pattern of the next few days never varied. One of them was always at Helen's side in ICU holding her hand, reading the paper to her, or just talking to her; neither one sleeping much on the uncomfortable sofa in the waiting room, eating little, but drinking copious amounts of coffee.

Little by little, Helen's vital signs improved as they weaned her off the sedation until finally they removed the breathing tube; each step towards recovery celebrated with cautious smiles. It wasn't until Helen opened her eyes that they let themselves hope for the best.

"That was quite a nap you had," Ben told her with a smile that lit up the dark room. "How are you feeling?"

"Better than you two by the looks of it," Helen quipped with a voice raw from the intubation. "Why am I in the hospital?"

Ben and Jordan exchanged quick looks.

No one had said anything about Helen not remembering.

"I'm kidding," Helen said with a weak attempt at a smile. "I might be eighty, but I'm not senile. Is Bear all right? I wouldn't be able to forgive myself if something..."

"He's fine," Jordan quickly reassured her. "Safe at home with Pete and missing you I expect, but seriously how are you feeling?"

"Like I got hit by a truck, but grateful to be alive. I'm sorry I worried you both."

"Nonsense. I wasn't worried for a minute. I knew you would never leave me until the house is full of babies you can tend to," Ben joked.

"Maybe that will happen sooner than I thought," she said to their surprise as she looked from one to the other. "But now I think I might just close my eyes for a minute if you don't mind."

And just like that she had fallen back to sleep, this time the peaceful sleep of a healing patient. Each day after that was better than the last until finally her steady improvement was enough to convince her doctor she would be safe in a regular room and they moved her to a wing of the hospital where both Jordan and Ben could visit at the same time. Until she kicked them out, that is.

"It's not that I don't love seeing you both, but isn't it about time you headed for home? I'm sure the dogs would love to see you and there has to be a client or two that needs your services Ben. You don't have to sit here and babysit me."

"Stop it. I'm not going anywhere," Ben told her with a smile. "But Jordan should go. She can check in at the office and see if there is anything needing attention. Maybe pay a few bills. You can take the truck."

Jordan, who had been sitting near the window reading a book, looked up as decisions were apparently being made without her. Truth be told, she would love a hot bath and a change of clothing. Neither she nor Ben had packed a bag in their haste to get to the hospital that first night causing a trip to a local mall to purchase a change of clothing. The days of sitting had left her feeling lethargic, and she longed for a run and a decent meal, but she didn't want to leave Helen alone.

"Why don't you both go?" Helen suggested again. "It makes no sense for you to sit here all day when I'm on the mend. You'll only be a phone call away if I need you."

Jordan and Ben looked at each other, both unwilling to be the one to admit they could use a break until finally Jordan opened the door.

"I suppose we could drive back for the day and then come back tomorrow after work. Ben what do you think?"

He looked from one face to the other in hesitation. "Well, I suppose it wouldn't hurt. As long as you're sure, Helen."

"I am, now the two of you skedaddle for home so I can get some sleep. It's tiring entertaining you all day!"

Within an hour the truck that had barely left the parking lot since the mad dash to the hospital was headed home. What hadn't changed since that scary trip, however, was the silence inside. They had spent days at the hospital, speaking only when necessary and only about Helen. Neither one had mentioned Jordan's marital status, but the look on Ben's face when she admitted the truth to him had never left her mind. Now, side by side in the small space, her admission loomed large between them and the never-ending countryside blended together as she stared out the window. Halfway home Jordan could stand the silence no longer.

"Are you ever going to talk to me again?"

To his credit he didn't try to be coy about what she was really asking. "What else is there to say? You're married, and you lied about it. That pretty much sums it up for me."

"I didn't lie and you know it."

"You didn't lie and while that might be the truth, what's also the truth is you let me believe you cared for me when the whole time you knew nothing would ever come of it."

He was right. She could have stopped it long before he developed feelings for her, but she was so lonely and so afraid of spending the rest of her life that way, she hadn't pushed him away when she should have. The hurt he was feeling was all on her.

"I'm sorry."

"So am I Jordan. So am I."

There was nothing more to say. Letting her guard down for the first time since fleeing from Richard had been disastrous and Ben had now become another regret she would have to live with.

CHAPTER ELEVEN

If the situation had been different, Jordan would have already cut ties with Ben, but there were things to be done at the house, not the least of which was catching up on the cases that had piled up in their long absence. As the community learned of Helen's accident, Ben's slowly growing client list had been patient with the delays but it couldn't go on forever. Out of sheer necessity, their trips to the hospital to visit Helen ended up limited to weekends.

Cutting ties was the only way she knew to lessen his pain, but it would be a long time before Helen recovered enough to run the household and Ben couldn't run the practice alone. She reported to work each morning expecting a frosty reception now that Ben knew at least the partial truth about her past. Instead, she got nothing. Ben was rarely in the office and had instead taken to leaving notes for her. He left before she arrived each morning and even though she waited dinner for him the first few nights; he was always a no-show.

Not having to face him should have been a relief, but Jordan missed their friendship. She missed their conversations and the way his laugh filled the entire house. She missed seeing the love he showered on Helen and the caring way he interacted with each client. She missed the way his presence filled the room and made her feel protected. Having only the dogs for company made the day lonely and more than anything, she wished she could turn back time and make everything between them better again.

But that only happens in fairy tales and her life was anything but a fairy tale. Dwelling in her misery, her mind flashed on something her father had told her after he found out she and Richard were to be married. *"That man will ruin your life,"* he had screamed. How profound that statement had been, even if she had been too blinded by love to realize it. Everything bad that had happened in her life traced directly back to Richard and she would never be shed of him.

Alone in the house yet again, she turned on her computer and typed the name Victoria Stevens into the search box. The screen populated with stories she had already seen a hundred times. Paging through the insignificant entries of her former life, something caught her eye that hadn't been there before—a brief mention in the society pages of the *Times*—but it was significant enough to make her blood run cold.

There, in black and white, was Richard's plea to help find his wife. Accompanied by a photo of him holding an old picture of her, he was asking for the public's help to find the wife he claimed hadn't returned from a trip to Europe. He had been very careful to say she wasn't missing or in any danger, but had simply extended her trip and he could not reach her. The story said that with sightings of Victoria surfacing all over Europe, the NYPD had determined her absence was a simple case of marital discord that wouldn't be further investigated. Of course, it was a total fabrication, as she had never gotten on the plane to Paris. She always knew that Richard had cops on his payroll, but this took it to a whole new level. The photo showed a grieving husband desperate to bring his wife home and was captioned with a plea for any information leading to her safe return along with a promise of a sizable reward.

Published months after she fled and well after she thought he had stopped looking for her, it was chilling. With renewed effort, she read every entry she could find but discovered nothing else. Going back to the *Times* piece, she looked at the photo more closely. In grainy black and white it was difficult to connect the face in the article with the face she now saw in the mirror each morning, but even if most people wouldn't see the resemblance, anyone who knew her from her life in New York might recognize her. After months of feeling safe again, the fear was back, and now she didn't even have Ben to help.

The ringing of the phone startled her, and she quickly cleared the search history on her computer and picked up the phone.

"Anderson Law office," she said.

"Jordan, it's me." Hearing Ben's voice on the line after looking at Richard's photograph made her feel guilty.

"Hello."

"I'm on my way home and I wondered if you would stay and have dinner with me tonight?"

"Ben, I'm not sure . . ."

"It would be just as friends, of course. I know that's all that's between us, but, to be perfectly honest, it's been pretty lonely without you."

Even without seeing his face, Jordan knew how hard it was for him to admit that after finding out she had lied to him. And she missed him, too.

"Sure."

"I can pick something up at the diner if that's okay."

"That would be fine. I'll see you when you get home."

As they hung up, Jordan reached in her desk drawer for the sketch of Ben she had kept carefully hidden. The eyes that had taken so long for her to finish stared back at her from the page with the same look of desire Ben had so often directed her way, and a wave of love for him washed over her. Having broken his heart already, she knew he must never know the true depth of her feelings. She prayed for the strength to keep it from him. Tracing her finger lightly over the drawing, she sighed deeply before putting it back in the drawer.

Jordan had finished her work in the office and was busy tidying the kitchen when he came through the door laden with bags from the diner. She waited for Ben to set the tone.

"I didn't know what you wanted to eat, so I got a few choices. We can always reheat whatever we don't eat tonight," he said, as if they had just seen each other that morning. "I've got burgers with tater tots or there's a bowl of chowder if you aren't hungry enough for a burger, and there's even a salad without tomatoes and dressing on the side just the way you like it."

He had remembered the first meal they had together that night in the diner when the waitress had been so rude to her. He remembered, and it touched her heart. She turned away so he wouldn't see the tears gathering in her eyes.

"What? Did I say something wrong? That's how you like your salad, right? I didn't screw it up, did I?'

"No, you got it exactly right," she said softly. "Thank you."

"Jordan, please look at me."

After the weeks of cold indifference he had exhibited towards her, the tenderness in his voice was completely unexpected and she did as he asked. He stood before her, a broken man, shoulders slumped, worry lines crisscrossing his brow, the sparkle in his eyes long gone.

"I've been an ass and I'm sorry."

"Ben please . . ."

"No, let me finish, please. It doesn't excuse my reaction, but of all the things you could have told me about your past, being married was never even in the realm of possibilities. To hear those words come out of your beautiful mouth, well, I guess I didn't know how to react and I struck out at you instead of letting you explain. I'm sorry for that."

"You don't have to apologize. I'm sorry for lying to you. I knew you were developing feelings for me and I should have told you the truth right away. Instead, I hurt you and I never wanted to do that. I thought I was protecting you."

"If there is one thing I have learned from my brother, it's how to protect myself from angry husbands."

His feeble attempt at a joke fell flat, and he smiled weakly at her. If he only knew the extent of the danger Richard posed to anyone in her life, he wouldn't have been so cavalier. For now, it was enough that he was talking to her again, and the darkness that had filled her heart for weeks was lifting.

"So, what are you saying?"

Desperate to have Ben's friendship back, she still wasn't brave enough to ask the question.

"I'm saying I want to be friends again and I've really missed you."

"Oh Ben, I've missed you too and, of course, we can be friends."

The girl who barely believed in God had now had two prayers answered. Helen was on the mend, and the man she cared more about than any other was back in her life. What had she done to deserve such happiness? The nagging feeling that it was too good to last gnawed once again at the pit of her stomach before she willed it away and she and Ben sat down to eat.

.   .   .   .   .

Within days, things were back to normal.

Ben's practice was flourishing and the firm, which was now drawing clients from several area counties, was busier than ever before. Smiles which had been difficult to find after Helen's accident and Jordan's big revelation were now commonplace in the house and they had regained their easygoing companionship.

"Ben, please stop at the market on your way home tonight and pick up some laundry soap. We're all out."

"Sure, but once again, you don't have to do my laundry. I can figure it out on my own," he said with a smile.

"It's no bother to throw a load of laundry in the washer during the day and besides, something tells me if I let you handle it, all your nice white shirts would end up varying shades of pink," she teased.

They had already discovered with great hilarity, that the accomplished attorney, having already turned several very expensive dress shirts into colorful rags, was no match for the laundry room.

"Thanks for reminding me," he said with a chuckle. "Let's just keep that between us when Helen comes home, okay? She would never let me live it down."

"Neither will I," Jordan teased. "But you better get going or you'll be late for court. Your case files are in the box next to the front door."

"What would I do without you, Jordan?" he asked as he grabbed his briefcase. "See you tonight."

The sound of his truck tires on the gravel had already faded away when the phone rang.

"Anderson Law Firm."

"Jordan dear, hello."

"Good morning Helen. You just missed Ben on his way to court. How are you? We miss you so much."

"I'm doing much better and, in fact, they are letting me out on Friday. I was just calling to make sure you could come and pick me up.

"That's wonderful news and, of course, we'll be there to collect you. In fact, I can't wait. I've made up the bedroom off the kitchen for you so we can wait on you for a change."

"Thank you for that. I have to admit, I was afraid of being alone in the cottage for the first few days. But now tell me, how are you both?'

"Busy, but well. Ben has more business than he can handle, but I've never seen him so happy."

"Hum . . . I wonder if that has more to do with you than the firm."

"What do you mean?" Jordan asked in surprise.

"There's something in your voice when you talk about Ben that wasn't there before. Is it possible that while I've been away, something has happened between you two? If so, it's about dang time!" she exclaimed.

"Helen! Stop it. There's nothing going on between Ben and me. We're just friends and you know that."

"You know something, Jordan? When you're as old as I am and you've experienced life like I have, you'll know not to kid a kidder. There is definitely something between the two of you and you can deny it all you want, but I think you two are falling in love."

"Helen!"

"Don't Helen me. I know I'm right and you know something else? I'm glad about it. You two are perfect together and whether or not you want to admit it, you need each other. Hopefully you won't wait too long to admit it either. Now . . . tell me everything I've missed this week."

·　　·　　·　　·　　·

After the call with Helen, Jordan buckled down to catch up on her work, knowing that she and Ben would most likely collect Helen together the following day. Tempted to call him with the good news about Helen's release, she waited to share the news in person so she could see his reaction. By the time the Courthouse closed, she was sitting at the kitchen table drumming her fingers while impatiently waiting for him to walk in the door. The hour hand had already made a full sweep of the clock before the phone rang.

"Anderson Law Firm," she answered.

"Jordan, it's me. I'll bet you're wondering where the heck I am." Admitting her impatience to him wouldn't do any good, so she held her tongue.

Ignoring her silence, he continued. "I'm sorry I'm late, but we just got out of court. The Judge didn't want to keep the jury another night, so he let them keep going on their deliberations, but in the end we won our case and I'm just leaving for home now. Only problem is I can't remember what type of laundry detergent you asked me to buy."

"It doesn't matter. Just hurry home, okay?"

As she said the words, Jordan realized too late how it might sound to a man who just recently had hoped for more between them. "I mean, there are a few things I need to go over with you before Pete and I head home for the night."

"I'll be there soon."

While she waited for the hour Jordan knew it would take Ben to arrive, she dug through the fridge intending to make dinner for him. Mexican food was his favorite, and she put together a quick chicken enchilada bake and popped it in the oven just as he walked in the front door.

"Jordan, I'm here," he shouted. Pete and Bear raced to his side, with Jordan not far behind, wiping her hands on a dish towel as she walked out of the kitchen.

"Did you get the...?" she asked before Ben handed her the detergent. "Thank you. I just popped your dinner into the oven. It will take about an hour if you want to get cleaned up first."

"You didn't have to do that; I know you want to get home. What did you want to talk about?"

"It can wait. Go get cleaned up and I'll finish a few things in the office until you're ready. I thought maybe I'd join you for dinner."

He cast a suspicious look her way, and she didn't blame him. The last few minutes of their phone conversation had seemed so natural and so right. She found she didn't want to leave for home. If only she had never married Richard. If only she had listened to her parents. If, if, if. The man she had waited her entire life for was standing in front of her and she could never be with him because she had made the worst decision of her life with Richard. Despite it all, she just couldn't stay away from Ben.

He smiled brightly at her. "Great, I'll be back down in a flash."

True to his word, he showered and changed and was back downstairs well before dinner was ready to come out of the oven. He found Jordan hard at work in her music room office.

"You know most volunteers are happy to go home at quitting time," he said as he walked in the office, running his hands through his still wet hair. "What are you working on?"

Jordan had been studying the sketch yet again, and she hurried to pull a file on top of it before Ben could see. No matter what Richard had thought of her work, she knew the sketch was by far the best thing she had ever done. Unfortunately, she was the only one who would ever see it.

"Nothing," she said quickly. "Just finishing up some loose ends. Dinner should be almost ready."

Leading him back to the kitchen, she knew instinctively his eyes were watching her and a thrill spread throughout her body at the thought. She would never get over the excitement of knowing how much he wanted her, even if nothing would come of it.

"Something smells terrific," he said before taking a seat at the table. Originally set only for one, Jordan had put out a place setting for herself as Ben changed.

"It's Mexican, so I think you'll like it," she told him as she removed the dish from the oven and placed it on the table between them. "Help yourself while I get us something to drink. I have some good news."

As she turned towards the fridge to grab a pitcher of ice water, she relayed Helen's news.

"That's fantastic," Ben said with a beaming smile. "It will be great having her home again and you know something? I think a celebration is called for. Let's break out some of that wine Mr. Grochow gave us last week."

He continued to receive the occasional gift instead of his fee, and a local vineyard had delivered a case of wine at the conclusion of the Grochow legal matter. Not much of a drinker, Ben had stored the wine in the basement until he could figure out what to do with it. Jordan, on the other hand, had become a bit of a wine connoisseur during her marriage and she readily agreed.

Opening the bottle with a flourish, Ben poured each of them a rather generous glass.

"To Helen's recovery and her return home," he said as he raised his glass.

"To Helen," Jordan echoed.

The food paired perfectly with the wine and before they knew it, they had drained the bottle and opened a second one. Somewhere in the back of Jordan's mind, she knew it was a poor decision, but she and Ben were getting along so well she once again pushed that nagging feeling of doom aside. They moved into the living room as Ben lit a fire against the chill of the night and Jordan closed windows in the room before joining him on the other end of the sofa.

"Thanks for staying tonight," Ben said as he stretched his big frame and put his feet up on the coffee table. "Dinner was great, but I think it was even better sharing it with you. You're just so easy to talk to."

"You're welcome, but when Helen's home, you'll have plenty of conversation again."

"It won't be the same and you know it."

Turning to look Jordan in the eye, she saw the look. The look that said his mind was going well beyond the friend zone. She stared back at him as the same feelings of desire built in her. Every part of her said to look away, but she just couldn't. Maybe it was the combination of the warmth of the fire and the large amount of wine she had consumed, or more likely, her strong attraction for the man, but she turned towards him as his arm reached across the back of the sofa to touch her shoulder. The moment he did, a jolt of electricity shot through her and she dared not move a muscle.

"Say something please," he asked as they stared into each other's eyes.

This was the moment she had longed for. A moment that should never happen, but one she longed for with every part of her soul. A moment that once surrendered to would change everything between them and she didn't care. Reaching up, she took the hand on her shoulder into her own and pulled it to her lips as tears filled her eyes.

"Are you sure?" he asked gently in a way that was so Ben.

Not trusting herself to speak, she simply nodded her consent before he slid over to her side and took her into his arms, burying his face in her hair and breathing deeply before his lips found their way to her own. All their pent-up desire seemed to erupt in tandem, and they hurried to shed their clothing to feel flesh on flesh.

Every thought that should have prevented a married woman from cheating on her husband flew out of Jordan's mind as she felt her body respond to Ben. Her skin burned with his touch and still she wanted more. She pulled him closer until they joined as one in the timeless rhythm of love. Her senses awash with the feel and taste of him, she lost herself in an explosion unlike anything she had ever experienced before. As his desire also came to its inevitable conclusion, he collapsed on top of her, panting from the exertion. They lay that way, neither willing to break the moment until their breathing returned to normal and Ben rolled away.

Jordan's thoughts were flying. She had wanted Ben more than any other man, but now that he had satisfied his desires, what happened next? Had they both just made the biggest mistake of their lives?

"Talk to me," he said softly into her ear as he turned onto his side and pulled her closer. "Tell me what you're thinking."

"I'm not so sure you want to hear it," she said sadly.

"Please Jordan, don't ruin this moment with regrets. I don't regret what just happened and I don't want you to either. I never intended to have an affair with a married woman, but whatever the deal is with you and your husband, you can't deny what we share is special. I've never felt this way about anyone else, and I am willing to bet you feel the same. You just have to."

Jordan caressed his cheek and tried to find the words to say what was in her heart for the first time since they met.

"Ever since I was a little girl, I've dreamt of meeting someone just like you. Someone caring, smart, and loving. You Ben Anderson are everything I ever wished for in a partner and if we had met earlier, my life would have been so different. I would have spent the rest of my life loving you and raising a houseful of children with you, but that's not how it turned out for us. I don't regret what we just shared, but you and I both know it was wrong."

"That's a load of crap and you know it," he whispered. "If two people truly love each other, being together is not wrong. Marriage is just a piece of paper. You'll get a divorce and we can be together. I'll handle it all."

"No."

"What do you mean, no? You just said you wanted to be with me and build a life with me."

"It's not that simple. Divorce isn't an option."

"Why the hell not?" The words shouted in anger quickly turned to pleading. "Jordan, please, don't do this. Think about what's at stake between us. Please don't let whatever you're hiding ruin both of our lives."

Pushing him away, Jordan got up and quickly dressed as Ben looked on in shock.

"Where are you going?" he asked.

"I'm going home," she told him. "I'm sorry. It seems everything I do hurts you and I just can't do that to you anymore."

"Please wait," he begged before getting up and taking her in his arms once more. "You're not responsible for my feelings and I don't want you to go. Stay the night with me. I promise things will look better in the morning and then if you still want to go, I won't stop you. But please Jordan . . . stay with me tonight. Let me have just one morning of waking up with you in my arms. Please."

One memory. That's all he was asking for. Looking into those big blue eyes so filled with hope and longing, she couldn't deny him.

CHAPTER TWELVE

Jordan slept little that night. Alternating between her warm and safe position wrapped in Ben's arms and pacing silently around the bedroom, she prayed for a solution that didn't involve losing Ben.

The situation was hopeless unless she wanted to come out of hiding, file for divorce, and hand over everything she had so carefully hidden away as protection from Richard. She had no illusions that the search he had undertaken was to bring her back to him because he loved her. By now he had certainly discovered the missing flash drive and to protect his many dangerous secrets, any of which she suspected would put him behind bars for life, he would leave no stone unturned to find her.

Like all creatures backed into a corner, she knew he would take all measures to silence her, including carrying out his threats against her family, and she just couldn't let that happen. She also knew she couldn't walk away from the best thing that ever happened to her.

"If I die today, I will die a lucky man waking up to your beautiful face," Ben said softly. Staring at the ceiling, she had been going through every scenario of how to keep him in her life and she hadn't noticed when he opened his eyes to look at her.

Ben was more than just a warm body to fill her bed. He was a man of compassion and joy and he brought safety and happiness to her life besides what she was suspecting was true, unadulterated love. Wavering back and forth all night, it wasn't until the first pink rays of sunrise broached the horizon that she had decided.

"Good morning," she said quietly.

"How long have you been awake?"

"To be perfectly honest, I don't think I've slept yet. There was a lot to think about."

Instantly on guard, he sat up in bed to look down at her.

"Please don't tell me this is over," he pleaded. "You mean everything to me."

"This might be the stupidest thing I've ever done," she said as the corners of her mouth began an upward turn. "But if you can live with being involved with a married woman, I'm not going anywhere."

"Say it again," he asked as his own smile began.

"I am not going anywhere."

The months of pretending there was nothing but friendship between them were finally in the past even though the uneasiness that had dogged Jordan for months was still deep inside her warning her not to get too comfortable.

Richard was out there somewhere, looking for her and posing a threat not only to her family, but now also to Ben. Instead of her life getting better as time passed, she had just made it a hundred times more complicated, but didn't she deserve happiness? She was a good person who had suffered at the hands of a cruel man, but should her poor judgement in marrying Richard doom her to a life devoid of love and laughter?

Those were the questions she had weighed while Ben slept. What it all finally came down to was her need for love. How many more chances would she get to find a man who could make her feel the way Ben did? In the end, she wasn't willing to take the risk of losing him and now, because of her selfishness, she might have put him in danger he would never expect. It would be up to her to remain vigilant, to mitigate whatever risk there was to Ben, and if the time came that Richard posed an immediate threat, she would disappear once again to protect the man she loved. For now, she would grab whatever happiness Ben could offer and what would make her happy right now was feeling Ben's skin under her hands. Reaching for him, she let her worries slide away and lost herself in his arms.

·   ·   ·   ·   ·

The couple that arrived to collect Helen was the complete opposite of the one that had arrived the night of the accident.

Smiling from ear to ear, always within touching distance of each other, it was obvious something significant had changed in their relationship, and Helen pounced on it immediately.

"Well, would you look at the two of you," she gushed with happiness. "It's about time."

They didn't need to ask what she was referring to. The dopey look of a man in love covered Ben's face and Jordan blushed a brilliant shade of crimson.

"Yeah, I always knew I would win her over if I kept at it," he said with a smile before bringing Jordan's hand to his lips and giving a kiss. "But she was worth it."

"We're so happy you're coming home," Jordan said to divert some of the attention away from their new relationship.

Richard had never been one to show affection outside of their bedroom, but Ben was the complete opposite and seemed intent on letting everyone know they were together. While thrilled to have him at her side, the rather public displays of affection would take some getting used to.

"And I'm thrilled. As nice as everyone has been to me, I hope this is the last I see of these four walls," Helen said as a nurse helped her into a wheelchair and Ben loaded up a utility cart with the many cards, balloons, and bouquets of flowers that had filled her hospital room. It would definitely be a fragrant ride home.

"We'll miss you, Mrs. Patterson, but I hope we don't see you again either," the nurse teased. "Follow the doctor's instructions and you'll be your old self again in no time."

"Ashley, you have been a wonderful nurse. If you're ever my way, please stop in and say hello," Helen said as she gave her nurse a hug. "Now let's go home!"

Non-stop conversation filled the truck as they made their way home. Helen demanded to know everything she had missed starting with the night of the accident and they were happy to oblige.

"But what about you two?" Helen finally asked when they had finished catching her up. "I keep waiting for you to tell the story of how you ended up together."

Admitting that they finally gave in to their feelings after one too many bottles of wine wasn't quite the romantic tale Helen might have been hoping for, but Ben answered without giving away all their secrets.

"I suppose being alone in the house, my charm and sophistication was just too much for Jordan and before I knew it, she had seduced me."

"Ben Anderson!" Jordan exclaimed in embarrassment. "That's not what happened and you know it. If you must know, Helen, it was all Ben. He's right, I kept fighting him off, but still he wouldn't admit I would never fall for him and eventually I felt sorry for him and threw him a bone."

They both erupted in laughter at their fabricated versions of the truth, and Helen laughed along.

"I don't really care which of you is telling me the truth," she said, smiling from ear to ear. "I'm just glad you finally realized what I've known from the moment I first saw you together."

"Oh yeah, and what was that?" Ben asked as he risked a glance away from the road to look at the two women beside him.

"That you were destined to be together, of course. It wasn't just that you make a striking couple, but there has always been electricity in the air whenever you look at each other. And Ben, you never take your eyes off the girl when you're together. It's like you couldn't stand to have her out of your sight. Even when you stood at the top-floor window every day hoping for a sight of Jordan as she ran by. Smitten is what you were."

Helen was even more observant than either of them had given her credit for, but while her observations might have been correct, the reasons behind them were anything but as Jordan well knew.

Ben had spent all that time looking at Jordan because she had seemed so familiar to him and he had been fixated on figuring it out. It wasn't because he was interested in her as a girlfriend.

Jordan, on the other hand, seemed to have had no choice after Ben blackmailed her into staying with them after the accident. One thing Helen was right about though—if not for a cruel twist of fate, Jordan would have agreed they were destined to be together.

"Well, Ben might have been smitten back then, but that certainly describes me now," Jordan said as she reached for his hand just as they pulled up to the house. "Enough about us though. I think your welcome home committee just spotted us."

Jordan was becoming quite adept at deflecting the attention from herself and as both Pete and Bear barked in tandem at the sight of them on the porch, they braced for the welcome they would receive from the large dogs. Although still frail from her near-death experience, Helen didn't hesitate to kneel and wrap her arms around both of the massive wiggling bodies as the dogs bestowed kisses all over her face. When she could take it no more though, she shooed them gently away and reached for Ben's hand for help standing.

"I think that's about all the excitement I can handle for today," she exclaimed. "Ben, could you help me back to the cottage please?"

Jordan looked at her in surprise.

Had Helen forgotten about their discussion about staying in the house?

"Helen, I should have mentioned this earlier," Ben interjected. "But while you're recovering, I thought it might be better if we put you in the downstairs bedroom. That way, you have easy access to everything you need and I can hear you if you need something."

"Oh my no. You and Jordan need your privacy. I would never dream of intruding on that," she gushed, although they both could see the idea of moving into the house at least temporarily was something she was interested in.

"Helen, Ben and I . . .," Jordan began before her cheeks flushed at what Helen was assuming.

"What Jordan is trying to say is that she's not living here. You wouldn't be intruding on anything." That, of course, wasn't the whole truth, but it was a big house and if it turned out it wasn't big enough for them to steal a private moment or two, they always had Jordan's cabin.

"Well, if you're sure," Helen said hopefully.

"We are. Now let's get you settled."

All the activity of coming home seemed to have taken more of Helen's energy than they would have expected and once they brought her things from the cottage and placed them within easy reach, Helen seemed drained. She perched gingerly on the edge of the bed.

"Whew. I didn't realize how tired I would be after all this excitement. Would you two mind if I took a nap?"

"Are you sure you wouldn't like to eat something first?" Jordan asked. A cool, crisp salad with veggies straight from Helen's garden waited in the fridge.

"Thank you, but maybe later, dear. Ben, why don't you take those hounds out for some fresh air while I ask Jordan to help me change into my nightclothes?"

Her unexpected frailty surprised them both and Jordan watched from the hallway door as Ben placed a gentle kiss on Helen's forehead.

"Sleep tight, you wonderful old woman," he whispered before he and the dogs left the room.

"Are you sure you're feeling okay?" Jordan asked as she came to Helen's side. She shared Ben's concern. Helen had always been slight, but she had never been frail, and now that's how they both saw her.

"I'm fine, but I'm not as young as I once was and this whole thing has taken more out of me than I thought. But being home with you both is going to speed up my recovery, I'm sure."

Minutes later, Jordan was tucking Helen's covers in.

"Just promise you'll call if you need something."

"Of course. And Jordan...?"

"Yes?"

"I really am happy for you both."

"Do you think we should have insisted she eat something?" Jordan asked as they went to the kitchen in search of a very late lunch.

"I think she'll be okay. She's not a young woman anymore and even though she was released, that doesn't mean she's back to full strength. Sleep's probably the best thing for her right now, but I'll check on her later and see if she would like something to eat.

By the time they had lunch at the table, Jordan was eager to discuss their new relationship and how they would now interact with each other.

"Have you given any thought to what happens now?" she asked between bites of her salad.

"What do you mean?"

"With us I mean."

Raising his head, he looked back at her with concern.

"You're not having second thoughts, are you? I thought we settled this. I understand you're married and I fully understand the implications of that, so what am I missing here?"

"You're my boss and, well, I don't know what you expect from me."

"Oh, is that all?" he said, as his shoulders relaxed again.

"Is that all?" she exclaimed. "What will people think when they discover you're having a fling with the help?"

"First, please don't denigrate what's between us. This isn't a fling, Jordan, and I think you know that. Second, you're not the help. You're a volunteer, remember!"

His attempt at making her smile nearly succeeded, but she wasn't finished with her questions.

"In the office, maybe I should address you as Mr. Anderson?"

"Of course not. Nothing needs to change between us unless you're uncomfortable with the way things were before. Workplace romances happen all the time and unless the company has a policy against them, which the Anderson Law Firm does not, nothing needs to change between the two of us, whether we are at work or out in public. I'd venture to guess people are going to be happy we found each other. So, does that ease your mind?"

"It does, but can I ask you one more thing?"

"Of course. What is it?"

"Can we keep my marital status just between you and me? It's no one else's business, but even so, I would be more comfortable with people knowing we're together if they didn't know that little detail."

"Of course. Look Jordan," he said as he reached for her hand across the table, "your happiness is important to me. I hope that in time, when you're more secure in this relationship, you'll feel the way I do and maybe then you'll let me help you with a divorce so we can plan a future together. But until that happens, let's enjoy what's happening between us and see where this goes, okay?"

"That sounds good to me," she told him with a warm smile.

.   .   .   .   .

Every new relationship includes a period of adjustment and for Jordan and Ben, it was no different. By day they tried to be professional, but their growing desire for each other made it difficult to keep their hands to themselves. On more than one occasion Helen had nearly walked in on their display of affection. The excitement of getting caught seemed to be a turn-on for Ben, but Jordan was decidedly less than enthused with the idea and she had made him promise to try to control himself until after office hours.

Helen's exhaustion after each of her bi-weekly therapy appointments offered plenty of time for exchanging a kiss or a quick cuddle. It had never been more than that until recently. With Helen's nap pattern firmly established, Ben's desire flamed a mere fifteen minutes after Helen's bedroom door had closed. Jordan's need to feel Ben's body next to her own matched his own desire, and they hurried to undress in Jordan's office before freezing in surprise at the unexpected sound of Helen's door opening, followed by her calling out to Jordan.

"I'll be right there," Jordan replied as she hurried to put her clothes back on and smooth down her hair. Her cheeks still flushed with desire, she glared at Ben. "Ben, we have to stop doing this. What if she had walked in here and saw us?" she whispered.

"Do you really think she'd be surprised?" he told her. "But I know it makes you uncomfortable, so I'll try to control myself. You have to admit, that if you'd just move in, we wouldn't have this problem."

Since Helen had moved into the house, they had found their opportunities for making love to be fewer and further between than either of them would have liked. Ben's solution had been simple: Jordan needed to move into the house. Ben was wonderful, but Jordan had jumped into that situation before with disastrous results, and she wasn't looking for a repeat. As much as they both hated it, Jordan continued to go home to her cabin after spending the early hours of each evening in Ben's bed.

But it was more than that. In her heart, she knew the cabin represented an escape route. She cared deeply for Ben and couldn't imagine a future where he would turn into Richard, but having been so hurt in the past, she wasn't willing to let the cabin go.

"I know you think that would make everything perfect, but it wouldn't. Things are great the way they are. Let's not jeopardize that, okay?"

"I'm not giving up on the idea, but I've already proven how persuasive I can be and I'll bide my time. Let's go to the cabin tonight. I'll get one of Helen's friends to stay with her until I get back. Promise me one thing, though."

"What's that?" she whispered as he pulled her close and nuzzled at her neck; something he knew full well would send her desire into overdrive.

"Promise that for the rest of the day you'll think about exactly how much you want me at this very moment," he whispered huskily in her ear.

As if she could forget. Her knees were already weak at the thought of what he would do to her and all she could do was mumble, "okay" as he pulled away.

Giving her face a few quick pats to focus her attention once again, she went to Helen's aid.

· · · · ·

That night in the seclusion of Jordan's cabin, the desire that had been building in her ever since Ben's whispers in her ear erupted in an explosion of tingling nerve endings and soul searing orgasm that left both of them too weak to move.

"That was . . .," she said.

". . . bloody fantastic!" Ben finished the sentence. He was breathing so hard Jordan turned to place her palm lightly on his chest.

"Are you okay?" she asked with genuine concern.

"Okay doesn't begin to describe what I feel right now," he gushed as he covered her hand with his own. "Jordan, I'll admit I've been with my fair share of women, but never have I experienced anything like that. It was like every part of my body was on fire and still I wanted more of you. Being with you is mind blowing, and I hope you realize that."

Sex with Richard had never been like this. In fact, making love with her husband had been more of a chore than something to be enjoyed; a fact he had never failed to point out to her. Even now she could hear the snarl in his voice as he told her he only screwed her to prove he owned her. Shivering at the memory she pushed it out of her mind to avoid ruining what was turning into a night to be remembered with Ben.

"Now aren't you glad we waited?" she asked as she trailed a finger down the hair on his chest before it disappeared beneath the covers. As her fingers arrived at their destination, Ben gasped in surprise.

"Oh my God Jordan you're going to be the death of me . . . but if you are, I'll die a lucky man," he told her before covering her body with his own as their need for each other built once again.

By the time they had finally quenched their desires for the evening, Jordan fell asleep while Ben held her close. As tired as he was after their love making he still couldn't get enough of seeing her in his arms and he was determined to convince her to move in with him. She had never admitted it, but he knew the cabin made her feel safe and at least for now she wasn't willing to give that up. Someday soon he hoped to convince her it was him that would keep her safe and not just a small cabin in the woods.

Unwrapping Jordan's arms from his body, he eased out of bed to dress and go home when he noticed Jordan grow restless. She moaned in her sleep and quickly began to toss and turn in the bed before suddenly screaming in terror as Ben rushed to her side.

"Jordan wake up," he begged. "You're having a nightmare. Come on Jordan, open your eyes. I'm here and you're safe."

Her eyes snapped open, and she looked frantically around the room before locking eyes with him.

"I'm sorry," she said as tears came to her eyes.

"You scared the heck out of me, but you don't have to apologize. It was just a bad dream. You're safe now and I won't let anything hurt you." He used his fingers to wipe the tears from her face.

"I'm fine," she told him even though she clung to him with more strength than he had realized she was capable of.

"I was just heading home, but I'll stay instead," he offered as he stroked her hair. He could feel her heart racing as she clung to him and it frightened him.

"No, please. I'm okay, really. You need to get home in case Helen needs you. I'm fine. It was just a dream."

"Do you want to talk about it? Tell me what scared you."

It had been months since the nightmare had invaded her dreams and in the interim she had told herself it was all finally behind her. The first few months after she fled from Richard the dream came every night; so often in fact, she did whatever she could to avoid sleep. It was just too frightening to close her eyes and now the dream was back-just when her life seemed to be the happiest it had ever been.

"I . . . I don't remember," she lied.

The dream was always the same - Richard killing her entire family before putting the gun to her head.

"*No one ever leaves Richard Harvey,*" he snarled over and over, always just before he pulled the trigger.

In the dream she could feel the bullet as it entered her brain before shattering into a million pieces while her mind's eye saw the dark pool of blood that quickly flooded the floor around her limp body.

It always played like a movie reel over and over in her head before she screamed and eventually woke up leaving her too frightened to sleep again.

"Are you sure?"

"Ben, I told you I don't remember," she said abruptly before softening her tone at the hurt look on his face. "Go home. I'm fine, but exhausted."

He knew her well enough by now to know she was lying, but he also recognized the stubborn streak she exhibited whenever she wasn't ready to share what was really going on.

"Well then why don't you sleep in tomorrow? We've only got one client coming in and I can deal with them myself. Just come in when you feel like it okay?"

He pulled her to him for a slow kiss, hoping to feel her relax in his arms, but as he pulled away, she still looked scared to death.

"Jordan?"

"I'll see you tomorrow," she said before she turned away from him and pulled the covers up to her neck. "Goodnight Ben."

Once she heard the front door close and the sound of Ben's truck driving away, Jordan threw off the covers and got out of bed. Wrapping her worn sweater around her she went down to the kitchen to start a pot of coffee and coax some life into the old stove in the corner. The chill she felt had nothing to do with the temperature in the house and everything to do with her husband. There would be no more sleep for her tonight.

Why, after all this time, was the nightmare back? She was happier than she had ever expected and there had been no sign of Richard, so why now? Pete followed her every step as she paced around the small kitchen desperate for answers. Richard had been a forceful advocate of therapy and a wry laugh escaped her lips as she imagined what one of his doctors would say—that her dreams were manifestations of her guilt over having started an affair with Ben even though she was still married. But she knew it was more than that and a chill washed over her as she remembered the dream and the vision of her parents being gunned down by Richard. In the dream neither of her parents spoke and her father always looked at her with pure hatred while her mother's eyes radiated love before they both lay dead at her feet.

Ben had been wonderful of course but she could never explain why the dream frightened her so much without revealing the rest of her secrets. She also knew that if the dreams continued, he would eventually demand to know what was going on and the only solution was to make sure he never spent the night again. Just how she would pull that off without hurting him or raising suspicions would be a challenge for another day. Finishing her coffee, she glanced outside to see dim light created by the nearly full moon. Only one thing could clear her head.

"Come on Pete, let's go for a run."

. . . . .

Fear of Ben witnessing more of the nightmares kept Jordan from fully relaxing as they cuddled together at the end of each evening.

She had used the excuse of Helen needing them within earshot to prevent Ben from spending the night at the cabin and at the end of each day they made their way to Ben's bedroom to satisfy their never-ending need to join in the most intimate of ways. Ben realized that when he woke, Jordan would have already left for the cabin and he had expressed his disappointment on more than one occasion.

It was never an argument thankfully. While they often had differences of opinions, they had yet to experience an outright fight mostly because neither one of them felt the need to be right. They just agreed to disagree. It was one thing she so appreciated about Ben.

Richard was the polar opposite of Ben including always needing to be right. There was never discussion with Richard; only a one-sided diatribe where he always had the last word. At the beginning of their marriage it was exhausting; by the end it was frightening. Once unleashed on her, the temper she had never seen in the early part of their marriage had been explosive. Looking back, she suspected that in his business dealings it had always been that way. Why else would a man who was so successful need so many security people around him? His temper and need for power must have created many enemies over the years.

That's what had initially triggered the nightmare—his direct threats to her family—but after almost a year with no harm coming to any of them, the nightmares seemed to have ended. So why were they back now?

Back at the cabin in the middle of the night she still tried to grab a few hours of sleep, but once unleashed the nightmare pattern quickly reestablished itself and within an hour of falling asleep she was covered in sweat and screaming in terror. Disoriented yet still enveloped by the terror she had experienced, she would look frantically around the room, sure that Richard lurked somewhere in the shadows. Pete, who normally slept at the foot of the bed, was always the first to sense her agitation and by the time she woke he was firmly planted at her side as a low growl emanated from him at the unseen enemy.

Waking from the nightmare when the pattern first began, she had calmed down and convinced herself it was simply a dream and had gone back to sleep. But as the days wore on the nightmare always came back and the entire episode repeated itself. Finally, too scared to close her eyes again, she would get out of bed to pace around the room before giving up and going on a good, long run. After weeks of the pattern, she was physically and mentally exhausted and everyone around her noticed including the ever-observant Helen.

"Jordan dear you look like you haven't slept in a week."

While Helen's recovery continued, Jordan had shouldered the lion's share of Helen's duties besides her own work, but she didn't mind. Everything she could do to keep busy kept her mind off the need for sleep but the night before had been brutal. Too rainy to run, she had spent hours sketching, leaving the cabin littered with half-finished ominous sketches that all included the shadow of Richard's face. It had been the first time she had picked up a pencil to sketch since Ben's portrait and it should have made her happy. Instead, the only images that flowed from her hand were manifestations of her fear and anxiety.

"I haven't been sleeping well," Jordan admitted.

"It's the nightmare again right?" Ben chimed in as he came up behind Jordan and kissed the top of her head.

"What nightmare?" Helen asked.

"It's nothing," Jordan said even as she gave Ben a warning glance.

She should have realized that even though Ben hadn't brought it up again, he hadn't forgotten either.

"It's not nothing and you know it, especially if you aren't sleeping because of it. Maybe it's time you spoke to someone about it."

"You mean a shrink? Not a chance," Jordan said firmly. Not only was she not about to share her story with a complete stranger, but Richard had spent a lot of money on his psychiatrist and look how he turned out.

"Jordan, don't be foolish. Helen's right. You look like you don't sleep at all, you can barely get through the day and at some point it's going to affect your health."

She may have started the discussion, but Helen was quick to realize this was about more than Jordan not sleeping and she slipped out of the room and closed the door behind her as Ben and Jordan squared off.

"If you think I'm not doing my job, then just come right out and say it. I'm a volunteer right? I'm sure you can find someone else to take my place, but maybe you'll have to hire two people since I've been doing the work of two people without complaint for weeks now."

As soon as the words left her mouth, she realized she had gone too far. Ben had never asked her to take over Helen's responsibilities around the house and now she was using it as a weapon against him.

"Ben, I'm sorry. I didn't mean that. You're right. I'm over tired and not thinking straight. Maybe I should see someone, but it can't be a shrink. It just can't."

Tears of frustration fell from her eyes. Her exhaustion was overwhelming, and she knew Ben was right. She needed help.

Pulling her close, he wrapped his arms around her as she laid her head on his chest. The strong beat of his heart and the warmth of his touch calmed her down.

"Sweetheart I'm so sorry I didn't realize the toll all this was taking on you and I'm going to get you some help with the house."

"Really, there's no need. I can handle it all and I'm sorry I said that. I love being needed. It's just that I need some sleep."

"Why don't I call the clinic here in town and see if we can get you in today?" he suggested. "Just a regular old family doctor—no shrink—and I'm sure you'll feel better in no time."

A reminder that he cared for and would always protect her was what she needed most and she released a slow breath at the thought that some relief was within sight. From the very moment she met him he had always made everything in her life better.

Tempted for a moment to share her remaining secrets with him to make the nightmares disappear, she hesitated. It was lack of sleep and not logic that put the thought into her head. After all, he was an officer of the court and he would have been duty- and honor-bound to turn the Harvey family in to the authorities. She was part of that family even if at this point it was in name only. She had benefited and lived the high life because of Richard's illegal profiteering and she would go down with him. If the day ever came when Ben learned who she was married to and the illegal business dealings Richard was part of, their relationship would be over.

In the end, the doctor's visit was easier than she expected. A kindly old man whose practice was comprised of runny noses and the occasional broken bone had asked few questions about her inability to sleep. His solution had been to pull out a prescription pad, and she went home with the solution to her problem in a little amber bottle of sleeping pills. Healthy all her life, save for being knocked down the ravine by Bear, she had never been one to take pills, but now she looked at the large white tablets and prayed for a good night's sleep.

"Here you go," Ben said as he placed a glass of water on the bedside table next to her. "Did the doctor tell you what to expect? What kind of side effects we should look out for?"

"Not really. He said they would do the trick, whatever that meant, but all I want is to sleep through the night and if that happens I don't care about any side effects. Besides you'll be here with me right?"

It had taken some persuasion to convince her to stay the night, but in the end Ben's argument had been a convincing one. They had both heard stories of people on sleeping pills walking in their sleep or something even worse and he had insisted on her spending the night at his house so he could monitor her.

"I won't leave your side all night," he promised.

"Well okay then, here goes," she said before downing one pill and getting in bed next to him. "Do you mind if for tonight we just hold each other?"

More than anything she just wanted to feel safe as she slept. Spooning together, the warmth of his skin on hers, she closed her eyes. She fell asleep almost instantly.

. . . . .

Opening her eyes to see it was still dark outside she was disappointed to realize she hadn't even slept through the night. Ben, contrary to his vow to not leave her side, was nowhere to be found, but she could hear voices in the house and she hurried to dress and make her way downstairs.

"Hi," she said softly as she entered the kitchen where Ben and Helen were cleaning up after what appeared to be a midnight snack.

"Good evening," Helen said with a smile. "I'll bet you are feeling so much better."

"What do you mean?" Jordan said in confusion.

"Hello sweetheart," Ben said as he came to her side and pulled her close. "We were a little worried about you."

"What are you talking about?" she asked again. "Obviously the pills didn't work if I couldn't even make it through the night."

"Actually, you've been sleeping for a couple of days," he said as he looked down at her tenderly.

"No, that can't be."

"Jordan, it's eight at night and it's Thursday. You've slept this entire time and without a hint of a nightmare I might add."

"Seriously?" The surprise on Jordan's face caused them all to chuckle.

"Yup and I have to admit it was a little scary. I kept checking on you and even called the doctor, but he said when you're that sleep deprived the pills can sometimes have that effect at first. He suggested you cut the dosage in half next time though. Frankly, I think he was a little cavalier about the whole thing, but he insisted you would be just fine and from the looks of it he was right. How do you feel?"

"Like a new woman," she said with the first genuine smile she had on her face since the nightmares returned. "Like a new woman."

CHAPTER THIRTEEN

Life couldn't have been better. Jordan was sleeping soundly for maybe the first time in ten years and was more content than she had ever been. Ben was blissfully happy with Jordan at his side, and his practice was flourishing. Helen was actually enjoying her semi-retired status and was so active they rarely saw her during the day. She had moved back to the cottage, but they still shared a meal together, cooked by Helen, each evening. They had become the happy little family Jordan had always dreamt of and she went to sleep each night looking forward to the next day.

"What are you doing for Christmas?" Ben asked out of the blue as they walked hand in hand. It was a gorgeous fall night with a clear sky lit by a full moon and Jordan was as relaxed as she had been for weeks, but Christmas was months away.

"Is Christmas coming earlier this year, and no one told me?" she quipped. "What brought that up?"

"I was just thinking that with the practice doing so well and all, maybe you and I could go somewhere together for Christmas."

"Somewhere like Hawaii? Somewhere they have beautiful white beaches and tropical drinks?" she asked happily.

"I sure wouldn't object to seeing you in a bikini, but maybe later for that. I was thinking New York."

For just a moment, Jordan froze and gripped his hand a little tighter before realizing what she was doing and letting go completely.

"You mean to see a Broadway show or something?"

"We could do that, but I was thinking it's about time I introduced you to my family."

He had been hinting at the subject for some time now, and she had always put him off with one excuse or another. Even though she had only met them once or twice in her former life as Victoria, the mere idea they might recognize her scared her to death.

"Ben, we've already discussed it. It's important to you, but the married woman you're having an affair with isn't exactly the girl you bring home to meet the folks, if you know what I mean. I thought you understood that."

"Sweetheart I understand your hesitation, but they don't have to know everything. I just want them to meet the woman I'm in love with."

Jordan's surprise when he mentioned New York was nothing compared to her shock now.

"You love me?" she whispered. She hadn't even dared to think that he might be in love with her, although she knew full well she loved him with her entire heart.

Reaching for her hand again, he pulled her slowly into his arms.

"Of course I do, and I've been waiting for just the right moment to say it. You're everything to me, and you must know that by now."

"Why?"

"Why?" he repeated with a deep laugh that echoed in the still of the night. "Because you're smart and funny and patient and kind and beautiful and caring and loving and everything else that is good about a woman. You make me feel like I could do anything and be anything and when I'm with you, and I never want to be anywhere else, that's why."

Everything he said was exactly how she felt about him and before she could stop herself, the words slipped out.

"Me too."

"Me too, what?" he prompted.

"I love you too," she said louder and with a smile that rivaled his own. "I love you Ben and I can't imagine loving anyone else, but you have to . . ."

"Wait . . .," he cautioned, holding a finger to her lips. "Please don't say it. I don't want to hear the word 'but' come out of your mouth. Let's just enjoy what we have now and figure out the future later, okay?"

· · · · ·

Having admitted the extent of their feelings for each other, Jordan found a new confidence. Richard was now her past and her constant checking up on him and worrying about him finding her was waning. While she would never be truly free of him, she and Ben were happy, and that's all that mattered. There seemed to be nothing but blue skies in their future until the phone rang.

"Ben? Phone," Helen shouted up the stairs.

Office hours were long over and Jordan and Ben were in his bedroom, getting ready for a weekend getaway to Casper.

"Gosh, I hope that's not a client," Jordan said disappointedly as Ben reached for the phone.

It wouldn't be the first time their plans had been cancelled because of a client emergency, but she had been looking forward to this trip for a week now and had even bought a new dress to wear.

"Whatever it is, it can wait until Monday," he said as he picked up the call. "Ben Anderson."

Jordan had turned her back on him as she finished packing, but the silence in the room was unusual and she turned back to see what was going on.

"No, you listen to me. You got yourself into this mess and you need to get yourself out. You're a grown man, for Christ's sake. Father was right, you need to live within your means and stop trying to buy half of Washington."

It was Brandon, of course, which explained the angry look on Ben's face as he stood silently listening to what his brother had to say back.

"Don't even try to play the brother card with me, Brandon. You burned that bridge long ago when you destroyed my career. I will not let you do it to me again. There's no need for you to come here and I will not change my mind," he said angrily. "I'm serious Brandon. I don't want you here. Goodbye."

He slammed the phone back on the receiver and turned to look at her, his eyes cold and hard. He was so angry that at first she didn't realize what he had said, but then she realized all at once and she trembled. When he noticed, he came to her side and took her into his arms.

"I'm sorry I frightened you," he said, as if his anger caused her fear. "In case you didn't figure it out, that was Brandon."

"He's coming here?" she asked quietly. Her heart was racing so fast she was afraid for a minute she might collapse, and she pulled away and sat on the edge of the bed. "Your brother is coming here?"

"He wants to, but you heard me tell him not to. Apparently, he's got even more money problems. I suspect he thinks if he comes in person, he can get me to loan him what he needs. My practice is going well, but even if I had that kind of money I would never loan it to him. I'm done getting him out of jams."

"But will he come, anyway?"

Ben's anger at his brother made the otherwise normally observant man miss the fear in Jordan's question. Her face had gone pale and her hands continued to shake. Brandon was a direct connection to Richard, and she knew he would recognize her immediately no matter what color her hair was. He would ruin everything.

"Even he wouldn't be that bold. I'm sorry this is how we're starting our weekend. I wanted everything to be special for you and it still can be. Let's just put Brandon out of our minds and enjoy ourselves, okay? Are you ready to go?"

Nodding her head, he picked up their suitcases and, after saying goodbye to Helen and the dogs, they started the long drive to Casper. Still consumed with his anger at his brother, Ben said little on the trip until Jordan could stand the silence no longer.

"I'm sorry he upset you," she said before taking his free hand in her own. There was no need to ask who she was talking about.

"You're lucky you don't have any siblings," he said sadly. "He's never going to learn."

"It's really not my place, but why do you keep taking his calls if it always ends in a fight?"

"Honestly," he told her as he shook his head in confusion. "I guess I still believe he might change; that he might call just to ask how things are going. I suppose that makes me the stupidest guy on earth for thinking he's ever going to be the brother I hope for."

"Or maybe it's that you are the most kindhearted brother he could ever have and you see some redeeming quality in him that gives you hope. Maybe it's like you are with me; trying to accept us with all the baggage that comes with being flawed."

"I'll give that Brandon is flawed, but you're anything but," he told her as he pulled her hand to his lips for a soft kiss. "But enough about my brother. Let's talk about something else. Did I tell you what happened in court yesterday?"

Jordan had become quite adept at turning a discussion away from topics she didn't want to talk about, and it appeared Ben was learning a thing or two. As he talked, she ran through the different scenarios that could happen if his brother really showed up. Obviously she couldn't be around him, but that also meant not being around Ben. She needed a plausible excuse with an unlimited timeline for her absence: something like a vacation. Ben was sure to realize something was going on, but if Brandon figured out who she was, Ben would finally learn the secrets she had worked so hard to protect and she would lose him. She couldn't let that happen.

By the time they pulled up to the hotel, she was no closer to an answer, but she had an idea.

"You were awfully quiet on the drive. Is everything okay?" Ben asked when they reached their room. "I'm really sorry I got so upset when Brandon called, but please don't let it ruin our weekend."

"It's fine, really," she said as she walked to the sliding doors and stepped out onto the balcony. "This is a beautiful view, don't you think?"

"I think you're beautiful, but why are you changing the subject?"

"I'm sorry, and you're right. We don't want your brother to ruin the weekend, but it got me thinking. It's been a very long time since I've seen my parents and one of these days, I think I might take some time and go home for a visit."

"Really? I thought you had no contact with them—other than that one call to your mother, of course."

It surprised her he remembered their conversation about that from months ago, but then again, he seemed to remember everything she told him.

"You're right and I have no firm plans, but one of these days, if you're okay with it, I'm going to just up and go for a visit."

It was the best idea she could come up with. There was no timeline involved in going or returning, and even though she had no intention of actually visiting her parents, he would never realize she was actually holed up in a cheap motel far away.

"Why don't we plan a trip to see your folks together?" he suggested. "It only makes sense if we're planning to visit mine at Christmas. I'd love to meet them."

"Ben, you know that will not happen. Your parents might not know I'm married to another man, but mine certainly do. How would I explain you to them? I'll be lucky if my father doesn't slam the door in my face the way it is. I love that you want us all to be one big happy family, I really do. But you have to realize that's never going to happen. Can't we just enjoy what we have together without dragging others into it?"

Her objections couldn't have been a surprise to him, yet he stared at her with the same look he had when they first met: a look that said he knew there was more to what she was telling him than she was letting on. Maybe she should have just kept her mouth shut, but how else could she explain her sudden departure if Brandon really showed up in town? Laying the groundwork now had seemed a logical course, but now she wasn't so sure.

"Against my better judgement, I can't say no to you. Go when you want and make peace with your family, but make sure you come back to me, okay?"

The question, as innocent as he probably meant it, caught her off guard. If Brandon discovered her true identity before she could leave town, she would never come back to Ben and it would devastate both of them.

"Just try to keep me away," she said with as much bravado as she could before turning her back and unpacking.

. . . . .

As promised, Ben had delivered a perfect getaway. Good food, superb wine, great music, a bit of dancing, and more than a bit of lovemaking had pushed any worries out of Jordan's mind. Their only focus during the weekend was each other and she couldn't have been happier, but now it was time to go back to the real world and Ben had a full slate of client meetings and court appearances all week which meant Jordan was also busy; too busy, in fact, to even think about Ben's brother.

"Jordan? Telephone," Helen called up the stairs. Jordan hadn't even finished dressing yet, but in a law firm, clients called at all hours.

"This is Jordan. Can I help you?" she asked as she picked up the extension in the bedroom.

"Jordan, I hope I'm not calling too early. It's Casey from the paper."

Now that Ben's practice was flourishing and money was no longer an issue, Jordan had suggested keeping it that way by placing an advertisement in the local paper.

She had emailed it over the day before, but maybe she had missed something.

"Thank you for calling. I hope we can still get the ad in next week's paper. I wasn't sure what your deadline was," she said as she held the phone to her ear with her shoulder while she tried to button her blouse.

"Next week will be fine, but there is a slight problem."

"I don't understand."

"Remember when we met, and I told you I had trouble keeping designers? My last designer quit yesterday, no notice at all, and I'm in a bind. Ben said you were an artist and I wonder . . . I mean, I know this is really last minute and all, but would you consider giving me a few hours of your time? You'll be paid of course and I have a full slate of advertisements and no one to put them together for me."

"Casey, that's really nice, but I am not a graphic designer. I draw, that's all. I know nothing about advertising."

That wasn't exactly the truth. In high school, she had made pocket money designing simple advertisements for businesses owned by her father's friends. But that was when she still thought she had talent as an artist.

"But you are an artist and that means you have a good eye," he continued. "Look, it won't be for long and I will take whatever hours you can give me—I know you're busy working for Ben—but if I don't have those ads, I have no revenue. It would only be for a few weeks before I can get someone in permanently. Won't you please consider it?"

She might have been too soft-hearted for her own good, but the idea of using her creative talents again was enticing. Other than the sketch of Ben that remained hidden from sight in her desk drawer and the ominous drawings influenced by Robert, she had done nothing creative in ages. There was also genuine desperation in his voice.

"I guess I could give it a try, but before I give you my final answer, I have to make sure it's okay with Ben," she told him. "He's got a court case that will keep him in Casper for the next couple of days, but when he gets back, I'll ask him."

"I don't know how to thank you, Jordan, and I'll talk to you soon."

With Ben away for the next couple of nights and Helen once again on her own in the cottage, there was no reason for her and Pete to stay in the house. With both dogs in tow, she headed to the cabin. Now that she was in most respects living with Ben, the cabin had been empty for a few weeks. Determined to keep it up, she had gotten in the habit of stopping in as part of her run each morning to water the plants, pick up her mail, and tidy up a bit; after all, it was still home to her, but without Ben with her to fill the void, she discovered it was lonely there. Thank goodness she had Pete and Bear for company.

The dogs loved the smells of the forest and their noses were on the ground the minute they arrived. From her perch on the porch steps, she watched them explore the glade until her artist's eye recognized what a great sketch the view would make. Collecting paper and a pencil, she went back to the porch. In what seemed no time at all, she had an acceptable sketch of the dogs as they nosed around the yard. Even as rusty as she was, the sketch was good, and a smile came to her face as she studied it before reaching for a clean page. Richard and his constant negativity about her work had chased the confidence out of her, but after all this time with Ben, she was pleasantly surprised to find it was back. She had just put pencil to paper when she remembered something.

In just a few weeks' time, it would be an entire year since making her escape from Richard. There continued to be occasional mentions in the society pages of her disappearance, but those were becoming more sporadic and she wondered if those in his circle of wealthy friends even cared what had become of her. It didn't really matter to her. All that did matter was their marriage remained legally valid.

Everything in her life was perfect, save for her ties to Richard. Maybe it was finally time to trust that Ben could keep her safe. But was that all just wishful thinking? Was it better to let their relationship continue as it was than to open the door to the danger Richard posed to everyone she loved?

As she considered the possibilities, her hand moved almost of its own volition and she sketched as she thought until she realized that the face she had been drawing was Richard's and it startled her so much she dropped the page. Tears filled her eyes, and she stared down at the wretched face staring back at her as her cell phone rang.

"Hello gorgeous," came the welcome sound of Ben's deep voice through the phone. "Do you miss me yet?"

"More than you know," she assured him. "I decided to stay at the cabin while you're gone, but didn't realize how lonely it would be without you. I've been sitting on the porch sketching Pete and Bear."

"Jordan, that's terrific! How does it feel to be sketching again?" His excitement matched her own, and she loved that he understood the significance of it all.

"Pretty good, actually. If you like, I'll show you what I'm working on when you get back," she said, surprising even herself. She had always hesitated to show anyone her work and yet she had offered it to Ben without a second thought. "How's the case going?"

"Unfortunately, not so well. I had a witness do a one-eighty today on the stand. As much as I pressured him, even reminding him of the penalties for perjury, he wouldn't budge and it was really harmful to our case. If tomorrow doesn't go any better, my client will look at the world from behind bars for the next few years."

"I'm sorry about that, but I'll wager you'll figure something out. The client is lucky to have you."

"Enough about me. How was your day?"

"Well, funny you should ask. I got offered a job!" she proclaimed.

"You have a job," he said in confusion. "Why would you be applying for other jobs?"

Not wanting to cause him any pain, she hurried to explain.

"And it would only be temporary and Casey said I could work whenever I want so it would work around my schedule at the office. I'd still be able to get things done around the house and . . ."

"Whoa Jordan, wait up!" he said with a laugh. "It sounds like you've already decided to take the job and I'm happy for you. And if it helps, I can get some temporary help in the office so you can have more time working for Casey."

She knew he wouldn't hold her back from the opportunity, but she also didn't want him to replace her.

"Please don't do that. I love my job and this thing on the paper is only for a little while until he gets a replacement hired. It might seem silly to be so excited about it, but it's the first time anyone has hired me for my artistic skills. It might also be the last if I'm no good at it, but Ben, the sketch I did tonight? I think it's really good."

She had no intention of telling him about the sketch of Richard.

"I can't wait to see it," he told her. "I'd love to spend all night on the phone with you, sweetheart, but I have hours of work to do before court tomorrow. Are you sure you're okay out there in the woods all by yourself?"

"I'm not by myself. I have Pete and Bear, but I can't wait until you're home," she reminded him. "Call me tomorrow and let me know how the case goes, please?"

"Of course. Jordan?"

"Yes my love?"

"I love you. Sweet dreams."

Buoyed by his call, Jordan picked up the drawing of Richard and scrawled "bastard" at the bottom before crumbling it in a ball and walking into the cabin, where she promptly threw it in the trash.

"Pete, Bear, come on boys," she called through the open doorway as the dogs raced inside. "Let's find something to eat."

CHAPTER FOURTEEN

If a life that for years had been so fraught with angst could become perfect overnight, Jordan's had. The dubious anniversary of her flight from Richard came and went without so much as a hiccup and for the first time in that entire year, Jordan was relaxed and happy. The voice of doom was nowhere to be found, and it was all down to one thing—the man who was currently making advances.

"You're making it awfully difficult for me to concentrate on the brief I'm writing," Ben said as he came up behind Jordan to wrap his arms around her waist and nuzzle at her neck.

"Don't be silly," she told him before continuing to organize the papers on her desk. "I'm not doing anything out of the ordinary, and you were in another room."

"Oh, but you were. I could hear you humming. Am I wrong, or was it that slow song we danced to that night at the dive bar? You know . . . the one that led to all this?"

Not only had she been humming the song, but before he came in, she had also been swaying along with the music in her head.

"How do you get any work done if all you do is think about me?" she asked. Turning in his arms, she let him pull her even closer, discovering physical proof of where his thoughts were leading.

"My point exactly," he insisted. "So, what are we going to do to solve my dilemma? Let's go upstairs."

Slipping up to his bedroom in the middle of the workday because of his seemingly unending appetite for her was flattering, but not very practical in an ever-busier office.

"Some employees might call that suggestion sexual harassment," she pointed out.

"And what would you call it?"

"How about a perk of the job better left for a more appropriate time and place?"

"When it's the only perk you're getting, I guess I don't have a choice," he said in disappointment before he disengaged from her arms and dropped into a nearby chair. "But now that you've brought it up, I should remind you that you're building a nice little nest egg in my safe. Isn't it about time I pay you like an actual employee and we put that money in the bank?"

Months ago, when Jordan had insisted on being a volunteer instead of an actual paid employee, Ben had just as insistently started converting her wages into cash that was kept in the safe in his office.

"Things are just fine the way they are. I don't need your money and I won't take if it you offer it."

"Be serious Jordan. Everyone needs money, or do you have a secret stash of cash hidden away somewhere? Is that husband of yours sending you an allowance? Maybe you're a wealthy heiress living in the cabin to throw people off. You need a paycheck."

Choosing to let the errant comment about her husband pass without comment, she looked him square in the eye. "Nope, I don't."

"That makes little sense. And besides, if I don't pay you, I can't bill clients for your work. If you look at it that way, you're really costing me money instead of making me money. You need to be paid, and we have to get this straightened out before the IRS comes knocking on my door."

Repeatedly having to defend herself in the same argument was tiring.

Exasperated by his dogged determination to push the issue, she had had enough.

"Who's going to turn you in? Certainly not me," she said with a smile. "Seriously, Ben, we've had this conversation way too many times. I don't need your money. Anyway, I'm practically living here for free as it is, so what do I need money for?"

"Good lord woman, but you are exasperating sometimes!" he exclaimed.

"And yet you love me anyway," she teased.

"That I do."

•   •   •   •   •

After a very busy week working for Ben, running the household, and starting her new part-time job at the newspaper, Jordan was exhausted. Instead of another evening in the kitchen she suggested dinner at the diner. It was where they had had their first "non-date" and now that everyone in town knew they were a couple, Jordan had no qualms about going back to face the waitress who had so tormented her that night.

The woman had been so solicitous to her on their subsequent visits to the diner, Jordan suspected Ben had paid her a quiet visit somewhere along the line to straighten out her behavior and she loved him for it.

"Good evening folks," the waitress said with what was a passable smile at Jordan. "Can I start you off with something hot to drink?"

After they placed their orders and the waitress went back to the kitchen, Ben's cell phone began to ring, but he made no move to answer it.

"Aren't you going to get that?" Jordan asked. It was unusual for him not to do so.

"Nope. I already know who it is and I don't want to talk to him," he said as the waitress returned with coffee for them both.

Jordan raised an eyebrow at his comment and waited for the waitress to leave for more explanation.

"It's Brandon," he said when they were alone again. "He's called about a dozen times today."

"What does he want?"

"I don't know and I don't care," he said as he poured cream into his coffee. "You had a point when you asked why I continue to talk to him. My life would be simpler and a lot less stressful if I just cut him out completely, so that's what I'm doing. I will not take his calls anymore and hopefully he'll get the hint and that will be the end."

"Are you sure? I know you were hoping things would change between you."

"Yes, I'm sure," he said before reaching for her hand across the table. "I have everything I need to make me happy right here, so Brandon is no longer part of my life. Now where's our food? I'm starving."

Hearing him say so was music to Jordan's ears. With Brandon out of the picture, the last impediment to fully enjoying her new life was gone and along with it all worries about Richard finding her. She was beaming from ear to ear.

By the time their food arrived, Brandon was long forgotten. Jordan had been so busy all week that she and Ben had barely talked and once she started talking about her new job, she barely took a breath.

"To be honest, I never expected to enjoy it so much and I'm learning a lot. Casey has been great showing me how to use the software they use and so far he said he likes what I've shown him."

"I knew you would be good at it," Ben said proudly, "and that was even before I saw any of your sketches. Like I said, I think the sketch you did of Pete and Bear that day at the cabin could be in a gallery somewhere."

He had been vocal in his praise of her work when she finally shared her sketch and that boost to her confidence was just what she needed as she began work at the paper. So far, she had only finished three advertisements, but Casey seemed thrilled with the results.

"I don't know that I would go that far, but honestly? I think it was pretty good, too."

"Are those the type of drawings you normally do?" he asked. "I mean when you were younger."

"Actually no, I did portraits. Faces were my specialty, and it's harder than you think. It's easy to get the features right, but much more difficult to convey anything about the person in a simple drawing. I always thought it was the eyes that were the most difficult to capture, especially if the person was very complex. Shallow people have empty eyes, but then there are people like you whose character would be difficult to capture entirely. For those portraits I would always do the eyes last."

Little did Ben know that was exactly what had happened with his sketch. The temptation to share the sketch with him was there every time she looked at it, but so far she hesitated and she couldn't figure out why that was the case.

"Someday maybe you could do a sketch of me," he suggested.

"Someday," she promised as they finished their meal. "For now though, why don't you take me home and I'll show you what other talents I have?"

Ben didn't need further explanation or encouragement, and they headed home.

. . . . .

"Ben, if you don't mind, I thought I'd take some time this afternoon and get some errands done in town," Jordan said as she walked into Ben's office the next day. After a memorable night when neither of them got much sleep, she could hardly keep her eyes open. She hoped a change of scenery might help wake her up and she could get some of the little chores done she had been putting off, including updating Pete's vaccinations with Dr. Norris.

"If you want to wait until the end of the day, I'll go with you," Ben suggested.

"I appreciate that and maybe we can take a walk later tonight, but some shops will be closed by five, so I thought I'd go right after lunch—if that's okay with you, of course. I'm going to take Pete with me so he can get his shots."

"You know, Jordan, you don't have to ask my permission. It's not like you're an actual employee, right?"

Earlier in their relationship, she might have worried about that comment, but the wink he gave her and the smile on his face gave away his teasing.

"Ha, ha," she told him. "I should be back before supper, but don't wait for me if I'm not. Casey asked if I would stop in and look at a new ad he got this morning. It shouldn't take too long, though."

"Great. Enjoy your afternoon and I'll see you when you get back."

⋅ ⋅ ⋅ ⋅ ⋅

"Hey Casey," she said as she walked in the front door of the newspaper office. "I know I said I'd stop by later, but I'm parked right out front, so I thought I would look at the ad now. Is it okay if Pete comes in? I don't want to leave him in the truck."

"Sure, bring him in."

She had quickly discovered that certain days in the life of a newspaper man, like the day the paper was printed, were more hectic than most, but looking at him sitting in front of his computer, she was glad to know this wasn't one of them.

"Thanks for stopping down. The local churches have taken out a quarter-page ad each week to advertise their services. It's a lot of revenue if I can show them something they like. They want to start it before Thanksgiving, so we have a couple of weeks to get it right. I thought it might be easier for you if you worked on it at home, so I put together what they sent me and copied the design program onto a flash drive for you to use on your home computer."

"That's great, but you didn't have to do that. Ben is fine with me spending time here," she told him as she accepted the folder of materials from him.

"Did you come into town together this afternoon?"

"No, why would you ask that?"

"I just saw him not twenty minutes ago in the diner. I didn't have time to talk to him though and assumed he had court or something since he was in a suit and tie."

Surprised that he would have come into town without mentioning it to her, she said a quick goodbye so she could drop Pete off at the vet and surprise Ben at the diner. A quick cup of coffee together would be nice.

The tinkle of the bell above the door sounded as she walked into the diner and looked for Ben. Disappointed not to see him, she turned to leave before the waitress stopped her.

"Are you looking for your boyfriend?" she asked as she poured coffee for another customer. "You just missed him."

"Thanks. Did you notice what direction he went?"

"It's really not my job to keep tabs on your man now is it?" the woman spat at her.

Apparently, the goodwill the woman extended only applied when Ben was around to witness it.

"Eva, stop being such a bitch to the woman," the customer in front of her said. "The guy in the suit who just left headed towards the motel."

"Thank you. You both have a nice day," she directed back at both of them. The smile she hoped to elicit from the woman was non-existent, but she was tired of trying to make the woman like her and she walked out without another word.

Turning toward the motel on the outskirts of town, she tried to figure out where Ben was headed, but nothing made sense. Scanning the street ahead, there was no sign of him. She was about to go back into town when she spotted him coming out of one of the motel rooms.

"Ben," she called loudly. Although he was close enough to hear, he didn't react to her call.

"Ben, over here," she shouted a bit louder, waving her arms above her head. Again, there was no response. What was going on?

She watched as he crossed the street, apparently headed back into town, and then she noticed a bag he was carrying. It was from the little gift shop in town; a store he wouldn't normally frequent. That explained everything. He hadn't told her about coming to town because he was buying her a gift. Throughout their relationship, he had surprised her with small, unexpected gifts like the flowers he had brought her from Helen's garden so long ago. That's it. He was going to surprise her with a gift. It didn't explain why he had come out of the motel, but she turned back the way she came so she didn't ruin his surprise.

Between the actual errands she intended to run and spending time visiting with people, Jordan barely made it home in time for supper. As she and Pete walked into the house, she could hear Ben on the phone and she popped her head into the office to give him a quick wave before putting her things down and heading into the kitchen. But she stopped suddenly when she noticed Ben wasn't wearing a suit. In fact, he hadn't been wearing one all morning, and he had no court appearance scheduled. Something was going on, but maybe it was all part of the surprise he seemed to be planning.

"Oh Jordan, there you are," Helen said when she spotted her in the hallway. "How was your afternoon?"

Jordan gathered the place settings and set the table for dinner as she told Helen about her afternoon. Not sure what Ben had planned and whether Helen was privy to it, she said nothing about seeing him in town.

"Ben mentioned you might take a trip to see your folks," Helen said as she put food on the table."

"He mentioned that to you?" Jordan said in surprise. "Actually, it was just a passing thought. I'm not sure I'll actually go."

"You know Jordan, I don't think it's ever too late to mend fences, especially with your family. Your folks would probably love to see you and see what you've accomplished with your life. You have a good job and a wonderful relationship and you've grown into a beautiful young woman. They should be proud of what you've achieved."

If only that were the case, but of course Helen didn't know the entire story. Ben would not have broken her trust on that issue, she was sure of it.

"Well, maybe, but like I said, nothing definitely planned," Jordan said, hoping that would be the end.

"Are you making plans without me?" Ben asked as he came into the room and gave Jordan a kiss. "How was your afternoon? Productive I hope."

"More than you know," Jordan said with a chuckle. If he had seen her on the street, he didn't let on and she played along.

"Did you finish the ad for Casey?" Ben questioned as they all sat down to eat.

"No. He sent some things home with me and after dinner, I thought I would work on it and then drop it off for him in the morning. He said there was no hurry, but he seemed anxious about it."

"Oh, that reminds me," Ben interjected. "My court hearing for Monday got moved up to tomorrow. It looks like I'll be back in Casper for a couple of days. Do you think you can hold down the fort for me?"

One thing Jordan had learned was that they seldom moved court hearings up in the schedule. Suspecting that Ben's excuse for going to Casper was part of her surprise, she asked no questions.

"Of course."

· · · · ·

Ben left early the next day and, with no appointments scheduled, Jordan easily breezed through her work. She had finished the church advertisement the night before and emailed it to Casey and now had the entire afternoon looming before her with nothing to do. With Helen off on a quick getaway with friends, Jordan was confined to the house to answer the office phone, and she was restless. Even Bear and Pete were no help, as both dogs were currently sound asleep in the living room. She needed something to liven up the day, and went in search of Ben's iPod. Ear buds in place, she turned the music up and soon was dancing around the house to the sounds only she could hear. She felt liberated and alive and was thoroughly enjoying herself until the muffled sound of the doorbell broke through. Pulling one of the ear buds out, she listened again, jumping when someone pounded on the front door.

Risking a quick look out the window, she saw a car she didn't recognize in the driveway. She hurried to turn the music off, smooth back her hair, and open the door.

"I'm sorry, I didn't hear the bell . . .," she said before stopping mid-sentence in total shock.

The man standing in front of her, reeking of alcohol in the middle of the day and weaving on his feet, was the spitting image of Ben. Only this time she knew immediately that it wasn't him; it was Brandon.

Through blurred eyes, the man looked her up and down, wiping the back of his hand across his mouth to wash away the spittle that had pooled in the corner.

"I'm here to see Ben," he slurred as he continued to stare at her in a way that, even if she hadn't already experienced his previous assault, would have turned her stomach.

The old fear he had caused at that party was immediately back and she trembled as she closed the door slightly to prevent him from coming in.

"He's not in the office today. You'll have to leave," she said with more bravado than she actually felt. She was alone with the man who had tried to rape her, and she was terrified.

"Are you the office girl? When is he coming back?"

"He'll be back on Monday. You can call him then. I'm sorry, but I have to go now. Please leave."

"Hey, I know you, don't I? What did you say your name was?" he asked as he moved a step closer and she moved to close the door even further.

"Please, will you leave? I really need to close up for the day."

"Don't tell me what to do," he thundered at her. He had gone from being a run-of-the-mill drunk to a man very much like Richard just before he struck her and her heart began pounding frantically.

His anger roused the dogs who quickly appeared on either side of her. They weren't fooled by the stranger who looked so much like the man of the house and sensing Jordan's fear, both Bear and Pete growled ominously at him.

"I think you'd better leave now," she said with deadly quiet. "The dogs don't like strangers very much."

Looking from her to the dogs and back again, he finally took a step back, and she closed the door and locked it securely behind her as the dogs barked furiously and ran from window to window before finally stopping in Ben's office where Jordan stood watching as Brandon poured himself into the car and left.

Her fun afternoon of dancing and music was over. None of the scenarios she had previously imagined included opening the door to find a drunk Brandon standing in front of her. Even in his deeply inebriated state he had thought she seemed familiar. When he sobered up, he might very well recognize her. She needed a plan, and she needed it in a hurry.

After checking every door and window in the house, with Pete and Bear shadowing her every step, she took a seat at her desk and burst into tears. Deep down she had convinced herself Brandon would never show up and she and Ben would have a long and happy life together. If only she had been paying more attention instead of dancing around like a teenager, she could have pretended no one was home and he would never have seen her.

Taking a deep breath, she tried to think logically. She hadn't worked so hard to escape from Richard to have Ben's horrible brother ruin it all. The thought suddenly occurred to her that the man in town, the man coming out of the motel the day before, hadn't been Ben at all. It had been Brandon all along. So why had he been in town for an entire day without letting Ben know? Ben would be furious when he found out Brandon was here, but she wouldn't be the one to tell him.

If she had had more courage, she would have packed her things and headed out on her pretend vacation. But she couldn't just yet. Once Brandon figured out who she was, she might never have time to see Ben again before she ran for her life. She had to see him one last time. He would be home the next night and if Brandon paid any attention to what she had said, he wouldn't come back before Monday at the earliest. That would give her the weekend with Ben before she disappeared.

She tried to imagine what he would think when she didn't come back from her vacation. Would he search for her? She was positive his love for her was strong enough that he would move heaven and earth to find her and it warmed her heart, but she also knew that his persistence would put him in jeopardy. As much as it pained her to think of hurting him she would have to break his heart now to save him from danger later. With a heavy heart she began writing a goodbye letter.

Tears staining the pages, she poured out every secret she had been keeping and her willing participation in the felony theft of Richard's documents. By the end, hoping to soften the blow of her departure, she carefully outlined the danger she had put him in and provided detailed instructions on where and how to access the flash drive and financial records that would put Richard away for the rest of his life should anything happen to her. Even if it destroyed her life, the least she could do was take Richard down with her and she knew Ben would do just that in her absence.

When she finished the dozen pages, she resisted the temptation to end it all with the words of love that were in her heart. Once he learned her secrets, he probably wouldn't want to hear her declarations of love, anyway. Signing the letter, she folded it carefully and put it in an envelope before remembering the sketch still tucked away in her desk drawer. It was the one thing she would take with her from this place and the one memory she could leave for Ben. Long ago she had adorned the sketch with words of love for Ben and she knew she should remove them, but before she could change her mind, she made a copy for herself and placed the original in the envelope before tucking it into the back of the heavy law book sitting on the corner of her desk where he might someday find it.

Unwilling to stay alone in the house, even with Pete and Bear for company, Jordan turned on the answering machine, gathered her things, and they headed for the cabin. She spent the rest of the night packing the few belongings she would take with her. When Ben called she tried hard to sound normal but he immediately sensed something was off.

"Are you okay?" he asked not long into the conversation.

"Sure, I'm fine," she said in what she hoped was a confident voice. Seeing Brandon at the door had rattled her, and she was having a hard time concentrating.

"Are you sure? I can't quite put my finger on it, but something seems off with you tonight."

"Really, I'm fine. But I miss you. What time do you think you'll be home tomorrow?" she asked. Torn between wanting him home next to her, she feared Brandon would connect with him before she could leave.

"Midafternoon most likely. You know as much as I love Helen, I'm glad she's gone for a few days and we have the house to ourselves for the weekend. In fact, I might never let you out of bed."

She could hear the smile in his voice through the line and imagined the look of desire in his eyes. It was the look in the sketch; the one she would hold dear long after she was gone.

Trying to divert him from thinking something was wrong, she admitted she wasn't opposed to the idea of staying up in the bedroom all weekend at the cabin. Every final moment she could spend with him was a memory she would never forget.

"That will be terrific," she said finally. "But I wanted to tell you something. Remember that trip back home I was considering? I've decided that after the weekend I'd like to go."

"I think that's a fantastic idea Jordan. Have you called your folks to let them know you're coming?"

The lie just slipped out of her mouth.

"I have actually and I told my mother I'd leave late Sunday or early Monday if that's okay with you. I know it's short notice but I'm all caught up at the office and Casey told me he has a couple of designers coming in for interviews tomorrow so I think now is a good time."

"If that's what you want, sure, but I'm surprised at how quickly this is coming together after all this time estranged from your parents. Will you fly?"

He had never come right out and asked her where home was and she had never offered the information. The less he knew about where she was going the better it would be for everyone. Of course, she had no intention of going home to her family either.

"I thought I would drive. It's beautiful at this time of year and it will give me time to think about what I want to say to my family when I see them again."

Lies, lies, and more lies . . . justified only by the need to protect him from what was coming. What surprised and disappointed her most of all was how easily lying was becoming for her.

·　·　·　·　·

That night, for the first time since she saw the doctor, the nightmare returned, only this time it wasn't just Richard's face she saw, it was Brandon's. She woke up screaming just as he was about to rape her. Drenched in sweat, shaking from head to toe, she couldn't stop crying. Ben had been the only person who could soothe her after one of the nightmares and now she didn't even have him.

Too afraid to sleep again, she got dressed and went downstairs to sit on the porch. The glade was so still not even the sound of an insect was heard. Lightning flashed in the distant sky and there was the smell of rain in the air, a fall rain that would be as cold and dismal as she felt. She pulled her knees to her chest, wrapped her arms around them and let silent tears fall as the dogs tussled together in the wet grass of the early morning. She sat that way, unmoving, until the sun finally reached for the sky. The rain was coming, but with the sunrise piercing the storm clouds it was light enough to run.

Leaving the dogs behind, she went through the motions while the thoughts of how much she would hurt Ben played repeatedly in her mind. Every time his face flashed in her mind she told herself he would be just fine without her. With Helen he wouldn't be alone and in time he would forget he ever had feelings for Jordan. At least that's what she kept telling herself. It would just take time. In time he would understand her actions were to protect him.

She remembered all the times he had expressed his dream of filling the house with a family of his own. Being with her meant that would never happen and logically that meant she was really doing him a favor—freeing him so he could find the woman who could be mother to his children and his lifelong partner. Someday he would thank her for it. She wasn't naïve enough to believe his thanks would come soon though and she would have to be strong enough to do this for both of them.

The rain finally began as her feet pounded on the pavement and her arms pumped in rhythm to her steps. Her breath was coming faster and faster and the rain blinded her vision, but still she ran as if the devil himself were chasing her. Like Ben had once upon a time, anyone watching her would wonder what she was running from and no one would realize she was running away from the love of her life and the piercing blue eyes that knew her better than anyone.

Drenched by the chilly rain, she wiped aside the wet hair plastered to her face, concentrating only on the exercise. Running had always helped her find clarity, but this time her heart wouldn't let her and miles down the road the picture of Ben's face and the agony that would be there when he discovered she was gone for good was all she could see. Stopping at the side of the road she fell to her knees as sobs of grief erupted from her thin frame.

"Oh my God Jordan are you okay?"

The familiar voice failed to register until she felt a hand on her shoulder and she leapt back in surprise as Dr. Norris looked down at her with concern. So consumed with her sadness she hadn't even heard his van pull up.

"Jordan what's wrong? Are you ill? Did you hurt yourself?"

He peppered her with questions while she hastily used the back of her sleeve to wipe the tears away and think of some excuse she could give him.

"I'm fine," she said abruptly before getting to her feet and walking a few steps away, disappointed when he followed her and placed his body in front of her.

"I'd say you're anything but fine," Dr. Norris said as he reached out to place his hand on her shoulder. "And what are you doing out here in the middle of nowhere? Did you really run all this way?"

She looked around in confusion before checking the fit tracker on her wrist. She had run almost twenty miles already. It would be another twenty miles back and she wasn't sure she could do it in her present condition.

"Oh, I guess I lost track. I rarely run in this direction and I just lost track of where I was. I'm fine though, really."

"Why were you crying? Has something happened? Please Jordan. Help me understand what's going on."

Of course he wanted to help. That's who he was, but she could never admit what had brought on her anguish.

"Could you give me a ride home? I don't think I have the stamina to run all the way back," she told him without answering his question.

"Of course," he said. "Let me help you in the truck."

As they drove away, Jordan immediately trembled and Dr. Norris turned the heat on full blast. But her trembling wasn't from the cold nor the wet clothes. It was knowing she would soon rip the heart out of the man she loved. They were silent on the way home, but she saw the sideways glances he continuously cast her way as she stared out the window consumed with misery.

"Looks like you have company," Dr. Norris said when he turned into the glade surrounding the cabin.

He might not have recognized the truck sitting in front of the cabin, but Jordan did and her eyes scanned the yard looking for its owner. As Dr. Norris helped her from the truck, Ben and the dogs appeared from the back of the cabin and walked towards them.

"Oh, it's the attorney," Dr. Norris said. He was disappointed and didn't even try to hide it this time.

"Thank you for the ride. I really appreciate it. Maybe I can take you to lunch soon. I'll call you later and we can sort something out." Ben's appearance had startled her into yet another lie.

Kevin's face transformed with a wide smile as he directed a look of conquest Ben's way.

"I'm just glad I could be there for you in your time of need and I'd like that lunch very much Jordan, but I better get going. Talk to you soon."

He hurried back to his van just as Ben reached Jordan's side and with a half-hearted wave, he drove away.

"What are you doing here?" Jordan said giving him a quick kiss on the cheek while trying not to get him as wet as she was. "I thought you weren't coming home until tonight?"

"The prosecutor had some kind of family emergency and the Judge delayed the proceedings until late next week. I thought I'd surprise you. Are you okay?" he asked softly into her ear.

He was standing just inches away but made no move to touch her. More than anything she wanted to melt into his body, but subconsciously she felt herself pulling away from him even then.

"What did you need that the good doctor helped you with?"

"It was nothing. I just ran a little too hard and too far this morning and got caught in a downpour. He offered me a ride home."

"And for that you agreed to go on a date with the man?" Ben said.

"It's not a date. It's just lunch to say thanks is all. You should go open the office. I'm going to take a warm bath."

"Maybe the office will be closed this morning," he suggested. "It's been a while since I inspected your bedroom. What do you say we remedy that?"

Every moment spent together at the cabin was one less chance for Brandon to appear on their doorstep before she left for good and she took Ben's hand in her own and led him into the cabin without another word.

The rain she hadn't been able to outrun eventually made it to the cabin and she and Ben spent the day together exactly as he had hoped - in bed. When they were too tired to do much more than talk, they went out to the porch swing. It was a crisp, cool fall evening, and the sounds of the forest had just begun to sing around them. Bear and Pete relaxed comfortably at their feet and Jordan felt safe and content wrapped in Ben's arms. The rain had cleared the air and even though the faint sound of thunder could still be heard in the distance, starlight shone brightly from above and Jordan realized how much she would miss this place after she was gone.

It hadn't been that difficult to convince Ben to spend the weekend with her at the cabin and she was grateful. Brandon would never find them here. She forced herself to relax and be as normal as possible so Ben wouldn't suspect what was to come.

"I've been meaning to ask you something," Ben asked as they looked up at the stars.

"What's that?"

"What would you think about building a house here?"

"There's already a house here," she reminded him.

"I know and I realize how important the cabin is to you and how much you enjoy the solitude out here, but I thought the cabin isn't big enough for an entire family."

Sitting up straight she looked him dead in the eye, instinctively knowing where his conversation was heading. His timing couldn't have been worse.

"Ben, I . . ."

To her unmitigated surprise, he unwrapped his arms and slid down onto one knee as she watched in astonishment. Digging in his jeans pocket he pulled out a small black velvet box.

"Jordan, my world changed the moment I first laid eyes on you. You consume every waking moment of my life and you're every thought I have.

You've become my reason for living and for being the man I want to be. My life means nothing without you in it and even though I know there is a huge reason I shouldn't be asking this question, I just can't wait another minute. Will you please marry me?"

He opened the box to reveal a gorgeous ring featuring a deep red ruby surrounded by a circle of diamonds.

It was as untraditional an engagement ring as their relationship and it took her breath away. She reached out her hand to touch it before remembering what was at stake and she pulled back, tears flooding her eyes.

"Say something please," Ben begged. "Don't leave me hanging here."

"What do you want me to say? I'm married," she said sadly.

"Don't think I have forgotten, but isn't it about time to admit you're never going back to him? Let me help you get a divorce so we can start our life together. We can sell my house and tear down the cabin and I'll build you the home of your dreams here where we can raise our kids and live a long and happy life together the way it should be. You and I deserve this. We deserve to share our lives with the one person we are destined to be with—you and me baby—building a future together. Please say yes."

"Ben please don't do this. I might not be the most religious woman in the world, heck I'm probably already destined for hell after this affair, but divorce is impossible and I've told you that already. Please get up," she asked before pulling him to his feet and patting the spot next to her so she could look him in the eyes. Instead, he put the ring down beside her and crossed his arms in front of him as he towered above her.

"You're seriously turning me down? But you love me. I know you do," he said quietly as she reached for his hand and stood.

"I've waited for you my entire life Ben Anderson and like every little girl before me, I've dreamt of this moment when the man I love would get down on one knee in front of me and offer his heart. But I don't deserve you and I never did. We were just kidding ourselves into thinking that we would ever have a future together. The mistakes of my past will always be there, keeping me from you and keeping me from the life I want. I can't marry you and I am sorrier than you could know, but I think it's time to admit all this was a huge mistake and let you move on with your life."

"So that's it then? Can't we just forget I bought this and go back to way things were an hour ago?" he asked as he picked up the ring with tears rolling down his face.

Her heart broke into a million pieces to see it. The last perfect weekend they would have together was over before it really had begun and yet she knew that this would be a better ending than her plan to flee. There would be pain and anguish for both of them, but he would be free to find a woman who could give him the future he wanted.

"What good would it do? We'd both still be lying to ourselves about a future we'll never have. Trust me. It's better to just make a clean break from each other now both personally and for the firm. I'll come by the house to collect my things in a few days. Ben, I am so very sorry."

Expecting a fight, it shocked her when without another word he went back into the cabin, returning with his suitcase and stopped only to stare at her. The agony on his face was excruciating for her and she longed to take back everything she had said but she just couldn't.

"I'm always going to love you," he said softly before turning to leave with Bear trailing behind.

She said nothing even though every fiber of her being wanted to shout it back to him and rush into his arms. She said nothing because there was nothing left to say.

CHAPTER FIFTEEN

To know the true agony of love lost, it seems one has to have truly loved someone, and Jordan had now learned that truth in the most painful way. Ben had been the most important part of her life and in one heartbreaking moment, she had thrown it all away.

Afraid of running into Brandon, she had never collected her belongings from Ben's house.

In the days that followed, her life became a sad routine of twice-a-day runs, long walks in the woods surrounding the cabin, playing with Pete, and at night doing anything to avoid going to sleep where sweet dreams of Ben and the tender way he once held her alternated with the nightmare of Richard and Brandon.

She saw no one other than Dr. Norris and rarely ventured into town for fear of running into Ben or Helen.

The promised lunch for Dr. Norris took place at the cabin and it had been a disaster. She spent the entire meal comparing his every word and action to Ben and feeling guilt over how unfair it all was to the man in front of her. He, of course, noticed none of it and since that time he had been extra attentive even though she had given him no reason to hope for anything between them. If she had been in her right mind, she would have ended things with the man before hurting him also, but lonely for human companionship, she said nothing and instead learned to tolerate his occasional visits to the cabin. His timid attempts to entice her into a repeat date fell flat and she did not try to explain.

Pete was the only ray of sunshine on her otherwise drab day. Twice-a-day runs occupied a good chunk of their day although it was an alternative route that kept them far from the house on the hill and the eyes she knew would watch for her from the top-floor window. Pete was her constant companion and only comfort and yet she recognized how much he missed Bear. They were both miserable.

She had taken to spending much of her day on the computer—Ben's computer—looking for any bit of information about Richard. At some point she suspected Ben would remember the bill he was paying for internet service at the cabin and shut it off, but for now she made use of it.

Logging in yet again, she immediately went to Richard's secret accounts. Perplexed when an error message popped up, she entered the password again. Still no access. Had he realized after all this time that she had been in the accounts? She had never moved money or done anything other than copy the records, so how could he have known? Maybe it was a temporary glitch. Closing the laptop, she vowed to try again later.

"Come on Pete, let's go berry picking."

A large patch of wild blueberries was located not too far from the cabin, and the fresh berries would make a wonderful pie. It would be a nice way to thank Dr. Norris for his friendship and give her something to fill a few hours of the day. The outing was a pleasant diversion from her normal routine and the pair started for home with enough berries to make not only a pie, but a few jars of jam as well. Jordan remembered with fondness her mother teaching her to make jams and jellies, and an overwhelming desire to hear her mother's voice washed over her.

As they neared the clearing, Pete froze in place, ears standing at attention.

"What is it, boy?" she asked, her voice a mere whisper.

Her heart raced and her breathing became ragged. Was it possible Brandon had recognized her and gotten to Richard? Grateful her vantage point offered a clear view of the back of the cabin with plenty of foliage to camouflage their location, she didn't move.

Pete took a step forward and she grabbed for his collar before he could give their hiding spot away; the sudden action causing her to drop the berries, which rolled everywhere underfoot.

Straining to hear what his sensitive ears had and hers could not, she ordered Pete to stay. She heard nothing and crept forward as quietly as the woods allowed, crouching low to avoid being seen. Finally, at the edge of the forest, she heard a faint voice.

"Jordan, dear, are you home?"

It was Helen.

"Won't you please come to the door?"

Jordan waited a few more moments before stepping through the brush and into the glade.

"Helen, I'm out back," she shouted before releasing Pete to greet their guest. He nearly knocked Helen over in his exuberance, and Jordan hurried to restrain him.

"Hello stranger," Helen said with a laugh as Jordan wrapped her arms around the frail body. "I'd nearly given up on you. I've been knocking for the longest time, but I was sure you were home because your truck was in the driveway, but then I realized you might be out running. Unless you've taken to running in the woods, that would be wrong, I'm guessing."

"Pete and I went blueberry picking. I was going to make a pie," Jordan said as they locked arms and turned towards the cabin.

"Ah, that explains the blue stains on your fingers," Helen laughed, "but where are all the berries?"

How could she explain her hesitation at the edge of the forest and dropping the berries? But as with so many things these days, a lie came easily.

"There weren't quite enough, and those I picked ended up in my mouth, I'm afraid. But why don't you come inside for some coffee and we can talk?"

As excited as she was to see the woman who meant so much to her, Jordan knew the real reason for inviting Helen in was her desperation to find out how Ben was doing. She put a pot of coffee on while Helen took a seat at the table. Although she appeared to have fully recovered from her accident, she now walked slower and with the aid of a cane.

"I'm sorry I didn't say goodbye. But . . . well . . ."

"It's okay Jordan, I understand. After days of moping around the house without you, Ben finally shared with me some of what happened between you and I'm sorry for what you both have gone through. Admittedly I thought there was a future for you two and I'm sorry it ended badly."

"I'm not sure what Ben told you," Jordan told her, "but this is all my fault. He'll get over it eventually and maybe in the future we can be friends. Do you think that will happen?"

"No dear, to be perfectly honest, I don't think Ben will ever settle for a friendship with you. It's probably not my place to tell you this, but I honestly don't think he will ever get over you. I think he was in love with you even before he met you, and he's devastated."

Helen's bluntness, when she had to know Jordan would feel tremendous guilt at her words, was shocking. Maybe there was more to this visit than Helen was letting on.

"Will you be honest with me, Helen? Did Ben ask you to come here today?"

"Not in so many words, but he's been to town so many times in the last few weeks, I'm sure it was in the hopes he would catch a glimpse of you. He won't come right out and ask, but he's desperate to know if you're all right. I just thought maybe I could put his mind at rest."

"As you can see, I'm fine," Jordan lied. Truth be told, she was anything but fine, but admitting it to Helen, as much as she loved her, would serve no purpose.

"I can see that and even though you and Ben won't be together anymore, that doesn't mean we can't still be friends . . . if that's okay with you, I mean."

Reaching across the table to take the blue-veined hand in her own, Jordan smiled at her. "It's more than okay. Now why don't you tell me how you've been?"

"Well, there have been some changes at the house," Helen said as Jordan poured coffee for them both. "And not all for the better, I'm afraid."

"What do you mean?"

"Ben's brother has moved in."

That was the last thing Jordan expected, and her jaw dropped as her hands trembled. Having no contact with Ben, she had assumed wrongly that Brandon was long gone.

"But I thought they didn't get along."

"That's true, but he showed up at the door just a couple of days after you and Ben . . . well anyway, he claims he's broke. His wife threw him out and Ben's mother and stepfather wouldn't take him in and he needed a place to stay. You know how kindhearted Ben is, and even with as much aggravation as that man has caused for him, Ben couldn't turn him away. So he's living in the house, sleeping until noon every day, drinking all of Ben's liquor, eating all of his food, and expecting me to wait on him hand and foot. And he's always underfoot. He never leaves the house and I can't get a moment of peace with him there."

"Oh my!"

"But what's really upsetting is the way I've seen him act around some of Ben's younger female clients. Honestly, he scares me the way he looks and talks to them."

Helen would never know, but Jordan had experienced it firsthand, and she hoped Ben was smart enough to realize it before Brandon caused him trouble.

Desperate to know more about him, but afraid too many questions would shine a light where she would rather not, she was grateful when Helen moved on to other less contentious topics. By the time the last drops of coffee had grown cold in the bottom of the pot, Jordan realized that even if she couldn't be with her own mother, Helen was the next best thing. As she walked back to Helen's car, she promised they would keep in touch.

"You're welcome here any time," Jordan assured her.

"I'd like to say you're welcome at the cottage too, but I understand that might be awkward with Ben and all. Before I go, can you answer one more question for me?"

"Of course."

"You loved him, didn't you?"

"How could I not?"

"Then whatever is going on between you two, hold on to that, my dear. This too shall pass."

Her cryptic farewell aside, Helen's visit had meant the world to Jordan, even if the news about Brandon moving in was troubling. She would need to be extra careful on those rare trips to town.

•   •   •   •   •

"Damn it all to hell," Ben shouted in the empty room. His temper had been short and quick for weeks now and Helen was becoming all too used to such outbursts; still, she came running at the sound.

"What is it? Are you all right?"

"I'm fine," he said, although the unusual crimson hue of his face said he was anything but. He stood behind his desk, holding his keyboard upside down as liquid drained from it. "I just spilled coffee all over my desk. Can you get me some paper towels, please?"

Returning with the requested paper towels, she helped him mop up the mess.

"Why is it everything goes wrong when I'm on a deadline? I spent all night last night working on that summation only to have my computer freeze up and then got no sleep because of the stupid coyotes howling, which Bear was happy to take part in, and now this. It's like fate has turned against me."

"When are you going to admit it?" she told him before throwing the damp towels in the trash can.

"What are you talking about? Admit what?"

"It's not fate. It's you and the situation with Jordan. You're been off your game ever since she left. If you'd just for once admit that you're in pain, maybe you could let some of that go."

"Helen, you know I love you and I respect your advice, but you're way off base on this one. Jordan was my employee. Nothing more. In some respects, it's a relief she's gone. Maybe now I can hire a professional paralegal.

"Ben William Anderson, how dare you? How dare you so easily dismiss that woman and what she meant to you? Every day I watched the two of you together and she might be the single best thing that ever happened to you and you know it. She brought laughter and joy to your life, not to mention one of the brightest legal minds I wager you have ever encountered. Do you think you would have won half of your cases without her? Of course not, so don't you dare say such things about her."

Such fury coming from a normally unflappable woman was startling, but it turned out it was just what Ben needed. He dropped into his chair and buried his head in his hands. Her words had struck a nerve, and she took her own seat across from him and waited for him to speak.

"How am I supposed to just go on with my life as if she was never part of it?" he asked softly. When he looked up, the pain in his eyes was heart wrenching. "I'm in love with her."

The admission, while long in coming, was no surprise to Helen. She had watched their love story unfold.

"I know you are and that's why everything seems to go wrong in your life. You miss her. Surely there must be some way to salvage whatever it is you did."

"What do you mean? I did nothing."

"My dear boy, I know you would like to think that, but I also know that there is something in Jordan's past that she didn't want to share with us and yet repeatedly you badgered her about it. I'm not saying that's what caused her to leave, but . . ."

"She's married."

Helen wasn't easily surprised, but his admission startled her into near silence.

"You're wrong. You must be," she whispered.

"She told me she's married. She wouldn't say much more than that, but I offered to help her get a divorce and she wouldn't even consider it."

"Oh Ben, I'm so sorry. Maybe if . . ."

"Don't think whatever you're going to suggest I haven't already thought of, it's no use. I doubt she'll even talk to me. Besides, I don't even know if she's still in town. For all I know, she packed up and left."

"She didn't."

"How could you possibly know that?" he asked. Hope had replaced the pain in his eyes. "Have you seen her?"

"Well, I wasn't going to tell you this out of fear it would be even more painful for you, but I went to see her just a couple of days back. I took her things to her, and we had coffee."

"For God's sake Helen, why didn't you tell me?" he exclaimed.

"Because she didn't want me to. I was worried about her being all alone, but she's doing fine. She's very thin, even more so than usual, but she appears to be fine."

"And did she ask about me?" The cautious hope in that statement made her choose her words carefully.

"Only to ask if you had sent me to see her, and I told her you knew nothing about it."

Ben slumped back in his chair and stared at nothing.

"I'm sorry Ben. I know you were hoping she would reconsider, but what did you expect? If what you say is true and she really is married, you shouldn't be involved with each other. As hard as it is, my darling boy, you need to move forward and forget about her. A good way to start would be to clean up her office and start finding a paralegal. I don't relish the thought of going back to helping you in the office again. So, that's my sermon for today. Now let me see what I can find for your lunch."

She was hardly out the door before Brandon sauntered in and plopped down into the chair Helen had just vacated.

"So, little brother is having an affair with a married woman," he exclaimed. "Never would have seen that one coming."

"Didn't mother teach you eavesdropping is wrong? It's not what you think," Ben said angrily.

Having Brandon in the house had been a difficult adjustment and the interaction between them continued to be tense. Brandon claimed poverty and judging by his refusal to leave, it might be the first time he was telling the truth, but having him around all day was proving stressful.

His time in Washington had only made him more arrogant, even when he apparently had nothing to back it up. He had further irritated Ben by insisting on being introduced as "Senator" Harrington and on the rare occasions when he interacted with Ben's clients, he treated them as peasants unworthy of his time, leaving Ben to apologize for his behavior. Frustrated didn't begin to express how Ben felt about having him in the house.

"It never is, is it Benny boy? So where is she? How come I haven't met her yet?"

"If you must know, we're not together anymore," Ben admitted before his eyes went to a picture of the two of them on the bookshelf.

Brandon noticed the look and retrieved the picture.

"Wow, that woman is gorgeous and . . . strangely familiar, I must say. Did she work here? I'm pretty sure that's the woman who threw me out of your house when I first got to town."

"What the hell are you talking about, Brandon? Jordan was already gone by the time you showed up here."

"Well, that's not exactly what happened," Brandon admitted. "A few days before we hooked up, I came here looking for you, and this woman," he said, tapping Jordan's picture, "this woman opened the door and told me to leave. In fact, she threatened to sic your dogs on me, so I left. Didn't she tell you I was here?" he asked innocently. If he had known how intoxicated he was at the time, Ben would never have let him stay. "Probably a good thing she's out of your life, Ben. She was a real bitch."

Ben leapt out of his chair, launching himself across his desk to grab Brandon by the throat before he just as quickly realized what he had done and let him go.

"Jesus Christ Ben, what the hell was that?" Brandon said as he backed away and rubbed his neck. "You always were one to care a little too much about a good lay. You had your fun with the woman and now she's gone. Don't blame me for it, for Christ's sake."

"Get the hell out of my office, Brandon," Ben told him through clenched teeth. He had never wanted to strike another human being as much as he did at that moment. He clenched and unclenched his hands. "Don't you ever mention Jordan again, do you hear me? See if you can find something else to do today; preferably something out of my sight."

Brandon scurried out of the office while Ben tried to cool down. He had to put Jordan out of his mind, but it was easier said than done and Ben was having a difficult go of it. Ready to call out to her with a question before remembering the office next to his was empty was a common occurrence in those first few days without her, and there were reminders everywhere that made it impossible to forget her. How many times had he already opened a case file to find Jordan's handwritten note buried in the documents? Intended to remind him of a particularly salient point to make during the trial, her feminine handwriting stirred up a host of emotions as he pictured her pouring over his law books or doing research on the computer.

Each time he passed the open door to her small office it reminded him of Helen's advice to clean up Jordan's space, but with no applicants coming in for the paralegal job he had finally advertised, there was no pressing need to move ahead.

In some respects, seeing the messy desk and the files piled ever so neatly in an order only Jordan seemed to understand made it seem like she had just gone out for a walk and would be back shortly. Barely able to admit it to himself, much less Helen, it was the reason he didn't touch her office. Jordan still held a large part of his heart and he just hadn't been able to let her go. But she had been gone for weeks already and while he still made frequent trips to town in the slim hope of seeing her, he continued to come up empty. Admittedly, it was time to move on. Picking up the draft of the paralegal ad, he headed downtown.

"Hey Casey," Ben said as he walked into the newspaper office. His help wanted ad had resulted in a grand total of zero applicants, but he couldn't give up on finding a replacement. He was already drowning under an ever-expanding case load.

"Ben, hello," the newspaper editor said as he walked to the counter and extended his hand in greeting. "It's been ages, man. How are you?"

"Doing well. The practice is busier than ever and I'm swamped. Do you think you can run that ad for me again and maybe include it on your website this time?"

"Sure, we can do that, but what's Jordan think about sharing her position with a stranger?"

The question caught Ben off guard, and he cleared his throat before answering. "We're not together anymore."

"Sorry man. I didn't realize since she's not working here anymore either. That's too bad. Charlie was just talking about Jordan the other day. She saw her run past our place and suggested we have you both over for dinner one night. We were kind of hoping to find another couple to be friends with."

"Yeah, well, if you could just get that ad in for the next couple of weeks and send me the bill, I'd be grateful. But I better run. Bear's in the truck. See you soon."

Hurrying back to the truck, Ben felt the pain of losing Jordan all over again. They had been building a life together even if they didn't realize it at the time and it would have been everything he could have ever wanted. In a sudden moment of clarity, the pain he felt over losing her became anger. Anger at Jordan for keeping her secret. Anger at not being able to do anything to help her and, anger at himself for falling in love with a woman who would never truly love him back.

Even though she said she loved him, how could she? She belonged to another man. He had let himself see emotions in her that never existed and, just like Brandon, she had let him down. The two most important relationships in his life had ended exactly the same way—in disappointment and regret.

As if he had conjured him out of thin air, Ben's cell phone rang and he looked at the display and swore under his breath while letting it ring.

"Brandon, what do you want?" he asked brusquely just before the call would have gone to voicemail.

"Hey Benny boy . . . for a minute there I didn't think you were going to answer. I just wanted to remind you about stopping in at the bank and seeing about that loan."

With Ben unwilling to loan him money, Brandon had suggested he instead help him get a loan. In such a small town, being a United States Senator opened a lot of doors, but even the local banker was unwilling to loan Brandon money based on his word alone. The man had insisted that Brandon have a co-signer and Ben was his only option. Resistant to the idea at first, having Brandon in the house was becoming intolerable and against his better judgement, Ben was considering signing for him just to get him to go home.

As Brandon had gotten more desperate for money, he had let slip some important details about his current situation. His D.C. lifestyle had nearly bankrupted him and creditors had been hounding him day and night. Filing for bankruptcy wasn't even an option. As a junior member of the Senate's Finance Committee, filing for bankruptcy would cost him more than just embarrassment. His desperation for a bailout had turned him into a dog with a bone he wouldn't or couldn't let go of.

"Damn it Brandon, I told you I'm not ready to consider it yet. Let it go, will you please?"

"What do I have to do to convince you to sign? It's already mortgaged to the hilt, but I can put your name on the title of my D.C. townhouse. It's worth a couple mill at least."

"You know what I would really like?" Ben asked. "I'd like you to stop being such a freeloader and get off your ass and help around the house. Do you think you could do that for a change?"

"You mean like the help? Isn't that what you have the old woman for?" Helen hadn't even tried to hide her disdain for Brandon and the feeling was mutual. The two had consistently butted heads since his arrival.

"You can start by treating Helen with more respect and doing some chores. Start with taking Bear to the vet this afternoon. He's due for his annual checkup. Appointment is at four. Helen will give you the directions."

"Fine, but if I help out, then you'll co-sign for the loan?"

"If you can prove to me you've changed, then I'll consider it, but you've got a lot of work to do to make up for what you cost me in D.C."

"Fine. I'll take the dog, but rental car or not, there is no way that animal is going in the Lexus."

CHAPTER SIXTEEN

"Jesus, Mary, and Joseph," Jordan shouted to an empty kitchen before reaching for a kitchen towel.

After weeks of eating Helen's frozen meals, the freezer was now empty and Jordan had spent most of the afternoon preparing soup. The small kitchen counter was littered with the remnants of the vegetables she had been peeling, dicing, and slicing, but now she had cut her hand on the dull knife.

Never overly fond of the sight of blood, she tried not to look at the red stain that had already seeped through the towel. What else could go wrong? Wrapping a plastic bag around the towel in her hand she grabbed the truck keys and raced into town. In less than an hour, she had been examined, the wound had been cleaned, and six stitches had been placed and covered by a mound of white gauze. Her reward for the little misadventure? A bill she couldn't afford.

Her hoard of cash was getting low, and she looked toward the newspaper office as she walked to the truck. Maybe Casey would let her do some work for him again, but then again, that might not be such a good idea. When she had asked to be paid in cash, he looked at her suspiciously while she offered a lame excuse about not trusting banks, but she could tell he didn't buy it. She didn't relish another person with a curious nature questioning her like Ben had in the beginning, but she needed to make some money.

When she turned back to her truck, it surprised her to see Ben's truck parked in front of the veterinary clinic across the street and the man himself exiting the building with Bear in tow. It was the first time she had seen him since she turned down his proposal and she wasn't sure what to do. He had looked right at her before looking away as if she was a complete stranger. Should she ignore him back? Should she talk to him? Their friendship had been what drew them together at the beginning and she missed that as much as his love.

In the end, still unsure how he would react to seeing her, she walked across the street to at least say hello. Reminiscent of how they had first met, Bear spotted her and pulled the leash out of Ben's hand to race to Jordan's side, nearly bowling her over in his excitement. When he calmed down a bit, she grabbed his leash and walked him back across the street, where Ben continued to stand next to the truck.

"Hello," she said softly, unable to look him in the eye. "How have you been? I've missed you."

"Yeah, I tend to have that effect on women," he told her, causing her head to snap up at the unfamiliar voice.

"You," she spat.

"Yup, it's me, Brandon. I don't think we had a chance to meet when you threw me out of my brother's house, did we?"

As he spoke, he had moved closer to her. She stepped aside, realizing too late she was now trapped between the open door of the truck and his body. Flashes of the night he had pinned her against the wall at the party crashed through her mind and her breathing became fast and ragged.

"And now I find out that you're not only the hired help, but the married slut who stole my brother's heart."

He reached out a finger to her chin, touching her gently before letting it trail down her throat to her chest where she finally slapped it away. The mere thought of him touching her again made her want to vomit. She frantically tried to figure out how to get away from him without making a scene.

"Leave me alone," she ordered.

"Not yet. My brother showed me a picture of the two of you and you looked so happy it made me sick, but then I had another look at it. Why do you look so familiar to me? We've met before, haven't we? I just can't place it, but I know I've seen you before. I've been with a lot of women, but I think I would have remembered you. You look like...."

"Please just let me go," she pleaded as she looked away from him and let her hair fall across her face. The longer he looked at her, the more likely he would remember exactly how he knew her.

"Jordan, are you okay?"

She had never been so relieved to hear her name come out of Dr. Norris's mouth and, with Brandon distracted by the question, Jordan slipped under his arm and moved away from him.

"I'm fine," she told Dr. Norris before hurrying across the street to her truck and quickly driving away.

Brandon's overly pungent cologne filled her nostrils, and she rolled down the truck windows, hoping to wash it away. He may be identical to his brother in physical features, but everything else about him was repulsive and a sudden urge to vomit overtook her. Stomping on the brakes, she pulled to the side of the road, slammed it in park and walked into the field to empty her stomach, unable to get the lecherous look on Brandon's face out of her mind. Like Ben, he was smart, maybe too smart for his own good, but because of it, she knew it was only a matter of time before he figured out how they knew each other. She needed to disappear, and quickly.

Back in the safety of the cabin, she implemented her plan.

She had little, but what she had was needed. She loaded the boxes filled with her meager possessions into the truck before pulling a tarp over it all and tying it down securely. Her carefully thought out escape plan was being executed like clockwork until she remembered a problem she hadn't counted on.

Too proud to take the salary Ben had offered her, she was now almost broke and there was no way she could sell the cabin to raise money in mere days. She needed cash if she was to fund her escape, and unlike Brandon, she couldn't ask Ben for it.

But there was one option—one she had promised she would never use, and it was the money Ben had been squirreling away in the safe for her—her wages for the last several months. She had said she would never need it, but he had promised it was hers to do as she wished. The only problem was it was in Ben's safe in Ben's house where Ben's brother now lived, making it impossible for her to access it without telling Ben why she needed it. Or was it possible? Helen had offered her help if Jordan was in need and now, she needed her help desperately.

The kitchen clock showed it was close to midnight, but Helen had always been a night owl. Hoping this wasn't the one night she went to bed early, Jordan placed a call. It rang several times before Helen's pleasant voice answered.

"Helen, I'm so sorry to call so late. I hope I didn't wake you."

"Jordan, how lovely to hear from you," she said warmly. "And you didn't wake me up at all. I'm watching an interesting biography of the First Ladies on public television. How have you been?"

Unsure how to ask, Jordan ended up just blurting it out.

"I need a favor."

"Of course, dear. You know I'd do anything for you."

"I'm in a bit of a bind you see and I need money but . . . well . . . all the money I brought with me when I came here is mostly gone and I don't know what to do. I was wondering if you could help me out?"

"Of course, I have a little money tucked away for emergencies. How much did you need?"

"Helen, I'm not asking for a loan; I'm asking if you might get the money from Ben's safe for me. The money he was putting away for my wages all these months? He said I could have it whenever I needed it and I need it now."

"Oh Jordan, I know Ben was putting that money away for you, but honestly I don't think it's my place to give it to you. If you just call him tomorrow, I'm sure he'd be happy to give it to you."

A long, drawn-out sigh escaped Jordan's lips. Helen would not help her.

"Oh wait . . . ," Helen said. "I see the problem with that. You don't want to see him in person, do you?"

"Yes, that's the problem," Jordan responded, latching on to the excuse Helen had so conveniently provided. "You know how much I hurt him and I've been purposely avoiding him so he can move on. I don't want to bring up all those feelings again with something as simple as handing me what he has repeatedly said was mine whenever I want. You understand what I'm saying, right?"

With every fiber of her being, she prayed Helen would believe that excuse. After a moment of silence, Helen agreed.

"Of course I do, and I'm happy to help. Ben's up in Casper for a few days for a big jury trial and when he comes back and opens the safe up again, I'll grab the envelope and bring it out to you. I'm sure he would be fine with that. Will that be soon enough?"

She had hoped to disappear tonight, but if Helen couldn't access the safe on her own, she had no choice.

"Helen, thank you. You don't know what this means to me. I'll wait for your call."

Everything else was ready, but with days before she could get the cash, her life had now turned into a waiting game.

CHAPTER SEVENTEEN

Brandon was bored. Everything about the hick little town was the same every damn day, and he was bored with it all. Ben had left a couple days earlier for an out-of-town trial and left Brandon with only the old woman for company; a fate that was turning out to be worse than death. They didn't like each other and neither one took any pains to hide that fact. How Ben had put up with the old woman for so long was beyond him, but since he still hadn't agreed to co-sign the loan, Brandon was forced to be nice to the old bat and it was getting harder each day. She continuously found fault with everything he did, and it took everything in his power to thank her for it.

"What are you doing in your brother's office?"

He hadn't heard her sneak up on him as he snooped around the office and realized too late he should have been paying more attention. She always seemed to appear out of nowhere.

"Not that it's any of your business, but I was just looking at his photos," he lied before spotting the picture of Ben and the married woman and picking it up. "Did you know his girlfriend? What was her name? Janet?"

"It's Jordan," Helen corrected as she grabbed the photo from his hand, wiped a speck of dust from the frame and put it gently back in its place. "Her name is Jordan, and I don't think Ben would appreciate you being in here when he's gone."

"Ben's in love with her, isn't he?" he continued. One thing he had learned from the weeks living in the house, the old woman loved a good conversation.

"Not anymore," she said wistfully. "They were a good match though and I could see a future together for them, but it didn't work out."

"Because she's married, right? I never would have thought my brother would have an affair with a married woman, but he's an attorney. Why didn't he just help her get a divorce?"

"He offered, on more than one occasion actually, but she wouldn't hear of it. At first he thought it was due to religious beliefs, but Jordan has always had a lot of secrets and there must be more to the story than we know."

"Like what?" he asked. The more the old woman talked, the more he was learning about this Jordan.

"It doesn't matter anymore. She's moved back to her own place and Ben is moving on. Close the door on your way out. I have work to do and I'm done babysitting you."

She walked away as the lightbulb went off in Brandon's head and he finally remembered exactly who Jordan was. It was the look in her eyes the day before when he had her pinned against his truck. It was the same look she gave him years earlier when he had his hand up her skirt at his parent's anniversary party. Her name wasn't Jordan. It was Victoria, the missing wife of his onetime business acquaintance Richard Harvey.

Her hair was different, her eyes were different, but there was no mistaking her face or the goddess-like body he had so lusted after the night he first met her.

Unable to control his desire, he had risked Richard's wrath when he trapped her in the bedroom and began to have his way with her at the party before being interrupted. He had never gotten over his anger when one of Richard's security guards had burst into the room before he satisfied his lust and it was years before his thoughts stopped replaying what almost happened that night.

And then she disappeared and everyone in their circle of wealthy friends and business associates knew it. Having heard the stories of the physical abuse Richard used to keep his women in line; many of them, himself included, assumed Richard had taken his particular form of abuse one step too far and killed the woman. His half-hearted public pleas for her safe return fell on deaf ears and it hadn't been long before he moved on to another woman, who looked very much like Victoria. Yet here she was, hiding in plain sight in a backwater town in Wyoming with a new name. No wonder Richard hadn't been able to find her.

Tempted to finish what he started that night at the party, another thought occurred to Brandon. There was a reward. He was clueless why Richard would want the woman back after all this time, but if the reward was still in play, it would be more than enough to get him out of the hole he was in and get him back to D.C. where he could start his life over. And if Richard refused to hand over the cash, Brandon might just threaten to leak a few of the more salacious details about the woman's disappearance to the media. For a man like Richard, with secrets of his own to hide, that should be enough to force his hand.

Pulling out his cell phone, he scrolled through his contacts to find the number that would put him back in the game. Fifteen minutes later, the plan had been agreed to. Now he just had to figure out where to find the woman.

Originally, his plan had been to search property tax records using Ben's computer, but having found him in the office once already, Helen had locked that door tighter than Fort Knox. With the Senate out of session and being persona non grata with his office staff for all the negative publicity he brought to their office, he didn't dare ask for their help. It appeared he had few options to search for the girl until realizing that if he was careful, the good folks of the town would be sure to open up to him. While Helen was hanging clothes on the line, he slipped into Ben's bedroom, borrowed a set of his clothing and headed to the center of town.

Several people had already exchanged greetings with him as he wandered around trying to find someone to question, but it wasn't until he entered the diner that he hit the mother lode in an overworked and aging waitress who immediately started flirting with him.

"Mr. Anderson, what a treat to see you today," the woman said as she put a glass of water in front of him and poured him a cup of coffee before he had even asked. "It's rare we see you in here alone."

From the way she cocked her head and licked her lips, Brandon was sure the woman had a thing for his baby brother and he knew immediately he would work that to his advantage.

"Now why would I need anyone else around me when I have someone as pretty as you are waiting on me?" he told her with even more than his usual load of charm and saccharine.

A rosy blush immediately appeared on the woman's cheeks and she actually giggled like a schoolgirl.

"You know, I always thought there might be a little something between you and me," he said, hoping he was reading her correctly. One thing that had allowed him to get where he was in life was using people's vanity against them, and this woman was proving no different. Within minutes, he had her eating out of his hand. "Maybe you'd like to have a drink me with me sometime?"

"Well, that would be wonderful," she gushed, "but what about your girlfriend?"

"What about her? What she doesn't know won't hurt her and I'm sure you would be a lot more fun, if you know what I mean." The wink he added at the end of his statement elicited another giggle from the woman, who now leaned over the table in a blatant attempt to attract his attention to her oversized breasts.

"Now that's what I like to hear," she said as she swung her bosom just inches from his face while he fought the urge to move away from her. The stench of old grease and onions surrounded her. "That skinny bitch can rot out there in that cabin while we—shall we say—satisfy an itch."

"How do you know where she lives?" he asked, trying not to show his excitement at this stroke of luck.

"Everyone knows the old Olson place on Route 15. From what I hear she didn't even bother to change the name on the mailbox. Just paid cash for the place and moved in. Rumor has it she's sitting on a load of cash since she doesn't have a bank account. But enough about her. I can meet you after work tomorrow. I get off at eleven. Meet me at the bar on the corner and we'll see where the evening takes us."

"Thank you, my dear," he said, offering his most charming smile. "It will be an interesting evening for sure.

Wondering at what point the woman would realize he was a no-show the next evening, he left with a smile on his face. There was something immensely satisfying knowing that even here, he could always get what he wanted. By the time tomorrow was over, he would have solved his money problems and be on his way out of this depressing town with his meal ticket in tow.

.   .   .   .   .

Helen had shown up with the thick envelope of money just as promised, and Jordan was relieved. The hours had slowly ticked by since their late-night phone call, and every sound in the glade had set her on edge. Convinced that by now Brandon had certainly sussed out her true identity, she had put on miles pacing around the cabin and she wanted nothing more than to load Pete into the truck and drive away from this place that had meant so much to her all these months.

The last thing she expected as Helen drove away was to see a shiny black Lexus pull up to the cabin shortly after. She raced inside and slammed the door, peeking out the window as Brandon got out of the car and sauntered to the front door like he hadn't a care in the world.

Too late to do anything about it, she remembered she hadn't locked the door behind her and Brandon walked in like he owned the place. Staring at her while he casually lit a cigarette, his gaze took in the room while Pete's nose sniffed the air at the unfamiliar odor before issuing a warning bark, causing Jordan to reach for his collar.

"So, this is where you've been hiding?" he asked with a look of derision as he blew the acrid smoke into her face. "I never would have expected Victoria Harvey would be reduced to living in such squalor."

There it was, finally. He recognized her, and she didn't even bother trying to deny it.

"What do you want, Brandon?"

"A week ago, I would have said I want what was denied to me that night at the party. In fact, I've spent a lot of time thinking about what it would be like to screw you. But a few days ago, when I remembered who you really are, I realized you're worth more to me than a quick roll in the hay."

His words should have come as somewhat of a relief, but that voice of doom she had been carrying around for so long was now tolling loud and clear.

"What exactly does that mean?"

"Well, you might not realize it since you've been hiding out here, but your dear and loving husband has offered a substantial reward for your return. A reward that will be quite beneficial in my current financial situation and I intend to collect on it. Once I let Richard know where he can find you, I will be rolling in it thanks to you."

"So why haven't you called him already?"

What was the sense in fleeing now if Richard already knew where to find her? Even with the money Helen had delivered, it wouldn't be enough to run and establish a new life somewhere else. Her dreams of a life free from abuse were gone and all the bravado she had tried to present for the past year suddenly evaporated. But maybe not all was lost. That he hadn't called Richard already might mean he was willing to negotiate. If money was all he needed, she might get out of this yet. Her mind working a mile a minute, she tested that theory. After all, what did she have to lose?

"If I remember correctly, you were never one of Richard's biggest fans. If money is all you're after, maybe we can make a deal." She could see his mind working and realized she might be on to something. "I have some cash I might part with in exchange for your promise to forget you ever saw me."

"Keep talking," he told her as his cigarette finally burnt out and he threw the butt in the kitchen sink.

"I have about ten grand in cash." It was all the money from Ben's safe and would leave her with nothing.

"Did I forget to mention the reward Richard was offering was a substantial sum?" he said smoothly. "What you're offering doesn't even come close."

Having seen the article on the internet, she knew exactly how much Richard was offering and she knew she couldn't come close to that kind of cash. But she had one thing left to offer.

"Wait a minute, you didn't let me finish. I also have this property, and I can sign it all over to you."

Offering him the cabin would wipe her out, but what good was her freedom if she couldn't even feed herself?

"This piece of shit? What in the hell would I do with this?"

"I thought you were a big shot developer?" she taunted. "Isn't that how you were making money before you got into politics? This piece of shit cabin sits on hundreds of acres of untouched forest land that is prime for development. Hunting, fishing in the stream nearby, logging . . . you name it. This land is worth millions more than I bought it for. Why, I've already had three people try to buy it from me in the short time I've lived here. You would never have to come to your brother begging for money again."

Lies, lies, and more lies, but this time she felt no guilt about any of it. There really were hundreds of acres of land, but it was swamp land. She had paid just a few hundred dollars an acre and it would never be developed in a way that would make someone money. But by the time Brandon figured that out, she would be long gone.

"And you would just sign it all over to me?" he said.

Saying a silent prayer that his greedy nature would blind him to the due diligence he should have been doing, she stood stock still, her face a blank slate to ensure she gave nothing away.

"I would if you would give me an ironclad agreement to forget you ever saw me. I can draw up the papers and we can meet again tomorrow for you to sign."

She prayed he was greedy enough to jump at the chance she had offered him and, without hesitation, he took the bait.

"Tomorrow then. I'll be here at six and you better not be screwing with me because I have your husband on speed dial and if you're lying, I will finish what I started that first night before handing you back to Richard."

Slamming the door behind him and this time locking it firmly, she shook uncontrollably as the sound of his car slowly faded away. Had she really just gotten away with it she wondered? One thing was for sure, by this time tomorrow she would either be flat broke and on her way to yet another new life, or right back where she started.

CHAPTER EIGHTEEN

"Looks like this is the last meal we'll be sharing for a while," Brandon said as the brothers sat down to lunch. Unable to stomach Brandon any longer, Helen had taken to eating a solitary meal in her cottage and it was just the two of them left in the house. Even Bear had made himself scarce after Brandon had tormented him one too many times under the guise of "playing" with the dog.

Had he heard him right Ben wondered? Something had definitely changed in his demeanor since yesterday and now suddenly he was leaving. The brother who had moped around the house for weeks was suddenly happier than Ben had seen him in years.

"I thought you were penniless and had nowhere to go?" he asked with an eyebrow raised in disbelief.

"There's no harm in admitting it now, but you're right. I was dead broke. Not a penny to my name, and I owe everyone from the dry cleaner to a loan shark. But all that's changed now. By tonight, my problems will be solved."

"Brandon, what's going on?" Ben asked. It was all too suspicious to be believed. He had known Brandon far too long not to suspect something underhanded was going on.

"Nothing except for the fact that I just walked into the sweetest land deal I've ever been part of. But I'm not able to talk about it publicly if you know what I'm saying. Not yet, at least."

Torn between wanting him gone and worrying that he was involved in something illegal, Ben didn't know what to say until he remembered his vow to distance himself from all things involving Brandon.

"So, you'll be leaving? What time?"

"Late this afternoon. I have a few things I have to take care of first, and then I'm out of here."

•   •   •   •   •

Just a few hours later, the brothers said goodbye with little fanfare. Brandon was jumpy as all get-out and Ben was just glad to see the backside of him. Even Helen appeared on the porch to give a half-hearted farewell. By the time his car was out of sight, neither one could quite believe he was actually gone. The atmosphere in the house, which had seemed so tense since Brandon's arrival, already felt lighter and now that Brandon appeared flush with cash, Ben hoped never to see him again. It was a sad way to think about his brother, but his life was already too stressful to want anything different.

It wasn't until he walked back into his office that he noticed the door to the wall safe was slightly ajar and he walked over to it. He had opened it when he returned from Casper, but didn't remember closing the door in that same position. Opening the door fully, it seemed everything was where he had left it, but then he noticed something. The manila envelope of cash he had been keeping for Jordan was missing. God damn Brandon! Had he really stolen from him? Once again, Brandon had made a fool of him. Of course, he took the money. That's why he had been so eager to get out of town. There were thousands of dollars in that envelope; all the money that should have gone to Jordan.

Furious with himself and Brandon, he swore loudly just as Helen appeared in the doorway.

"Ben Anderson!" she admonished at his choice of language. "Whatever is the matter now?"

"That bastard brother of mine stole from me. That's what's wrong," he raged.

"What are you talking about? What did he steal?"

"The cash. He took Jordan's cash right out of the safe like a common criminal. Now what the hell am I going to tell her if she wants the money? There's no way I can replace that much cash on short notice."

"Oh my," Helen said as she wrung her hands on the dish cloth she had been holding. "I think I caused all this."

"Helen, not now. I don't want to hear anyone make excuses for my brother. I'm sick and tired of it."

"Ben, please listen to me. Brandon didn't take the money. I did," she admitted with tears in her eyes.

"What? Why would you do that? If you needed money, you could have just asked. You know I'd do anything for you."

"I know and I appreciate that, but it wasn't for me. Honestly, I thought it would be okay. You always promised Jordan you were just keeping the money until she needed it. I was going to tell you, but it just slipped my mind. Ben, I'm so sorry, but Brandon didn't take it. I took it from the safe and gave it to Jordan."

"You did? But why wouldn't she have come to me if she needed money?" he asked.

The anger had drained from him, replaced by profound sadness as he realized the answer. After everything they had been through together, Jordan didn't trust him enough to ask for her own money, and the thought tore him apart.

"You have to understand Ben, she doesn't want to see you. She won't admit it, but I think this whole breakup has been as hard on her as it has for you. At the time, I thought my bringing the envelope to her would be the easiest thing for both of you. I can see now how wrong I was."

"Did she give you any indication why she needed it now after all this time?" he asked.

She took a deep breath before answering. "I might be wrong, but I think she's leaving town."

His head whipped up at her words, and tears filled his eyes. "Why would you say that? You can't be right!"

"I'm sorry, Ben, but I don't think I'm wrong. When I dropped the money off, the truck was full of boxes and the cabin was almost empty. I think she left town."

"But that makes no sense," he said frantically. "She wouldn't just walk away from the cabin; she loves that place. Her whole life is here."

"That's not exactly true, and you know it. Again, I'm so sorry, but she had a life before she came here and maybe she decided it was time to go back. As much as we both love her, she has secrets we'll never know. It might be time to think about the possibility she went back to her husband."

"No, she would never do that. I know her. She loves me and she would never go back to him," he claimed before burying his face in his hands.

"I'm so very sorry, my dear boy."

The only thing that would mend Ben's broken heart was time and, placing a gentle kiss on his bowed head, she left him to his thoughts.

He sat unmoving for a long time, his mind full of memories of Jordan and their time together, the amazing smile she always directed at him, the way her entire body shook with her laughter at life's joys, and the gentle way she absentmindedly stroked Pete's fur when she was reading. Knowing he would never again experience any of it with her was devastating. Never had a woman more perfectly suited for him been created than Jordan Wheeler, and now she was gone and he was alone. He had given his heart away, and she hadn't even loved him enough to say goodbye before she left. Maybe she had never loved him at all.

His tears replaced by a growing anger, he rushed into her office and threw the door open. The only thing that would make any of this better was to erase every memory of her, and with one quick sweep of his arm he wiped everything from her desk, sending the papers flying across the room like a pile of leaves in a strong breeze.

His momentary anger left as quickly as it came upon him. He stood in the middle of the mess, breathing heavily as he eyed the chaos he had caused before his eyes landed on an upside down law book and an envelope bearing his name peeking out of the pages.

The handwriting was Jordan's, but he knew instinctively this was not another reminder about a case file. Hands still shaking from his fit of rage, he retrieved the envelope and fell heavily into Jordan's desk chair, staring at his name and running his finger lightly over the handwriting. The script was as beautiful to him as the woman who wrote it and he tore it open, pulled out the thick sheaf of pages, and read.

It took nearly an hour by the time he had read and then re-read it several times, not quite believing what Jordan had written.

The dozen pages said everything Jordan could not tell him since the day they met and as he considered the implications of that information, he finally understood why she had so carefully guarded her secrets and the danger she had been in this entire time.

The pages, covered in dense writing on both sides, contained a detailed account of every fraudulent, illegal, and downright cruel thing financier Richard Harvey had done to build his empire. If the proof Jordan had hidden away could be located, Ben knew Harvey would undoubtedly spend the rest of his life in prison.

This was ammunition the FBI and SEC spent years trying to gather on criminals and Jordan had just handed it all over in one fell swoop.

But more so than the allegations of crimes committed by the man, it was the admission that the very man she accused was her husband that terrified him.

Harvey was well-known to Ben's family, yet unlike so many in their wealthy circle of business associates, Ben's father had never done business with him. His father had recognized what few others did not. Harvey was a man for whom ethics and morals didn't exist and he wasn't the type of businessman Ben's father had tolerated. Yet, the man had always seemed to worm his way into the lavish parties thrown by his parents and on more than one occasion, Ben remembered the man being quietly escorted to the door.

The flash of memory of one such moment brought with it another revelation and Ben finally realized after all this time why Jordan had always seemed so familiar to him. She was Victoria Harvey—the woman he had watched from across the room at his parent's anniversary party before she was spirited away by Brandon.

He remembered being curious that in a room full of people she had seemed so very alone and out of place and he couldn't look away from her all evening. She had the look of someone in desperate need of rescue. Even then she had pulled at his heartstrings. She had looked different, of course, but the way she walked and gestured and smiled shyly at those who addressed her was still there.

He had only seen her one other time that night, when she had emerged disheveled from a bedroom with tears streaming down her face after what he had assumed was a liaison with his brother, but he had never got her out of his mind.

An expert judge of character, he had never let himself believe she had been the type to hook up with a random guy in the middle of a party. Knowing that she was possibly married to Richard, he was surer of that than ever and he wondered what had transpired between Jordan and his brother in that bedroom so long ago.

And that's when the lightning bolt struck him.

If he recognized Jordan from that party, Brandon surely had also, and he had as much as admitted she looked familiar to him. Like pieces of a puzzle, it all suddenly fell into place in his mind. Jordan had asked for the money he was keeping for her. Brandon had suddenly come into money. Brandon had to be involved in her sudden decision to leave town. He had to stop both of them before he lost her forever. Grabbing his truck keys, he raced outside, hoping he could still catch her before she left.

CHAPTER NINETEEN

It had been a stressful day of waiting. Everything was packed and stowed in the truck and she had spent most of the day wandering through the woods with Pete or sketching furiously from the porch swing to preserve every memory of this place she loved.

The land transfer documents she had prepared using the knowledge she gained from working for Ben lay on the table, waiting to be executed. That and handing over almost all of her cash was all that remained before Jordan could make her escape. The only thing left to do was pray Brandon showed up.

Six o'clock came and went with no sign of him and just when she was ready to give up and leave town anyway, Pete's ears perked up and Brandon's rental car pulled to a stop in front of the cabin.

The evil smile on his face sent a shiver through her as he got out of the car. Being alone with the man was as uncomfortable now as it had been all those years ago, and she swallowed the bile that had risen in her throat and reminded herself why she was doing this. They stared at each other for a moment before he strode past her and into the kitchen without a word.

"You're late," she said simply because she wasn't sure what else to say.

"Do you have the paperwork?" he asked, as if he hadn't heard what she said. "I've got a plane to catch, so let's get this done with."

"It's there on the table if you want to read it over first," she gestured as she moved to the far corner of the kitchen.

He may have been picking up on Jordan's stress, but Pete planted himself firmly between Jordan and the stranger in the kitchen as a low growl emanated from him. Brandon looked up in surprise and more than a bit of fear.

"Get the dog out of here," he demanded as Jordan's hand automatically went to Pete's collar.

"No, he stays," Jordan said with more assertiveness than she actually felt. Pete was the only thing standing between her and the man who had tried to rape her.

"No, he goes or I place a call to Richard. Your call, but I'm sure you'll do the right thing."

The smugness with which he spoke left no doubt who was in charge of the negotiations and grudgingly Jordan walked Pete to the bathroom and closed him in. Immediately, the dog started scratching at the door and barking furiously.

"Now let's get this over with before I change my mind," Brandon said over the din. "Where's the cash?"

Reaching into her purse, she retrieved the thick envelope.

"I have your word that once this is over, you'll forget you ever saw me?" Jordan wasn't stupid enough to believe he wouldn't go to Richard as soon as he was once again out of money, but it appeared she had no choice.

"Of course," he said smoothly. "Hasn't Ben proved to you we come from an honorable family? Now hand it over and sign the damn papers and if you even try to cheat me, I'll hunt you down and you won't like what I do to you."

Her hands shaking with fear and desperation, Jordan handed over the envelope before picking up the pen and signing away the last thing of any value she owned.

She threw the papers at him as Pete's continued barking became even louder. If she had been paying attention, she would have realized that the angry barks from moments ago had changed into something else.

Brandon calmly folded the papers in half and tucked both that and the envelope of cash into the inside pocket of his suit.

"You've gotten what you asked for. Now please get out," Jordan asked with tears in her eyes before she heard car doors slamming.

Her eyes wide with surprise, she hurried to the window before looking back at Brandon in anger.

"You promised me you wouldn't say anything," she screamed at him. "You promised."

Leaping at him, she punched, hit, scratched, and clawed in a feeble attempt to punish him for betraying her, but he simply wrapped his arms around her until she couldn't move.

She had lived in fear of this day for over a year, and now it had finally come to fruition. The men exiting the vehicles were all part of Richard's security teams. Brandon had betrayed her even though he accepted the money and the land.

"And why not?" he whispered into her ear as he held her prisoner. "I got what I wanted, hell what I deserved after being stuck in this shit hole town for all these weeks, and my good friend Richard gets his lovely bride back. Oh, and did I forget to mention he was so happy to know where you were the reward has already been transferred into my accounts?"

Pushing her away from him so suddenly she lost her balance, Jordan fell to the ground, hitting her head on the corner of the kitchen table on the way down. Blood oozed from a deep gash on her forehead and the room spun as she slowly got to her knees. She crawled on all fours towards the bathroom door and the protection Pete offered before being yanked away at the last minute while the dog's barking became even more furious at the sound of her cries. The bathroom door rattled on its hinges as Pete lunged at it repeatedly in his attempt to get to Jordan's side.

"Shut the damn dog up," Brandon instructed one of the men who had now entered the cabin.

Jordan watched in horror as the man took his gun out and aimed it at the door. She threw herself at his legs in a desperate attempt to save Pete's life, but she wasn't in time. The kitchen echoed with the sound of the gunshot, and Pete's brief cry of pain was all she heard before there was nothing but silence from the other side of the door.

"No!" she screamed before launching herself at Brandon. Unprepared for the onslaught of a woman mad with grief, she knocked him to the ground and pummeled him with every ounce of fury she possessed. The security men watched with amusement before coming to their senses and pulling her away from Brandon.

Getting to his feet, Brandon dusted his suit off before unleashing a slap that caused Jordan's head to snap back.

"You fucking bitch," he spat mere inches from her face as her head rolled from one side to the other with the force of the blow. "You deserve everything that's coming to you. Give her the injection and let's get the hell out of here."

The pain in her arm from the hypodermic needle barely registered before everything went dark and she collapsed to the floor.

CHAPTER TWENTY

All was peaceful as Ben pulled up to the cabin, relieved to see Jordan's truck still there. Racing to the door, he knocked before the door opened on its own, and what he saw caused his heart to stop. Blood spatter covered the kitchen and Jordan was nowhere in sight.

"Jordan! Damn it Jordan, where are you?" he yelled. The house was as still as death until he heard a faint whimper from the direction of the bathroom door. Only then did he notice the bullet hole in the door. "God no," he cried as he slowly opened the door, praying he wouldn't find Jordan's body.

As much as he hated himself for it, he was relieved beyond measure to discover Pete and not Jordan. The dog's thick fur was matted with blood but even with his wounds Pete tried to get to his feet, crying in pain with each attempt before collapsing to the ground again.

Grabbing a towel to stem the blood from the dog's wound, Ben pulled out his cell phone and called 911.

"I'm at the old Olson place and Jordan Wheeler is missing. There's blood everywhere and her dog's been shot. Please send help right away."

He didn't wait for a response and placed his next call to the vet, briefly explaining the situation and asking him to get to the cabin as quickly as possible before hanging up. More than anything, he wanted to keep looking for Jordan, but she would never forgive him if she came home to find he had abandoned Pete. It seemed to take forever before he heard sirens in the distance and the glade filled with law enforcement vehicles. The red, white, and blue of their strobe lights bounced off the trees surrounding the glade, creating a surreal atmosphere as their cars screamed to a stop and men flew out of the vehicles. Just a quick look around the cabin was all the Officers needed before fanning out into the woods to search for Jordan.

Dr. Norris wasn't far behind the deputies and, with just a quick look at Pete's wounds, he scooped the dog up and immediately raced back to the clinic with promises to do everything he could to save him.

Ben's heart was pounding in his chest, but knowing that help had arrived, he worked to calm himself down and provide as much information on what he thought was happening as possible. Pulling the Sheriff aside, he quietly explained who Jordan really was. Even folks in Wyoming had heard stories of Richard Harvey and the Sheriff quickly placed a call to the FBI field office in Casper. After several hours of searching and with no sign of Jordan anywhere near the cabin, everyone pulled back to the Sheriff's Office just as the FBI arrived.

"Mr. Anderson? Supervising Special Agent Monroe and ASA Sanderson from the FBI. The Sheriff has filled us in on Ms. Wheeler's disappearance and he said you have some evidence that might point a finger at her husband. Why don't you tell us what you know and how you know it?"

For the next hours Ben told them everything he knew about Richard Harvey and his illegal business dealings. The agents listened intently, jotting down the occasional note or stepping outside the interview room to make a phone call, and Ben was becoming frustrated. Nothing they were doing was helping them find Jordan, and the sun was coming up. She had been missing for hours and Harvey could have done anything to her in that time.

"And you say you have proof of all this?" Agent Monroe said.

"Not me, but Jordan. As I already told you, the letter she left for me says exactly where the information is."

"And of course, you'll hand over the letter," the other agent said.

Ben had spent some time thinking of just that and realized that everything in the letter could open Jordan to prosecution even if she hadn't realized it when she wrote it.

"That can be arranged in exchange for full immunity for my client."

The men exchanged glances and Ben kept silent. Jordan hadn't officially retained him as her attorney, but he couldn't sit idly by and watch her throw her life away for Richard Harvey either.

"As an officer of the court, I know you'll keep this under your hat, but the FBI has spent a year working with SEC and ATF officials on a case against Harvey. He's just savvy enough to have covered his tracks until now. So, I wouldn't hesitate to say that if what you've told us checks out, I think we could work a deal," Monroe told him. "Of course, it would be up to the New York State's Attorney to make the final determination."

"Then you better place the call because you're not getting anything without it," Ben said confidently. If there was one thing he had learned from all his years working in D.C., the feds would move heaven and earth to prosecute someone like Harvey. "Now, what are you doing to find Jordan?"

"It looks like Harvey has her."

Ben's blood ran cold at the words.

"A small Lear jet apparently landed several hours ago at a private air strip about an hour from here and it took off just a few hours later. According to the owner of the property, he was paid in cash to keep his mouth shut, but he thought it was all suspicious and was watching with binoculars when the men returned. He swears there was an extra man with them when they left."

"And what does that have to do with Jordan?"

"He claimed they carried something to the plane . . . something that looked like a body."

His breath caught in his chest as he processed what the Agent said and he tried to stay calm. Losing it just when Jordan needed him most wouldn't help her.

"But if they had killed her, why would they take her body with them? Why not just leave it here?" Ben asked.

"Our thoughts exactly. We think she's still alive."

CHAPTER TWENTY-ONE

Opening her eyes in the darkness, it was easy to believe she was still safe in the cabin, but Jordan only had to reach out her hand for Pete to remember the man that killed him and she immediately burst into tears.

Brandon had betrayed her, and she was now apparently Richard's captive. Everything that had meant anything to her was gone and even if Richard didn't kill her, her life might just as well be over.

Weak and dizzy from whatever they had injected her with, she seemed unhurt except for the cut on her forehead and a swollen cheek where Brandon had struck her and she tried to take stock of her surroundings. The unfamiliar room had only one small window near the ceiling. Too small to squeeze her body through, even if she could have found a way around the metal bars crisscrossing the glass, it was worthless to her. Moving her hands along the walls in the near darkness, she bumped into the door handle and pulled with all her might, but it didn't budge. Placing her ear to the door, she could hear faint voices, but nothing clear enough to make out what the people on the other side had been discussing. The only thing she knew for sure was she wasn't in the penthouse. If such a room had existed, she would surely have found it in all those years with Richard.

Just then, she heard a key in the door and she backed away in fear to the far corner of the room as the door opened. Light flooded the dismal space, and she turned towards the door, expecting to see Richard. Instead, she saw only Brandon. She felt a slight moment of satisfaction to see that her assault at the cabin had left its own mark. He sported two black eyes and a large cut on his lip.

"Where am I?" she demanded.

"What's the matter?" he sneered. "Accommodation not up to your usual standards? It's only temporary until Richard gets here, I assure you. That should be any minute now, although when he arrives I expect you might beg him to stay where you are. I've never heard him so furious with anyone. Apparently, you have something that belongs to him and he wants it back. That's the funny thing about all this. Everyone assumed he wanted you back, but I guess he doesn't give a shit about you. He wants what you took from him. Now he didn't actually tell me what that was, but judging by the millions he paid me to bring you back, I'll wager it's something pretty damning. Your wonderful husband hasn't always played by the rules and everyone around him knew that. But that's none of my business. With the money he paid me and the land you signed over to me, I'll never have to see either of you again."

As he was speaking, he had moved closer and closer and was now standing directly in front of Jordan; so close she could feel his breath on her face.

"But before hubby gets here, you and I have unfinished business."

Before she could react his hand reached under her dress and ripped her panties apart as he pushed her up against the wall. As he worked to unzip his pants, Jordan struggled ineffectively against his assault. Brandon was about to finish what he had tried so long ago, and there was nothing she could do to stop him.

"Harrington, you bastard, leave her alone."

If only the voice shouting into the room had been Ben's, Jordan could have relaxed. Instead, she opened her eyes to see the one face she feared more than any other.

"I told you I didn't want her harmed," Richard said as he took in the scene and Brandon hurried to zip his pants up. "Get out." As Brandon scurried out of the room, Richard's calm demeanor became more frightening than if he had been shouting and she trembled.

Richard wasted no time on small talk. His blow came hard and fast across Jordan's face, sending her flying across the room before he turned and walked out, locking the door securely behind him. Her hand to her throbbing jaw, Jordan struggled onto the cot and curled into a ball as silent tears wet the pillow. The blow was certainly expected, but why hadn't he said anything? None of this made sense. Was it simply psychological torture besides the physical abuse? She shouldn't be surprised by anything Richard did, but his unpredictability frightened her the most. What would he do next?

She didn't have long to wait. The scene was replayed several times a day for the next several days until Jordan was in too much pain to even stand when he came into the room. Filthy and starving, her determination to fight back waning, she looked up at the face she had once loved when Richard unexpectedly pulled a stool into the room and placed it in front of her cot.

"Where is it?" he asked quietly. She had known it all along. The only thing that mattered to him was the flash drive and he apparently now felt he had broken her down enough to get her to talk.

"Some place you'll never find it and my attorney has instructions to release it to the feds if anything happens to me," she whispered. She had always known how this would end, and she didn't care anymore. At least if he killed her, the torture would be over and Ben would eventually find the letter and make sure Richard got what was coming to him.

"Come now, my dear, that's not true and we both know it. You would never have been so clever. I'll ask you once again, where is it?"

"I told you. And if you do anything to me, all the horrible things you have done will become public and you'll spend the rest of your life in an orange jumpsuit. But if you just let me go, no one will be the wiser. I'll disappear and you'll never see me again. Your secrets will be safe."

"Do you remember what I told you so long ago?" he spat at her. "No one ever leaves Richard Harvey. No, I think I will just keep you close to me until you tell me where the drive is and then I'll decide what to do with you. If the feds come looking for me, you'll be in that jumpsuit along with me and let me tell you something, my dear . . . orange is definitely not your color. But just in case that's not enough incentive, I want you to think about your parents and those people back in Wyoming who Brandon tells me mean so much to you. I've grown tired of this game we've been playing, so for everyday that I don't get what I want, one of those people you care so much about is going to die until you have no one left. You have one day to tell me where it is and if you don't, their death will be on you. Even someone as simple as you can understand that, right? The clock is ticking, my love."

Turning on his heel, he walked out the door.

CHAPTER TWENTY-TWO

It had already been a stressful week of empty leads and dead ends in the search for Jordan until they caught a lucky break. The owner of the air strip where the plane had originally landed finally remembered a portion of the plane's tail number. It wasn't the whole number, but the FBI quickly connected what he could remember to a plane leased to Richard Harvey. When faced with FBI agents at his doorstep, the pilot was more than willing to talk and they confirmed the passenger manifest had increased by two when the plane departed Wyoming headed for upstate New York. As the investigation moved to New York, Ben had two very important jobs to do before he could make his own way back east.

"How's our patient doing today?" Ben asked as he and Bear walked into the vet's office.

"Why don't you see for yourself," Dr. Norris said with a smile before opening the half door that separated his waiting room from the rest of the clinic.

The door was hardly open before Pete came barreling into the room, tail wagging furiously, giving happy little barks as he danced in excitement around Ben and Bear. Ben had visited every day since the dog had undergone emergency surgery to repair the damage from the bullet, and his recovery had been nothing short of miraculous. The only lasting reminder of that day was the large patch of shaved fur and the already healing incision. Jordan would be thrilled . . . if only they could find her.

"Like I told you on the phone, he needs to be kept quiet, if that's possible. No jumping or running. Just slow walks for the next couple of weeks."

"Helen will make sure of it," Ben assured him as he clipped Pete's leash to his collar. Tempted to run his fingers around the inside of the dog's collar, he resisted the urge until a more private moment.

"Any word on Jordan?"

As contentious as their previous interactions had been, Ben had realized over the last few days how much the veterinarian cared for Jordan. That shared concern seemed to have formed the basis for a friendship between the two men, and Ben smiled sadly at him.

"Nothing concrete, but the investigation is now focused back on New York. I'm headed there later tonight."

"Bring our girl home, will you?" Kevin asked, as the two men shook hands.

"I'll do my best."

•　•　•　•　•

Ben had one more stop to make before he could leave for the airport. When they reached the cabin, Ben helped Pete out of the truck and called both dogs to him. Taking a deep breath, he said a quick prayer before removing Pete's collar and feeling its smooth leather in order to find the bump that shouldn't be there. Pulling a small knife from the glove box of the truck, he carefully cut through the leather to reveal the out of place flash drive. Smiling to himself at Jordan's ingenuity to place the evidence in the collar of a dog who most people were too afraid to approach, he was reminded yet again of how much thought she had put into her plan. But had it been enough?

Who knew what kind of hell Harvey was putting her through if she was still alive? He was sure it was Harvey who had taken her and if Jordan's letter was accurate, Ben knew the man would use force against her now. They had to find her, and soon, before there was nothing left to find, and if the FBI couldn't do it, he would confront Harvey himself if that's what it took to get her back. But first, he needed to collect the rest of the documents Jordan had hidden in the woods. Following the very specific instructions she had left for him; he went straight to the large patch of wild blueberries along the trail behind the cabin and dug up the securely wrapped package before heading home to pack for New York.

.　.　.　.　.

The darkness in Jordan's prison room should have helped her sleep but since Richard's most recent threat, she couldn't close her eyes without seeing someone she loved being killed. She had spent hours laying on her cot staring into the darkness while running through every scenario in her mind.

Wavering between fear Richard would actually carry through on his threats and doubt he could actually take a human life, she didn't know what to do. The copies she had made and whatever was on the flash drive were the only insurance she had against Richard carrying out his threats and she prayed Ben had already discovered the information and gone to the authorities with it, but what if that wasn't the case?

Tempted to provide all kinds of false information that would lead Richard on a wild goose chase to forestall the inevitable, she hesitated. Any lies she might tell could mean someone she loved would die, and she wasn't willing to take that chance. Unless she actually turned the materials over, someone might die anyway. Either way, it would all be her fault and she couldn't live with that thought. The smart thing to do was to give Richard what he wanted and be done with it, but as he reminded her repeatedly, she wasn't exactly smart.

One thing she knew for sure, however. Once Richard had the drive and the documents, he would have no further use for her. A small part of her hoped he would just let her go once he got what he wanted, but logically, she knew that would never happen. She was a liability, a loose end, and Richard had always done whatever was necessary to tie up loose ends.

Trying to calculate how much time she had left before Richard appeared in front of her, all she could think about were the faces of the people she loved, who were now in grave danger even if they didn't realize it. Ben's face was front and center and tears came to her eyes at the thought of any harm coming to him. If she had succeeded in disappearing, her life would have been hard enough without him in it, but the thought of a world permanently without Ben was more than she could bear.

.   .   .   .   .

Since his arrival in New York, Ben had camped out in the office of the State's Attorney General working to hammer out an immunity agreement for Jordan.

He had played a cat-and-mouse game with the staff there as they demanded proof of what was contained in Jordan's evidence, but he demanded an agreement be executed before giving them anything. In the end, and after an entire year investigating Harvey with not enough concrete evidence to make an arrest, Ben prevailed and the Attorney General agreed to give Jordan full immunity. The deal had been signed, sealed, and delivered to Ben and he had turned over all of Jordan's evidence, leaving him with little to occupy his time.

Unlike back in Wyoming, where he could actually sit in on the investigative meetings, the joint task force in New York had shut him out completely, and now even SSA Monroe was refusing to give him updates on the investigation. The Agent had even suggested Ben wait some place other than FBI headquarters. Left with no choice, he called Helen and gave her a quick update before hailing a cab to his parents' home.

"Sweetheart, welcome," his mother said as she opened her arms to extend a warm greeting to her son.

The luxury brownstone was his childhood home and represented security and comfort to him. He felt it again the moment he stepped across the threshold. The mansion stood shoulder to shoulder with multi-million dollar residences in a quiet neighborhood across from Central Park. Growing up, it had been the perfect mixture of family life and New York elegance, yet these days the four-story brownstone was thousands of square feet more than his mother and stepfather needed.

Seeing his mother helped ease his worry about Jordan, and he wrapped his arms around her fashionably thin frame and pulled her close without saying a word. Always in tune with her children, she waited for him to release her before asking what was wrong.

"As much as I love seeing you, what's going on, Ben?"

"Oh, Mom, I don't even know where to start. Is Jim here? You both should hear what I have to say and I'm not sure I have it in me to tell the story more than once."

"What have you gotten yourself into now and how did Brandon convince you to do it?" came the gruff voice of his stepfather.

As the men exchanged their own greetings, they made their way into the expensively appointed living room. No prompting was needed for Ben to begin the story, going all the way back to the very first time he saw Jordan run by the house. The only thing he left out was the depth of Brandon's suspected involvement in it all. By the time he finished, the sun had long set, and they had moved into the dining room and were finishing their meal.

"I just wish I knew what was going on now," Ben lamented as he got up from the table and paced around the room. "It's the not knowing that's so hard."

"I can make a call if you think that would help," his stepfather offered. Unlike Richard Harvey, James Harrington was well respected by everyone at City Hall and at 1 Police Plaza.

"Unfortunately, I'm not sure in this case you'd get much further," Ben admitted. "I know you haven't had business dealings with Harvey, but like so many in your social circle, you are acquaintances and the feds are keeping a tight lid on whatever they are doing."

"Maybe I shouldn't ask this, Ben, but your interest in this woman . . . it's more than just friendship, isn't it?" his mother asked.

Unsure how to explain his true feelings for Jordan, he had left that important component out of his story but his mother had always been able to read him.

"I love her," he admitted. "And she loves me and I had hoped to spend the rest of my life with her, but she was so afraid of Harvey she told me it was over. I know she planned to leave town to protect me, but he took her before she could run."

"What am I missing?" his stepfather asked. "What is Brandon's connection to Jordan?"

"At first I didn't think there was a connection until I realized Brandon recognized Jordan." How could he possibly explain his suspicions about what Jordan and Brandon had been doing in that bedroom in this very house? But the time for secrets was long gone.

"Do you remember that big anniversary party you had here a few years ago? That's when I saw Jordan for the first time and also when Brandon met her. Just before you threw Harvey and his friends out of the house, I saw Jordan come out of Brandon's bedroom and she had been crying."

"Oh Ben, you don't think . . .?" his mother said, her eyes were wide with fear and revulsion.

"I don't know what to think about that night, but I know that Brandon thought he recognized her, and he's too smart not to have finally figured it out. It probably doesn't matter though because he had been staying with me and he left for D.C. hours before Jordan went missing."

"At the risk of causing any more drama, I think you should know that Brandon isn't in D.C.," James said.

"What do you mean, dear?"

"I really didn't want to tell you this, Lillian, but Brandon called me two days ago. He claimed to have come into possession of hundreds of acres of land prime for development, and he wanted me to partner with him. When I pressed him for details, he hesitated until I told him I wouldn't consider anything until knowing more. Then he said the land was in Wyoming and he had just flown back on a private plane after purchasing the property. He said he was in upstate New York."

He hesitated, as if unsure whether to continue.

"What aren't you saying?" Ben asked. Already, the hairs on the back of his neck were standing at attention.

"The plane was Richard Harvey's."

"Oh my god. If he was on Harvey's plane, the same plane the FBI is convinced was used to bring Jordan back to New York, then Brandon is involved in all of this. I'm going to kill him!" Ben shouted.

"Please Ben, don't say things you don't mean. I know it looks bad for Brandon, but maybe it's all a coincidence," his mother cautioned.

"Mom, I know you want to believe the best of your sons, but it's time we all admitted that there is something wrong with Brandon and there always has been. He's up to his eyeballs in this mess and if any harm comes to Jordan, there won't be any place on God's earth that Brandon can hide from me. Thank you for dinner, but I need to let the FBI know what you just told me."

After exchanging quick goodbyes, Ben headed for the FBI office at Federal Plaza, armed with the fresh evidence.

.   .   .   .   .

"I should have known Brandon was involved," Ben stated after sharing what he knew with the investigators. "It was too much of a coincidence that he just up and left after pleading poverty all those weeks."

"Is there any chance that he might have been on a legitimate business trip to buy this land?" Agent Monroe asked.

"He owes money to everyone on the east coast," Ben assured him. "If he came into possession of the land, there was something illegal about how he got it, I guarantee it."

For a few minutes, the group was silent as they considered Brandon's involvement in Jordan's disappearance.

"If your brother is still with Ms. Wheeler, we might be able to target their location through his cell phone. Do you think he would take a call from you, or would he suspect something was up if you reached out to him?" Agent Monroe asked.

"Brandon is the most egotistical person I have ever met and he would never suspect I figured out his connection to Harvey. I'm sure he would take the call."

After a bit of coaching on what to say, they arranged the call with technicians seated nearby to make the trace.

"Hey baby brother! Miss me already?" Brandon said happily.

Knowing that he might very well be involved in Jordan's disappearance, Ben worked hard to control his fury and stick to the script they had provided him.

"Actually, I just called to make sure you made it home okay. That was a long drive to make by yourself."

"It would have been, but I ended up catching a ride with a friend. Flew home in style as a matter of fact on a private Lear jet. Nothing but first class for this guy, I'll tell you that."

"Oh really," Ben said sarcastically before Agent Monroe raised an eyebrow at him and waved his hand to indicate Ben should keep talking. "I talked to Jim today, and he said you asked him to partner with you on some land deal. You didn't tell me the land you bought was in Wyoming. Where exactly is it? Maybe you and I should do something together."

The line was silent, and Ben knew his brother was trying to find a plausible excuse to avoid telling the truth.

"I don't want to hurt your feelings, bro, but the amount of money we're talking about here is a little out of your league. Even Jim took a pass on it."

Just then, Ben noticed activity around him and realized the FBI had locked on to Brandon's location as agents flew out of the room.

"That's too bad. Listen Brandon, I'm late for a meeting, but I'm sure we'll be in touch soon. See ya."

If Brandon was at all concerned about the abrupt end to the phone call, Ben couldn't have cared less. He was up to his neck in this whole thing and, brother or not, Ben hoped he got what was coming to him.

Agent Monroe remained nearby as he stared at the computer screen the technician was working on.

"There it is," he said excitedly. "Harvey owns that abandoned warehouse, and I'm willing to bet that's where he's keeping Ms. Wheeler."

Grabbing his coat to leave, Ben's hand on his arm stopped the Agent in his tracks.

"Wait a minute," Ben told him. "I'm coming too."

"Regulations don't allow a civilian . . ."

"I don't give a damn what your regulations allow," Ben told him. "If this is going to lead us to Jordan, then come hell or high water, I'm going to be there."

After studying him for a moment, the Agent finally relented. "Well then, I hope you don't get air sick because the helicopter will be here soon.

CHAPTER TWENTY-THREE

By the time Richard finally returned to the dank little room, Jordan was sick with worry but also brimming with confidence. Of all the evil things he had done, murder was never on the list and she just couldn't let herself believe he would risk his empire now by harming the people who were important to her. And to convince her to keep her mouth shut, she had another sign. The voice of doom that had been nagging away at her for months had completely disappeared and as the minutes ticked by before Richard's ultimatum, the strength she would need to do what was right after all this time was growing by leaps and bounds. As he walked up to her, she straightened her back and stood up, standing toe to toe with him.

"Well, what is it to be?" he spat at her. There was no emotion in his face and for a moment she stared at him, trying to remember what about the man had so captivated her so very long ago.

"I've already told you. The flash drive and all the information I copied are already in the hands of my attorney. Even if I wanted to give it to you, and trust me, I don't, it's too late."

She braced herself for the blow she was sure would follow her declaration and yet other than a slight narrowing of his eyes, he didn't move.

"Pick one." His voice was devoid of any emotion.

"One what?"

"Pick the loved one you want to die first. I told you what would happen if you didn't cooperate and their death is going to be on you. So, pick one."

"I won't and you know something, Richard? You're not going to kill anyone and you know why I know that? Because you would rather die yourself than spend the rest of your life in prison, that's why. You know I'm telling the truth and hurting someone I love still won't get you what you're looking for. I'm telling the truth about my attorney having the evidence, and you know me well enough to know it."

"Would that be the same attorney you've been shacked up with for the past year?" he sneered. It did not surprise her that he knew about Ben. Brandon's words flowed like vomit when he wanted something, and she was sure he had filled Richard in on everything between her and his brother.

"Brandon's brother, right? Harrington, get in here," he shouted over his shoulder.

"Did the bitch give you what you want?" Brandon said as he walked into the room. "Maybe now I can get what I want from her."

"Keep your dick in your pants," Richard told him angrily. "Where's your brother? The attorney. Where is he right now?"

"How the hell am I supposed to know?" Brandon exclaimed. The look of superiority that had been on his face since she had signed over her land disappeared at Harvey's question; replaced with a look of concern. "I suppose he's still in that horrible town in Wyoming. Why? What does it matter?"

"Because if what she says is true, we're going to make a trade. Get him on the phone."

"Now, Richard," Brandon said hesitantly, "we don't need to involve my brother in this. I thought I was just supposed to deliver the bitch to you and that would be the end. I don't want to bring my brother into it."

Snapping his head around, Richard thundered at him. "You stupid fool, he's been involved from the beginning! For all I know, they cooked up her disappearance together. He has the flash drive and something tells me he knows exactly what to do with it. Now get him on the phone."

Jordan had been listening carefully, but she was also watching the sizeable gap between the men and the wide-open door. She moved so fast Brandon had to leap out of her way, but Richard was lightning fast and just as she reached the threshold, he grabbed a handful of hair, stopping her in her tracks as she screamed in pain. Dragging her back into the room by her hair, he threw her down on the cot.

"Try that again and I'll do more than just pull your hair," he spat at her. "Brandon. Phone. Now!"

Pulling the phone from his pants pocket, Brandon dialed the number and handed the phone back to Richard. Ben answered on the first ring.

"Brandon, I can't talk now," he said quickly.

"So, I finally get to meet the man who's been screwing my wife for a year. Ben, is it?" At the sound of Ben's voice, Jordan got up screaming from the cot before Harvey shoved her back down and clapped his free hand over her mouth.

"Harvey, I swear if you harm a hair on her head I'll kill you myself."

"Now why would you think I'd harm my dear Victoria? Excuse me, my bad. What name is it she goes by these days? Jordan is it? She's perfectly fine, as you can hear yourself. Come, my dear, say something to let your lover know you're okay."

Holding the phone out in Jordan's direction, all she could manage was a "Ben, I'm . . .," before Richard backhanded her across the face and she went flying across the room.

The sound of his blow and Jordan's cry of pain echoed in the small room and he let the sound sink in Ben's head before he said anything further.

"Well, maybe she's not exactly okay," Harvey laughed into the phone. "But she's well enough and funny thing is, it appears you're the only one that can keep her that way. Bring me the flash drive and I'll let her go. You have two days and if you don't show up, you can start looking for her body. I'll text you instructions tomorrow, but if you contact the police, you'll never see your girlfriend again."

"Two days isn't long enough. I don't even know if I can get a flight," Ben said, stalling for time.

"You'll make it work if you want to see her alive again," Richard told him before abruptly hanging up and staring at Jordan.

"Let's hope your boyfriend is as resourceful as his brother, or in forty-eight hours, you'll never see him again."

Shoving Brandon out of the doorway, Richard stormed from the room. To his credit, Brandon now looked like he was about to empty the contents of his stomach in front of her until he too gave her one last look and walked out as the door slammed shut behind him.

.   .   .   .   .

The call had come just as they were boarding the helicopter.

Harvey might not have realized it, but he had provided ironclad proof that not only was Jordan still alive, but he was the one who had her and Ben's own brother was definitely involved. With everything they now knew about the man, it seemed Harvey was getting more desperate by the hour, and Monroe signaled for the helicopter pilot to cut the engine as they pulled back to regroup after the latest development.

This time as plans were made for Jordan's extraction, Ben was included, mostly because he refused to be shut out again, but also because Harvey apparently had no clue the FBI was involved. Ben was expected to deliver the evidence that could put him behind bars.

Relegated to being a silent observer as the plan was laid out, Ben didn't mind. There were decades of expertise in the room with hostage negotiators, sharp shooters, technology experts, and others, all working in tandem to develop the plan. Richard's text had demanded delivery of the information to the same warehouse they had already identified as Harvey's, along with a not too subtle reminder to keep the police away or Jordan would pay the price.

To Ben more than any of them, the picture Harvey had also sent of Jordan cowering in the corner of a dark room was incentive enough to make sure they covered every probability. Jordan's life was at stake.

Just hours before the handover was to take place, the room was alive with activity. High on copious amounts of coffee and adrenalin fueled by the excitement of the chase, the strike team was at fever pitch. Agents packed their gear and double checked their ammunition while a technician threaded a miniature camera into the collar of Ben's shirt.

"Remember to be yourself, Ben. Anyone in this position would be nervous. If you look overly confident, it might tip Harvey off that we're in place," Agent Monroe told him.

"I understand," Ben assured him as he rocked back and forth on his feet. He was as jumpy as a cat and anything but confident. The smallest mistake on his part could cost Jordan her life and if that happened, he could never live with himself.

"The camera on your shirt and the drone above will be our eyes and ears while you make the handoff and naturally we're also going to put you in a vest just to keep you safe."

"But won't Harvey's men know I'm wearing a vest?" Looking around the room at the men as they suited up, the vests were clearly visible.

"Harvey's men have never met you and don't know your body type. With the shirt and jacket on, they won't even realize you're wearing one. Now, do you have the drive and the copies of Jordan's documents?"

Determined to make Harvey believe they were complying with his demands, a duplicate flash drive had been created, along with copies of the paper documents.

Unless Harvey immediately put the drive in a computer, he wouldn't know it was a fake until it was too late.

"Yes," Ben said as he reached for the satchel he would hand over to Harvey. "And I don't hand it over until Jordan is right in front of me."

"That's right. Once Harvey has the documents in his hand and you give us the code word, that's when we'll move in. If anyone looks like they intend to harm Jordan, the sharpshooters will take them out."

"Okay. I'm ready." The agent did not miss the slight tremor in his voice.

"Hey man, you know you don't have to do this. We can have one of our agents take your place if you want to back out. No one would blame you if you're scared."

"No, I'll do it. You might not blame me, but I would blame myself. I should have realized long ago that Jordan was in danger and I let her put me off too many times. This is my job and mine alone."

"You're a brave man," the agent said as he clapped him on the back. "Now let's go bring your girlfriend home."

. . . . .

Walking up to the warehouse, Ben's hands were so sweaty he felt his grip slip on the satchel and he quickly wiped them on his pants. His instructions had been quite specific. Under no circumstances was he to enter the structure. He stopped a good fifty yards from the building and looked around him at the rooftops and every window of the warehouse. He had been told to expect his every movement was being watched and even as Agent Monroe talked softly in his ear, he remained still. The creak of a metal door opening brought his attention back to ground level as Harvey, trailed by a handful of his men all carrying automatic rifles, walked towards him. Scanning the group Ben was relieved to see Brandon wasn't among them. As furious as he was with Brandon for his role in Jordan's disappearance, Ben couldn't help but be grateful he wouldn't be involved should the exchange go bad.

"If I didn't already know you were a twin, I might have easily mistaken you for Brandon, but then again, there's something less weasel-like about you I think," Harvey said with a laugh when they were only twenty feet apart.

"Where's Jordan?" Ben asked immediately. There was a time for small talk and this wasn't it.

"My aren't we the eager beaver. She'll be along shortly, but first let me see my property."

"It's in the bag, but you're not getting it until I see Jordan."

Harvey considered his demand for a moment before whispering something to the man on his right. The man and one of the others immediately turned back to the warehouse and disappeared inside as Ben and Harvey stared each other down without a word. It didn't take long before the door opened once again and Ben got his first look at Jordan.

Dirty and disheveled, her face and body covered in bruises and congealed blood, the men had to help her walk as they came forward, but even so Ben's heart filled with love and his back straightened with resolve. One way or another, he vowed to himself, they were going to get out of this unharmed. It took a moment for Jordan to realize Ben was standing in front of her. When she did, she immediately tried to go to him, but Richard's men held her firmly in their grasp.

"Are you okay sweetheart?" Ben asked gently. His blood boiled at what Harvey or his men had done to her and his hands curled into fists at his side.

Tears now falling freely down her face, she could only nod her head in response as she tried to smile back at him.

"Isn't that sweet," Harvey mocked. "Do I need to remind you that's my wife you're addressing? So now you've seen her. I want the drive so hand it over."

Mindful of what the agents had instructed him to do, Ben didn't move.

"You're the ones with the guns, so hand over Jordan first and then I'll give you the bag." Opening the bag, he showed them the contents before closing it securely again. "See it's everything you asked for. Now let her go."

For the first time Harvey actually hesitated before looking at the same man who had brought Jordan out. The two consulted for a moment before Harvey nodded his head and the man grabbed Jordan's arm even tighter and walked her forward. When they were within arm's reach of Ben, the man shoved her forward and she fell into Ben's arms. More than anything he wanted to wrap his arms around her and run, but the deal wasn't done yet and he eased Jordan behind him.

Picking up the satchel at his feet, he tossed it to Harvey who grabbed greedily for it, rummaging inside to find the drive which he quickly pocketed in his inside suit coat pocket.

"Thank you," he sneered. "I have to hand it to you, being Harrington's brother and all, I really didn't think you'd show up. It took a lot of balls I'll give you that."

"So, we're free to go?" Ben asked. He had been repeating the line over and over in his head. It was the previously agreed upon code that the deal was done and the feds could move in.

"Not quite," Harvey said smoothly before turning to face the men at his side. "Get rid of them."

In tandem, the weapons of all of Harvey's men pointed at Ben and Jordan as red dots danced across their bodies. Jordan looked up at Ben in horror before a shot rang out and one of Harvey's men dropped to the ground as the others looked around in confusion.

"FBI," came the voice over the bullhorn. "Drop your weapons."

While his men immediately complied, Harvey took off running for the relative safety of the warehouse as the agents surrounding the property gave chase. With only a hasty apology to Jordan, Ben joined the chase. His speed no match for the much older and out of shape man, Ben quickly caught up with him and leapt onto his back. Harvey flew face first into the dirt.

Ben's pent up rage and fear took over, and he flipped Harvey onto his back before closing his hands around his neck. Harvey's eyes bulged with fear and his face was mottled in crimson as he fought ineffectively against Ben's onslaught. As his eyes rolled back in his head Ben eased his hold.

"Anderson you have to let him go," Agent Monroe told him as he came up from behind. "We've got this now and he'll never hurt you or Jordan again."

It wasn't until Ben felt Jordan's hand on his cheek that he released his hold. Shoving Harvey's head once more into the dirt, he got to his feet and took his first deep breath since discovering Jordan had been taken. With tears in his eyes, he pulled her to him as the FBI cuffed Harvey and took him into custody.

"I knew you'd come," she whispered, her arms securely around him. "I just knew it."

Ben had spent days thinking of what he would say to Jordan if he could only see her again and now, overcome with emotion, he was speechless. Lowering his lips to her forehead, he placed a gentle kiss on the one spot not covered in bruises.

"Let's go home," he whispered into her ear before taking her hand.

"Ben," came Brandon's cry from the door to the warehouse. "Tell them I had nothing to do with this. Harvey conned me. This is all a mistake. Let me go, you son of a bitch. That's my brother—he can vouch for me."

Two agents were dragging an uncooperative Brandon from the warehouse.

"Sorry man. I know he's your brother and all, but . . ." the Agent holding Brandon said as they came closer and Brandon continued to struggle.

The pleading on Brandon's face was something Ben had seen his entire life, but he had finally had enough.

"I don't have a brother," Ben said before taking Jordan's hand and walking away as Brandon began screaming obscenities at them.

"Are you sure you don't want to help him?" Jordan asked. "I don't want you to have any regrets."

"My only regret is that I didn't do it earlier. Let's get out of here."

CHAPTER TWENTY-FOUR

After an overnight stay in the hospital, the rest of her time in New York had been spent with attorneys and investigators from the State's Attorney General, the FBI, and the SEC. Even as battered and bruised as she was, Jordan didn't hesitate to tell her story repeatedly. Whatever it took to put Richard behind bars was fine with her and each night when they returned to Ben's parents' house, she was asleep as soon as her head hit the pillow.

As news of Richard's arrest hit the airwaves, a ripple effect had gone through the New York elite. Anyone who had even the remotest association with him in the past worked frantically to disassociate themselves from him. The man who had instilled such fear in his business associates was now reviled by poor and rich alike and no one wanted to be tainted by any connection to him.

Ashamed of the notoriety she had caused for Ben and his family, Jordan had at first resisted when Ben suggested they stay with his parents. Not only were they now aware of the sordid details of her marriage to Richard, but also of her affair with their son and she was sure they would hate her for it. But quite the opposite happened. Ben's mother welcomed her with open arms and with an intuition very much like Ben, her focus was more on Jordan's well-being than the drama that had brought her to their doorstep. Within days they had made Jordan so comfortable she began talking about what she had gone through with no prompting, surprising not only herself but Ben as well.

Jordan's part in the investigation completed for now, she had been told it would be months before she would need to return for the court case against Richard. They could finally return home, but their departure was sure to create yet another media spectacle.

Jordan's picture had been plastered across the globe as the international ramifications of Richard's misdeeds became public knowledge. She couldn't so much as step outside without someone photographing her. Never comfortable in the spotlight, she dreaded the scene that was sure to erupt at the airport until learning Ben's stepfather had arranged for a private plane to take them home.

Ben hadn't left her side for a moment and even when they were sitting side by side on the plane, they held hands. After weeks of stress and worry, she could finally relax. He turned to look at her as she emitted a deep sigh.

"Everything okay?"

She had been about to tell him she was fine, but remembered there would be no more secrets between them.

"I'm tired, but happy," she told him truthfully. "I can't wait to go home."

"Would you hate me very much if I told you we are going to take a brief detour? There are some people who want to see you."

Her eyes began to tear up, and she knew instinctively he was talking about her parents.

"Ben I'm not sure that's a good idea," she said. "My dad, well you don't understand how angry he is at me."

"Actually, he's the one who reached out to me. Jordan, he wants to see you. He wants to tell you how much he loves you."

The tears now fell in earnest. "Are you sure?" she asked in a whisper.

"Have I ever lied to you?" he answered with a smile. "Just a quick visit for now and then who knows? Maybe we'll have that family Christmas yet."

If she needed any more proof that Ben was the man for her, she had only to remember what followed as Jordan's reunion with her parents exceeded her wildest expectations. She had been trembling with nervousness as the plane taxied to a stop at the private airport, her hand grasping Ben's tightly as they walked into the terminal where Ben had arranged for her parents to meet them. Then she saw them and just like that, her fear went away.

Her mother rushed to gather Jordan into her arms and over her shoulder Jordan could see her father, reserved as always but directing a smile her way; a smile she hadn't seen in a dozen years and Jordan reached out her hand as he too rushed to hold his long-lost daughter. Once they started they never stopped talking and apologizing to one another. The scheduled one-hour meeting turned into two before it was time to go.

"Call us when you get home so we know you're safe," her mother said as she hugged Jordan tightly.

"I promise Mom," Jordan assured her with a laugh before walking into her father's outstretched arms and burying her face in his chest.

"I love you Dad."

"I love you too, but can you ever forgive me for being such a stupid old man?" he asked. The tremor in his voice did not go unnoticed by his daughter.

"There's nothing to forgive and I am happy to once again be Jordan Wheeler. I'm sorry Dad. I don't know what I was thinking back then. I never meant to turn my back on the family name or you."

"I know that but there's something else I know."

"What?" she asked in confusion.

"Something tells me that soon enough that young man there is going to give you another last name and when that time comes, you have my blessing. Now you better skedaddle before that fancy plane takes off without you. I love you my sweet girl."

When she looked up at him, there were tears in her father's eyes and she mouthed "I love you" before taking Ben's hand and walking to the plane. She had never been happier, and it was all thanks to the man beside her.

•　•　•　•　•

Helen wasted no time pulling Jordan into her arms when they finally arrived back home.

"Welcome home," she said warmly. "We've missed you something terrible."

"Thank you. It's good to be back," Jordan assured her.

It was good to be home but after everything that had happened in the last few weeks and indeed the past year, Jordan was mentally and physically exhausted. Like the first time she had come to Ben's home, she was covered in bruises and cuts, but unlike then, she was free of the secrets that had hindered her relationship with Ben. Thanks to several days of questioning at the hands of the FBI and with Ben at her side in his new role as her attorney, he now knew absolutely everything about her past.

As the three of them walked into the house Jordan realized something very important was missing.

"Where's Pete?" she asked.

Consumed with grief after they had shot Pete, she had cried her eyes out over the loss, but it was one of the first things Ben had told her after they reunited. Even though they couldn't be together, every call back to the house found Helen holding the phone up to Pete's ear so Jordan could talk to him as he looked around excitedly trying to find the woman whose voice he heard in his ear. It made little sense that he hadn't come to the door to greet her.

"Pete told me he needed to make a grand entrance," Helen said mysteriously. "I'll go get him."

As she walked away, Jordan looked up at Ben. "What's going on? Do you have something to do with this?" she asked with a smile.

"You'll see," he said with the same air of mystery Helen had exhibited.

The sound of nails clicking on the wooden floor announced Pete and Bear's arrival as they rushed to Jordan's side and she knelt down to gather them into her arms. Licking, whining, and dancing around, Pete could barely contain his excitement at seeing her again. It wasn't until he settled down that she noticed the bow around his neck and she looked up at Ben with a raised eyebrow.

"What's this?" she asked with a laugh as Pete licked her face once more.

"Why don't you take it off and see," Ben suggested.

Carefully removing the bow, she gasped in surprise as the large ruby and diamond ring she had seen once before caught the sunlight and sent a cascade of light throughout the room.

"Ben?"

Pulling her gently to her feet, Ben took the ribbon from her hands and removed the ring. Holding it up in front of him, he got down on one knee while Helen looked on with a knowing smile on her face.

"Maybe I should wait until your divorce is final, but I'm not taking any more chances. Jordan Wheeler, if there was ever a woman more perfectly suited for me it's you and I will love you until my dying breath. Please be my wife."

.   .   .   .   .

That night Jordan and Ben were finally alone after weeks of drama. Helen had gone back to the cottage after outdoing herself with a fantastic welcome home meal and the dogs were asleep on the floor near the fireplace. Even the welcome home phone calls from what seemed half the town had finally died down and the house was quiet save for the news program playing softly on the TV and the occasional snap of burning logs in the fireplace.

Jordan's head rested on Ben's shoulder as they took a collective deep breath.

It had been a long few weeks, but they were finally home and with Ben already having filed for her divorce from Richard, it wouldn't be long before they could announce their engagement to family and friends.

Jordan toyed with her new ring which for now rested on a chain around her neck, happily imaging what it will be like to finally be Mrs. Ben Anderson, when Ben turned up the TV at the sight of Agent Monroe addressing a crowded room of reporters.

"*Harvey remains in custody and bail has been set at twenty million dollars. I want to say again that his arrest results from a multi-year joint investigative effort between the FBI, SEC, and ATF, but none of it would have been possible without the heroic efforts of Harvey's wife. Jordan put her own life at risk to ensure Harvey would face justice and it was only her ingenuity in securing the documents while hiding in plain sight that ultimately allowed us to get the evidence we needed to arrest her husband. She is to be commended for her actions and on behalf of the Bureau; we thank her for her courage.*"

Ben clicked off the TV and waited for Jordan to say something. He looked down expecting to see tears. Instead, he saw the beginning of a smile.

"He's right you know," he said softly. "Harvey might have gotten away with all of it if it wasn't for you."

"I used to regret that I waited so long to leave Richard, but now I'm glad I did."

"Why would you say that?" Ben asked. "When I think of everything he put you through my blood boils."

"Because if things had been different I might never have met you and that isn't something I want to think about.

"I know you believe that, but not me. What we share is meant to be and you and I were destined to be together no matter what. I just wish I had realized it when I first saw you at my parents' party. We could have been together long ago. But now we have our entire future in front of us and we can do anything we want."

"I'm glad you brought that up because I've decided. Now that Richard is behind me, I think I want to go to art school. It's always been something I dreamed of and now that I have the cash and my cabin back from Brandon, I can afford it. What do you think?"

"I'll be right back," he said as he disentangled himself from her arms and walked out of the room returning with a familiar piece of paper in his hands. Finding his seat next to her again, he unrolled the sketch he had discovered when she went missing.

"I think if this is any sign of your abilities, you've been wasting your life not doing it professionally," he said with conviction.

Running her finger over the sketch, she basked in his compliment. "This might be the best sketch I've ever done," she told him. "But then again, I've never drawn a man I loved before."

"But you know something? Something's still missing from this drawing," he told her as he pulled her onto his lap.

"What are you talking about? What's missing?"

"You. I told you the last time I proposed—it's you and me my love. Together forever."

ABOUT THE AUTHOR

Author Barbara A. Luker is a master at weaving romance with suspense in stories that will leave readers turning the page until the very ending. She and her rescue cat Annie live in southern Minnesota, and to this day, she remains her third-grade piano teacher's greatest disappointment.

OTHER TITLES BY BARBARA A. LUKER

NOTE FROM
BARBARA A. LUKER

Word-of-mouth is crucial for any author to succeed. If you enjoyed *Hiding in Plain Sight*, please leave a review online—anywhere you are able. Even if it's just a sentence or two. It would make all the difference and would be very much appreciated.

Thanks!
Barbara A. Luker

We hope you enjoyed reading this title from:

www.blackrosewriting.com

Subscribe to our mailing list – *The Rosevine* – and receive **FREE** books, daily
deals, and stay current with news about upcoming
releases and our hottest authors.
Scan the QR code below to sign up.

Already a subscriber? Please accept a sincere thank you for being a fan of
Black Rose Writing authors.

View other Black Rose Writing titles at
www.blackrosewriting.com/books and use promo code
PRINT to receive a **20% discount** when purchasing.

www.ingramcontent.com/pod-product-compliance
Lightning Source LLC
Chambersburg PA
CBHW030808210726
48290CB00002B/488